WHITE
NIGHT

WHITE NIGHT

ELLIE MARNEY

ALLEN&UNWIN
SYDNEY • MELBOURNE • AUCKLAND • LONDON

This project is supported by the Victorian Government through Creative Victoria.

First published by Allen & Unwin in 2018

Allen & Unwin
83 Alexander Street
Crows Nest NSW 2065
Australia
Phone: (61 2) 8425 0100
Email: info@allenandunwin.com
Web: www.allenandunwin.com

A catalogue record for this book is available from the National Library of Australia

ISBN 978 1 76029 355 0

For teaching resources, explore www.allenandunwin.com/resources/for-teachers

Excerpt on page 69 is taken from *Ranger's Apprentice Book One: The Ruins of Gorlan* by John Flanagan. Copyright © John Flanagan, 2004. Reproduced by permission of Penguin Random House Australia.

Cover and text design by Debra Billson
Cover and text images by Dario Sablijak and Vladimir Caplinskij/Shutterstock
Set in 10.5/15.5 pt Janson Text by Shahirah Hambali

Printed in Australia by McPherson's Printing Group

10 9 8 7 6 5 4 3 2 1

For Deb, who always thinks the best of everyone

Three things are all over my feed on the first day of school: the skate park's being shut down, Mr Showalter is losing his nut, and the new girl is a feral skank.

Teo saw Mr S talking to himself at the IGA. Lozzie's avatar is a dancing tulip.

Showalter = do not care. I'm barely awake. Lying in bed moving my thumbs is all I can manage. *New girl – how you know?*

Deep Throat sources, Sprog types.

Cam sends an eye-roll. *Means he has no idea.*

Sprog sends a pic of his middle finger.

Loz clears the air. *Homegroup homies say Newgirl = Eden commune feral.*

That's when I notice the time. I've got to move or I'm gonna be late.

I bail out into the kitchen, look around. Dad'll be in the garden, but Mum's not here – unusual. I go for a hunt, only make it halfway to the back verandah.

'Bo, is that you?'

I follow her voice left, walk down the hall and stand in the doorway. 'You all right?'

Mum's sitting on top of the doona in her PJs, shoulders propped up on pillows, waving me in. 'Come over here, big fella.'

I sit gingerly on the edge of the bed, trying not to dip the mattress. Mum's real round now, and she rolls easy. Her belly juts forwards like the prow of a ship, and her long black hair streams out behind her. I still can't get my brain wrapped around the idea that I'm gonna have another sibling. Mum's due in April, which doesn't seem that far away anymore.

'First day back,' she says.

'First day, same old stuff. Whatcha doing in bed?'

'I didn't sleep that well.' She stretches, puts a hand on her back. 'Thought I'd get a lie-in before making you kids breakfast, but...'

'Too late now. I've got to go in ten minutes. You need anything?'

'I'm good. Only I need to go to the loo again, as usual. Help me up?' She slings her feet over the edge of the bed, and we laugh a little as I lever her up. Once she's standing, she winces and puts a hand under her belly. 'Right. Now I *really* need to go to the loo.' She pushes at me. 'Get ready. Don't forget to take a water bottle. And don't eat all the bread.'

Mum shuffles off to the bathroom. I race between the laundry pile, my bedroom, the kitchen. No time to cook a decent breakfast. I'm shovelling bread and jam into my mouth and my books into my backpack when Dad and Connor walk in from different directions.

Connor dumps his bag near the kitchen island, tries to grab the bread. 'Dude, it's so lame we have to go to school again.'

I snag another slice before I hand it over. 'Du-ude, you sound like you've been watching too much *Regular Show*.'

'Boys, don't eat all the bread.' Dad swats Connor. 'And keep your mouth sweet about school. I pity your teachers more than I pity you. Where's Mum?' He scans around the kitchen, before his eyes settle on me.

I speak through my mouthful of bread. 'Barp'oom. Gotta go.'

He stills me with a hand on my shoulder. 'Work hard. I know it's only the first day back, but show them you're keen. If you want to make it big on the field, you need discipline. That starts at school. And when you get home, I'll need you to help me pull some concrete mix outta the ute before you go to footy training.'

I groan.

'No groaning. Is Mum okay?'

I swallow my mouthful. 'She said she's tired.'

He nods at me, and I nod back. We're almost eye to eye now – I did a bit more growing over the summer holidays. Me and Dad will probably end up the same height. We've got the same eye colour, the same build, the same hair. My skin's not as dark – I got a mix of Dad's tan and Mum's paleness – but me and Dad are similar in almost every other way.

Dad gives my shoulder a squeeze. An understanding has passed between us – *take care of Mum.*

I'm cool with that. Dad and me share the load around here. Dad's the sun my planet orbits around. He's strict, intense, subject to random flare-ups – like firestorms on an actual sun – and fast on his feet. He'd still do okay on the footy ground, even though he gave up the game fifteen years ago. He's got quicksilver under his skin, in his blood and bones.

I like to believe I'm just like him.

*

'*Right,*' Mr Showalter shouts, 'everyone please *shut up.*'

We all smirk at each other as the fans spin in wobbly circles overhead. Mr Showalter was on leave – stress leave, I'd heard – last year, and if this is his classroom management strategy on day one of the new term, he's toast.

Sprog grabs me at the bell. 'What's this shit about the skate park closing soon?'

I shrug. 'Mate, the council's been wanting to shut down the skate park for ages. Dad reckons it got pushed along cos those guys got busted dealing there.'

'We're fucked, then.' Sprog looks depressed. He hangs at the skate park a lot, when he's not hanging with me or checking out chicks on Gough Street.

'Don't lose hope.' I clap him on the shoulder, hoist my backpack. 'What's next?'

He scans the timetable. 'English. Great. Another year of listening to Smallie rave on.'

'And watching him scope out Kaylah's legs.'

'I do a bit of that meself,' Sprog admits.

We get out of Room 323, hit the corridor. Lamistead Secondary is the only high school in the district – kids are bussed in from outlying farms. People are spread thinner out in the farming areas, though, which means there's only three classes of Year Eleven. There's enough of a population mix to provide some variety, but the town kids – including me, although I don't live right in town – make up the majority. First day back is like a cattle stampede. I exchange nods with Joel Harvey across the hall while walking against the crush. Junior kids give ground, but you've still gotta push. There's a year to go before we acquire Year Twelve Rock God status. Sprog already carries himself like he thinks he's a Rock God.

Second period has started and everyone has found appropriate seats, according to the current pecking order. Our English teacher, Mr Small, is stacking paper on his desk – probably in an attempt to make himself look more efficient at the beginning of the lesson. The usual hum of conversation quiets when this chick walks in.

She has frizzy, dirty-gold hair, kept back from her face with a band of tie-dyed scarf. The fringed ends of the scarf tangle with the straps of the overalls she's wearing over a white singlet. Who wears overalls to school? Strappy sandals on her feet, no make-up. A nose-stud. A canvas knapsack instead of a backpack. Yep, she looks feral.

I can see straight away she's out of her depth – the weight of books in her knapsack, the map of the school in her hand. She waves her hall slip at Mr Small. She has an honest-to-god flower in her hair. 'Um, hi. I have a note from Mrs Wagner at the office…'

Mr Small breaks out his cheesiest smile. 'Ah – my new student. Welcome. It's Aurora Wild, isn't it?'

'Just Rory is fine.' Her voice echoes in the space left by the conversational buzz.

'All right, Rory.' The smile again, god. Mr Small waves a magnanimous hand towards the rest of us. 'Well, we have free seating in this class, so find a pew anywhere you like.'

He thinks he sounds cool when he says that. *Find a pew* – wow, what a cool guy. I roll my eyes.

The girl nods. 'Thanks, Doug.'

I hear an almost audible *ping* as fifteen other students suddenly register what New Girl said. She seems oblivious as she heads for a free desk near the front.

'Doug' lifts a finger to grab her attention. 'Aurora? It's Mr Small in class.'

New Girl pauses. 'Oh, right. Sorry.'

Yeah, thanks for that, Smallie. Making sure we all understand the rank-and-file system here, good to know. Mr Small's roving eye seems to be exempt from the 'you, student – me, teacher' rule, but New Girl doesn't get that yet. I wonder if he'd still let her call him Doug outside of class. Small's a dickhead and a sleaze, and he basically destroyed my enjoyment of this subject last year, which was a shame, cos I liked English in my first three years with Mrs Vernon.

Mr Small claps his hands together as he sits on the corner of his desk, in the accepted 'groovy teacher' fashion. 'Welcome back from holidays, everyone. Now, we have a few books on our reading list this term, and I thought we'd ease in with some short stories. Has anyone read *Island* yet?'

New Girl raises her hand. I nearly groan aloud. Ohmigod, *why*? Why would you poke your hand up first thing in a new class at a new school?

Mr Small looks around the room. 'Yes, Rory?'

'I've read it,' she says.

Good for you, sister. I want to bang my head against the table.

'Well, that's great,' Mr Small says. 'That's a good start to the term's—'

'I've read all of them.'

Mr Small squints. 'Pardon?'

Kaylah stops bouncing her tanned leg on her tanned knee. Shandy gives New Girl the dead-fish glare from the other side of the aisle.

But New Girl doesn't seem to notice the looks she's getting. 'The books you set. *Wuthering Heights*, *The White Tiger*... *Maus* was my favourite.'

Maus was listed for fourth term. Which means, if I'm hearing this right, she's hoovered up a whole year's worth of English novels before February's even started. First the overalls and general feralness, now this. She's a try-hard, mouthy participator. Awesome.

This chick's gonna fit in just great at Lamistead.

After breakfast on Tuesday, I have to help load the post-hole digger into the trailer hooked up to the ute. The post-holer is a solid piece that Dad inherited from his mentor, Harry Krane.

I remember Harry as an old guy with gnarly fingers who used to rub my head with his knuckles when I was six. Harry was a man from the local mob, living on his own country, sure and proud of his identity; Dad was dumped at a Queensland hospital as a baby, grew up in institutions, and still has no idea of his heritage. They couldn't have been more different if they'd tried. Dad says he owed Harry a debt he couldn't ever repay, and that's why he was happy to buy the business when Harry retired. Now Dad's got business cards – *Mitchell's EarthMoving* – stuck up in the windows of all the shops in town.

Some people collect teapots, or paint kit aeroplanes, or obsess over cars; my father gets a hard-on for digging equipment. Mum's always joking that if they ever got divorced, he'd marry the bobcat in the shed. But Harry's post-holer is one heavy son of a bitch. By the time we get it sorted, I'm running late for the school run.

I end up meeting Aurora Wild for the first time on the same day I get my first ever detention.

We meet over a broken bike chain, which is not a first. I mean, I've fixed broken bike chains. Not this one, though.

'It's rooted.' I squat in the dust on the side of Fogarty's Hill Road, where the eucalypts are too far back to give proper shade. School is in the opposite direction to town from our place, and all the roads in are lined with bush.

Aurora spills off her haunches and onto her knees. 'I was hoping you weren't going to say that.'

'I'm real sorry, hey. But see that link there?' I point. 'It's come apart in the centre and jammed in your gears.'

I'm still trying to figure out why I stopped for her. Powering my way to school, I saw a flash of gold hair, movement: Aurora Wild was kicking her bike by the roadside. I did a screechy to stop, telling myself I felt bad for the bike.

She squints. 'If we had a screwdriver, couldn't we pop out the bad link and click the chain back together?'

'You got a screwdriver?'

'A pocketknife.' She digs around in her knapsack.

Naturally, Aurora Wild carries a pocketknife. I don't know why I'm surprised. New Girl needs some serious enlightenment.

'Um, did you know you can get in the shit for carrying a knife at school?'

'Really?' She pauses. 'Even just a pocketknife?'

Dad always says the opposite of a poker face is a gin rummy face. I don't know what the hell he means, but I think Aurora Wild might have one. 'Yep, if you get busted, it's a suspension.'

She pulls out the knife. 'They'd really suspend me for carrying this?'

The knife is an antique Swiss Army number, with obsolete attachments – a tiny file, a Bakelite toothpick. I have to admit, it doesn't look like a weapon of mass destruction.

'Fair enough.' I turn my attention to the task at hand. 'Nah, still can't do it. I got skillz, but I'm not MacGyver. You need someone with proper tools to have a look at it.'

What it needs is a whole new chain. She's sailing a real old ship here. The bike is fuzzy with rust; cobwebs dangle under the seat and in the spokes. Chances are high it needs more than the chain replaced, it hasn't been used in so long.

'Crap.' Aurora slumps in the dust. Thin metal bangles – so many bangles – chime together on her wrist as she flaps at a fly near her cheek. 'Okay, thanks for stopping, but I've held you up. You should go. You'll get in trouble with Mrs Franklin if you're late to homegroup, won't you?'

I stand up and clap my palms against my legs to brush off the grime. We're about five kay from school, so more than halfway, but the hill ahead is a total bastard – we're sitting in the gulley about halfway along Fogarty's Hill Road, and they call it Fogarty's Hill for a reason. If I really churn it hard I could probably make it right on bell time.

I don't wanna abandon New Girl, though.

A constant refrain of Dad's comes back to me: *Don't be a dickhead, help your brother out*. He usually says it about two seconds after Connor starts whinging, but all the same, it pulls me up. My little brother can be a pain in the arse, but he's still a human being. Everybody needs a hand sometimes.

I yank out my phone and try to call the office to report

that we're going to be late. No reception – that's right, we're in the gulley. Aurora watches me tuck the phone away.

'It's all good.' I lean down and pull on the handlebars of her bike until we've got the old ship standing. 'If we can get this thing in to school, Mr Fennelli will fix it for nothing.'

She clambers up. 'I can wheel it myself.'

I shake my head. 'Your back tyre's gonna drag with a stuck chain. It's a long way. I'll carry it, you wheel mine.'

I heft the bike up and lay the crossbar on my shoulder. I was right, the bike's old – it weighs a fucking ton.

'We'll take it in turns,' Aurora says quickly.

I must've winced. I try to shove the bike higher. 'Uh, yeah, okay.'

Aurora wheels my bike and I lug the Titanic on my shoulder. Sandy dirt crunches under my boots, flies make suicidal circles. The heat of the day is bleeding out of my skin, and it's only eight-thirty.

'Thank you,' Aurora says. 'For stopping.'

I'd shrug, but my shoulders are occupied. 'No worries. It's crap, being stranded. I got stuck last year. Blew a tyre halfway to school, no patch kit. Had to carry the bloody bike the rest of the way, like this, then hunt around all day getting it fixed for the ride home.'

She grins in sympathy. Her frizz of hair is what I imagine a spume of expensive champagne might look like. It turns to darker, thicker ringlets where it meets the perspiration at the base of her neck. Her face is incredibly freckled, and shadowed with dirt; Mum would be tutting, and pushing her towards a hot shower. The bridge of her nose is sunburnt, but the tiny jewel on the side flashes green in the light.

11

She's got some kind of knitted headband keeping her hair back today, and she's wearing the overalls again with a grey tank top. Her pale shoulders are exposed – she'll be red as a smacked bum by the end of this arvo, but by the look of her nose, maybe she's used to it?

'So … who's MacGyver?' Her hands, on the handlebars of my bike, are strong, callused, with a confident grip. Hard-working hands.

'Sorry?' I realise I've been checking her out, force myself to stop. Concentrate on trudging up Fogarty's Hill.

'I don't get the MacGyver thing.'

'Ah.' I laugh, and the metal of the bike frame scratches against my neck. 'MacGyver is this guy from a TV show. He can fix or build anything from whatever he's got. Like, give him a piece of tin foil and a bottle cap, and he'll make you a radio.'

'Seriously?'

'Yep. Every episode, he outwits bad guys with his ex-military fix-it skills. My dad thinks he's God.' It's hard to keep a straight face while explaining MacGyver. 'I've tried to explain that he's fictional, but I don't think Dad cares. He just likes to believe there's another guy running around in the world with spark plugs and wire in his pockets.' I glance at her. 'You don't watch TV?'

'Nope.' She shakes her head over the handlebars. 'No TV.'

'Really? How do you … y'know … live?'

She laughs. 'I get by.'

According to the local rumour mill, most commune folk get their education in-house. I turn my head forwards and watch my footing as I ask the next obvious question. 'How long were you homeschooled?'

'Nine years.' She straightens her arms to keep my bike ahead of her as we climb the hill. 'From when I was about seven.' She notices my expression and smiles. 'Can't quite imagine it?'

'Um, not really.' Sweat is trickling an itchy line down my nape, and I hope I don't look too horrified. Wouldn't it be boring? Wouldn't you get lonely? Wouldn't being taught by your parents every day drive you fucking crazy? She looks away as she changes the subject. 'Your bike is great.'

'It was my dad's. It's an early model Cannondale. They don't make them like this anymore, and Dad took care of his, so he's always on my case to look after it.'

'My bike is awful.' She's matter-of-fact about it. 'Here, come on, we should swap.'

Aurora engages the kickstand on my bike, pushes her knapsack off her hip and slides it around behind her, holds out her hands. The Titanic drops off my shoulder with a thump, and as she hefts it onto her own, I notice she's got armpit hair. Woah. I don't know any girls who don't shave their armpits – or their legs, for that matter. Me and Sprog have joked that depilation seems to be a serious business among the chicks at Lamistead.

She grunts with the weight of the bike, and I can't help grinning. 'Don't know what you're complaining about. That's a real gem you've got there.'

She snorts, then steadies the weight. 'Oh, yeah, it's great. I borrowed it from Sally, my neighbour. I wasn't sure how long I'd need a bike for, so I kind of begged around.'

I grab my bike and we restart the trek. Then her words sink in.

'Are you gonna start getting a lift?' The bus doesn't run this route; I can attest to that myself. Maybe her parents are worried about her riding on the road and they're gonna drive her.

'What? No.' She laughs briefly as she trudges along. 'I'm not sure how long I'll last at school. Whether I'll like it enough to stay. My dad didn't want me to enrol. He's always going on about the factory model of education and how it destroys creative thought.' She blushes, kinks her neck against the bike frame.

'So you had to fight to be allowed to go to school?'

'Yep.'

I laugh. 'Man, that's flipped. Most kids would be fighting their parents to stay home.'

She seems surprised by the idea. 'I never thought of it like that.'

Now *I'm* thinking about it. She's never been to school before, so she probably didn't get the memo about compulsory classroom apathy. And she's gonna struggle with the social stuff, for sure. I wonder whether I should clue her in. If she thinks she's gonna magically break into friendship cliques that have been going since playgroup, she's about to be sorely disappointed.

'So do you have any mates at school yet?'

'No. But it's only the first week.' She smiles at me. 'And I just met you.'

'Yeah, you did.' My return smile is neutral. 'So when'd you move here? To the district, I mean.'

She wriggles the Titanic on her shoulder, keeps a hand on the frame so it doesn't swing. 'I guess it's been … five years?'

14

I pull up short. 'But I've never met you. I've never even *seen* you.' I take a couple of quick steps to catch up. I need to see her face so I can tell if she's bullshitting me.

'Oh, well…' She's puffing on the final rise to the crest. 'We don't get into town much. I went yesterday, for school. And to the library three weeks ago, to get books and stuff. And last year, for the Growers Market festival.'

She sounds almost proud about that. But the Market festival was…*last March*. Is this chick for real? Suddenly it's like I've got the whole picture, and it's the weirdest picture I've ever seen.

I shake my head. I could ride back past my place all the way to Lamistead in under thirty minutes from here. 'I'm having a hard time understanding how you could live so close to town and be so cut off. It seems kinda extreme.'

'Garden of Eden is an intentional eco-village that practises rewilding and radical zero-impact lifestyle as a sustainable alternative to the domesticated, techno-capitalist worldview.' She's obviously reciting. But then her voice becomes more normal. 'We're off the grid. No plastic, no appliances – and no TV. Permaculture food production, DIY building, low carbon…you name it, that's us. It's about reducing our ecological footprint to an absolute minimum.'

'That's…' I search around for a complimentary term. '…pretty hardcore.'

'I guess.' She pushes her hair back, bangles chiming. 'Anyway, that's why I've never gone to school here. But I wanted to see what it was like. See if I could make it work.'

We've reached the top of Fogarty's Hill. As I look down over the slope, I realise what I'm feeling: it's *wonder*. Like

I've discovered a new species, or some exotic kind of flower previously unknown to science. This girl is something else, something I don't think I've ever imagined existed. She isn't just a new student. She lives in a commune, completely off the radar. She only ever goes into town – town! That's, like, only twenty kay away! – about once a year. And now she's...

Shit – she's at Lamistead Secondary.

I know what people there can be like; I know what that's going to mean for her. The students of Lamistead won't exactly throw out the welcome mat. I can already imagine Shandy and Kaylah circling at school, plotting their attack.

But Aurora's put effort into this – the school books, the crappy bike, the long ride, the battle to be allowed to enrol. She's giving it a shot, when she could have opted out. She definitely gets credit for having a pair.

We've both stilled at the crest, panting for breath. I wave my hand at her load. 'Gimme that back.'

She slides the Titanic down with a grunt. 'God, that's heavy.'

'Only three more kay to school and it's all flat. Piece of piss.'

'Thanks.' She wipes her neck with one hand, looks grateful.

I pass her my bike. 'You should stick with school. People in class are tight, but they'll get used to you.'

'I'd like to stay,' she admits.

'Then stay.' I grin as I manhandle her bike back onto my shoulder. 'Stay at school, Aurora. Hang with the rest of us factory models.'

She smiles and turns to face the road. 'All right. I'll stay, because Bo Mitchell thinks it's a good idea. And it's Rory, by the way. Only my dad calls me Aurora.'

Sprog and Lozzie are already at our table in the grotty, suncloth-covered concrete space that admin has dubbed the 'senior area' when I dump my backpack beside them at lunch.

Sprog gives me knuckles and grins. 'Detention Boy.'

'News travels fast.'

'Is it cos you helped New Girl get her bike to school?' Lozzie swipes a hot chip through the tomato sauce she's smothered them with.

'Yeah, well, I missed homegroup and Mrs Franklin is a hard arse.' Actually, if I had to pick one teacher to drop into a volcano, I'd be torn choosing between Mrs Franklin and Mr Small. 'How'd you know about the bike?'

'Teo saw New Girl talking about it with Mr Fennelli.'

On the far side of the senior area, I spot Rory. She's sitting on a bench alone, eating something out of a paper bag and reading a book. She glances up and sees me, waves. I raise a hand back. 'New Girl's name is Rory. She's been homeschooled until this year.'

'I always thought people homeschooled cos their kids were

mentally retarded or something,' Sprog says. 'Y'know – faulty wiring.' He launches into his version of a 'retard' impersonation, hunching and squinting and making slobbery sounds.

'You're the one with faulty wiring, you dick.' I dig in my pocket for loose change for the canteen. I don't want to look up. I know Rory is watching Sprog's performance.

'It's called intellectually disabled, FYI.' Cam slides her bag onto the table. 'And it's nothing to be ashamed of, Dominic. We've known about your issues for years.'

Sprog gasps, clutches his chest over his heart and pretends to fall off the bench. But his face gets this flicker of hurt, which I think Cam's missed.

'Well, she's obviously not intellectually disabled,' Lozzie points out.

'Are we talking about New Girl?' Cam asks.

Lozzie nods. 'She's got hairy pits.'

'Really?' Cam looks shocked.

Joel interrupts all this when he comes over to ask Sprog about footy training. Joel and Cam exchange nods. Lozzie tells us her horse foaled last night, and shows us pictures of the new arrival on her phone.

Shared history is impossible to avoid in a country town so small you can practically list everyone by name. Sprog and Teo Trembath and Justin Fromer all live within a block of each other. Cam and Lozzie D'Onofrio – she's only 'Blossom' to her gran – are neighbours, besties since primary school. Everybody knows who's who and what's what, and we've all dated each other at different times, with varying results.

Sprog dated Breanna Fromer, Justin's sister, for a while. Me and Lozzie went out for a couple of months early last year. Lozzie's great – offbeat, funny, with this unself-conscious beauty – but it felt like I was dating my cousin. Joel and Cam went out for a while, now Joel keeps his distance. I think he liked Cam a lot, maybe still likes her – he doesn't want to look like he's pining.

Cam's probably had plenty of offers since then. Guys watch with their tongues hanging out as Camilla D'Amato goes by. Long black hair and long brown legs in combination are a bit hard to ignore, plus she's smart, and she can work her way around a netball court and outrun a guy on the track field. We dated – with aluminium pull tab rings – when we were both in kindergarten. I've known Cam long enough that we have a comfortable rapport, but she can be a bit intimidating.

'Oh shit,' she says now. 'Look. Shandy's making her move.'

Across the senior area, Rory's reading has been interrupted by the arrival of Shandy and Kaylah, who are chatting with her and waving their manicures. Shandy looks animated and confident.

Lozzie observes the scene with interest. 'Newbie's not actually going to fall for that routine, is she?'

'Her name's Rory,' I repeat.

'That girl,' Cam says, sighing, but I'm not sure which girl she's referring to.

Rory's expression is wide-eyed as Shandy sits down beside her. Rory shows a hint – my heart sinks – of pleasure at being noticed, spoken to. But Shandy Patterson's malicious streak radiates from her like a distinctive perfume. I don't know why Shandy's decided to set herself up as the biggest bitch in our year, and I don't wanna know. Kaylah Lanzzi is Shandy's

19

bestie, but the relationship is more like Master and Vassal: Shandy takes the lead, Kaylah follows obediently.

Does Rory realise that Shandy and Kaylah are sharks sniffing blood? I don't think she does, and I'm torn. Rory seems pretty likeable, but I don't know if I can be friends with someone that clueless.

Lozzie shakes her head. 'Shandy's practically sitting on her lap.'

'If Shandy wants to sit on someone's lap, I'm right here,' Sprog says, slapping his thigh in invitation.

Cam makes a face. 'There's not a girl alive who wants to sit on your lap.'

'Really? You think the size of my package is putting them off?'

'Don't be disgusting.' Cam gazes back at the scene with Rory. 'Crikey, she really hasn't got the foggiest, has she?'

'She's weird, for sure.' Lozzie lifts her eyebrows. 'Mr Ennis puts on a video in Biol – I know, right? We haven't even cleared week one and he's already into the YouTube – and it's like New Girl was hypnotised. We're all flopping around, chatting over the voiceover, and she's fully staring at the screen. Like this.' Loz bugs out her eyes at some fixed point in space.

'No TV in the commune,' I explain.

'No kidding. It made me wonder what else they don't have. I mean, check her out – it's like she's never seen make-up before.'

As we watch, Shandy draws one of Rory's hands to her for comparison, showing her where they attach the glue for false nails. I think of Rory's work-roughened hands from this morning, and my eyes narrow.

'You think that's weird,' Sprog says, 'you should see her food. Recess, right? She pulls out this big brown paper bag, and she's got a whole bunch of carrots. A *bunch*. With *dirt* still on them. She just brushes the dirt off and starts munching away. She's got a tin of tea leaves in there as well. And boiled eggs, homemade bread…'

'You sound hungry.' Cam grins at him.

Sprog stands up, grimacing. 'Not hungry enough to eat that crap. I'm gonna get a pizza.'

Cam extends a fiver. 'Here, buy me a slice.'

'Fuck off. Buy your own pizza.'

'Don't be rude, Dominic. Please get me a pizza.'

Sprog sighs, takes the money.

I wait until Sprog has grumped off before volunteering my intel to Cam. 'I helped her carry her bike in this morning. Broken chain.'

Cam stares at me. 'You helped her? Seriously, Bo, don't get involved. That shit is like quicksand. Hang on – is that why you were late for homegroup?'

'Yep.'

'And now you've got detention. See? Quicksand.'

I shrug and steal one of Lozzie's blood-spatter chips as Sprog returns, holding two hot-food bags from the canteen.

'Pizza's finished. I got you a sausage roll,' he says.

He offers one of the bags to Cam, who looks at him blankly. 'But I don't want a sausage roll.'

Sprog sighs, gives her the other bag. Then he opens the one she rejected and starts eating her sausage roll.

✳

21

Mum's not home from her work at the dental clinic – she's on reception three days a week – when I get in after school, but Dad's here, getting ready to have a kick in the back paddock with Connor. I dump my backpack, consider how to dodge the Detention Talk. I could say I'm hanging out with Sprog. I could say it's a footy training thing…

Shit, that's not gonna work. Tomorrow I'm supposed to meet Connor in town after school, then go to swimming squad at five. Neither of those two things can happen if I'm in detention. I'm stuck. I'll just have to suck it up and tell Dad what happened.

Dad is sitting at the kitchen table lacing his runners, still in his jeans and T-shirt from work. 'You get a chance to talk to Ross Willander's boy at school today?'

'Todd – yeah.' I open the fridge for the milk, grab a glass and spoon, get the Milo out. 'He said to give his dad a call about that retaining wall job, if you still want it.'

'I do. Thank you.' Dad double-knots on the left. 'All good today?'

'School was okay.' I stir the brown crust down into the white. 'I was late, though. Stopped to help that new Eden girl on the way in – broken bike chain. Mrs Franklin docked me for missing homegroup.'

Dad looks up. 'She docked you?'

'Yep. So that's detention. Tomorrow afternoon.'

'Bullshit.'

I'm not sure if he's swearing cos I got a detention, or cos of the reason why. 'I tried to explain, but Mrs Franklin is committed to being a complete bit—'

'*Bo.*' Dad tugs on his knots. 'Feel free to say whatever you want with your friends, but that's not the way we talk about teachers in this house. Anyway, it's the rules. You skip out on homegroup, it's a detention.'

'She could've listened to what I had to say!'

'Maybe so. Doesn't mean she can make an exception to the rules.'

The rules. Dad's so uptight about the rules, even the ones he hasn't laid down himself. What does it matter if I miss homegroup? I was helping someone out – doesn't that count for something? Was Dad this serious about the rules when *he* was sixteen?

He stands up, raises his eyebrows at my spoon clanking around inside my glass. 'You've told me about it now, anyway. Relax.' He ruffles my hair. 'Wanna come out for a kick?'

I shrug. 'Sure.'

'Well, when you've finished eating your bodyweight in Milo, get your boots on.' He grabs the footy off the kitchen table, tucks it under his arm as he heads for the verandah door. 'So the Eden girl must be a bit of a curiosity at school?'

'Yeah, she's …' I hunt for the word. 'Different.'

'She cute?' He catches my startled glance, laughs. 'Yeah, okay, she's cute. Ah well, no good deed goes unpunished, eh?'

I roll my eyes. 'Tell me about it.'

He's still grinning when he nods at me in reminder. 'Boots. See you down there.'

And that's the last I hear about it until dinner, when Mum gets the news.

'It doesn't seem fair to get detention for helping another student,' she says.

I hold my arms out, because *IKR?* Dad ignores me. I chew

my dried-up chop without further comment. There are about a hundred ways you can cook chops without turning them into shoe leather. Or potatoes without turning them into mash. I'd offer to show Mum, but she might wonder how I know. Connor shovels food into his mouth like someone's bought a world monopoly on mashed potato, and if he doesn't eat his fast enough it'll be taken away.

Dad serves himself another helping of peas. 'Anyway, how was footy yesterday?'

'Mullet was riding us – he made us do sprints. Bit rough for the first day back.' I grimace. It's pre-season, but shit, it's all taken very seriously.

'Mullet's a good coach. He wants you in shape early. He was saying there might be a rep squad scout around this season. What do you reckon? You'd be keen to try out, right?'

I shrug. I've heard the scout rumour before. And I know a few guys in the local development squad – they train fucking hard, hardly anyone makes it to the VFL, and they're all ready for knee reconstructions by the time they're twenty-five. Dunno if I'm sold on the idea.

'Nice to be back on the ground, though, yeah?'

It's the same ground I was on the last four months for the cricket season. 'The club needs to put the sprinklers on. The midfield is hard as a rock.'

'That pitch was too fast all summer,' Connor agrees. My brother, the nine-year-old reincarnation of Richie Benaud.

I help clear the plates, then do the dishes and feed Julie, our kelpie cross, while Connor reads aloud to Mum on the couch. Dad has started on business bookkeeping at the kitchen table when I go to my room under the pretext of doing some

English homework. I can't actually remember which part of the book I'm supposed to be reading. I text Cam about it, while getting in a sneaky Facebook scroll on my phone.

By nine-thirty, Connor's gone to bed, everything's tidy, and the lights in the house are dim. Pouring myself a glass of milk, I hear murmuring on the back verandah. Mum and Dad are sitting out there in the faint light from the kitchen, and something about the way they're sitting stills me.

Dad's reclining in the corner of the swing chair, and Mum's leaning back against him, her hands holding the front of her belly, her hair tumbling onto Dad's shoulder. Dad has his arm around her. Their bodies fit together – they've relaxed against each other. Mum lifts her chin and says something, so soft I can't hear it. Dad tilts his head, says something back, and Mum laughs, real quiet. She jiggles with it, clutches her belly. Dad's arm curves more firmly.

They look good together. Somehow, among all the people in the world, my parents managed to find each other. When I think of them meeting for the first time, I imagine it with the sound of two matching components snapping into place. I don't know if it was like that, but that's what I imagine.

✳

Later that night something wakes me.

I shamble out to the bathroom in my pyjama pants, eyes half open, head full of air. Take a swig from the milk carton in the fridge. Roll to the bathroom. Scratch my hair with one hand. Have a whiz. Wander back.

As I return to the kitchen, Dad eases into the house from the back verandah. He's dressed in a T-shirt and a pair of

25

Bonds trunks – daggy Dad sleepwear. He's got the home phone in his hand, and his face is grubby with whiskers.

'Whatcha doin'?' I tuck my hands into my armpits, crack my eyelids against the glare. The kitchen light is too bright. We leave it on for Connor, although it's been years since he woke up in the night.

'Wrong number,' Dad says, waving the phone.

I reach into the fridge, take a swig from the milk carton. It must've been nippy out there in his jocks. I look over at the clock. 'Who the hell calls a wrong number at one in the morning?'

'Go back to bed, Bo,' Dad says.

And that's what I do.

'I firmly believe,' Sprog says, 'that the rise of the hipster beard was directly related to the increased popularity of the Brazilian.'

I give him the side eye. It's too early in the morning for this shit.

'I'm totally serious. Blokes want fur when they go investigating down there.' He shrugs, as if this point is a given. 'If the ladies are gonna wax it off, the boys have gotta provide it themselves.'

'Can we not talk about pubic hair in homegroup?'

'Lighten up, Bo.'

'Fuck off, Sprog.'

'Mate, what's got your goat?'

'Dad was being a fucking grouchy arse at breakfast, and I'm a bit over it, okay? I'm in enough trouble with detention this arvo as it is.'

Dad *was* being an arse: he got up Connor for slobbing up his room, then gave me the full deal for making his and Mum's lives difficult by having detention. Dad's gonna have to leave a job early to collect Connor from school, cos Mum doesn't finish until after four. After yesterday's talk, I thought we were square – I didn't anticipate getting my head bitten off over my Weet-Bix this morning.

I didn't see Rory on the road to school, but Rory is not my problem. The last thing I need to be thinking about is a newbie with no instinct for self-preservation.

When I get called out of first period, my guts tighten until I remember it's scheduled.

'Mr Mitchell, you know what this meeting is about, don't you?' Mrs Ramanathan says, as I come into her office. 'Take a seat.'

I nod, plonk down on the plastic chair near her desk and put my backpack between my feet. 'First term of Year Eleven means careers counselling.'

'That's correct. Now, refresh my memory, please, Bo, and tell me what you put on your subject selection sheet.'

'English, Biology, Humanities, Business, Maths, PE, French.' I know I don't need to refresh Ramanathan's memory; she's as sharp as a tack.

'PE was always going to be a given…' Her expression is bemused. 'Will you pursue a career in sport, Bo?'

I shrug. I used to dream about playing in the AFL, but I figured out last year I'm never gonna make the big game. Now I need a Plan B. I'm thinking something a bit less brutal on my body. PE teacher, maybe? Dad would love to see me in the pre-VFL rep squad – he's been hinting big in that direction. I just wish I could drum up some enthusiasm for the idea.

Thing is, though, I still love to play footy. And it's more than just the game – it's all the added extras. Dad comes to every match. Girls give you admiring glances. The guys at the fish and chip shop know your name. Everyone loves footy players.

'Hm.' Mrs Ram runs one red-painted fingernail across the paperwork in front of her. 'And ... Biology. Why Biology, Bo?'

'Um, dunno. I did okay in Biology.'

'You "did okay" in Food Technology as well. You excelled, in fact. Is there a reason why you decided not to continue with that subject?'

I shrug. There's a reason, but it will sound stupid if I say it out loud.

Mrs Ram's wrinkles pucker. 'You made some wonderful dishes in my class last year, Bo. I'm disappointed you've chosen not to go on with a subject for which you seem well-suited. Remember, you're free to alter your subjects until the deadline in a few weeks.' When I don't respond, she looks away. 'Ah well, we shall move on. The French may be a problem. You'll have to do better in that subject if you want to keep up.'

'Yeah, I know. It was one of the subjects Dad said I had to keep, but.'

Mrs Ramanathan nods. 'A language will boost your score result, but only if you can lift your game with the work ...'

I glance around the room, tuning out. This office is like every other teacher's office in the school – cramped, full of outdated furniture, and shared by at least two other people. You'd think that Mrs Ram – a senior leading teacher – would qualify for something a bit classier. She's dressed up her desk with a pot plant and a few tubs of brightly coloured textas, but there's also the usual piles of paperwork, with a small stack of cookbooks in the corner.

A poster Blu-Tacked to the wall shows a marble benchtop with a selection of antique kitchen utensils and raw ingredients: eggs in a nest, unshelled nuts, cinnamon sticks, chunks of dark chocolate. You could make a nice flourless cake with that stuff. Or a—

'So what are you going to do, Bo?' Mrs Ramanathan asks.

I bring my eyes back to her. 'Um, I'm gonna lift my game in French.'

'No, dear.' She sighs, and her draped blouse flutters. 'I'm asking you what you want to do with your life. Where do you see yourself after high school? In five years' time?'

I ... actually don't know how to answer that. Most of the time, when I think about life outside high school, I think of me and Sprog hanging out. Or helping Dad with Mitchell's EarthMoving jobs, or playing sport, or watching movies, or maybe knocking over a few rounds of *Halo* with my brother. But we're talking about life *after* high school. That's a whole different barrel of monkeys.

'Um ...' I say.

'This is something that requires a little more thought, perhaps?' Mrs Ram's eyebrows lift. 'Bo, you're a good student. You behave well and you work solidly. But apart from your performance in my classes last year, you never quite shine. Why is that?'

I shrug again. What am I supposed to say? School is ... school. It's the bookend bike rides, and homework, and putting up with teachers with short fuses in classrooms that have had the baking heat of summer locked up inside them since the end of last year.

Mrs Ram's gaze is kohl-lined and intent. 'Bo, listen to me

carefully. In a few weeks, subject selections will be finalised. Then, even if you would like to switch into Food Tech, it will be too late.'

I bite my lip, and she notices.

'That's right,' she says. 'Now, I would like you to do something for me. Spend some time thinking about the subjects you've chosen. While you're at it, think about the things that are important to you. That mean something to you. Think about what you'd really *like* to be doing after high school. Then come back to me with your final decision.'

She turns back to her paperwork, and I realise I've been dismissed. I stammer out a goodbye and Mrs Ram waves – a kind of 'cheerio, but this conversation isn't over' wave – and I leave.

In Humanities, Mr Showalter is futzing around, starting another thrilling lesson on contemporary social movements. Something breaks the tedium, though: Rory walks into class. Except she looks … different. The baggy legs of her overalls have been hacked off mid-thigh. She's scraped her hair into a ponytail, and she's wearing an enormous brown flannel shirt – the tails of it flap at the back.

I blink at her as she slides into a seat at a desk on my right. 'What are you—'

'I've been transferred into this class,' she whispers, notebook and pens clutched to her chest. 'Mrs Perkins's class is full.'

I'm still recovering from the shock of seeing so much of her legs. They're toned and fawn-pale, with a light smattering of golden hair – again with the lack of depilation. Ringlets are springing out from her ponytail, refusing to be controlled. And the shirt …

31

Then I figure it out. She's altered her outfit so she's dressed more like the other girls at school. She's trying to blend in. But if I know anything about high school, it's that trying too hard at anything is a big No.

I glance around. Cam is two rows behind me, making this confused frown. To my left, Sprog is leaning back in his chair so he can scope out Rory's new look. His face is expressionless but his eyebrows are high.

The class is torture. Rory does her work without fanfare, but she raises her hand to answer questions with an obscene amount of enthusiasm. It's like she's actually read the textbook – even Mr Showalter looks shocked. People start sniggering. By the end of the period, Rory's got sweat beading on her top lip. It must be hot as hell in that shirt. Or maybe she's realised being a big class contributor isn't winning her any friends.

At bell time, Sprog bumps me on the shoulder to get my attention as I watch Rory practically sprint out of the classroom.

'That is one freaky chick.'

I bump him in return. 'Give her a break. She's from Eden, man. She is unfamiliar with our ways and customs. Did you know she's lived out there for five years?'

'The whut?' Sprog screws up his eyes. 'So she's been in the district five years, and no one's ever seen her? That's messed up. That's like, child abuse, man, locking your kid up like that.'

Sprog clearly doesn't get the sense of wondrous discovery I had when Rory explained her background to me. It's just another factor of weird I've added to her public persona. Maybe I should've let Rory explain it herself.

'Did that girl read *all* the course texts, or something?' Cam asks as she walks over from her desk. Being on top of classwork is usually her area of expertise, and Rory's just knocked her off the perch.

'She did in English,' Sprog informs her.

'Jesus Christ.' Cam tucks her hair behind her ears and crosses herself in a perfunctory way, something she does every time she takes the Lord's name in vain. She told me once it's so she doesn't feel guilty when she goes to visit her nonna.

'Maybe it's easy to get more reading done without a TV around,' I suggest, as we start walking towards the senior area for recess. 'Or maybe she likes discussing politics ...'

'... or maybe she's a giant brainy-brain,' Sprog says, taking up position beside Cam, 'and you're gonna have to up the ante to stay Queen of the Smart Folk.'

By the time we've made it to the senior area, Rory's ripped off the shirt and loosened her hair, which falls around her face in a cloud of summery curls. When she sees me, she comes over, still red-faced. 'I didn't catch you on the ride in this morning.'

Before I can reply, Cam lifts her bag from where she's plonked it on the bench. 'I'm going to find Lozzie. I think she's at the netball courts.'

As soon as Cam leaves, Sprog exits too, saying he wants to buy a drink. So Rory arrives and both my friends clear out. Rude, much?

I reach for something, anything, to smooth things over. 'Uh, yeah. You'll miss me this afternoon, too. I've got a previous engagement. Detention with Mr Small at three-thirty.'

'Detention?' Rory looks at me blankly.

'Yeah, y'know? When they keep you at school for extra time, for doing the wrong thing?'

'What did you do?'

I shrug. 'Ah, it's cos I was late the other day, hey.'

'But that was—' Her mouth opens in shock. 'You were helping me get to school! You shouldn't get a detention for that!' She seems appalled by the idea, now she's realised the role she played in it. 'Oh god, that's terrible. I should go to Mrs Franklin and explain.'

'Rory, it's fine.' I shrug. 'I'm not getting caned or anything.'

'They *hit* students for breaking the rules?' Her eyes nearly fall out of her head.

I touch her shoulder to calm her down. 'Nah, mate, I'm kidding. They don't cane kids in school anymore.'

'Right. Not *anymore*.' She puts a hand on her breastbone, like she's giving herself a heart massage.

'Not that they wouldn't like to,' Sprog interjects. He's slurping on an Oak from the canteen, and he sticks his whole self between us, hoisting his jeans up. 'Shit, I'd like to, if I was a teacher. Keep the little brats under *control*!'

He whoops, heading out of the senior area, swinging his backpack around above his head. I snort. 'That's, um, Sprog. I'll introduce you properly another time.'

Rory watches Sprog's departure. 'Your friends don't like me.'

She catches my glance and shrugs, daring me to deny it. That's the most awkward part of it. Rory *knows* what she looks like – too passionate, too vulnerable, too weird in every way. And she's totally right – my friends don't like her.

I make my expression firm. 'They don't know you. They'll come around.'

But I don't know whether I'm saying that for her sake or for mine.

✳

My phone pings with a message from Sprog – *U still in detention? Ditch that shit* – at the exact same time Mr Small levers himself out of his chair.

'Time's up.' Smallie scans over all us losers in the classroom. He seems to reserve a dirty look just for me. 'Please don't let me see you in here again.'

I go hard on the ride home, chasing lost time. Magpies swoop at me half-heartedly from the box gums on the road shoulder. The whole time I was in detention, I kept circling back to that conversation with Mrs Ramanathan. I liked her classes. I was good at them, too. But a sports guy like me, choosing cooking? That'd be a total shame job.

Her other questions cut even deeper: *Where do you see yourself after high school? In five years' time?* I don't have an answer, and I feel like I've failed some kind of test. A few years ago, I'd have been able to give Mrs Ram something. But this isn't like wanting to be an astronaut or a fireman when I was a kid. What's important to me *now*? Am I supposed to know? I'm only sixteen years old – I haven't got a clue about my 'career', or my 'long-term future', or any of that shit. Except for Cam, nobody really seems to take it seriously. All the teacher-talk about *grasping your potential* is just a cue for Sprog to make a series of wanking jokes.

I'm done with detention, I know that much. The afternoon

is hot and bright and seems pretty damn nice after being stuck inside for an extra hour and a half against my will. Coasting down the other side of Fogarty's Hill Road, I'm somehow not surprised to see the shimmer of gold near the bottom of the gulley.

I pull up beside Rory in a dry spray of dust. 'Whatcha doing here?'

'Waiting for you.' She rises out of a cross-legged position, keeping the forefinger of one hand in the middle of her book to mark the page, slapping at her butt with the other hand.

I still can't get used to the fact that I can see her legs now she's chopped off her overalls. I try not to stare. 'It's only detention. I survived.'

'No much fun though, right? I wanted to say sorry again. And I brought you something to make it up to you.' She grabs for her knapsack that's sitting on the ground beside the Titanic, and starts rooting around inside with her free hand.

'You didn't have to do that,' I point out.

'I wanted to. I believe in fair trade. You got your time wasted because of me. Here.' She lifts up a jar, which looks like it used to hold coffee. Now it's chock-full of thick, golden darkness. 'It's honey.'

The joke's right there. 'Sweetening me up?'

'No!' Then she realises I'm only teasing. 'Funny.'

'Rory, you don't have to give me anything.' She looks at me, and it's like our eyes get caught in the honey, viscous and sticky and delicious. I have to look away. 'But hey, this is nice.' I peer at the contents of the jar. 'It's got honeycomb in it!'

She shrugs. 'Homemade. Most commercial honey is a mix of different types, but this is straight from our hives.'

'Well, thank you. This is awesome.' I tuck the jar into my backpack, avoiding her eyes when I ask my next question. 'You gonna ride in tomorrow?'

'For sure. My bike's fixed now.'

I look up. She's nodding eagerly, which is good. I'm not the only eager one, then. I decide to state my case. 'I come past here about quarter to eight every morning.'

'Okay. I'll be here.'

'Cool.'

I wish I *was* cool. Or even that I could *act* cool – that'd be nice. I'm pretty sure I'm blushing as we say our goodbyes.

It's nearly half past five by the time I get home. Mum's cruising around in the kitchen; the kettle is boiling and she's still in her work clothes. Dad's bustling through the house, collecting Connor's training gear. My brother is lolling on the couch, eating peanut butter toast, making no attempt to do anything at all.

'Right, you made it,' Dad says, catching sight of me. 'Please avoid detention in future. It's a pain in my butt.'

'I'll try my best.' If his tone is any indication, Dad's anger seems to have burnt out, which is a relief. I fumble in my backpack for Rory's jar. 'Mum, hey, I've got something for you. That girl from Eden—'

'The one who got you into detention?' Mum's eyes narrow.

'That wasn't her fault. Anyway, she gave me this.' I pull out my prize. 'It was her way of saying sorry.'

'Honey! Oh my god, it's still got the comb in it.' Mum cracks the jar open and dips a finger in to taste. 'Yuuum. Okay, I change my mind. I like this girl.'

Dad gives her a gentle look. 'You – rest. I'll get fish and

chips for dinner.' He glances at Connor. 'You – get your training bag, or we'll be late.' I get the final nod. 'And you – get your homework and chores done. Help your mother.'

Dad and Con bustle out the door, and my phone buzzes as I walk to my room.

'Mate, where are ya?' It's Sprog.

'Ah shit.' I dump my bag on the bed. 'Detention's over, but I'm on house arrest.'

'Detention blows.' Sprog would know. 'Skate park, however, is jumpin'. Me and Jem Reynolds are doing one-eighties. Crew is cheering.' He must hold out the phone, because I can hear the sounds of the skate park boys, then I hear Sprog sigh. 'This sucks. Why can't they keep the park open, hey?'

This complaint again. 'Mate, the ramp's falling to pieces. The whole site's dangerous. Cam said the council's asking for development submissions. They've even had an offer from a supermarket.'

'That's bullshit. Why can't they find another piece of ground somewhere in Lamistead to build their stupid supermarket? I mean, where else are kids in town supposed to hang?'

'I dunno, mate. You got me. It's a dumb decision, but we's teenagers – what can we do about it?'

'Fuck all.' Sprog sounds disgusted, but I can't tell if it's at the council's decision or at his own powerlessness.

Crazy thing is, Sprog's not really that good a skater. He just likes the skate park cos it's a place to go. Which is fair enough: I've been to his house, and it's bloody depressing. His mum's empty bottles sit out on the front porch like an honour guard. Even when his brother, Curtis, isn't home, the place reeks of tension, and the smell of Salvo's furniture and unwashed dishes.

When Curtis *is* home, Sprog's anxiety level skyrockets. Will Curtis and their mum, Heather, get into it tonight? What will the screaming match be about this time? I don't visit too often. Sprog always prefers to meet up elsewhere.

We chitchat for a bit longer – Sprog wants to talk about the chances of a rep squad scout showing up at footy, I'm less enthused – but it's getting late. Mum calls out for a hand with chores, and I've still got to finish my homework before Dad and Connor get back with the fish and chips.

Potato cakes are Dad's version of an apology. He's trying to make up for this morning, smooth over his sharp words and other jagged bits. But there's obviously something else going on. Dad isn't acting or sounding much different, but I can tell something is bugging him. I'm strangely relieved, cos all day I thought what was bugging him was me.

*

In bed that night, I'm well ready for sleep. But for some reason, I roll around in the sheets, can't find a comfy spot. When I finally drop off, I dream about honey.

Warm golden globs of the stuff are running in a stream right in front of me. I want to taste it, but bees have been drawn to the same spot. They buzz around me, threatening to sting. I wave my hands uselessly as the swarm of bees hums and thickens…

I wake up covered in sweat. Lie there for a second as my body settles. There's still a buzzing in my ears. Then I realise it's not buzzing – it's voices. Low, angry voices from the bedroom on the afternoon-sun side of the house.

My parents are arguing.

'So that's not like them?'

'No.' I glower at the ground ahead as I push my bike. 'I mean, they're normal – they argue over stuff. But usually, they're really tight. You know, walnuts in the shell? The way there are two halves that are completely different, but the seam in the centre where they meet is perfectly aligned? That's my parents.'

Rory nods, taking it in. We stopped for a drink about two kay from school, started talking, and never got back in the saddle. The Titanic is actually looking better – Rory said Mr Fennelli gave it a full service. It can't quite keep up with the Cannondale, but Rory pedals harder than me, so we're almost even.

Rory's voice is placid. 'Bo, I don't know anything about your parents, but I don't think you should worry. Your mum's having a baby soon. That's got to be making her tired, and that puts extra stress on your whole family, especially your dad.'

I shake my head. 'It's not Mum. Mum's steady.'

'Maybe it's something financial that you don't know about?'

I push hard over a bump in the road. 'I don't think so. I think it's Dad. There's something up with my dad, and I don't know what it is.' My feet start plodding as we get closer to school, and I sigh. 'I feel like cutting school today.'

Rory's eyes widen. 'You want to cut school?'

'Yeah. But I won't. Too much hassle. A few people I know cut, but nobody from our group.'

'Not even Sprog?'

I grin. 'Nah. He's one of those guys who wags school then shows up at lunchtime. He's got nowhere else to be, and all his mates are at school.'

'Well, I'm not going to cut,' Rory says firmly. 'Double Art today. I like Mr Ong, and he said I can use clay for my first term project.'

'Clay, huh?'

'Yep. He said we could choose any medium. I like to sculpt. I use clay from the riverbed at home ...'

Her voice undulates on the day's breeze as she explains about local clay, natural versus commercial clay, the ways you prepare it, how glazes work, and I'm distracted from my problems for the rest of the walk. We make it to school right on bell time and by then I feel better.

Chatting to Rory has a calming effect. She listened to all the stuff about my folks – didn't try to offer solutions, just listened. And her own stuff is interesting: she talks about different things, not school social politics, or sport, or movies, or gaming. I didn't realise how similar all my conversations with my friends are until I started having different ones with her.

I ride the wave of Rory-generated calm right through to my second class.

'*Bonjour*, M'sieur Mitchell.'

I've been partnered with Lozzie for conversation work. Her white-blonde scruff is pulled into a ponytail, and she's wearing her riding jeans – she looks like she's come straight from the paddock.

I settle in the chair opposite her, grumping as I hunt for my French dictionary. '*Je déteste le langue française.*'

'You mean, *Je deteste* la *langue française,*' Lozzie replies. 'But hey, points for effort.'

We swap questions and answers for a few minutes, scrabbling through our dictionaries for words we don't know or can't remember. I do more scrabbling than Loz – she aces this class.

'It's from doing dressage,' she explains. 'Half the horsey terms are in French.'

'Lucky you.' That gives me a thought. 'Hey, would you be interested in helping me in this subject? Cos Mrs Ramanathan is worried about my marks.'

'*Bien sûr.* I'd get to brush up on basics while I'm at it, so double happiness.' She smiles brightly. 'What's this I hear about Saturday? Sprog's organising a party?'

It's the first I've heard, but when we're gathered at recess, Sprog confirms the rumours. 'River party, Saturday night. We all good to go?'

I shrug. 'Dunno, hey. Dad's got a bug up his arse about something. It would involve some negotiation.'

'So negotiate. It's gonna be warm on Saturday,' he says, wheedling. 'I know your dad wants your nose to the grindstone now school's back, but it's only one party. Or don't tell him. Say you're hanging at my place.'

'Cos he'll totally believe that,' I say, with a bit too much acid. I catch sight of Sprog's face, and suddenly wish I'd been more diplomatic. 'Look, man, I'm keen, but think about it – I say I'm at a mate's place, Mum and Dad hear on the grapevine that there was a party on the same night, they rightly assume that's the real story, and then I get keel-hauled. Not fun, yeah? If I'm gonna do this, I gotta do it right.'

Sprog's time is totally unsupervised and largely his own, so he doesn't always get why I put up with my parents' bylaws. But they're pretty clear-cut laws: keep up with homework and sport, do your chores, lay off the phone usage, and – the key item – not too much socialising during term time.

The prospect of a river party is tempting, though. I'll have to figure out some way of getting permission to go. Normally I'd ask straight out, but with the strange tremors at home, I might have to lay some groundwork – extra chores, sucking up, that sort of thing.

'Can I invite Rory?'

Sprog makes a face. 'What is it about you and that chick?'

'She's nice.'

'Fine. Invite the feral.' He sighs, looks over at Cam. 'You coming to the thing?'

Cam keeps her eyes focused on the notes she's transcribing. 'It's my birthday. I'm definitely coming.' She pauses to give him a look. 'Did you organise this party cos of my birthday? You know I hate birthday parties.'

'The thought never crossed my mind.' Sprog waves a hand airily.

I'd actually forgotten it was Cam's birthday. She's usually low-key about it, but now I understand why Sprog's set on making this party happen, which only reinforces the impression that his last line is the most unbelievable thing I've ever heard.

Cam obviously doesn't buy it either. 'Don't play games with me, Dominic,' she says, deadpan.

'I never play games with you, Camilla,' he replies, equally deadpan.

But in that moment, their eyes lock, and suddenly I get it – the snarking, the bullshit, the tension. I get all of it. As I figure it out, they both look away.

Sprog continues talking in the same casual tone. 'Hey, I just figured it's gonna be hot, and summer's nearly over. Let's make the most of it.'

I should be excited about the idea of a party, but I feel out of whack. If Sprog had suggested a quiet night at the river, with him and me and Cam and Lozzie, I'd be more enthusiastic. Right now, the idea of being stuck in the middle of a big group of people leaves me cold.

Shandy and Kaylah sit across from us in the senior area. At least they're not bothering Rory today, but that's probably because she's not around to bother. She's not around at lunchtime, either, though, and for a second I think she's ditched school after all. I try to take my mind off it with a game of basketball in the PE pavilion, where Teo smashes me a few times during centre passes and Sprog cowboys the ball around. My brain is just starting to feel more normal when Mrs Ramanathan shows up.

At first, I think I'm in trouble. Then she explains why she's hunted me down, and I *know* I'm in trouble. 'So if I want to change into Food Tech, I'd have to drop PE?'

'Those subjects are on the same timetabling line.' Mrs Ram points to the relevant spots on the print-out in her hand. 'You can't take both.'

'That…' I wipe my sweaty face on my T-shirt to hide my expression. I've been thinking I could drop Biology, placate Dad by keeping PE. And that's another shock – I've really been *thinking* about it. This is serious. 'That makes things more complicated.'

'I understand, Bo.' Mrs Ram's face is sympathetic. 'Perhaps you can talk to your parents about your options? But the final choice should be yours. Let me know what you decide.'

Great. All her suggestions are impossible.

My brain's still buzzing at bell time. Double English after lunch is traditionally tiresome, but it's also when I finally get to see Rory again. She cruises into the room, bangles chiming, cheeks flushed. Then she sits at a desk on my right, so I can see the message she scrawls in the margin of her English notes: *Art rooms at lunch. There's a kiln!!*

I raise my eyebrows at the news.

She scrunches her nose and writes again: *That's exciting, you know.*

Sounds thrilling.

It is! She's left-handed, I realise, which works well in this situation.

More thrilling than this class?

She rolls her eyes. The class is mostly Mr Small rhapsodising at length about the story we've been set to read, followed by comprehension questions. He spends most of the lesson casually walking past desks, giving Kaylah special attention while Kaylah simpers. The only thing Kaylah seems to be learning in this class is how to switch the shine on for middle-aged sketchy dudes. Life goals, man.

I tap my pen on Rory's notebook to get her attention. *You coming to the river party Sat night?*

She glances at me. *Am I invited?*

I just invited you.

To hell with Sprog. If Rory's at the river on Saturday, at least I'll have some enthusiasm for the party. After the final bell, at the bike racks, I fill her in on where and when to meet for the party. Then I'm busting arse to get home, eat and change for footy in town.

During term time, it's the tedium of school followed by the regular regimen of after-school sport, homework, chores, sleep. There's a brief respite on the weekend, but on Monday morning I wake up and do it all again. Mum and Dad deal with routine constantly with work, looking after me and Connor, and keeping the house together. I wonder if that's what my life's going to be like after I've finished school. The same old things over and over…

Mum comes in from the garden as I'm standing at the island, shovelling Weet-Bix into my mouth. There's dirt under her nails, and she has to reach up to stroke my hair back off my forehead. 'When did you get so tall, big fella?'

I dump the empty bowl in the sink. 'Well, I got home the other day, hey, and there was this little cake in the fridge with a label on it, saying *Eat Me*. And when I ate the cake, my whole body started expanding…'

'Lol lol lol,' Mum says, which is even funnier cos she never uses lols or emojis in texts. 'Got your boots?'

'Yep.'

'What d'you think about this VFL scout business? Is the team excited?'

'I guess.'

Mum squints at me. 'Thought you'd be excited too.'

'Yeah, I dunno.' As I say it, I feel a strange flutter against my hip.

Mum smiles, puts a hand on her stomach – it was her belly nudging me. 'Did you feel that?'

'Yeah.' I grin. 'Wow, you've got another footy player in there.'

'Or maybe a netball player, who knows?'

'Nah, if it's a girl, she can join the girl's footy team.' Then I ask her, cos asking Mum these questions is always easier than asking my father, 'What were you and Dad arguing about last night?'

She sighs, pushes on her lower back. 'You heard that, did you? Sorry. We didn't mean to disturb you.'

'You didn't disturb me,' I lie. 'I'm already a disturbed individual.'

'It's nothing you have to worry about right now,' Mum says. She presses a kiss to her thumb, then presses her thumb between my eyebrows. 'We sorted it out.'

That's the problem with asking Mum about stuff. She's easier to ask, but ninety per cent of the time her answers are just reassuring, or so vague that you don't understand anything better than you did before.

I don't know if they really did sort it out, either. Dad comes home late, after dinner and my post-training shower, and I can tell from his breath that he's been out having a few beers with his mate Bruce. Bruce is an okay guy, but he gets on the sauce a bit. I know Mum doesn't approve.

Dad's mellow enough for me to ask about the party, though.

'How small?' Dad asks, hacking into his reheated chop and veg.

'Small.' I'm standing in the kitchen with my hair dripping and a towel wrapped around my waist – not exactly a position of strength for bargaining. But Dad was the one who brought it up. He'd heard about it from Bruce's daughter, Chloe; I was right that word would get around. I'm glad I didn't try to wing it with a fib, like Sprog suggested.

I dig for something suitably vague. 'It'll just be a swim in the river, a bit of music … I'll be home early.'

Dad makes a show of contemplating the meat on the end of his fork. 'First week back of term …'

'I swear I'll be home early. It's Cam's birthday, and she wanted it to be low-key.' A slightly underhanded move on my part: both my parents like Cam, cos she's academic and hard-working. Leaving out the fact that Sprog initiated the party is only good sense.

Dad sighs, and I know I've won. 'Fine. Go. But on Saturday, you slave for your mother and catch up with schoolwork. And you're home by eleven.'

'Eleven is great.' Eleven is actually right about when things will be kicking off, but I'm not gonna push it.

'Good. That's settled.' Dad dips his forkful in tomato sauce. 'Now go put some clothes on. And don't you have homework that needs attention?'

I do, and sadly, it won't attend to itself. While half my mind's going over the French verbs Loz emailed me, I keep

48

returning to Mrs Ram's questions. What's my life plan? Not the same old boring shit every day of the week, every week of the year, that's for sure. I tolerate school, and I love footy, and hanging with my mates, but there's got to be more to life.

More *what*, I don't really know.

'Ohmigod, we've been waiting for *aaages*,' Lozzie complains. 'Did you two actually ride those machines, or walk them the whole way to town?'

We've made it to the shade of the big maples near the IGA car park. I'm locking up the Cannondale, so I don't think Lozzie sees me flush. Me and Rory actually did walk some of the way, talking. We got back on for the final stretch, whizzing past the primary school, and Camp Reserve Oval – where I seem to spend half my life – then onwards from the Criterion Hotel on Gough Street to our meeting spot.

Rory dumps her bike beside mine – she doesn't have a lock – and edges towards Cam. 'Hey. Bo said it's your birthday, so I brought you this.'

Cam glares at me before accepting the brown-paper-wrapped package. 'Oh. Wow, that's… I don't usually make a big deal out of it, but… thanks.'

There's a lot of eye movement between Cam and Lozzie that I don't quite get, and Rory looks confused by the way Cam shoves the parcel straight into her backpack without opening it. Before things deteriorate into some kind of uncomfortable girl-hell, Sprog saunters over. The bottles in his backpack are clinking; nobody is under any illusions about what Sprog's plans for the night involve.

'So, did ya bring your bathers?' He lumps an arm over Rory's shoulders, and I remind myself firmly that he probably tanked up before he arrived here. 'Cos you've gotta have bathers, mate. It's a swimming party.'

'Are we buying sausages?' Lozzie yanks at the sides of her bikini top. 'Sprog, what's the deal with food?'

'Harvey's got them – we're just picking up snacks.' Sprog sees my expression, removes his arm from Rory and waves us towards the supermarket. 'Behold, the IGA. Let the pillaging commence.'

We move off as a group. I catch Rory's eye as she sidles behind, keep my voice low. 'Have you been to the IGA before?'

Her reply is equally quiet. 'I've seen it on supply runs for rice and oil. But I haven't actually been inside.'

Once we're through the entrance, Sprog grabs a trolley. Rory stares as he pushes the metal cage in loopy circles.

'You've gotta get a trolley. It's all part of the supermarket experience.' My god, he's on a roll, and it's only five-thirty in the afternoon. He makes an elaborate bow towards Cam. 'Your carriage, m'lady.'

Cam clambers into the trolley, all gangly brown arms and legs, smiling in her white tank top and cut-off jeans. Lozzie makes her hold the bags. Sprog pushes – erratically. Somehow we make it to the lolly aisle in one piece.

Rory's gazing in astonishment at the internal landscape of the IGA. I've been into this supermarket so many times it's like my own backyard, but for once I see it from the perspective of a newcomer. I've got to admit, it's bizarre. Towering shelves, row upon row of packaged goods... I don't even know what half of them are used for. Mum follows pretty much the same list every time we shop.

'There's so much *stuff*,' Rory says. 'Who *buys* all this stuff?'

'Normal people,' Sprog says, with a sneer.

She looks around the aisle we're in – Biscuits and Confectionary – with appalled awe. 'Why do you need twenty different varieties of rice crackers?'

It's a fair question. I don't think it's one I've ever asked myself before, but why the heck *do* you need so many varieties of rice crackers? Or lollies, for that matter? We move along the aisles, picking up giant bottles of soft drink and mega bags of chips, passing through massive selections of condiments, entire walls of cereal, ramparts of ready-meals. It suddenly occurs to me that Sprog was right about the proposal for a new supermarket. It's crazy. How can Lamistead possibly need another chain grocery store? The town isn't that big, and there's so much stuff in here already.

And the food seems ridiculous, now I'm looking at it. Irish stew with potatoes – in a can! Fifteen different flavours of tuna! For someone like Rory, whose lunches are like a poem to simple food, the sight of all this processed food must be horrifying.

I check her face, feeling strangely embarrassed. 'Are you okay?'

'I don't think I've ever seen so much plastic in one place before.' She looks pale. 'Ray's right. The supermarket industry and Big Agriculture are out of control.'

I don't know who Ray is, and now doesn't seem the most opportune moment to ask. I file it away for later. By the time we reach the checkout, I'm relieved we're getting out of here. Rory's practically hyperventilating. She has a full-on spasm when it comes to the plastic bags.

'Ohmigod, stop! We can put the stuff in our bags – that's why we *have* bags. We don't *need* plastic bags.' She clutches her head, starts snatching up packets of chips before the checkout lady can deal with them.

Sprog groans. 'For fuck's sake.'

Rory turns to Sprog. 'There's a stretch of ocean in the North Pacific that's larger than Texas, and it's filled with *three million tonnes* of plastic. Most of it is plastic bags. Oceanographers call it the Great Pacific Garbage Patch.'

'Seriously?' Lozzie looks confounded.

Rory nods. 'They reckon that plastic debris is now the most common surface feature of the world's oceans. And eighty per cent of it is discarded on land.'

'Jesus.' Sprog grabs up his bags. 'You do what you like, I'm taking the plastic.'

Rory gives me a stricken look. I don't know what to do – Sprog is my best mate, but he can get feisty when his hackles are up. And when he's tanked, he's completely unpredictable. I shrug helplessly at Rory as Sprog marches off.

We're catching a ride in Teo Trembath's ute, the bikes tossed in the tray. The atmosphere in the dual-cab is awkward. Cam sits between Sprog and Teo, directing the conversation onto safe topics like footy and netball. Lozzie makes stupid jokes, squashed beside me and Rory in the rear. Slowly the tone lightens. By the time we get to the river, things are

53

chilled, and I'm still holding out hope that this evening won't be a total disaster.

There's already a small group gathered at the river bend, positioning cars and setting up picnic blankets on the bank. More people are walking it in, and the atmosphere starts to get festive. Folks see Teo pull the ute around, and a cheer goes up.

Sprog leans out the window, waving his arms and bellowing. '*My people! I have arrived!*'

'You're gonna fall out of the cab, you dork!' Lozzie yells, right near my ear.

'It's okay. I've got him.' Cam rolls her eyes and shows us how she's holding onto his belt.

Someone has put NERO on the dock, and my spirits lift as I climb out of the rear with Rory and Loz. It's a party night – I shouldn't be such a downer. Everyone's happy to see us, Rory's taking it all in with big round eyes, everything will be fine.

Sprog pulls a black-labelled bottle out of his backpack, holds it high. 'Here's to the first week of school being *over*!' To general applause, he unscrews the bottle and takes a raw, wet-mouthed swig.

This little stretch of river has been a teenage hangout for longer than my parents have been together. Joel's mob have been on this land forever, and give access to people who ask permission and are respectful. Our parties here can get rowdy, but we all make sure we don't wreck the place. The swimming spot is deep; you can fish for redfin here, if you're into that, or you can sit in the shade of the trees and watch the dark water swirl off around the corner.

People are talking, drinking, dancing, jumping in and out of the water. Joel and Justin load the rusted-out forty-four-gallon drum that everyone uses for bonfires. Before they ignite it, Sprog steps forwards, bottle in hand, and splashes the woodpile with whiskey.

His grin is sharp-pointed. 'Light me up, bitches.'

'Waste of Jack,' Joel says, shaking his head.

'It's Curtis's booze,' Sprog says. 'Fuck him.' He grabs the matches from Joel, as the background bass ramps high. When he chucks the lit match onto the wood, the fire goes up with a *woof*, sparks exploding skyward.

I step back too fast, bump into Rory. 'Shit, sorry. You going okay?'

'Fine.' She nods at Sprog. 'Is *he* okay?'

'All good,' I say. To be honest, I'm not really sure, but he's here with us, so he's safe. I'd like to know what's been going on at Sprog's place lately, though. He seems even more hyperactive than usual. I stand beside Rory and watch him throw himself off the rope swing and into the river with an animal howl.

Evening is coming on now, and the night is sultry. I sit on a picnic rug beside Rory in the flickering light of the flames, offer her a beer, which she accepts, and suggest a swim, which she's not sure about.

'I only have shorts and a singlet under this,' she admits, pointing at her overalls.

'No bathers?' The thought of Rory rising out of the river in nothing but shorts and a wet singlet makes my throat go ever so slightly dry.

She shakes her head, then looks over my shoulder. 'Um, I think your mate needs a hand.'

Joel flashes the tongs with a slightly desperate grimace – he wants help with the sausages.

'Go, go,' Rory says.

I'm enjoying myself more than I thought I would, but it's strange, being here with Rory. I keep an eye on her while I help Joel wrangle the cooking. 'You want the rest of these snags on the hotplate?'

'Yeah, load 'em up.' As I lay out the uncooked sausages, Joel turns the half-done ones with the tongs. 'You're mates with that Eden girl now?'

'Sure.' I pull the cling wrap off another meat tray. 'She's still figuring things out, hey. She's never been to school before – can't be easy.'

'Eden hippies.' Joel frowns at the flames, spits on the ground. 'Dunno what their deal is, on the Bowyer property.'

I'm curious about what Joel knows. He and his family understand more about the land around here than anybody else in school. 'Did they get permission to live there?'

'Yeah, they talked to the land council when they started up ten years ago, did it the proper way.' He shrugs. 'But Mum reckons they're weird. They've cut themselves off – no one knows what goes on out there.'

'Rory says they practise rewilding. That doesn't sound too bad. Like reveg, maybe?'

Joel snorts. 'Who knows? Do they contribute to the community? No. Do they respect the old places? Nobody's got a clue.'

'Maybe they don't know which places are important,' I suggest.

Joel raises his eyebrows, glances at Rory. 'Have they ever bothered to ask?'

Rory is sitting on the riverbank, alone. Nobody approaches

her, and she watches the action in the water while sipping her beer and making sculptural piles of river stones on her towel. It's like she's living inside a Social Reject bubble and I'm damned if I know how to break her free.

Once Joel has cooked the sausages, I take one over to her as an excuse to touch base. 'Here you go – specialty of the house. D'you want sauce?'

She gazes down sadly at the sausage-in-bread in my hand. 'Oh, Bo, thanks for thinking of me, but I'm a vegetarian.'

'You don't eat meat?' Shit, now I'm stumped. I've never had a friend who's vegetarian. In a farming community like Lamistead it's really uncommon.

'Sorry.' Rory shrugs. 'Any lentil burgers?'

'No.' My shoulders slump. 'You should've said something at the supermarket.'

'I didn't realise there'd be a fry-up.' Her tone is matter-of-fact. 'But don't worry about it. There are potato chips and stuff, right?'

I eat the rejected sausage while we watch half a dozen people take turns on the rope swing, whoops and yells flying as they hit the water. Sprog is paddling on a lilo; he's directing the action, King of All He Surveys. Shandy is down by the waterline, dipping her toes and squealing at the cold, while Todd Willander and two other boys from 11C dance attendance.

'Shandy's having a good time,' Rory notes.

I laugh. 'Yeah, she's in her element, for sure.' Shandy's got the best make-up, the cutest bikini, the fakest tan. 'She never swims at these things, only paddles. I think she's worried about messing up her hair.'

Cam beckons to me from down by the water's edge.

'Bo,' – Rory nudges me with her elbow – 'you should go hang out with your friends.'

'*You're* one of my friends,' I insist.

'Really, I'm fine. You don't have to chaperone me all night.'

I feel like I'm split in two, stuck on the fault line between Rory and my friends – each equally deserving of my attention, each pulling me in a different direction.

'Look, I'll go for bit. But I'll be back soon.' I rise up off the towel and meander towards Cam.

She's been chatting to Ebony Roscoe from netball. For all intents and purposes, Cam looks like she's having a great time – she's snaffled a bonfire sausage, the blackened grease staining her hands, and she's laughing. But I've known Cam a long time, and I'm not a complete idiot. Her eyes keep straying to Sprog.

'How much has he had to drink?' I ask quietly.

'More than enough, and then some,' she says, sighing. 'I hate it when he's like this.'

'It's just a bit of booze, Cam. We all do it.'

She makes a face.

Sprog strokes his way to shore and clambers out, powerful muscles bunching. He lifts Lozzie up then runs back into the water and dumps her. She's fully clothed, shrieking and laughing. Cam's laughing too, but not in the same way as the rest of us.

'Just tell him,' I say to her.

'You of all people should know you don't just *tell* Dominic anything. Especially not about his drinking.'

'I wasn't talking about his drinking.' I meet her eyes deliberately.

She looks away. 'I don't know what you're—'

'Cam. It's me.'

She swallows, says nothing.

'You should tell him.'

'That's … a really terrible idea.'

'Then – shit, I dunno. Grab him and kiss him right on his face!'

She blushes. But she's still shaking her head.

'For god's sake, what's your problem?'

'My *problem* …' She sighs again. Then something uncorks inside her, and all the words come out in a rush. 'My problem is that Dominic is screwed up about his mum and his brother, and he doesn't want me to see it, and I can't figure out how to get it through his thick skull that I *already* see it and I don't care. Plus he's always been so freaked about the fact that I'm smart and he thinks he's dumb, and we've been friends for so long, and it feels weird, and it's … basically a big fat mess.'

'I don't know why you two have to be so complicated,' I say, snorting despite myself.

'Shut up!' Cam pushes me on the shoulder as the music switches from Desiigner to Kaiydo. 'Anyway, what about you and …'

She cuts her eyes to Rory, but I stop her with a glare. 'That's just mates right now, thanks very much.'

'*Right now*, is it?'

'She's got enough on her plate already.'

'No kidding. I'm changing my mind about her, though. She's a bit obsessed with the enviro-stuff, but she's kind of sweet. She gave me hand-knitted socks for my birthday. She must have gone to a bit of effort.'

'She likes to give gifts,' I say.

'Showing she cares…okay, I'll buy that. She might be socially inept, but she's trying.' Cam glances over at Rory again. 'And look at that. Progress.'

'What?'

I follow Cam's line of sight, see that gold flash, and my heart stutters. Rory's down at the waterline, standing in the short queue for the rope swing. Her arms are crossed over her chest, and she's stripped off her overalls. She's down to her singlet, plus a pair of what looks like old running shorts – it's a pretty winning combination, as far as I'm concerned. It might be unconventional next to the other girls' bikinis, but some people are swimming in their jeans, so she doesn't look completely out of place.

She really is trying: she's out there, chatting to the people in the queue, ready to throw herself in. I'd give her a cheer, but then I see something that turns my heart murmur into full-blown arrhythmia.

Rory's taken her place at the front of the queue, and one of the boys from 11C is pressing the rope into her hands. High above her, Todd Willander has shinned up the tree: he's stretched full length along the top branch, where the rope connects. He's holding something shiny in his hand, and I have a terrible feeling I know what it is.

When I scan the bank, I find Shandy and Kaylah standing together; Kaylah's dressed in a hot pink bikini, and her face is pensive in the hellish firelight. Shandy looks gleeful. I see her glancing up, trying not to give away what's going on with a too-obvious display of interest. She has her phone raised, and it's focused on Rory.

'Shit,' I say, and I'm already moving.

Cam calls out behind me, 'What the hell? What's Shandy doing?'

I don't have time to reply, because I'm bolting for the swing.

I shove through bodies, knowing I'm not going to make it in time, yelling, '*Willander! Don't you fucking dare!*'

A couple of people look up, but it's too late. Rory grips the rope and runs off the bank – she arcs out as I reach the tree. Her expression is open, alive with excitement and the thrill of the swing's momentum ...

Right up to the moment when Todd slices through the braided rope.

Five metres of rope snakes around Rory as she flails, shrieks, and drops into the water with an ungainly splash.

Justin Fromer is the only other person to realise that Rory being tangled up in rope at the bottom of the river is a genuine issue – he wades in from the other side as I dive. The murky brown water kisses me in a cold shock, and I can't see shit. I keep searching, my hands outstretched...then my fingers touch slick skin, rough braided hemp, and I've got her.

We break the water with a double gasp. Rory has seaweed-strips of hair on her face, too disoriented to know which way is up. Justin helps me get her to the shore, pulling the coils of rope away from her as we go, like we're disengaging the arms of some particularly malicious octopus.

'Shit.' I'm panting, soaked and dripping, my shoes leaking water – I never expected to be diving in in my clothes. 'Christ, Rory, are you okay?'

'Oh—' She coughs up water, leans over her knees, coughs some more.

'She all right?' Justin asks.

Rory's nose is leaking blood and her cheeks are flaming, pink mixing with the red already on her face as she gets her coughing under control. 'Fine. I'm … fine, really.'

'Was that Willander?' Justin says.

I nod, my whole jaw clenched.

'What a tool. I'm gonna have a word.' Justin frowns and disappears.

People are looking on, but most of them are too blazed or distracted to realise that this isn't part of normal programming. Some of them are even applauding Rory for such a spectacular jump. A lot of them are laughing.

One of the people laughing is Shandy.

A flush of rage boils through me. I want to go over there and wipe that smile off her face, but Rory starts to shiver. She needs my attention more. 'Your nose is bleeding. Here, you've got to pinch it.'

'I can do it.' She pinches, tips her head back. The rope must've hit her on the face as she fell.

'That *cow*,' I say, glowering at Shandy. 'What's her problem?'

'She wasn't in line, it wasn't her,' Rory says, eyes watering.

'It was her lackey, which is just the same.'

'I don't understand,' Rory says sadly. Her nose is bruised, and there's a scrape over her eyebrow. 'I don't understand people.' She looks tired.

I don't either, I've realised, and it's beginning to get to me. I thought I understood my parents. I thought I understood the school social order, my place in it. I knew there was a shitty side, like this, but I've always been safe. Rory isn't, though, and it's driving me crazy.

She drops her chin forwards and swipes her face with the

back of her hand, leaving a watery pink smear. 'Bo, thank you.'

'You don't need to thank me.'

'I think I'm going to go home.'

I swivel towards her. 'Ah, man, don't go.'

'No, really. It's been a big night, and I still have to ride home.' She looks away.

'Rory, you can't let them win.'

She hesitates, then she sighs, turns for her towel and clothes. I swear under my breath.

'I'll come with you.' I walk beside her. 'We can ride back together.'

'No,' she says, all shaky firmness. 'I'm okay.'

'Rory—'

'Please, Bo. It's all right—'

'It's *not!*'

'It will be.' She touches my arm. 'I'll be fine. Please stay. You're having a good time.'

'Shit…' I scrub a hand through my wet hair. 'At least let me walk you to the end of the property.'

But when she's yanked her overalls and sandals on, and we get to the Titanic, we find it's been defaced. Spray-paint and texta have been slathered all over the frame, shouting slogans like *Free Love Right Here* and *Hippie Bike*. Rory sees the damage and seems to deflate in front of my eyes.

'*Seriously?*' I'm fully pissed off now. I stare at the kids laughing by the light of the fire. 'Why are some people such absolute *shits*?'

Rory sighs, like she wishes she knew the answer. 'Thanks for inviting me, Bo. I had a good night up until…' She waves a hand helplessly.

I got nothing. I hardly know what to say in return. This was supposed to be a fun night, but it hasn't turned out to be much fun for Rory. 'Mate, I'm really sorry.'

'It wasn't your fault.' She slips her knapsack strap over her shoulders, swings her leg over her bike, leans forwards and squeezes my damp hand with her own. 'I'll see you at school on Monday.'

Then she cycles away.

And I go back to the party to explain a few things to Todd Willander with my fists.

✳

Rory doesn't come to school on Monday. But the footage of her falling into the river has gone viral, thanks to Shandy's Facebook upload. There's been a lot of jokes about new students making a 'big splash' at school, and I feel as if I've been gritting my teeth all day.

People are fucking vindictive. I mean, I knew Shandy was a piece of work, but I never expected this. I'm not even a hundred per cent sure what my friends think. Cam and Lozzie made disapproving *tsks*, but I wonder how deep their disapproval goes.

What I do know is that word about my stoush with Todd Willander gets around faster than lizard spit. By the time footy practice starts in the afternoon, people have already taken sides, and by dinner, Dad's quizzing me about why I got into a punch-up with one of his client's sons.

'It's over,' I say. 'Not a big deal.'

'Well, it's a big deal if I lose the contract with Ross Willander,' Dad points out.

I sit back as Mum puts the pot of pasta on the table. 'Todd's dad is gonna dump you? That's bullshit.'

'Bo.' Mum reaches for the cutlery on the table. 'Language, thanks.'

'But it is!' I look at Dad. 'You're the best landscaper in town, and he knows it.'

'I haven't had a chance to talk to Ross about it yet,' Dad says, as he dishes up for himself. 'Don't dodge the issue. Why did you and Todd get stuck in?'

'Because,' I explain, as I ladle sauce onto my pasta, 'Todd is a dropkick and a dickhead.'

'Bo,' Mum reminds me again, 'your brother's at the table.'

Connor grins, following the conversation avidly.

'Right.' Dad narrows his eyes at my neutral expression. 'Any particular reason for that assessment?'

I ladle on maybe too much sauce. 'He played a trick on Rory at the party on Saturday night. She was hurt and embarrassed. And he messed with her bike.'

'Ah.'

'So I hit him.'

'Hm.' Dad lifts his eyebrows and tackles his pasta. 'Well, that clears things up. I'll mention it to Ross.'

'Aaron.' Mum stares at him across the table.

'Yes?'

Mum looks between me and Dad. 'So... are we going to have a chat now about how hitting people generally doesn't solve problems?'

'Huh?' Dad looks blank, until he sees Mum's expression. 'Oh, right. Well, yeah. Bo, hitting Todd didn't solve your problem, did it?'

'No,' I agree. 'Todd is still a dickhead.'

'*Bo!*' Mum says, while Connor snickers.

'So what's a better solution, d'you think?' Dad asks.

'I really don't know.' I chew thoughtfully. 'I could try kicking him instead?'

Dad snorts, Mum says, '*Aaron!* You're not helping!' and Connor bursts into peals of laughter.

'It might not cure him, but it'd make *me* feel better,' I point out.

Dad laughs outright, then, with Mum pushing on his arm in exasperation, and for a moment my family is normal again – we're relaxed with each other. I sit up, smiling around my forkful of slightly underdone pasta, and everything is right with the world.

Dad gesticulates with his own fork. 'Seriously though, son, your mother's right. Hitting Todd probably didn't make *Rory* feel better, did it?'

'At least someone was sticking up for her,' I say.

The phone rings, and Connor jumps to answer it.

'Yes,' Mum says, 'but doesn't it make things more difficult for her at school?'

'Good point,' Dad says. 'Was Todd giving her grief today? Because if she's—'

'Da-ad,' Connor says, waving the home phone. 'There's a man called Liam on the phone and he wants to talk to you.'

It's like all the air gets sucked out of the room in an instant. Dad stops dead. Mum, too. Both of them are caught mid-action, like they're in suspended animation: Dad with his fork raised, Mum reaching for her water glass.

I look between them. Even Connor seems confused.

'I'll…' Dad clatters his fork down, pushes clear of his chair and holds out a hand. 'I'll take it, Connor, thanks.'

All the blood has drained out of Mum's face. She finally lifts her glass with a shaky hand as Dad walks out onto the verandah with the phone, closing the door behind him.

Mum sips at the water, sets her glass down, stands up slowly and turns to me. I'm scared by how ashy she looks. There's no dramatics with Mum, which somehow always makes me think the worst. 'Bo, I'm going to have a lie-down. Can you do the dishes and feed the dog, and make sure Connor gets organised for bed, please?'

I nod. 'Sure, Mum. Go have a rest.'

She walks around the table and down the hall to the bedroom and closes the door.

That's two closed doors.

I sit at the table for a moment, wondering what the hell this strange disease is that's afflicting our family right now. A disease characterised by silence, secrets and a complete absence of understanding. Somehow the worst thing about it is that it doesn't seem to have a name.

Connor and me go through the motions of finishing dinner. I clear the plates while Connor gets organised for bed. I feed Julie – she's the only one in the house right now who seems obliviously happy. She licks my hand in gratitude, and I give her a scratch behind the ears before I start on the dishes.

'Bo, I need to do my reading,' Connor says.

I pull the plug on the dirty water in the sink. 'What?'

He stands in front of me, clutching his library book. 'Mrs Barton says we have to read aloud to our parent every night.'

I wipe my hands on my jeans. 'You don't want to give it a miss tonight?'

Connor is blank-faced. 'Mrs Barton says.'

'Okay. Sure, bro. Where you wanna read?'

'On the couch, like I do with Mum.'

Once I'm settled in the corner of the couch, Connor flomps down and tucks himself against me. It's strange, cos apart from competing against each other on the Playstation sometimes, me and Connor never really hang out. Not like this, anyway.

'What are you reading?'

He holds up his book. '*The Ruins of Gorlan*. It's good.'

I check out the cover. 'Looks okay. All right, lemme have it.'

Connor makes a bit of a production out of finding his bookmarked place, then launches in. '*They had eaten breakfast well before sun-up, and Will had followed Halt into the forest…*'

It shouldn't be like this, though. Connor should be reading to Mum; I should be doing my homework; Dad should be doing bookkeeping or finishing off some household job. It's like we've all fallen into some whacked-out version of normal family life.

Connor snuggles into me as he reads, encouraging me with nudges to put an arm over his shoulders, needing that contact in a way he usually pretends to dislike. He might be a kid, but he's not clueless; he's picked up that something's wrong.

After ten minutes, he finishes up his paragraph and I tell him it's time for bed.

'Bo, it's too early!'

'Early night tonight.' I pull all his dark hair to stand up on end. 'No whinging. Go brush your teeth, do a piss, then go say goodnight to Mum.'

'What about Dad?'

I look out to the verandah, where Dad is still pacing and talking on the phone. He's got one hand on his hip, the set of his shoulders taut. His face is pinched as he gazes towards our backyard.

'Don't bother Dad right now, sport,' I say. 'He'll come in and kiss you goodnight later.'

Connor comes back from our parents' bedroom with a glum expression. 'Mum said she's sleepy. She's lying on the bed. Do you think being pregnant hurts?'

'What?' I draw the covers for him, shove on his front so he falls back onto the bed. 'No, mate. I mean, look, I don't *know*, hey, cos I'm a guy, so not much chance of me ever finding out. But I don't think it's supposed to hurt. Mum says it's kind of uncomfortable sometimes, but only *having* the baby hurts.'

'Why does having the baby hurt?'

'...*aaand* that's a question I think I'm gonna leave for Mum.' I make sure he's got his feet tucked in before I pull the covers up. 'Con, it's fine. Mum's okay.'

'Really?'

'Really.' I lean down and noogie him, blow in his ear, and he honks out a laugh, more relaxed. 'Now go to sleep. And stop being a stresshead.'

'Bo...'

'Yeah?' I turn with my hand on the light switch.

Connor is gazing up at me hopefully. Then he exhales,

70

shakes his head and looks away. 'Nothing. It's cool. G'night, lamer.'

'G'night, lamest.' I grin at him one last time, hit the switch, walk out of the room.

I only get as far as the dining table. Stand there for a second, touching my fingertips to the wood. We were all eating dinner and laughing here only a little while ago. What happens next? Should I go talk to Mum? Wait for Dad to come in, demand some answers? Would either of those things help? Part of me wants my mother and father to explain what the hell is going on. Another part of me is scared of the explanation. Let's face it – if it's freaking out my parents, it can't be good.

And another part of me is plain pissed. Whatever's happening, could it really be worse than the anxiety created by all these looks and whispers? It's like my parents think me and Connor are stupid, that we haven't noticed something's up. Well, newsflash, folks, but if a nine-year-old can figure out there's a problem, it's time to stop pretending.

I wish I could talk to Rory about this – actually, I wish I could talk to Rory, full stop. Her not showing for school today was a bad sign. The last time I saw her was Saturday night; I don't even know if she made it home okay.

I could go visit her – just get on my bike and roll. But I don't know what the deal is with the Garden of Eden community, and if they allow visitors. I'm not even certain Rory had permission to be at the party on Saturday night. If I get her into strife at home, especially if her family are already hostile to the whole public-school education thing, it could mean she misses even more days of school.

I walk through to my room, flop on my bed. I don't feel

like talking to mates, or doing homework, or reading a book. I don't want to 'consider my life goals'. Mrs Ram has asked me again if I've made a decision about Food Tech, but I don't have the brain space to think about it right now. My only life goal at this moment is to figure out what the fuck's going on with my family.

My parents continue to be baffling over the next few days.

There's a lot of talking behind closed doors and meaningful glances over meals, but no other clues. Dad has me helping him to load some equipment for a new landscaping job, and Mum's been weeding up a storm in the garden: they're both keeping themselves busy.

Rory actually makes it to school on Wednesday – I get to the Bowyer Track intersection and there she is. We're running late, and there's not much chance to talk on the ride in, but I ask about Saturday night as we're locking up our bikes.

'The party wasn't a perfect night,' Rory admits, 'but it was a start. I got a feeling of what it might be like to be a part of everything. I want to make this work. I made a promise to myself to give school a chance. I'd like to think I can last longer than a week.'

I grin at her. 'So you're kinda stubborn.'

'People say that about me *all the time*,' she says, laughing.

Her hair is braided along both sides of her head today. She's taken out her green stud while the bruise on her nose heals. But she's left the graffiti on her bike, although she's painted over *Right Here*. Ironically, Todd and Shandy and the others didn't label her bike all that differently from how she would have done it herself. The Titanic was always a *Free Love Hippie Bike*; now it's just self-identifying.

'So why'd you skip?'

'One of my neighbours had to go to the doctor.' She eases out from between the rows of bikes. 'Star had to drive, and she asked me to babysit her son.'

'Is your neighbour okay?'

'Not really.' She waves a hand. 'It's complicated.'

Being near Rory gives me a warm, hopeful feeling, and I want that feeling to stick around. 'Come and sit with us at recess. Cam and Loz were asking if you're all right.'

'How was Sprog's hangover on Sunday morning?'

'Fucking horrible,' I say cheerfully. 'He wouldn't even answer my texts until midday, and then it was just barfing emojis.'

'Oh, hey, I have something for you.' She fishes something out of her knapsack, hands it to me – it's an origami lotus flower. She nudges me, her smile sharing a secret. 'Unfold it.'

Unfolding the origami reveals a handmade invitation, delicately painted with blue swallows and garden vines.

'I turn sixteen on Saturday,' she says, her face lit up. 'Cam said she doesn't make a big deal out of her birthday, and usually I don't either. But I thought it might be fun to have some friends over for a change.'

She leans closer to show me the handful of lotus flowers in her knapsack, and I have to steer my mind off the question of whether or not she's wearing the running shorts underneath her cut-off overalls.

'I've made invitations for the others,' she says. 'So ... d'you think you'll be able to come?'

'I'll make it happen,' I say.

That'll be two parties in two weeks, but I don't care. For the first time in my life, I think about deliberately disobeying my father.

*

It's not all smooth sailing before the party, though. On Friday Sprog gets called out during fourth period and doesn't come back.

Cam hunts me down at the start of lunch. 'What the hell's going on? Is Sprog in trouble? He's not answering my texts.'

'Chill, mate.' I put my hands on her shoulders. 'It's probably a careers counselling thing. But even if it isn't, I'm sure he's fine.'

'Sure.' She shakes me off, starts burrowing in her bag for her lunch. 'You're right. He's fine. This isn't a big deal.'

'So not a big deal,' Lozzie says, yawning at her greasy chips. She was up late with her new foal again last night. 'We *are* talking about Sprog here.'

'But ... I have been worried about him and Curtis,' Cam admits.

'What?' I give her a frown.

Cam chews her lip. 'I think Sprog's scared of him.'

'Yeah, well, Curtis is scary when he's screaming. But he's all noise. Look, don't stress. I'll ask around.'

Joel and Teo don't know any more than we do, and when Sprog still hasn't shown up halfway through lunch, I walk across to the Design Tech wing. I'm dreading what I'm about to do, but I can't see any other option; Mrs Ramanathan is the only teacher I'm comfortable enough with to ask.

'You've come about your subject selections,' she says, looking delighted.

I'm a single-celled organism. I'm pond slime, scuffing my feet. 'Um, no. I'm real sorry, Mrs Ram, but I didn't come about that. Have you seen Dominic Hamilton? He got called out of class…I thought he might've been on his way to you.'

Mrs Ram wilts. 'No, Dominic isn't here. Have you asked at administration?'

By the time I get back to Cam, lunch is nearly over. 'He's not here. Someone in admin got a call for him and he left. That's all I could find out.'

Cam gnaws on the nail of her little finger. 'At least we know he's not in Mrs Franklin's office.'

Saturday morning is when the next thing happens. Mullet – our footy coach, Darren Mulligan – has scheduled a practice match between the Lamistead and Tarrakan footy clubs. The season is nowhere near ready to start, so it lends authority to the scouting rumours: Mullet wouldn't have gone to this kind of effort for no reason.

But when I get to the change rooms, Sprog hasn't arrived.

Mullet lifts his chin at me, calls me outside. 'You'll have to handle this one without your wingman. Sprog's been detained.'

'*Detained?*' I'm having sudden visions of my best mate in a jail cell somewhere. 'What the hell? Did he—'

'He's busy,' Mullet clarifies. 'His mum's crook, so you're on your own today. At least the rep squad bloke will get a good long look at you.' He peers at me. 'Didn't Sprog let you know?'

'No,' I say, dazed. 'He didn't tell me shit.'

Sprog never misses footy. And he's been excited about this scout business. I'm worried now. I scrabble out a quick text: *Mate where are you? Mullet said ur mum's sick? Call me later.* It adds itself to the bottom of the long chain of unanswered messages on my phone screen.

It's an okay match, but despite Mullet's urgings, I don't know whether I give it my best. Too much other stuff is racing around in my head. I ride over to Sprog's house after the game, but the only person at the house is the person I'm least hoping to see. Curtis Hamilton sits in an old camp chair on the front porch, wearing a Jack Daniel's singlet and jeans, sucking on a cigarette. His dry blond hair stands on end, and his eyes are red-rimmed and dangerous.

'Do I look like Sprog's social manager?'

'I thought you might know where he is.' I'm standing at the foot of the porch stairs, the Cannondale acting as a protective barrier. Curtis might be shit-faced most of the time, but he's got the Hamilton physique, and he's six years older. I don't really think there's anything solid in what Cam said yesterday, but I'm cautious. I'd be no match against Curtis in a fight.

'Hospital, I guess.' Curtis shrugs. 'Mum can't hold her liquor, that's all. Crazy old bitch.'

I'm not sure I heard him right. 'So what's wrong with her?'

'Jesus, I'm not a fucking doctor!' Then his face changes. 'Hey, man, you got a ten-spot? I just need—'

'Nah, man. I'm broke,' I say, backing away.

I text Cam after I leave the house. She'll be at netball with Loz, so she won't get the message until after the game, but she'll want to know what's going on – and chances are that

Sprog will take a call from Cam when he might not take one from me.

Then I realise something else. Sprog might be having personal dramas, but he's not my only friend with stuff happening today.

I'm late for Rory's party.

*

I ride like I'm auditioning for NASCAR on a bicycle.

On Fogarty's Hill Road, I careen down to the bottom of the gulley, searching for the entrance to Bowyer Track. This is the first time I've ever ridden this way. The path isn't signposted, and it's barely wide enough for one car. It's little more than a sheep trail, and I have to ride high in my seat to protect my balls.

After a good ten minutes of nonstop bouncing, the track veers to the left and climbs. At the top of the rise, there's a marker of piled-up river stones and a sign with a name burnt into the wood: *Garden of Eden*. Rory's standing by the sign, flowers scattered in her hair.

'You made it!'

'Sorry I'm late, hey. Sprog was having some drama with his mum.' I dismount and look around, as if more partygoers might materialise from the nearby scrub. 'So it's just me, is it?'

'Looks like it.'

'Shit.'

'It's okay. It was always a long shot.'

'Cam and Lozzie would've come, but it's a direct clash with netball training.'

'I didn't know about that.'

She wouldn't, I realise. She's never participated in local junior sport. 'They would've come,' I repeat.

'Don't worry about it.' She shrugs. 'Anyway, it means we get all the party food for ourselves. Come on in. You can park your bike anywhere.'

I lean the Cannondale against the sign and walk with Rory over the rise into Eden.

The land sprawls down into a shallow sunlit valley – the river must run along the bottom of the property. Enormous towering gums create a natural boundary around the site on either side, and I can make out buildings dotted here and there. But it's like someone sprinkled Jack the Giant Slayer's magic beans over the whole place: everything I see is covered in vegetation.

Fruit trees rise up at random, as if they sprouted wherever seeds fell. They're mixed in with lantana and mulberry and she-oak. I know at least some of the plants, from Mum's gardening obsession. A loquat tree grows happily beside a stand of bamboo. Clumps of artichoke party with wild blackberry. Sunflowers and corn hang loose with kangaroo apple. There's a lot of bush-wood trellis, but no fences of any kind.

Vines meander across dirt pathways, and in through the windows of dwellings. Some of the buildings look derelict. Others have an inhabited look, but it's not like any habitation I've encountered before: huts are cobbled together with mudbrick, bits of corrugated iron, windows that don't belong. Sun glints off a rammed-earth shed with glass bottles built into the walls. An ancient bus sits against the edge of the bush, shadowed by the giant trees, sunk on tyres that have long deflated.

But you hardly notice the buildings or the bus – they're hidden among all the *jungle*.

'Holy shit.' I stand beside Rory, trying to take it all in.

She looks at me. 'Is that the good shit or the bad shit?'

'Oh, it's the good shit.' I laugh. 'This is definitely the good shit, right here. Mum's always trying to get more stuff to grow at our place. She says the land around here's really dry. How'd you get it all so green?'

'It wants to be green,' she says, shrugging. 'We give it a push, then try to keep out of the way.'

Rory takes my hand and pulls me along a track. We weave around bunches of kangaroo grass and stands of waving corn and emerge before what was once a large wooden farmhouse. Half the roof has been removed, along with the wall that should be facing us. Cam's got an old doll's house at her place, one of those ones you can swing open at the front: this looks exactly like that, only on a much larger scale.

Rory leads me up a short path of decorated tiles to the wide stone steps that take us inside. The house's internal walls have also been demolished. A farm-style kitchen is set up in the rear left corner. Someone has dug a wide circular fire-pit straight into the slate floor. Beanbags, old couches, bark-stripped logs and moth-eaten easychairs are sprawled around the pit, where Rory has set up stuff for the party on tartan rugs and quilted blankets, just like it's a picnic. A whole watermelon sits on a tray beside bowls of trail mix, plates with scones and thick slices of homemade bread, jars of preserves, and an old bone-handled butter knife. Rory's gone to a fair bit of effort. I still can't believe I'm the only guest at this party.

Rory kneels on a rug and starts chopping into the

watermelon. It's not like one of those giant watermelons you get at the supermarket – this melon is small, and it's *yellow* inside. I didn't even know you could get yellow watermelon.

'Here, you'll be thirsty.' She hands me a chunk.

The juice clears the dust from my throat, dribbles off my chin. 'Wow, that's good.'

She cuts another slice for herself.

I glance around the farmhouse, the strangeness of it. 'I brought the dock.' It's the first thing I think to say, and as soon as it's out of my mouth I feel stupid. This is the last place you'd want jangly dance music blaring. The background noise of insects summer-humming in the grass seems a more appropriate soundtrack.

'Great.' She gives me an awkward smile that changes into a genuine grin. 'It's all right, y'know. I was incredibly nervous about the party thing anyway.'

I step in closer, dump my bag. 'Well, the party's still on, right?'

She bites her bottom lip. 'I have one guest, so I suppose that's a yes. And I don't get nervous around you, which is a plus.' She switches her gaze quickly back to the food. 'Hey, let's crack open the bottles.'

'Sounds good. I'm parched.' The bottles in question are brown glass, unlabelled, and the liquid inside is golden and frothy. 'Home-brew?'

'You wish.' She offers me a mug. 'It's ginger beer.'

It *is* ginger beer, probably the best ginger beer I've ever tasted. It's nothing like the stuff you get at the shop – it's tart, not over-sweet, and it tingles on my tongue. 'My god, that is freaking fantastic!'

'Ray brews it. He's pretty good at it.'

The mysterious Ray again. 'I've never had home-brewed ginger beer before.'

'We grow all the ingredients on-site,' she says, pouring herself a mug. All the mugs are squat pottery, with thick rims and no handles. They fit nicely in your hand, like they were made to be held. 'Actually, we grow pretty much everything we eat here. The ginger comes from a big patch over behind the house. Ray's been experimenting with natural sugars from beetroot and honey...' She blushes, rolls her eyes. 'Listen to me, I'm rambling about ginger beer.'

'I thought you said you didn't get nervous around me?' I grin.

She snorts. 'It's not that. I've never had a party before, so I wasn't sure what to prepare...' She scans the rugs and food. 'Actually, you know what? Since it's only two of us, let's move everything down to my place. I think we might be more comfortable there.'

I glance around, mug in hand. 'This isn't your place?'

She laughs. 'Oh, no. We all use this space, mainly for shared meals and meetings. D'you wanna help me carry the stuff over?'

'Sure.' I sling on my backpack. 'Partying at your place. Excellent. Lead on.'

'So who does all the gardening?'

I follow Rory out the back exit, carrying my armful of bottles and mugs and platters into the green. The garden here isn't politely cultivated, like at home. It's as if the plants have taken over.

'Oh, everyone. And nobody. The area around the houses is mostly wild, or home garden stuff, so a lot of it is self-seeded.' Rory's voice is a bit stiff. I think she's excited to share Eden with someone from outside, but maybe she's also worried about my reaction.

I put her straight on that score right away. 'Well, it's freaking amazing. I've never seen anything like it. I didn't know there was a place this lush in the whole district.'

The wilderness of garden smells raw, sap-filled. This is Rory's world – and I'm starting to understand how it sets her apart from every other person I know.

We follow a gentle decline, moving further into the Eden jungle, then the path widens out. Rory nods her chin forwards to show me, cos her hands are full. 'Welcome to my place.'

We've arrived at her front yard, if you could call it that – there's no manicured lawn, though. Plumped garden beds sprawl with tomatoes, cucumbers have colonised a wire bed base, forty-four-gallon drums overflow with potato leaf.

On the left, beyond a hose-pipe archway, an old couch is plonked in the middle of the garden. Vines and grass curl around its base, as if the couch took root here; it's a bit like seeing the lamp-post in the middle of the Narnian forest. A perforated metal drum from the inside of a washing machine sits nearby, blackened with use. This is an outside living room, I realise, with its own fireplace.

Rory leads me under the archway, covered with dangling strawberries, to a collection of gnarled tree stumps near the couch. 'Here. Dump everything before you drop it!'

We settle the party provisions on the tree-stump tables, then I take off my backpack and try out the couch. The seat and back are cracked leather, weather-worn but comfortable.

'What do you think?' Rory asks shyly.

'It's *awesome*.' The 'living room' is in dappled shade from the big trees nearby. A rainbow-painted metal whirligig spins gently on a pole. Terracotta sculptures peek out from behind the leaves. In fact, there are a lot of sculptures – some of them are people, or animals, but most are rounded abstract shapes. 'You should have a party here at night. Candles, the fire going, some chilled-out music... It'd be ace.'

Rory smiles at my idea. She rubs her biceps. 'Hey, I know you've just ridden over, so you're probably hot and sweaty, but I need a jumper. Pour yourself another drink. I'll be back in a sec, okay?'

She dashes off behind the couch. I'd like another mug of that ginger beer, but I'm intrigued about where she's gone. I turn around, and what I see is a bit mind-blowing.

Half-hidden in the leaves behind the couch is a tiny hut. It might have been attached, at one time, to a mudbrick house on the left, but that house has crumbled away – only two corner walls and a slanting roof remain. The hut itself seems barely more sturdy. It's a wooden lean-to, with a corrugated iron roof slanting almost to the ground on the right. The only signs that someone lives here are the whitewashed door that looks freshly painted and the red curtains covering a four-pane window.

'Rory?' I walk up a short path of cracked pavers to peer through the door she's left open. Once my eyes adjust, I see … the inside of a shed. Pine floorboards. A camp bed set up on the right, with blankets and quilts laid over it to make a soft nest.

At the foot of the bed, Rory burrows through a huge wicker basket full of random clothes. 'Oh, hey – sorry, I'll find it in a minute.'

'It's fine,' I say. 'No hurry.'

Scarves and multicoloured cloths are tacked up on the wall behind the bed. In the nearby window dozens of glistening ornaments hang on string lines. Books are stacked on makeshift shelves – and on one shelf is a collection of the same small terracotta sculptures I saw in the garden. They're organic-looking, curved and fat.

On the left is an ancient wood-fired range. I see a kettle, a couple of cooking pots and, beside the range, a small water drum covered with a wooden lid, a dipper resting on top.

An antique wooden dresser stands nearby, with a few bits of crockery and a calico-wrapped lump, which I think might be a loaf of bread, sitting on top.

Rory definitely lives here. The shelf of books holds all our English texts, and the copy of *History Alive!* from our Humanities class. I recognise the scarves on a hook as the ones she wears to school.

'This is…' I'm still coming to terms with it. 'This is your place?'

'Yep. I've got my own little hut.' Rory stands up, smiling proudly, shimmery pink fabric in her hand. 'It's not fancy, but it's liveable.'

It's definitely not fancy. On the windowsill to my right is a metal pannikin with a toothbrush in it, a jar of white paste nearby – homemade toothpaste. Rory's already told me they don't use commercial stuff like toothpaste and shampoo in Eden. A candle sits in a holder on a tree-stump nightstand near the bed.

My head is spinning. She must do all her schoolwork by candlelight. How does she handle living like this? How does she make the transition from *here* to *school*?

But then I think about it some more. 'You've got your own house,' I say.

'Yep.' Rory pulls on the pink cardigan, bunching her fists through the sleeves.

'You're independent. You can make your own rules.'

'Yep again. Come on, we should eat. And drink the rest of the ginger beer before it goes flat.' She grins at me, and I start to understand how this place, this tiny house tucked inside a secret garden, could be a little magical.

I'm following her back into the garden when I notice somebody walk past the furthest archway.

Rory calls out, 'Ray! Hey, Ray!'

The man checks his progress, makes a detour in our direction. So this is the famous Ray: anti-supermarket propagandist and ginger-beer maker. He's wearing a work shirt with the sleeves cut off – like my dad sometimes wears on jobs – and a pair of shorts with hiking boots. His legs are long and dark and thin. He's actually so dark-skinned that I think he's black, at first. As he gets closer, I realise he's just really really tanned, the kind of tan some white people get from being outdoors every waking moment of the day.

The only hints to his age are the liberal salt-and-pepper in his long, ponytailed brown hair, the out-of-fashion moustache, and the grooves of wear on his face. He's maybe late fifties, but he's lean and stringy-muscled, like a runner. The way he moves – in long, loping strides – is very fluid. He's either younger than he looks, or he's pretty fit.

As he gets closer to us, his hand extends. 'Hey there, nice to meet you.'

'Bo, this is Ray Carl,' Rory says.

Something about Rory's tone tells me I should be on my best behaviour. I shake Ray's offered hand without comment. It's leathery and dry.

'Bo, is it?'

'Yeah, hi.' I nod.

His eyes aren't a particularly spectacular colour – just a regular shade of brown – but the intensity of the guy's stare is kind of hypnotising. 'So, Bo, have you come to drink the Kool-Aid with us?'

Rory glares at him. 'Ray, that's not funny.'

'Oh relax, Aurora. I'm only teasing.' He looks back to me. 'What do you think of the place?'

That's an easy question to answer. 'It's a bit different to what I'm used to, but I like it.'

Ray doesn't smile, but I get the sense that he's amused by my reaction. 'I'm glad you could come, Aurora's been tripping about this party for—'

'Ray!' Rory blushes.

Ray pats her on the shoulder. 'Come on, now, don't take everything so seriously. Anyway, Bo, it's great you could make it, and I hope you'll join us for Meeting later.'

'Meeting?' I heard the capital letter on the word when he said it, like when Rory talked about the Meeting House.

'That's not why he's here.' Rory turns to me. 'You don't have to, Bo. It's not compulsory.'

Ray holds out open hands. 'I just thought Bo might like to come and share some food with us.'

'Sure,' I jump in. I want Rory to feel comfortable with me being here. 'I'd be happy to come. And if there's food – well, I'm always up for food.'

'Excellent.' Ray nods, looking oddly satisfied. 'Well, I'll see you then. Again, nice of you to come, Bo. See you later, Aurora.'

Rory rolls her eyes, her voice sing-song. 'Bye, Ray.'

Ray Carl stalks off into the garden maelstrom. I'm not sure what the tension was between him and Rory, and I hope it didn't have anything to do with me. 'Did I say the right thing?'

Rory sighs. 'There's no right thing or wrong thing. It's fine. Come on, let's eat.'

I walk over, pushing jasmine vine aside, and flump back down on the couch. 'So…what's a Meeting, exactly? I haven't signed up for an all-night session of gardening lectures, or people singing "Kumbaya", have I?'

Rory laughs and settles herself opposite me, slipping off her sandals and crossing her legs. 'Well, there might be some gardening talk. And I can't guarantee there won't be singing.' She hands me a slice of jam-slathered bread, collects one of the brown bottles from the stump, pours the liquid into my mug and passes it over. 'But it's mostly just the evening meal. It's a chance for everyone to get together after a long day.'

'Sounds okay.' I relax into the couch. The food is simple but delicious: the taste of the jam popping in my mouth, the bread thick and soft and nutty. 'How many of you are on the property? It seems like there's more plants than people around here.'

'There used to be more of us. But some people decide it's not for them, or maybe they're not as committed to the lifestyle, so they move away.' Rory spreads jam on her own slice of bread. 'Right now, there's me, and my mum, Star, and her partner, Stuart, and their little boy, Daniel—'

'Wait – Star's your mum?' I'm surprised by that, I don't know why. It's not like Rory sprang to life fully-formed; she's gotta have parents here somewhere.

'Yes. But she and Stuart have their own house. Sally and Ilona live nearby, in that direction…' She waves her free hand to somewhere off behind us. 'Then there's Kell, and Allison – they have a cabin each. Virginia and Jules live in a house on the far side of the property. And then there's Ray.'

'He has kind of a boss-man vibe,' I say.

'What? No, he's not the boss. It's a consensus community.' She shrugs. 'Well, actually, Ray *is* sort of the mediator and spokesperson for the community, so outsiders might think of him as our leader. But if something needs to be worked out, we all talk about it as a group.'

I look around our location again as we feast. 'This place is cool. Did you do all this gardening yourself?'

'Most of it, yeah,' Rory says as she chews on a crust. 'I'm self-sufficient with vegies now, plus a lot of the produce goes to the kitchen in the Meeting House, for group meals. We all help with the cooking. I've started doing dinner now, cos of school.'

She offers me some trail mix, but I shake my head. 'You come home from school and get straight to work?'

'Three nights a week.' She helps herself to some nuts, returns the bowl to the stump. 'It's not hard when we're working in pairs in the kitchen, plus I get a break from dish duty those nights. Do your parents prepare all the food at your place?'

'Mum, mostly. I dunno why, really – she and Dad both work. But I guess Mum's only working three days a week, so she's more free.'

'On the weekends?'

'Nah, she still does it on the weekends, too.' I think about that. 'We should do more to help her out. I mean, she's having a baby in April. If we haven't figured out how to fend for ourselves by then, there's something wrong with us, I reckon.'

Rory washes down her mouthful of food with the ginger beer, then wipes her lips with the back of her hand. 'A baby, wow. Are you excited about having another brother or sister?'

'I don't know. It's a bit freaky.' I haven't actually talked to anyone about the new baby before, and now I'm wondering why. 'I guess it'll feel more real when there's a baby crying down the other end of the house while I'm trying to do my homework.'

'Daniel was such a cute baby,' Rory says, grinning. 'I took care of him sometimes, when Stuart was working and Star was busy. But all he did was sleep! I thought a new baby was all action, y'know? Waking up in the night, and needing to be bathed and changed and fed. But Daniel was a great sleeper, which was kind of boring.'

I snort. 'I'm sure his parents didn't complain. But was it weird when your mum started a new family without you?'

'Yeah, but Star's her own person.' She contemplates a piece of coloured glass hanging nearby. 'I'm glad she's found a situation that makes her happy. Daniel's a sweetheart.'

'How come you don't live with your mum?' I ask suddenly.

Rory sets down her mug. 'We haven't lived together since we moved here. We shared a different hut for a while, but … it was cramped. I decided I wanted my own space about three years ago. At Meeting we discussed whether I could run my own house, and Ray was on board with it. It's meant a bit more work, but it's not that big a deal.'

I take that in for a second. She's been living alone, running her own house, for *three years*. 'You haul water every day?'

'From the river, yeah. It's not that tough. Other chores are worse.'

'Like what?'

Rory scrunches her nose, ticks off on her fingers. 'Making soap – the smell of lye makes me sick. Field work is kind of boring. Milking the cow is time-consuming in the morning.'

'You have a cow?' I swivel my head, as if I'll see the cow just by looking around.

'It's the community cow. But Kell does most of the milking – he's our animal guy. We have bees and chickens, too.' She shrugs. 'But then there's cutting brush – I hate brush-cutting.'

I gape. 'Jeez, you have about a hundred times more work to do than me. I only do the dishes every night, feed the dog. Sometimes I help Dad on jobs on the weekend.'

'Landscaping? That's hard work.'

'It's okay. But yeah, foundation work is hard. Dirt's heavy.'

'I like dirt.' Rory grins at my expression. 'I told you, I'm into clay. Hey, you want to come see the river? I get all my clay there. We can take a shortcut through the hut.'

She uncurls her legs and stands, heads off along the cracked pavers to the little white door, with me tagging behind. Passing through the inside of the hut, I cast my eyes around again. How does she do all this by herself? I have trouble getting myself up in the morning, pouring out of bed to grab a coffee and eat some cereal or toast, pack my bag for school, stuff in my pre-prepared lunch…

'Sorry, it's a bit messy,' Rory says, grimacing.

'It's not. Anyway, it doesn't matter. It's your house, you can do what you like.'

We go through a door at the back, follow a winding path downhill. A set of natural stone steps leads up in another direction, back towards the Meeting House, I guess.

'Don't you worry about bushfire?' I ask.

'Of course.' Rory's golden curls bob around her face as she

turns her head. 'But the gardens act as a firebreak, and we can always retreat to the river.'

We walk under a canopy of gums and over a sturdy bridge of fitted planks, then we're on grass. Rory turns right near a stand of wild blackberry and we walk upstream, arriving at a place where the track ends at a sandy bank. Giant gums cast shade, a kookaburra starts warbling overhead. Muted sun glances off the river water and the slabs of bordering rock – it's a beautiful spot, like a private waterhole. Suddenly I remember the 'old places' that Joel spoke about, and wonder whether we should be here.

There's a length of red fabric hanging on a spray of native broom nearby.

Rory stops. 'Give me a minute.' She pushes me back towards a jumble of small boulders, walks closer to the bend of the water and calls out. 'Sal? It's Rory. There's a boy with me – are you nearly done?'

I edge around, peer over her shoulder to see who she's talking to. A woman stands knee-deep in the water, a sarong swaddling her hips, the clear current swirling around her brown legs. She's in her forties, I guess, and she's bare-breasted and wet. I gasp and immediately back up.

Rory turns. 'Bo, it's okay.' She calls out again to the bathing woman. 'We can come back later if you like?'

'Oh, no. I'm done now.' The woman splashes her face, completely unconcerned about her nakedness. She wraps the damp sarong around her body, tying it tightly under her arms, then gathers up an armful of sopping clothes and wades towards us, smiling. 'Hi, there. You must be Bo? I've heard a lot about you.'

'Um, yeah, hi.' My face is on fire, and I'm not sure where to look.

'I'm Sally. Sorry, Rory. I didn't know you'd be coming down, or I would've washed earlier.'

'We're the ones interrupting,' Rory says, handing Sally a pair of dark-rimmed specs that were balanced on a boulder. 'Don't forget your glasses!'

'Oh, ta.' Sally slips the glasses on, looking fresh and relaxed. She has short black hair, dripping from her bath, and her face is pockmarked with acne scars. 'Nice to meet you, Bo. How's the party going?'

'It's, um, great.' I decide that the best place to focus my eyes is straight on her face.

'Sounds good. Is Rory dragging you along to Meeting?'

'Maybe.' Rory glances at me. 'But I'll be there, even if Bo isn't.'

'Hey, I'll come,' I say. 'I'd like to come.'

'Then I guess I'll see you there – with my clothes on, I promise!' Sally grins, dumps her soggy bundle into a metal bucket near the water, grabs the red cloth marker off the nearby branch. The bucket handle clanks as she picks it up and starts walking off. She calls over her shoulder. 'We're not all nudists here! You just caught me at the wrong moment!'

Rory and I both laugh.

Once Sally is gone, I look around more freely. 'So this is your washroom?'

'Yep. We bathe here. There's a spot for clean water collection upstream. The rocks make this a good place to do laundry. No soap, though, only blackwood leaves – they lather up in water. We don't want to pollute the river. In winter, I heat water on the stove and wash inside. Toilets are elsewhere, if you're wondering.' Rory grins. 'Although I sometimes do a sneaky pee in the river, I admit.'

I laugh at the guilty look on her face, then shake my head. 'You have a pretty amazing life, Rory.'

She shrugs. 'I don't know about amazing. It takes a lot of effort. But if it means we get to keep the beautiful places, like this river, then I think it's worth it.' She touches my sleeve. 'Come see the clay.'

She draws me further upstream to a tributary off the main course of the river, shows me the place where she's dug the rich red clay out of the bank, demonstrates its plasticity and daubs some on my wrist to explain the colours. Light off the river water makes her nose-stud flash and reflects in her hair. She's so relaxed here, way more than she is at school. Everything about her fits into this landscape of water, earth and green growing things – she looks like she belongs.

The way she lives, in that tiny hut among the riot of garden… I think about the exoticism of it, but also the isolation, and the effort involved in maintaining this lifestyle. Rory believes in it, really *believes*. It's something she's fashioned her life around, this care for the environment. It's a hell of a commitment.

It makes me wonder what *I'm* committed to. Footy? My friends? My family? I don't have a religious system, or a cause that moves me. What do I believe in? I think and think, and…nothing comes.

We wander back downstream, cross over the bridge and return to her outside couch to finish the food while we talk.

'…so Cam basically knows *everybody*,' I say, as I polish off the last of the scones. 'Her mum is a big deal in town. She's on the council. Cam knows Shandy and Kaylah through netball, and me and Sprog cos it's a joint football–netball club. But she gets on with the academic kids too, cos she's dux of the school.'

'She and Lozzie are pretty close, huh?'

'Yeah – their mums are mates, so they practically knew each other in the womb, I reckon.' I brush crumbs off my front. 'So what's the deal here? Did Ray start the commune?'

'No, the community's been active for at least ten years. Well before we arrived, anyway.'

'And it's totally plastic-free, tech-free, gluten-free?'

She laughs, wiping watermelon juice off her fingers onto her overalls. 'We just don't buy into the accepted view of the world as something you use up and throw away. You can live on the earth without trashing it.'

'How d'you eat?'

'Pretty well, as you've seen.' She raises an eyebrow at the now-empty scone plate. 'We don't eat meat. Eggs and milk and cheese come from our own animals. We grow all our own vegetables – we're not a big community, so we can do that. For soy and oil and lentils and salt and stuff, we trade. Honey, fruit, blankets—'

'Blankets?'

'We make blankets from yarn discarded by the woollen mill. Also pottery, and some other craft stuff – Jules makes carved doll furniture. Stuart's a lawyer. He works part-time for the Lamistead council environment service. It's hard to stick to zero impact when you work out in the regular world, though.'

I empty the last of the ginger beer into my mug, thinking of the candles in her hut. 'No electricity?'

'There are solar panels for the larger houses. I'm not hooked up, though – it was too much hassle. And we have wood heating, from coppiced trees cut on-site.'

'What about sewerage? Medical?'

'Pit toilets with sawdust. Most of us use medicinal herbs or homeopathic remedies. And, there's Ilona – she used to be a nurse.'

'What if someone breaks a leg?'

She shrugs. 'Then we'd set it and fix it.'

'What if you get an infection? Or a toothache?'

'Then we pull out the tooth and pack the cavity with a ti-tree oil and slippery elm poultice, and drink willow bark tea for the pain…' She gives me a droll look. 'I'm kidding. We go to the doctor if we need to, like Sally did the other day. For a serious emergency, we'd go to the hospital in town, I guess. I've taken paracetamol before. But I've never been to a dentist.'

I stare at her. 'Bullshit.'

'Really. And I've still got all my teeth, see?' She smiles widely to demonstrate.

I squint. 'That's … bizarre.'

'Bizarre that I have all my teeth?'

'Come on, you know what I mean.'

Her face goes serious. 'Eden really is committed to zero impact. That means we make do without a lot of the regular stuff that most people take for granted.'

'Like Western medicine.'

She piles the empty bowls and plates on top of each other on the stump. 'There's a lot of advantages in learning to take care of yourself without the easy fix of modern medicine.

But hey, we're not that extreme. There's an intentional community in Wales that hasn't had contact with the larger world for nine years. They don't even have a phone.'

I do a double take. 'Do you have a phone?'

'Sure. Stuart and Star have the phone at the moment. I mean, they have the phone a lot, because of Daniel. Ilona and Sally use it too, sometimes…' Her mouth makes an odd twist, then she continues with the tidying up. 'It gets handed on from family to family. There's a roster.' She looks up in time to see my freaked-out expression. 'What?'

'There's a roster for the phone. You make your own toothpaste.'

'I know it must seem strange.'

'How can you not want…everything that's out there? Hamburgers. Air-conditioning. TV.'

'I didn't grow up with any of that.' She stands up to carry the crockery to her hut, and I realise I've done nothing to help her pack up. I get up too, grab some stuff.

'But I do think about it more,' Rory says, as we stroll with our load of dirty dishes. 'I have to, now I'm at high school. Before, I used to dream about what the larger world would be like… It seemed kind of magical. Does that make sense? I knew it was out there, but sometimes it seemed like something from a fantasy.' She shows me where to stack the dishes in a metal bucket outside the door of the hut. Her expression changes as she continues. 'Not always a beautiful fantasy, either. Sometimes the outside world seems excessive and destructive and dangerous – a dark fairytale. I'm sorry, I don't know if I'm really expressing it properly.'

'No, I get it,' I say. I've seen the local supermarket through her eyes, now, and I've watched enough news reports about climate change and polar ice caps melting and shit like that to understand why Rory believes it's important.

She turns towards me. 'So...you want to come to Meeting?'

The spell breaks for a second. I look around: the sky above us is changing colour, and the air is starting to cool.

'Ah, crap – what time is it?' I grab my phone to check, get a shock when I realise it's nearly seven. I've been banking on Mum and Dad assuming I'm with Sprog. It's a Saturday evening, I've done my homework and footy training... The hell with it.

'Can you stay?' Rory asks.

I turn my phone off, slip it away. 'Absolutely. Free food, right?'

'You just ate half a dozen scones!' Rory goggles at me, laughs. 'And fair warning, we might make you do dishes.'

I grin. 'Dishes I can handle. Just don't make me sing.'

As the light darkens towards evening, people begin to arrive at the Meeting House.

Me and Rory end up settled together in front of the fire-pit on an old lounge chair. A woman who introduces herself as Allison comes and sits on Rory's other side, and we're pushed closer together than I expected – the scent of lemon myrtle in Rory's hair is driving me a little crazy.

Sally rocks up with another woman, both of them lugging a side of a big pot.

'Hey again, Bo,' Sally says, smiling. 'It's usually Rory's turn to make dinner, but we thought we'd give her a night off. Birthday privileges, yeah? This is Ilona.'

Ilona is a tall, strong-looking Anglo woman wearing a sleeveless burgundy smock. 'Blessings on your birthday, Rory dearest.' They put down the pot, and Ilona walks over and kisses Rory's cheek, shakes my hand.

'Ilona made the dhal,' Sally says, grinning. 'There's fresh paneer cheese, too, if you want it.'

Another couple – both white, both quite elderly, both

dressed in old-fashioned clothes – walk up the concrete steps arm in arm. The woman delivers a plate of flatbreads to the side of the fire-pit. With her white hair drawn up into a dramatic roll and her long skirts, she looks as if she's walked straight out of a period stage play.

'Jules,' the man says to me, as he helps his partner into an easychair, 'and this is Virginia.'

I remember what Rory said about Jules making doll furniture as I shake his hand. 'I hear you're a woodworker.'

'Ah. Young Rory has been divulging all our secrets, I see.' Jules adjusts his braces, smiling as he takes a seat of his own. 'Yes, I like to keep up the old crafts. Whittling, carving, parquetry—'

'And he likes to talk about them ad nauseam,' Virginia says, leaning forwards as if sharing a confidence. 'Don't get him started, unless you want to be here all night.'

'Oh, pshaw!' Jules leans back, laughing.

I can't help grinning. It's the first time I've ever heard anyone use the word 'pshaw' outside of an old movie.

A guitar starts playing, and I lift my head to see a shaggy-looking white guy enter the circle from the rear doorway, tuning his instrument as he walks. There's another guy with him – a taller man, Japanese maybe, with cropped black hair and a guitar of his own, although he's not playing it yet. They're engaged in conversation, and followed by a woman with a child on her hip and a pot of roast vegetables crooked in an arm.

'Star!' Rory calls, and the woman sets down the pot and sweeps closer to kiss her awkwardly, while balancing the boy on her hip.

Star's younger than I would've thought, maybe mid-thirties. She's wearing faded grey fisherman's pants and a blue singlet top, with a multitude of leather and string and bead necklaces. Her skin is creamy-pale, like Rory's, and her hair is curly in front in the same way, but it's a darker gold, and twisted into dreadlocks that have been bound into a thick rope that falls halfway down her back.

'Oh, peace and love for your birthday, darling,' she says, distracted. 'Would you hold Daniel for a sec?'

'Sure. Come here, sweet.' Rory holds out her hands, and the boy leans off Star's hip and tumbles into Rory's arms. His face is tear-streaked, and he's holding a wooden spoon. Rory coos at him, then turns to me. 'Bo, this is Daniel.'

'Uh, hi.' I give him a wave, but he hides in Rory's shoulder.

'Oh, Daniel!' Star's straightening her clothes and tucking in dreads that have come loose while she was holding her son. She sighs at Rory. 'He's been driving me crazy all afternoon, fussing over everything. Maybe it's his teeth. He's not enjoying life much today.' She sees me, and smiles. 'You must be Bo. Welcome to Garden of Eden – peace and love to you. I hear you're a good soul.'

I don't know about the state of my soul, but I want to make a good impression on Rory's mum. 'Uh, thank you. Nice to meet you.'

'Wow.' Star looks me over, her eyes glowing. 'You have a strong aura. Lots of purples and reds and blues.'

'Um … okay,' I say.

'Happy birthing day, Star,' Ilona calls out from the other side of the circle.

Rory nods at her mother. 'That's right – happy birthing day.'

The black-haired guy with the guitar steps closer and

wraps an arm around Star's waist, so I'm assuming he's Stuart. 'Yes, congratulations, groovy mama.'

He kisses her right there in front of everybody, as they cheer – and it's not a quick peck on the cheek, either. I keep my eyes focused on Daniel in Rory's lap. My parents are tender at home, but they don't pash on in front of people. Rory is obviously more used to public displays of affection than I am.

The shaggy guy with the first guitar joins the group and starts strumming. Everyone picks up the melody, as Rory hands Daniel back to Star, and people settle themselves into chairs, beanbags and couches, around the fire.

I'm still getting used to the way they talk – it's all 'peace and love' and 'groovy', like something straight out of the sixties, but they're completely straight-faced about it. And they seem open-hearted, genuine. The song isn't one I'm familiar with, something about a circle being unbroken, but it's pretty cool listening to folks sing so unselfconsciously. They're really singing it like they mean it.

I don't realise that Ray Carl has joined the gathering until the song finishes and he stands up, across the other side of the fire. He's changed into long pants, but otherwise he looks the same. His voice isn't loud but it carries, as he raises his Eden-style mug.

'Peace and love to you, Aurora Nightingale Wild, on the day of your birth. Blessings on all your labours. And we thank and praise you, too, Star, for bringing Rory to us.' He takes a draught from his mug, as people around the fire smile and toast in Rory's direction. She's radiant from the attention. Ray holds up a plate from a stack near Ilona and Sally's dhal pot.

'I'd like to say that I'm grateful to everyone for celebrating with Rory, and I'd especially like to welcome Bo, who's visiting us today. Now dig in – the grub's getting cold.'

'Hear, hear!' Jules calls, to a lot of laughter. 'Welcome, Bo! And happy day to you, Rory!'

There's a lot of back-slapping and cheerful calling out to me and Rory, which I try not to feel too embarrassed about. It's nice to be welcomed, but I can't help comparing it to the reception people have given Rory since she arrived at Lamistead Secondary. Even *I* wasn't welcoming, that first day in class. Now here I am, the only person from school to show up at her birthday party.

'That food looks great,' Rory says, as I sit back down with a plate of dhal and vegetables and flatbread on my lap.

'I reckon,' I say. 'Hey, I haven't even wished you happy birthday. Or brought you a present. I was going to get you something in town, but then I had to run over to Sprog's place—'

'Don't worry about it.' Rory leans against my shoulder, her smile brilliant. 'You showing up to my party is the best gift you could give me.'

'But I wanna get you a present,' I blurt out.

Her eyes are shiny, her lips pink and full. 'Then I'm sure you'll think of something.'

Our faces are so close I can see all the freckles across the bridge of her nose… but then I remember where we are.

I drag my head sideways. People are chatting, moving around the fire. They're easy with each other, like it's a family get-together. Then I remember: these people live and work in unison every day, largely isolated from the outside world. They *are* family.

The food disappears quickly, and Kell, the shaggy-haired guitar player, brings over a metal tub so people can dump their dishes. Stuart pours in hot water from the big billy sitting over the fire, and starts washing. Virginia sits in her chair with a tea towel, passing wiped dishes to Star, who re-stacks them. Ilona sits back on the beanbag, smoking a bidi – one of those Indian leaf cigarettes Teo sometimes steals off his dad – and chatting to Allison.

The smell of fire-smoke and the sight of all the stars above us makes me feel like I'm in another world. I'm more relaxed than I've been for ages. I even get caught up in a conversation with Jules about woodcarving, which sounds cool.

'It's an easy skill to learn, but you need some patience,' Jules says. He seems tickled that I'm interested. 'And you have to expect to get a few cuts and nicks, when you first start.'

'Yeah, I'd guessed that,' I say, smiling.

'My tools are all back at the ranch, but I can show you, next time you come.'

He seems totally confident that I'll be returning to Eden. I'm confident, too. I've been accepted into the group without question after only one meal. It seems crazy to me now that I was worried about visiting. And Rory's here – of course I'll be back.

The fire's been built high, so we're all bathed in warmth and light. Star has settled a sleeping Daniel across her lap – he has his father's straight black hair. Sally returns from the kitchen to cuddle up with Ilona on the beanbag. Then Ray stands and perches on the arm of a lounge chair, across from me and Rory, and all the conversation slowly dies down.

'Thank you, folks. That was a good meal,' he says. 'I don't

think many people in the district would have eaten as well as we have tonight. Seasonal produce, grown right here in the summer sunshine in rich organic soil, weeded and harvested by hand, beautifully prepared and eaten with friends... That's what I call real food.'

There's a murmur of agreement around the circle. Everyone has turned their faces towards Ray, and I get the impression that he speaks at Meetings regularly.

Ray is smoking the end of a bidi; now that he's got everyone's attention, he tosses it in the fire. 'It sounds crazy to say that gardening is radical. That cooking is a political act. But that's the truth of it. I mean, does your family still have dinner together, Bo?'

'What?' All eyes turn in my direction, and I swallow. 'Um, yeah. Yeah, we still have family dinner.'

'You're lucky.' Ray nods at me. 'The family dinner is going out of style, which is a shame, don't you think? Meals eaten together are when we learn the habits of community – the art of conversation, how to be polite, to take turns, to share. But now, people eat a quarter of their meals in their car, or in front of the television.'

When Ray's gaze shifts to circle the rest of the audience, I feel relieved – he's an intense guy. But what he's saying is starting to grab my attention.

'The nature of meals, of food, has changed. Fifty years ago, food cost nearly thirty per cent of most folks' income. Now it's less than ten per cent. That sounds like success, right? We've got cheaper food, so we can feed more people.' Ray smiles, and people around the circle nod. 'But there's a hidden cost, and most of you know about it. That cost is modern society's

106

regime of industrial food production, which is divorced from any idea of ecological reality. Lab-designed fruits and grains, potatoes that produce their own pesticides, cattle raised on diets of corn and meat meal...'

It takes me a minute to realise Ray's orating; his voice isn't raised, his manner is low-key and sincere. But his voice doesn't need to be loud. Everyone is listening. His casual tone makes what he's saying even more compelling. His speech seems as factual and genuine as any documentary. If there are deliberate pauses, and words paced for effect, the worst you could say was that he was warming to his topic.

'Food like that is fuel for workers, not nourishment for people.' Ray accepts a mug from Ilona, clears his throat, talks on. 'There are ten corporations in the world right now that control almost every item sold in supermarkets and fast food franchises. You all know how processed food is made palatable: with additives to make it smell and taste and look good, additives that are also found in cosmetics, and perfume, and house paint.'

I whisper in Rory's ear. 'House paint? Is he for real?'

She nods at me, her eyes sad.

Sally, along with other people in the circle, is shaking her head in wordless disgust. I'm a bit disgusted myself. I've never thought about food this way before.

Ray walks around the circle as he speaks. 'Pesticide use alone has increased six hundred per cent since the seventies. Six hundred per cent! And more than half the antibiotics produced in the US are fed to livestock. Meanwhile, people are getting sick. Millions of people are overweight and unhealthy, because the quality of their diet is so poor...'

Ray seems different when he talks like this. When I met him this afternoon, he was kind of serious and terse. He looked like a hillbilly, with his greying ponytail and moustache, and I got the sense he wasn't thrilled about a stranger coming into his world.

But maybe my first impression was wrong. Now, his voice comes alive, and his deep-set eyes engage with every person in the circle. He goes on explaining about fast food: thousands of acres of feedlot cows crammed knee-deep in their own manure, production lines that move so quickly there's no time to clean off that manure so it's sprayed with antibiotics and mixed in with the meat, packaging compounds that leak into the food...

The whole thing seems completely staggering. I've heard Mrs Ramanathan talk about processed food in Food Tech, but for the first time it's like the concept fits into a larger picture. And it's a pretty bloody alarming picture. It jars my head, jars me into speech.

'But organic food is really expensive. Not everyone can afford it.'

Ray's head swivels in my direction. 'Good point. But I guess people have to weigh up whether they want to spend their money on better quality food or on medical bills down the track. You have to wonder – what are the antibiotics and pesticides in processed food doing to people?'

'Is that even legal?'

'Well, in some places, it's not. But industrial food production is about making money, so many corporations cheat. Plus, there are always legal loopholes. And a lot of people don't even realise what they're eating. Did you know about this?'

I shake my head.

'There you are.' Ray narrows his eyes. 'And I hate to say this, Bo, but there's another reason. People don't care.' He shrugs. 'That's the way the world is now. People like things convenient, fast and cheap. They don't like to think about the consequences.'

Ray's attention passes to Virginia, as she asks a question, but my brain is still reeling.

Rory tilts her face close to mine. 'Are you starting to understand?'

I feel a bit shell-shocked. 'That's why you guys don't shop at the supermarket.'

'That's right,' Rory says. 'Processed food is terrible for the environment, and all those additives and hormones... Nobody knows what the effect of them will be.'

'Not everybody eats corporate.' Ray has overheard my exchange with Rory, and now he addresses me directly. He gestures around the fire-pit. 'There are pockets of resistance. We resist. We farm our own food, make our own bread... There's more we could be doing, though, which I've mentioned before.'

'Are you talking about the river paddocks?' Ilona asks.

Ray nods. 'We've cycled the crops there, but we've only ever had one crop per season. We've had discussions already about transforming those sections of the property – monoculture is Big Agriculture's way, but it's not our way. I think it's time to act on that. Start growing more plant families, companion crops.'

'It'll make harvesting tough,' Kell points out.

'But we'll get better yields, and longer harvest periods.

The land won't get so exhausted, and what we harvest will be higher quality.' Ray grins. 'It'll be good for the land, for the plants, and for our stomachs.'

'I like it.' Jules slaps his knee. 'It's a fresh approach, and nobody here is afraid of more work.'

Discussion breaks out as ideas are passed back and forth. There's a sense of excitement, which I can't help feeling a part of. I'm seeing the Eden community in action: working together, deciding on their future together.

The Meeting breaks up soon after, and Ray walks over to where Rory and I are standing. Again, I notice the way he moves – lithe and unhurried, clasping hands with people along the way.

'Bo, apologies for giving you an earful tonight.' The lines of wear on Ray's face seem mellowed by the firelight. 'You probably didn't expect to come to a birthday party and get your mind blown.'

'It's okay,' I say, pulling on my backpack. 'I think I can handle a bit of enlightenment. And it's important stuff – I'm glad I know about it now.'

'Makes you think twice, doesn't it?' He puts his hands on his hips. 'I might've been too cynical when I said people don't care. Folks here care. More people, like yourself, are figuring it out all the time – the world needs people like you.'

I extend my hand. 'Thanks for making me welcome, sir.'

'No need to call me sir.' He laughs, shaking my hand. 'You're your own man, Bo – just Ray is fine. And come over anytime.'

Rory and I have to take a path through the group to leave, and once everyone realises I'm going, they all want to hug me, or pat me on the back – it's weird but nice, like I'm saying goodbye to a bunch of close friends. The fact that most of them have only known me for a few hours doesn't seem to matter.

Flushed and smiling, Rory walks me out to the Cannondale. The last thing I want to do is leave, but I have to ride home. And then explain why I was out late to my parents – that's gonna be the hard part.

'I hope you weren't too freaked by the Meeting,' Rory says, 'Ray can really roll once he gets going.'

'God, don't apologise!' I laugh as I prop up the bike on the *Garden of Eden* sign. 'If I'm eating manure, I actually want to know about it.'

'Well, I thought you took everything in your stride.' She smiles, as the cool night breeze plays with her hair. 'And thank you for coming to my party.'

'Thanks for asking me, I had a good time.'

'I guess I'll see you on Monday, on the way to school.' Her hands are resting next to mine on the handlebars of the bike.

'I guess you will.' I hold her gaze. 'I know I've asked you a lot of questions today, but can I ask one more?'

'Sure.'

'Is your last name really Wild?'

She laughs. 'Oh! God. Yes, by deed poll. Now I have to ask *you*.'

'What?'

'Is Bo short for something?'

'It's embarrassing,' I say.

She looks at me with dry incredulity. 'And Aurora Nightingale isn't?'

'Bodeen.' I bite down hard on my grin. 'Bodeen Lionel Mitchell. Mum chose my first name, and my dad has always loved Lionel Rose, the boxer.'

We're standing close, leaning towards each other over the handlebars of the Cannondale. The moon is high above us, touching everything with a white-opal glow. Kissing Rory now would be the perfect end to what's been a perfect afternoon. A live current seems to be arcing between us, like those electro-balls in Biol. I can almost see the streaks of purple lightning connecting us everywhere we come close enough to touch…

But it's such a good feeling, I want to drag it out. Kissing would almost make it too intense, and I'm still not sure how Rory feels.

'I have to go,' I whisper.

'Okay.' Rory's voice is soft in reply. She opens her arms and stretches forwards to hug me. 'Ride safe, Bodeen.'

The feel of her body on mine is intoxicating. Her breasts are soft against my chest, her skin smells amazing. When I put my arms around her, I feel like I've been entrusted with holding something warm and precious and sensuously alive.

I clear my throat. I don't want to let her go, but I force myself to pull back, yank on my bike gloves, smile at her before I head the Cannondale down the track. 'Happy birthday, Aurora Nightingale!'

She laughs, and waves me all the way out.

'Okay, let's hear it.'

'I went to Eden for Rory's birthday party. She invited me to stay and have dinner with all the folks there, so I did. I would've texted you, but I had trouble getting reception in Eden.'

'You didn't think to ride out until you got a signal and send us a message so we knew you were still alive?'

I chew my cereal evenly, swallow. That would actually have been a good idea. 'No, I didn't think to do that. I'm sorry.'

'Even if you had, you know that you still would have been deliberately breaking the rules about socialising during term time?' Dad's face softens. 'We don't make these restrictions up for no reason, Bo. You're in senior high school, now. You won't meet your responsibilities at school and at footy if you don't set limits on your extracurricular events. Do you get it?'

I get it. I've heard this speech, or variations on it, a thousand times before. Dad sounds so reasonable, so mature, when he talks like this. I try to keep my tone calm, meet him on his level. 'I didn't plan to stay out so late. I know I worried you and Mum, and I'm sorry. But I was the only person from school who showed up for Rory's birthday. She was really excited I made it, and it would've been rude to leave.'

'You were the only guest?' Mum's leaning against the kitchen island, holding her mug of tea. She and Dad exchange glances. They're tough on me, but they're not unfeeling.

'Yeah. No one else could come.' I could elaborate about the Meeting, but I'm a bit over getting the third degree. 'It was just dinner around the fire. I talked to one of the guys there about woodworking. I had a good time.'

Dad spreads margarine (genetically-modified canola oil – *The Healthy Choice*) onto his toast (production-line white bread – *Low GI*) while he mulls things over. Mum's having toast, too, and I think of all the additives and crap that she's unconsciously consuming – her, and the baby growing inside her. That can't be healthy. Counting up the staggering number of processed foods in our kitchen is a good distraction from worrying what Dad's going to say about my escapade last night.

I sit opposite him with my cup of instant coffee (freeze-dried – *New Improved Flavour*), and my bowl of cereal (wholegrain – *Now with Less Sugar*), reliving moments from the party in my mind: the Narnian couch, talking by the river, the sense of community around the fire, Ray's lesson on food. The shape and colour of Rory's lips, the two of us sitting close, the warmth along all our points of contact, like the lick of flame in the fire-pit...

Finally, Dad lays down his butter knife. 'All right. I understand why you chose to stay without our permission.

114

That doesn't make it right, though. And you have to know there's gonna be consequences.' He picks up his toast. 'No evening events for a month. You go to footy and swimming like normal, but nothing after six p.m. No hanging out with Sprog, no Friday night movies at Cam's place—'

'For a whole *month*?' I haven't been grounded before. But then again, I haven't broken the rules like this before.

'Don't get shirty, Bo. If I didn't understand the circumstances, I'd have said three months.' Dad looks at me across the table. 'And there's something else. Don't go back to Eden.'

'What?'

'Don't go there,' Dad repeats. He breaks a crust off his toast. 'I don't want you getting mixed up with those people.'

I feel winded. 'But ... *why*?'

'Because they're fanatics.' He takes a bite of his processed bread, chews deliberately. 'Fanaticism makes people do strange things, and I don't want you getting involved with them.'

'The people I met there are nice.' I'm talking fast, while trying to stay cool. I promised myself I'd talk to Dad about this like an adult. I know it's the only way to convince him. 'There's nothing sinister about them, they're good people, friendly—'

'I don't care how friendly they are. I don't want you getting involved with them.' Dad lays down his toast and narrows his eyes at me. 'Are we clear on that, Bo? *Don't go to Eden.* I'm spelling it out for you, cos I know you like this girl, and I know it's hard to make the right decisions when you're emotional.'

'I'm not emotional!' I say, cracking the shits at last. Which, of course, makes me look emotional. I clench the spoon in my fist.

Dad looks at me. 'That's it. No more discussion. You do your time, and do as I ask, and at the end of a month you'll have all your privileges back.'

I get up, dump my bowl in the sink, don't meet anyone's eyes as I stalk back to my room. Why can't I keep my cool whenever I talk with Dad? And why doesn't he ever *listen*? He just dictates what can and can't be done, according to his own random idea of how the world should work.

What the fuck is wrong with Eden? What does he even know about it? He's never been there, never talked to the people, never met Rory...

Rory – god*dammit*. This means I'll only be able to see her at school, or on the weekends. But never at her place, in the place she feels most comfortable. I won't get to see her laughing, relaxed in her own home.

In her own home, where she makes her own rules.

It's ironic that Rory, who lives in an isolated, lifestyle-restricted community, has more freedom than I do.

*

'Did you make it home okay?' Rory asks. 'Was your dad upset with you?'

'Like you wouldn't believe,' I say. 'How are you? What's been happening?'

We're falling over each other to talk, in the little time we have in private before school. I've realised that when you can't text or call someone, seeing them is really important. How did anyone cope in the days before mobiles?

I don't tell her I've been banned from Eden. Why don't I tell her? I don't know. It doesn't feel right. She'd be really cut if she knew my dad disapproved of her and the community, and I'm still holding out hope that I can sneak over to her place when my parents' gaze is directed elsewhere.

'Tell me how it went after I left,' I ask, grinning. 'Did you guys all talk about me?'

'No, of course not.' Rory feigns a reproving look, then laughs. 'Okay, the general consensus seems to be that you're good people. But it's really nobody's business but mine, and folks respect that. We have to give each other some privacy, or we'd all go crazy.' She pushes her hair back off her face and turns to the road again. 'I still feel bad about your dad being angry.'

'Stuff him,' I say, wrestling the Cannondale onto the road shoulder. 'He's all about being adult when it suits him, but then he and Mum are playing secrets with this whatever-it-is they're both so stressed about. I can make my own choices sometimes. Dad's going to have to trust me to do that, eventually.'

'How's your mum? And your little brother is...Connor, right?'

'Yeah, it's Connor. He's good. And Mum's okay.' I look at her sideways. 'Except I'm a bit worried now about all the processed food she's eating.'

Rory yelps, covers her mouth with one hand.

'I'm serious! Ray's talk really made me think.'

Rory lets her hand drop. 'Then I'm glad you got to listen to him. Ray's a good speaker – he gives teachings every other night or so. It helps keep the community together. Reminds us of our purpose.'

'You guys already seem pretty purposeful,' I say.

'Yeah, but we're not part of the regular world. Sometimes we need to be reminded of what it's really like out there.' Rory shoves her bangle collection up her arm, pushes the Titanic forwards. 'People get complacent. Last year, two families moved away. Ethan's family used to live in the bus. Ethan was the only person my age in the community, but his dad, Merrick, had some disagreements with Ray about the way the community was being run. They'd been in the community eight years, but they still packed up and left.'

I think about that for a moment. 'You and this Ethan guy ... You were together?'

'Together? Like, you mean – oh, no, not like that!' Her freckles stand out as she flushes. 'We were close. But it was like everyone assumed we'd be a pair before we had a chance to work things out for ourselves. We got a bit sick of that.'

I'm not sure how I feel about the idea of Rory being a 'pair' with anybody else. 'Do you and Ethan still keep in touch?'

She squints at me. 'Are you jealous, Bo?'

'Nah, it's not like that. I just, y'know, wondered if you and Ethan were still ...'

'You *are* jealous.' She breaks into a grin. 'You don't have to be. One of the things we worked out was that Ethan isn't attracted to girls.'

'Oh.'

'He sends me letters sometimes. He and his family live in New South Wales now, near Byron Bay.' Her lips quirk. 'I might go up there one day, for a visit ...'

She side-eyes me, and I can't help laughing. I feel like a bit of a dickhead. 'Sure, go up to Byron. Sorry. But I thought if you already had a connection with someone, then maybe I shouldn't—'

I cut myself off, and Rory raises her eyebrows. 'Shouldn't what?'

I decide to be brave. Being brave isn't always about throwing your body on the line in footy clashes. Sometimes it's about letting your heart show in your face.

'I thought maybe I shouldn't get my hopes up,' I say.

I've never laid everything out for a girl like this before. But something about Rory is different. Somehow I know that, even if she's not interested, she won't take my vulnerability and wound me with it. I can trust her. Everything I've observed about her up to this point tells me this is true.

Right now, she's looking at me with something like wonder. She reaches out and cups my cheek in her hand.

'Are you still only *hoping*, Bo?' she says softly. 'Don't you *know* already?'

She smiles at me, and I feel as if I'm flying.

We finally make it to school, park our bikes and separate for homegroup. I'm feeling this strange sensation, like I'm glowing; Rory likes me, as much as I like her. I might be grounded, my parents might be losing it, my friends might not approve of my romantic choices, and my teachers might be putting the squeeze on, but there's a bounce in my step that I can't control.

I slide into a chair next to Sprog. When reception finally kicked back in on my way home from Eden on Saturday night, messages cascaded onto my phone screen like a meteor shower – but nothing from Sprog. 'Hey, man, what's going on? Missed you at footy on Saturday.'

Sprog keeps his eyes trained forwards. 'That's not all you missed.'

'Dude, I messaged you, but—'

'Forget it,' he says.

I peer at him: his T-shirt is worn thin, his hair is ratty, and he's refusing to look my way.

I try again when the bell goes at the end of homegroup. 'Is your mum all right? What happened with—'

'I don't wanna talk about my *mum*,' Sprog says, and he grabs his backpack and stalks off before I've even stood up.

Well, shit.

I make it to Humanities before Showalter arrives and corner Sprog near a desk at the back. 'Mate, you're obviously pissed about something, but you're gonna have to tell me what it is before I can apologise, cos I've got no fucking idea—'

'You've got *no fucking idea*,' Sprog sneers. 'That's the story of your life, isn't it?'

'Sprog...'

Rory enters the room, smiles in my direction, and something inside my chest jerks. She heads for a seat near the front, waves me over.

'Piss off, then.' Sprog's giving me the stink-eye. 'Go sit with your little feral chick, if she's more important than your mates.'

I open my mouth to give him a serve, but at that moment, Mr Showalter arrives and starts yelling at everyone to sit down. I bite my tongue, back away from Sprog, head for the seat beside Rory.

'What's going on with Sprog?' She's looking between me and the back of the room where Sprog's sitting.

'Ah, I dunno.' I pull out my books. 'Sprog's doing his nana about something, damned if I know what. I'll have to talk to him at lunch.'

Cam's giving me a 'what's that all about?' look from across the aisle, but all I can do is shrug. The lesson starts. We've been through Marxism, and Showalter is now trying to explain anarchism to a bunch of people who are probably still recovering from a pretty anarchic weekend.

'...a self-governed society based on non-hierarchical free association that was first correctly named by Pierre-Joseph Proudhon, a French philosophical anarchist, in his book *What is Property?*...'

Terri Thomas waggles her hand in the air. 'My iPod, sir – Nikki's taken it. That's my property.'

'What?' Mr Showalter falters, ploughs on. 'Um, yes, Nikki, if you could return the iPod please... So Proudhon coined the phrase "property is theft", which he later moderated to—'

'Nikki's the bloody thief!' Terri wails.

Nikki Wigen snorts. 'You *lent* it to me, you stupid cow!'

'That's enough, now!' Showalter is starting to sweat. 'Please. If you're not taking notes, you won't understand the—'

'Anarchism is about the Sex Pistols, right, sir?' Sprog calls from the back of the room.

'Er, yes, anarchism was associated with the UK punk rock movement in the nineteen seventies. But that's getting a little bit away from our original—'

Someone's phone – maybe it's Sprog's – starts blasting out a tinny version of 'Anarchy in the UK' and everybody breaks into laughter. Cam catches my eye and sighs.

'Excuse me, everyone...' Mr Showalter starts.

Bailey Debert stands up and says, 'I proclaim this class a self-governing society!' to generous applause and more whooping and hilarity. A few paper missiles are thrown across the room. Beside me, Rory is watching it all with appalled fascination.

'Class!' Mr Showalter is pink in the face. 'Excuse me! Everybody!'

Bailey bows, hand on his chest like Napoleon, and promptly scores a paper spitball in the face.

He raises a fist at Terri. 'That got me in the *eye*, you little shit!'

'*Everybody, please just*—' Mr Showalter lifts his hands. His face sort of shrivels and reddens. 'Everybody, please…'

He's blinking and blinking. It takes me a second to register that he's crying.

Mr Showalter raises his hand to cover his face. Everybody in the room has stopped talking and stilled. I don't know where to look. I don't want to see this.

'Mr Showalter?' Rory says softly.

'Is he all right?' Cam whispers. Her voice seems to fall into a well of silence.

In the deathly quiet, Showalter gasps out this sob. We all jump. It's awful. It's the sound someone makes when they're completely, hopelessly lost. Showalter sobs again, then he crumples. His body tilts forwards, and his arms go around his head, and he continues to sob, making these harsh, broken sounds.

I don't know what to do. I don't think anybody knows. We all just sit there. How is this happening? Is it possible for a teacher to lose it like this? Is it allowed? We're frozen, frightened. If a grown man, someone in a position of authority, can cry like this, can lose control in this way, what does it mean for us teenagers?

Then someone moves. It's Rory. She slowly gets up from her desk, walks over to Showalter, and puts a hand on his shoulder. What's she doing? Students don't touch teachers at school, and teachers don't touch students. It's written in the handbook somewhere. You can get sued for that crap.

I don't think Rory's read the handbook. She turns Mr Showalter, who seems incapable of anything now, and eases him into her arms. Hugs him. He cries and cries.

'It's Matt,' he sobs. 'My Matty…'

'Shh,' Rory croons.

'He's been in the hospital so long. He's in so much pain.' Showalter is gasping into her shoulder. 'My wife and I… we're both so tired… But he's my son. *My son* …'

This thick heaviness settles on me, a palpable sadness. Showalter's son is in hospital. I didn't know. None of us knew. His grief fills up the room, makes me want to cry myself.

Rory pats and hugs Mr Showalter. Then Cam rises from her chair and goes forwards, stands in front of Rory and Showalter, shielding them from the eyes of the class.

'Everyone sit down and do something quiet.' Her voice is formal and firm. She looks around. 'Bailey, could you get a glass of water for Mr Showalter, please? Bo, go down to admin and explain the situation, and ask for another teacher to come here as soon as possible.'

I get up, walk out of the room, moving forwards as instructed, like I'm a robot. All the way to the office, I'm turning it over in my head. Showalter's been under stress. We all knew; we all saw the signs. But we've been arseholes to him since we got back to school at the start of term.

What were we thinking? Are we all such losers that we thought it'd be a laugh, to drive this guy into a breakdown? Were we not thinking at all? And why did none of us react when he started to collapse? We all sat there, immobile. Where was our human response? Where was our compassion?

The only one in the whole class who comforted Showalter was Rory.

*

'That was fucking awful.' I'm pushing through bodies in the hall between classes, backpack over one shoulder.

Rory's sticking close. 'That poor man. He should be on leave.'

'He *was* on leave. Last term. Maybe he only came back cos they ran out of money for medical bills? Jesus.' The more I think about it, the worse I feel. And Sprog is still avoiding me. This day is deteriorating rapidly.

'We could do a collection?' Rory suggests.

'That's actually not a bad idea,' I say.

In English Mr Small tells us all to settle down. I get the impression that the collapse of another teacher is almost a personal embarrassment for him. It's a chink in the armour.

This class is determinedly normal. The only weird thing is Shandy and Kaylah having a titter-fest over on the far side of the classroom; they keep looking at Rory and giggling. I don't know what they're going on about; Rory's not wearing anything different from usual – no feathers in her hair, no radical hippie gear. Maybe it's blowback from the river party. It doesn't matter, either way, cos Rory's ignoring them.

Shandy and Kaylah bolt right on bell time, though, so that's one less annoyance. Sprog leaves almost as fast, which makes me fume. How am I supposed to figure things out if he won't even tolerate my presence?

'He'll come around,' Rory says, as she takes my hand.

I squeeze her fingers like they're a lifeline. 'Look, he might be at the basketball courts. I'll hunt for him there. Meet back up with you in the senior area?'

But Sprog isn't at the basketball courts; even Teo hasn't seen him. And when I trace my steps back to the senior area, Rory's not there, and neither is Cam.

'Where the hell *is* everybody?' I ask Lozzie.

'Cam had to go back to admin,' she says, 'to give her version of the events with Showalter. God, I heard about that – he shouldn't have been at school. Didn't any of the other teachers notice he was losing his shit?'

'I dunno, probably,' I say, distracted, looking around the senior area. 'Dammit, where's Rory?'

'Art rooms?' Lozzie chucks her apple core under a withered shrub in the garden. 'Isn't that where she likes to hang out?'

'She said she'd meet me here.' I look over and realise that Sprog's finally deigned to grace us with his presence; he's in the canteen queue, leaning on the metal-pole fence and exchanging comments with Shandy and Kaylah, as Shandy buffs her nails. I want to talk to him, but I'm not going up there while Shandy's hanging around.

'Right, well, that was exhausting. Jesus, what a mess,' Cam says, dropping her bag onto the table and making a sign of the cross. She lifts her hair off the back of her neck, grimacing.

'Mr Showalter's gone home. I think he's off for the rest of term, poor bastard. They're scrambling now to find a replacement teacher for Humanities. The school is communicating with the hospital to provide more support – we should pass the hat around in class.'

'That's what Rory said,' I point out.

'It's a good idea, I'll organise it.' Cam pulls out her container of fruit salad. 'I don't think Showalter is anyone's favourite teacher or anything, but come on. His kid's sick. As far as excuses for lousy teaching go, that's a pretty good one.' She glances around the senior area. 'Where's Rory? Maybe she could help me get the collection sorted.'

'She's not here.'

'Aren't you two usually joined at the hip?'

'I don't know where she is.' I'm getting frustrated now.

'Art rooms?' Lozzie suggests again.

'On it,' I say, grabbing my bag.

On the way out, I pass Sprog. When he sees me, he crosses his arms over his chest. Beside him, Shandy is smirking. She catches my eye, then turns to Kaylah and laughs, which gets right up my nose.

'What's your fucking problem?' I say to her.

'Nothing,' she replies, easing a strand of her fringe away from her face with a faux-genteel, pinkie-finger gesture. 'My problem is all sorted out now, thank you very much.'

I narrow my eyes. Then I realise that Sprog isn't just defiant. There's an edge to the way he shifts on his feet, the expression on his face, something more than mere glowering.

He looks *guilty*.

A brick drops into my stomach from a great height. My

facial expression flattens out as I step closer to the group. 'What did you do?'

Kaylah hitches her bra strap back and giggles. 'You'll find out.'

The hair on my arms lifts when I hear that giggle. I do what I should have done before – I run for the Art rooms.

I find her out in the covered courtyard area at the back of the rooms. It's where Mr Ong has set up the pottery workshop, with the kiln squatting over on the far right. She's sitting on one of the stools. A lump of raw clay is on the table beside her as she smokes a bidi. She's looking out past the workshop fence to the bush beyond.

I don't know what's going on, but Rory's expression is enough to tell me it's nothing good. 'Hey.'

She keeps putting the bidi to her lips and drawing, puffing out the revolting smoke. A bloom of panic unfurls in me – that she's smoking, cos that's not what she does; that she's smoking, cos she'll get into trouble for it, and me along with her if we're found together. I squash the panic back down.

'Are you gonna talk to me?' I ask.

She ashes the cigarette onto the concrete pavers. Her movements are measured, but her hand is shaking. 'You don't have to rescue me every time something goes wrong.'

'I know.' I shift on my feet. 'But I thought maybe I could help.'

'You can't.' She stares down at the pavers, snorts. 'Well, unless you want to help me clean out my locker.'

'What happened?' I say softly.

'Dog shit.' She closes her eyes. 'They put dog shit in my locker, okay?'

Shock runs through me like ice water. '*What?*'

Rory nods.

'Do you know who did it?'

'They didn't exactly leave a sign.'

But they didn't have to, did they? Bloody Shandy and Kaylah. I want to hit them. I want to hurt them, but you can't hurt girls. It wasn't only the girls, though: I think of Sprog's guilty defiance. He would've been recruited to pick the lock. And Shandy wouldn't have wanted to get her hands dirty – a couple of the other boys, Todd or Kevin, were probably involved. That I can do something about.

'I'm sorry. The way they're treating you is bullshit.' I stand there, my fists clenched. 'They're arseholes, and they're way out of line.'

A mix of fury and raw confusion is blended on Rory's face. 'Is this high school? Really? Or is it just me?'

I don't know how to reply. I mean, what's worse? To say, *Yes, it's just you they do this to.* Or to say, *Yes, this is high school* – because it bloody *is*. This is the animal pack mentality of high school: eat or be eaten, know your place in the social order, cringe and cower when you're expected to. If you're different, you're a target.

'Rory—'

'Don't.' She stubs her bidi out in the clay. Then she starts poking sinkholes into the great lump of clay, working the cigarette-end down deep.

'Did you know that ceramics are the longest-lasting art form?' Her hands squeeze and knead. 'Canvas and paper deteriorate. Wood breaks down. Dance and music are only temporary. Even stone wears. But ceramics outlast every other art form, because they're chemically similar to fossils. That's why, when archaeologists dig up historical sites, they find ceramics – pottery. They find bronze masks and swords and glass, too. But pottery is special. It lasts forever.'

Rory turns towards me, her hands still on the clay; now it's a pile of squeezed, misshapen brown dough. Her expression is more stark than I've ever seen it.

'I get that I'm a nobody at school. Everyone's a nobody, if you think about it on a geological scale. But I don't want to disappear without a trace. Even if no one remembers who I am, in a thousand years someone might dig at the place I lived and they'll find the things I made. And they'll wonder...'

I know what they'll wonder. It's the same thing I hope people will wonder about me. Who was this person? What did they believe? How did they live, and breathe, and walk on the earth? Even if it was only for a speck of time, in all of history...

Something stirs within me, something powerful, almost too strong for my ribs to contain. It wakes up at the sound of the things Rory's saying, the expression on her face, and explodes like a sunburst inside my head.

I look straight at her. 'I've got an idea.'

✳

It takes a lot less wrangling than I thought it would.

I go explain everything to Mrs Ram, who is suitably

130

appalled by what's happened – it's been a helluva day for the teachers – and gives me permission to skip Periods Five and Six. Then I race back to Rory.

First, we go to her locker and clean out all the shit, using gloves and a bucket we've begged from Mr Foran, the groundsman. Then we lug it back to the Art rooms. Still wearing the gloves, we work the whole disgusting mess into a big ball of clay. We laugh, and spend a lot of time swearing about the smell. Then Rory gets to work. By the final bell, she's got a sculpture made of dog-shit-infused clay.

We dump our gloves and the bucket into a bin bag, twist the top, then stand back – way, way back – and regard her creation. It's a tree, with a solid trunk and stylised branches reaching high.

'Are you sure this will work?' Rory asks. She doesn't sound grief-filled anymore; she sounds hopeful.

'It'll work.' I'm still reading about internal combustion ceramics on my phone. 'We talked about it in Art last year – this guy puts the fuel inside the clay by mixing fifty per cent manure and fifty per cent clay. It's inspired by Pre-Columbian pottery or something.'

'It's like raku,' Rory notes. 'Kind of porous.'

'You can even use human shit, apparently.'

Her eyes pop. 'I draw the line there.'

'Yeah, I don't blame you.' I tuck my phone back in my pocket, smile at her. 'It'd be really authentic, though, right? All you.'

'That's true!' she says, and she laughs.

It makes me glad to hear it. 'And ecologically sound.'

She pushes on my arm. 'I knew I liked you for a reason.'

We load the sculpture carefully into the drying room –

it's got to dry before it can be fired, apparently – and then I leave her. I'm late for footy training, but I don't care. All my righteous anger comes back in a head-splitting rush when I get to the ground and see Sprog loitering near the goalposts. Mullet is divvying up teams for the scratchie, and I make damn sure that me and Sprog are on opposing sides.

When I go in, I guts it to the max. Twice, I manage to beat Sprog to the ball, let him eat my dust. At one point, I scoop the ball from under his feet, handball it to Justin Fromer, then spin and shirtfront Sprog behind play.

Mullet calls us both over, sucking the inside of his cheeks. 'What's going on?'

'Nothing,' I say.

'Nothing,' Sprog says, more sullen.

'Well, whatever your nothings are, they're making you play like a pair of gorillas. There are opportunities for both of you here. But I can guarantee you the scouts aren't gonna be interested in signing up a coupla immature hooligans.' He points a finger at each of us in turn. 'Go get cleaned up. You're both done. And sort out your nothings before you get back on my ground next week, or you're both benched.'

We manage to keep it civil until we get inside the change rooms, then Sprog rounds on me, his face red with sweat and fury. 'You're really gonna bust my arse like this over a *girl*? What happened to bros before—'

'*Do not finish that fucking sentence.*' My jaw aches from clenching my teeth. 'Are you serious? You really want to make out like you're the victim in all this?'

'I didn't know they were gonna put shit in her locker!'

'Well, what the fuck did you *think* they were gonna do?

Leave her flowers?' I yank off my boots, pull on my runners. 'Use your fucking brain, mate!'

'Shandy said—'

'What, you're Shandy's lapdog now?'

'*Piss off!*'

'Thanks, I will.' I snatch up my gear. 'I don't know what I did that's got you so upset – I'm not a fucking mind-reader. But I do know that Rory isn't the person you're angry with. So if you're gonna take it out on someone, take it out on me.'

I should stay – I should stay and let him get it all out, whatever's eating him, but I can't. I feel like punching him in the face right now, and I don't want it to devolve into that. So I march the hell outta there, still wearing my dirty footy jersey. From outside, I can hear Sprog kicking the change room lockers, roaring in frustration. I think leaving was the right choice, but it doesn't make me feel better.

Riding home makes me feel better – clearer, calmer. It's the one thing I know I can do to release my pent-up energy in a constructive way. By the time I get home, I can talk and think and act normally. I sluice myself in the bathroom, change into clean clothes, come out to find Mum making dinner and Connor drawing at the kitchen table.

'It's a recurve bow,' he explains to me proudly. 'The boy in my book knows how to shoot arrows. And how to throw a knife, and skin a rabbit.'

'Nice. Dunno about the archery, but I can show you how to do the knife and the rabbit.' I ruffle his hair, turn to Mum. 'Where's Dad?'

'He had some work stuff to sort out. He'll be home later, after Con goes to bed.'

Mum peels potatoes serenely. It's impossible to know whether she's telling the truth about what Dad's doing – maybe he's dealing with whatever's been keeping him up at night, or maybe it really is work.

I get a zap of irritation, but then I look at her, standing there in her work clothes, her face tired, her belly bulging under her blouse and slacks. I remember what I said to Rory on Saturday night: *We should do more to help her out. She's having a baby in April…* It might be time to put those words into action.

'D'you need some help with dinner?'

Mum looks up at me. 'What?'

I take the peeler from her gently. 'I can do that, hey. You should have a cuppa, sit down. You've been working all day.' I edge into her spot in front of the kitchen sink, where the rest of the potatoes sit waiting their turn, the peelings collected in the basin. 'Are these spuds the only ones left?'

Mum gapes for a second, then she steps back. 'Yes, they're the last lot. They all need to be washed before they're chopped, though.'

'Sorted.'

'Thank you, Bo,' she says. She looks so amazed and grateful. I should have done this sooner.

I peel spuds, while Mum makes a cuppa for herself. It's weird that I haven't thought to offer Mum help before – not only cos it's obvious she needs the help, but because cooking is something I can actually *do*, even enjoy. Peeling, chopping, slipping the sausages under the grill, putting water on for carrots and peas… Cycling isn't the only thing that makes me feel better. As I go through the steady motions of food preparation, concentrate on the steps and timing, the last sediment of my anger washes away.

It gives me a chance to think about everything that happened today. Meeting Rory in the morning, the stuff she said… The messy business with Sprog, and Mr Showalter's breakdown… Then the way Rory and I worked together to make something good out of the literally crap hand she was dealt… I don't know if it's that memory or the heat from the stove that's making me feel warm.

Mum sits at the kitchen table, nursing her cuppa, nodding at Connor as he explains his drawing to her. She keeps glancing at my face as I work. I'm filling a pot at the sink and she smiles at me.

'What?' I say.

'You look happy.'

'I am.' It's true. In spite of all the crazy shit that's happened, I feel okay.

'What did you get up to today, to make you so happy?'

I can't say, *I made a dog-shit sculpture* – that'll sound nuts. 'I helped a friend. She was feeling bad.'

'Good for you,' Mum says.

I'm feeling generous with my happiness, decide to share it around. 'I can cook dinner tomorrow night, too, if you want a break.'

'Really?'

'Sure. I don't have any after-school sport, and it's early in the term, so homework's still pretty light on.'

I turn around for the carrots, put the pot on the stove, light the gas. I really am having a good time. I should do some of the meals I cooked in class last year. Meat and veg is okay, but it'd be nice to have a bit of variety. I think Mum mainly prepares simple things cos she's too tired and busy to go to more effort.

I clear my throat. 'Hey, Mum... Would it be okay if I did more cooking at home?'

Mum's mouth drops open again. 'What's brought all this on?'

I shrug. 'I just figured you might need help with the baby coming. That'd be good, right?'

Mum nods slowly, looking at me as if she's seeing me for the first time. 'Yes, that'd be good.'

'Cooking's okay, hey. I like it.' I've got to stop blushing when I say that.

'Well, if you like it...' Mum's smile spreads across her face. 'Bo, I'd be delighted if you did more of the cooking.'

Dad doesn't make it home in time for dinner – he walks in as I'm getting ready for bed, and I hardly get to say two words to him. But I'm fine with that. He'll figure this thing out, whatever it is. And I'll work it out with Sprog. And Rory will settle into school. And everything will be all right.

At this moment, life seems reasonably manageable. I've even got a few answers to those questions that Mrs Ramanathan asked. What are the things that mean something to me? Friends, family, footy, Rory... and cooking. I might finally be ready to admit that. What was it that Ray said the other night? *Cooking is a political act.* I'm not sure what that means, but I know cooking makes me relax, and I'm good at it. I shouldn't be ashamed of that. So what if it's not part of the image that I usually project? There's no law that says I'm locked into being a footy guy forever. And one of these days, I'll move out of home – I'll need to be self-sufficient, like Rory is at her hut.

There's something else that's important to me: sticking up for what's right. What I did for Rory today, I did because I care for her. I acted because it felt necessary – it felt right. Cooking for Mum was the same; she's my mum, and I love her, and I wanted to help her. I guess it was the same instinct Rory acted on when Showalter collapsed – the instinct to console and support, to do the right thing by another human being.

But Showalter was her teacher, not her friend. Rory's compassion extends to people outside her own circle, to the wider world – to the earth, even. Has growing up in Eden made Rory this way, or is it her nature?

Either way, I've got to lift my game. I can't just be helping out the people in my immediate circle and spitting on everyone else.

I lie in bed, my arms folded behind my head. These questions from Mrs Ramanathan have been kinda useful. Everything I've been taught so far at school about growing up has been about what skills I can acquire, what jobs I'll be fit for – I've never thought about what I really like, what's important to me. I've never considered the kind of person I want to be. I always figured it was all genetics, that you just kind of *evolved*, without a lot of conscious thought process.

But now I don't think it has to be like that. And it's a good time to start thinking about it. I'm sixteen, and I reckon I'm starting to get glimpses of the future ahead of me. It's a good feeling, knowing that I can make my own decisions: not only about the kind of job I want, but about the man I want to become.

I can be deliberate about the future. I can make it mine.

It's not until I'm in French with Lozzie that I realise she and Cam don't know about Sprog's involvement in the locker incident with Rory.

'Are you *kidding* me? And Sprog picked the lock?' Her jaw is fully dropped. 'What is wrong with that boy's brain right now?'

'Got me,' I say. 'But I wanna have a word with him at lunch.'

Loz blows a raspberry. 'You do that. Wait until I tell Cam – she'll be ropeable.' Her eyes narrow. 'I saw Shandy coming out of the principal's office this morning. I guess she had her wrist slapped. She was still grinning like an idiot.'

I shake my head. 'Shandy's got no shame.'

'Poor Rory.'

'She's fine,' I say. But I can't know for sure: Rory didn't meet me for the bike ride this morning, which is fair enough – it'd be a pretty intimidating prospect for her to front up at school again today.

'I'm not surprised she's getting picked on, though,' Loz continues.

'What do you mean?'

'Oh, come on, Bo. You only have to look at her to know she's a soft target.'

I put down my French dictionary. 'So she deserves what she got? Loz—'

'I didn't say that. Look, I get it – high school is hard. Not the academic stuff so much – that's just work – but the social stuff can be cut-throat. I still find it full-on sometimes.' She looks away, blushing – it's odd, seeing Lozzie blush – then looks back. 'But it makes you more resilient. You learn to stick up for yourself. And once you get a few mates, you all look out for each other... Rory's still figuring it out. She's too trusting, though, too open. It makes her an easy mark.'

'You think she needs to toughen up?'

'Well... yeah. Bo, she has to learn that the world isn't all rainbows and flowers.'

'I get that. But it's not fair to lay the blame on her. What, because she's vulnerable, she's asking for it? Don't you think that's kind of shit?'

Lozzie shrugs.

'If Rory wasn't the target, it'd be some other poor schmuck,' I point out. 'The problem isn't Rory, it's Shandy. Shandy preys on the weak, and we let her get away with it. It's like that stuff with Showalter the other day. Is that what we're all learning here? To keep kicking people until they toughen up or break?'

'You have to be a bit tough to live in this world,' Lozzie insists. 'I'm not saying it's ideal, but that's the way it is.'

It's a hard message to swallow. *That's the way it is*... It's the wrong way. We've set the bar for our behaviour too low.

If we expected more of ourselves as individuals, as a community, then the world wouldn't have to be like this.

And Lozzie's wrong. Rory isn't unaware of the nature of the world. She's not under any illusions. Rory knows the world is shit.

That's why she's hiding.

*

Sprog knows how shitty the world can be, too. I'm pretty sure that's why he almost looks relieved to see me when I show up at the basketball courts at lunch.

He's standing alone on the court, shooting for the hoop in a way that suggests he's not really invested in whether or not the ball goes in. His shoulders are low, and he looks tired.

I dump my backpack on the edge of the court. 'Camilla. You're pissed at me cos I told Camilla about your mum.'

Sprog collects the ball before it bounces away, keeps his eyes off me. 'It's none of her business. It's none of your business, either, if you really wanna know.'

I scrub a hand through my hair. 'Sprog, you're our mate. If there's a problem, we want to help.'

'It's not a problem youse can help with.'

'At least we can talk about it?'

'Spilling my guts won't make me feel any better.' He shoots again – the ball bounces off the rim and he catches it on the return. 'And I don't need the whole of fucking Lamistead knowing my mum's a—'

He cuts himself off before the words 'depressive alcoholic' can slip out. His face darkens, and he disguises it by lining up another shot.

'Camilla's not the whole of Lamistead,' I point out.

'You know what I mean.'

What he really means is that Cam's the only person in Lamistead he *doesn't* want to share this with. He doesn't want Camilla to feel sorry for him. He wants to maintain some dignity. He's always considered himself too low down in the food chain for Cam, and this incident with his mum is just another reminder.

I can see why he was angry with me, but I also know there's something crucial he doesn't understand. 'Sprog, how long d'you reckon we've been friends with Cam?'

The question shakes him out of his rhythm. He bounces the ball once, grips it tight. 'Since…a long time. Kinder, maybe? Whatever.'

'Right. Since kinder. And Cam's really bright, and Lamistead's a small town.'

'What's your point?'

'Cam knows about your family, mate. She's always known. And she doesn't give a stuff. She only cares about *you*. That's why I told her what was going on. She was texting me practically every half-hour on Saturday, trying to find out if you were all right.'

Sprog's jaw works as he stares at the ball in his hands, as he looks up at me. 'She was texting you?'

'Uh, yeah. Didn't she text you?'

'Yeah.' He sighs. 'Yeah, she did. And she tried to call on Sunday but I didn't pick up. Shit, she's gonna be pissed.'

'Well, Cam'll probably forgive you for the weekend. But that thing with Rory yesterday isn't going to work in your favour.'

He looks mulish. 'I didn't know they were gonna do what they did.'

'But you knew that Shandy's had it in for Rory since she arrived. You should've used your head. It's crap, the way they're treating her. You've gotta know that.'

He glowers. 'Why are you always sticking up for her? She's a freak.'

'Sure, she's a freak. We've all got freak parts – it's just we've known each other for so long that we're used to them. Rory might be a freak, but she's also a fucking person. And when people send her dog-shit presents, she feels it. Same way you'd feel it, if people did that to you.'

He winces, throws the ball down – it bounces away to the bleachers. 'Fuck, I've screwed this up, haven't I?'

Royally. 'Only one thing to do about it.'

'I'll apologise to Cam first.'

'I'd grovel, if I were you. She's not gonna be impressed.'

'Crap.' He chases back his hair. 'Look, I'm sorry I lost it yesterday at training.'

I step closer, grinning. 'Doesn't matter. I got you back.' Then I think about it. 'You're right, though. Your family is *your* business. I should've let you talk to Cam about it yourself.'

'Yeah, well, I didn't want to talk to her, did I?' He rolls his eyes. 'I think we've already established that I can be an idiot sometimes.'

I hoist my backpack, toss Sprog's into his arms. 'Come on back to the senior area, then, and all us idiots can hang out together.'

*

'That's awful!' Mum says, when I relate the story of what happened to Rory. 'What a thing to do to someone... No wonder she didn't show up at school today.'

We're sitting around the table after dinner. I made dinner again. It was a second night of chops and veg, but even if it had been cheese toasties, I think Mum would've been happy. She's stolen half a glass of Dad's beer, which he's drinking out of the stubby, and they're lolling in their chairs looking through the verandah windows at Con, who's bouncing on the trampoline out in the backyard, the crazy bugger.

Dad stretches in his chair. 'So Rory's had a tough run at the high school.'

'That makes it sound like bad luck or something.' I stand and start gathering plates. 'It's not about luck, it's about people being arseholes.'

'She's getting a few lessons in that, then.'

I breathe out my nose. 'I don't think it's something we should have on the curriculum, but yeah, she's getting a serve.'

'She's been homeschooled up until now?'

'Yes.' I stack cutlery on top of the plates. 'But she wanted to give high school a try. I think it would suck if she decided not to come back cos of the way she's been treated.'

'She's been very sheltered, though, hasn't she?' Dad slowly peels the label off his stubby. 'Eden's not the real world. It's just a refuge for people who can't cope with day-to-day life.'

'I don't know where you get all these ideas about Eden, Dad.' I've picked up my stack – now I'm standing here, staring at him. 'Have you been there?'

'No. But I don't need to go to Eden. I've met their sort before.'

'What sort?'

'Answer one question about Eden for me, first.' He takes a sip from his beer, looks at me. 'Where do they get their money?'

'What?'

'Their money. They need to have something to keep the community running. So where do they get it?'

'They're self-sufficient with food and power.' I carry the stack to the sink, walk back with a tea towel. 'They trade for supplies – they make blankets and woodwork, and they barter honey and eggs and stuff. Some of them have jobs – Rory's mum's partner, Stuart, he has a part-time job in town.'

'So this whole community of … how many people?'

'Eleven.' Distracted, I hand Mum a tea towel as she reaches over.

'Eleven people, right. And you're telling me they all live on one guy's part-time wage, plus what they grow or make and trade?'

'Yes.' I watch Mum swipe crumbs off the dinner table. I should be doing that.

'What about their building materials? What about things like fuel for their water pumps, repair parts for their solar array? Do they have a phone?'

Mum gives my father a look, and goes out onto the verandah to call Connor. I have to concentrate on the question. 'Yes, they have a phone. I don't know about the other stuff.'

'That requires money. Are they on welfare?'

'I don't know. I didn't ask.'

'A hundred bucks says they're scamming somehow.' Dad leans back in his chair as if he's proved his point. 'They're probably pooling their welfare payments and pensions to pay for necessities. So it's either my taxes paying for them to live out their utopian dream, or someone's bankrolling the whole thing.'

I frown. 'What do you mean, "bankrolling"?'

'Bo, do you understand the term "trust-fund liberal"?' When I shake my head, he goes on. 'It means someone who's got the time and energy to devote to a cause because they don't have to work, because they come from money. Most of those people in Eden, they live like ferals, but when they open their mouths to talk, their silver spoons fall out.'

'You've talked to them, have you?'

Dad waves the question away. He's already formed his opinion. He doesn't need proof.

'Dad, I don't know what your problem is with Eden,' I say firmly. 'And I don't know all the details of the community's background, or their finances. But they believe in something—'

'Environmentalism.' Dad shakes his head in disgust. 'It's just a cause. Doesn't mean it's not a good cause. But it's something people like that can pick up and put down whenever they feel like it.'

They're not like that! I want to say. *They're living it!* But I get the feeling I could talk until I'm blue in the face and Dad still wouldn't believe me.

'If you went to the community and checked it out—' I start, but Dad snorts, and I know he'd never go.

'You're just looking for a way to visit Rory,' he says. 'But

145

I've already told you, Bo, I don't want you going there. Make sure you stick to that.'

I roll my eyes and head for the kitchen, start running water for the dishes, banging the pots around. Dad simply will not budge. But it doesn't give me a solution to my problem. I want to see Rory. She can't come to see me, so I've got to go to her. I'm going to Eden again. There's nothing my father can say to convince me otherwise.

*

Wednesday starts off pretty normal.

I know I need to give Rory some space to figure things out, but being away from her makes me restless. In classes, I keep looking at the door, as if she'll walk in any minute. Rory's spontaneous like that – it's not out of the realms of possibility. I'm sure she'd get a kick out of the expression on my face if she did.

She doesn't walk in, though, and the day drags by. The only distraction is the drama between Sprog and Cam. Cam was horrified by the dog-shit incident, and she's been giving Sprog hell about it. At lunch, we're gathered around the table in the senior area when he arrives and dumps his bag. Cam glares. Me and Lozzie exchange glances, waiting for the fireworks to go off.

'You're sitting here, are you?' Cam regards Sprog, eyebrows raised. An Italian woman in a fury is a scary thing. 'We discussed this, didn't we? Well?'

'I haven't done it yet,' Sprog says wearily. He glances at her, rears back. 'Don't look at me like that! I can't apologise if she's not here!'

'You're one of the reasons she's not here.'

'Jesus Christ… Cam, I'm *sorry*, okay?'

'You don't need to say sorry to *me*,' Cam says. And without further ado, she picks up her bag and stalks out of the senior area.

'Cam.' Sprog sighs, watching her go. '*Camilla*.'

Then he picks up *his* bag and follows her out, and then it's just me and Loz.

I nod at Sprog's departure. 'How long are those two gonna keep arguing, you reckon?'

'Until Sprog apologises to Rory,' Lozzie says, checking messages on her phone. 'Or until he and Cam start kissing, I guess.'

'I give them a week.'

'Make it a week from when Rory gets back and you're on.' She tucks her phone away. 'When *is* Rory getting back?'

'Don't know.' I try not to sound too glum.

Lozzie sighs. 'I don't think I can put up with all this sexual tension for much longer.'

I grin at her. 'I'm sure Rory will keep your mental health in mind.'

My good humour only lasts until the end of lunch, when Mrs Ramanathan corners me on the way to fifth period. 'Did we, or did we not, have an agreement, Mr Mitchell? You were going to come to me with your decision about your subject selection.'

I war about how to reply for a second, then hang my head, realising I can only tell the truth. 'We did. We had an agreement. I'm sorry, hey. I got caught up with other stuff.'

'*Other stuff*.' Mrs Ram narrows her eyes. 'This is an

impolite way to refer to a girl.' She quiets me with a raised palm. 'Do you think we teachers are completely uninformed? I know you and Miss Wild have an attachment. What you did for her the other day was very honourable. I am not opposed to friendly attachments, but the task I set you is also important.'

'I'll have a decision for you by the end of the week,' I say firmly.

'You must dig a little deeper for me, Bo.' Mrs Ram waggles one finger in the air. 'Extra effort is required in some situations. I expect to see you at the end of the week.'

Extra effort – between my parents, school and my friends, my whole existence is about extra effort at the moment.

After the final bell, I ride into town and meet up with my brother outside the gates of the primary school. Connor bugs me until I buy us both potato cakes. The fish and chip shop on Gough Street is called The Codfather and it's run by Kaylah's grandad, Roberto Lanzzi. He always gives away extra potato cakes, which makes The Codfather the most popular after-school option for every kid in town.

Then we traipse over to the library to wait for Mum. While Connor veges out on the beanbags with *The Ruins of Gorlan*, I cruise the stacks. Lamistead Library is tiny, but it does have a good collection of cookbooks. I avoid the ones with photos of exotic ingredients, white tablecloths and silver cutlery on the cover – who cooks like that? – and look for titles that include the words 'wholefood', 'family' or 'classic'.

Neil, the librarian, gives my selections the once-over. 'That CWA one is good. Are these for your mum?'

'They're for me,' I say, a little stiffly.

Neil nods. 'A man's gotta know how to feed himself properly. It's the only thing that saved me when I left home. All my mates were living on instant noodles. One of them even got scurvy.'

'Seriously?'

'Yup.' He assumes a sage expression as he hands the books to me. 'Don't get scurvy. Keep cooking.'

Mum collects Connor about twenty minutes later, and I ride over to the pool for swim squad – it's the last session of the season, because the pool's about to close. The water is chilly, but once I'm moving I don't notice it.

By the time I get home, Mum's setting places for dinner. 'Did Rory come back to school today?'

'No.' I take off my bike gloves and wash my hands at the kitchen sink, grab the cutlery while she distributes the plates. 'Do you think I should go talk to her?'

'I don't think it's good that she's so isolated,' Mum says, moving awkwardly around the table with her baby belly. 'But I also don't think you should ignore your father's rule about visiting Eden.'

'It's a dumb rule.'

'You're very down on rules, lately,' she says, giving me the eye. 'Is there another way you can contact her? Can you text her?'

'She doesn't get much access to the phone.'

'Maybe you could write her a letter?' She laughs at my expression. 'I know, right? What a concept. But you could write to her and arrange a time and place to meet outside Eden. It's a thought, anyway.'

It's a thought that sticks with me while I call Connor in for

149

dinner, while I'm picking at my pasta. Rory's old-fashioned in lots of ways. Maybe she'd like a letter? But I'm desperate to see her. If I drop by her place early tomorrow and arrange for us to meet outside later, I won't actually be *breaking* the rules, cos I'll be setting things up to stay out of Eden. Right?

'No more sauce!' Connor complains, as Mum spoons out his extra helping.

'It's pesto,' she says. 'It's not going to kill you.'

'Yeah, bro, you can't just eat carbs.' I wipe my plate down with a piece of buttered bread. 'You'll get scurvy.'

'Bo, do we need to talk about scurvy over dinner?' Mum asks.

'What's scurvy?' Connor says, as Julie starts barking, and someone knocks on our front door.

Mum starts to rise, but I wave her back to her seat with a grin. 'I'll get it. You explain about scurvy.'

'It's probably Mrs Gillies,' she says, in a stage-whisper. Mrs Gillies is our nearest neighbour – she's sixty-three, and she runs sheep and agists horses on the paddocks beside our property. She lives alone, and if there's a problem she sometimes drops over and asks Dad to help. 'Tell her Dad's not going to be in until late.'

When I get to the door, though, it's not Mrs Gillies. It's a guy – early twenties, dark-haired and swarthy, solid-muscled. He's wearing jeans and a wrinkled black polo shirt, and he's got a backpack at his feet. He stands back from the door politely as I push Julie away with my knee and open the flywire.

'Hi. I'm here to see Aaron Mitchell.'

'Julie, shut up,' I hiss at her, then I turn back to the visitor. 'He's not here right now. Can I help?'

150

The guy sighs. 'Nah, it's okay. Thanks, though.' He leans for his backpack, and over his shoulder I see a red car parked down on the road.

I hold Julie awkwardly by the collar as she keeps trying to jump forwards. 'Whatcha need him for? Is this about work?'

The guy shakes his head. 'No, he's not expecting me. Sorry to interrupt your dinner, hey, but I've come a long way. D'you know when he'll get in?'

I shrug. 'I'm not sure.'

'Can I help you?' Mum says, wiping her hands on a tea towel. She's snuck up on my other side, and now it's getting crowded in the doorway, with me, Mum, Backpack Guy, and stupid Julie, who's practically pulling my shoulder out of its socket.

'I think I should come back another time,' the guy says.

Mum angles forwards. 'Do you want to leave Aaron a message? Or your number? He could call—'

'That won't work,' the guy says. He wets his lips. 'He won't call me. He doesn't want to talk. That's why I flew down from Brisbane.'

'You've come from Brisbane?' Mum's voice has gone flat.

'Yeah. Look, I'm sorry. I've gone about this arse-backwards.' He holds out his hand. 'My name's Liam Pettifer. I'm Lily Pettifer's son. Aaron is my dad.' He looks me straight in the eye. 'I'm your brother.'

I'm lying in bed with my shoulders propped up on pillows.

The problem is, I seem to have a head filled entirely with white noise and bullshit. The white noise started when Liam Pettifer said, *I'm your brother* – this great cloud of nothing, of *absence*, rose up inside me, making it hard to breathe.

He said 'brother', and I knew he really meant it, that he really was my brother. Not in the way Sprog sometimes feels like my brother, or how me and Teo and Joel call each other 'bro' all the time. Liam is my actual brother, the way Connor is my brother. A flesh-and-blood brother.

In the time it took me to process that, I could see it, too – he had my father's dark hair, the shape of his nose and chin... All those tiny details that spelt out the truth.

Why didn't I notice straight away? Maybe cos of all the bullshit in my head. The bullshit is the opposite of the white noise – blood-red and scratchy, like a series of etchings layered over the top of one another, the layers going a hundred-deep, so all you see is a jumbled mess of lines on the surface. It's a compost of all the memories, all the things

I've thought I've understood for the last sixteen years: of who I am, and who my father is, and how our family works, and what that all means. It's bullshit because all the memories and understandings are lies.

While the white noise made me quietly cloudy and vague and confused, the bullshit made me want to punch something. Liam, at first. I wanted to punch Liam. But then Mum, after a long silence, said, 'Liam, maybe you should come into the house,' so I was hamstrung, cos you can't punch a guest.

Mum turned to me and said, 'Bo.' Then she put a hand on my shoulder and said it again, '*Bo,*' and I said, 'What?' and she said, 'Bo, I want you to go to the kitchen and put the kettle on, all right?' So I kind of nodded and backed up from the door. Julie ran free, out into the front yard. Mum ushered with her hand and Liam stepped into our house, and I turned around and walked to the kitchen.

Connor was still eating his dinner at the table. 'Is it Mrs Gillies?' He made a face, kept chewing his food. 'I'm not chasing her sheep around in the dark again.'

I couldn't even talk, the noise in my head was that loud, so I shook my head. I filled the kettle and stuck it back into its bracket. My hands were trembling. I pressed the switch as Liam and Mum walked into the kitchen.

Mum looked pale. She was wearing a sleeveless top, and her bare arms seemed sinewy in the kitchen light. 'Connor, please put your plate on the bench and go to your room for a while.'

Connor blinked. 'But—'

'Take your plate with you if you want to finish your dinner. But I don't want to be disturbed for a while.'

Connor looked mystified, but Mum was using her

'Sergeant Major' voice, so he shrugged, grabbed his fork and plate and took off.

Mum turned to me. 'Bo, get down two mugs and make tea, please. Liam, how do you have it?'

Liam stood there, shifting on his feet. But his expression was staunch. 'Just black and one, thanks.'

Mum nodded and turned to me again. 'Bo, one for me, and one black with one sugar. Bring them out to the verandah.' Then she ushered Liam out the verandah door.

I should've felt pissed off. For a fleeting second I did, that I was being relegated to tea-maker. But then I reached for the mugs and realised it was good to have a task to perform, something that required me to focus on a series of small steps.

I waited for the kettle, watching Mum and Liam through the glass doors. Mum sat perched forwards on the swing chair, the weight of her belly in front making her look off-balance. Liam sat in the old wooden chair near the railing. Their voices were too quiet for me to hear what they were saying.

When the tea was ready, I ferried it out – Liam got up and opened the door for me, took the mug I offered, while I passed Mum hers. I paused then.

'Give us a minute, Bo,' Mum said.

I nodded and went back inside and to my room and closed the door. Suddenly this intense desire ran through me, to open the door again and go out of the house, grab my bike from under the eaves of the shed and cycle away. I could feel my legs twitching with the need to move. But then a wave of weird lethargy came over me. It drowned out the desire to leave, so I lay on my bed and looked up at the ceiling. I'm still doing that now.

This house was here on the property when my parents bought it, but Dad has made a lot of modifications over the years. The ceiling I'm staring at now is something he helped build with his own hands. Shadows gather like cobwebs in the corners as the night outside throbs its way over the land.

I stare up at the ceiling until I hear Liam leave, my mother's voice low as she shows him out. I hear a car drive away.

There's a long silence, then a clatter of plates as Mum cleans up the dinner dishes. I should help her. That's my job, and I promised to give Mum more help. But my whole body feels like it's coated in lead. I can't move.

I close my eyes so I don't have to look anymore at the inside of this room that Dad built. After a while – even though it's way early, even though I know that when I wake up, the world will be a vastly different place – I fall asleep.

*

I slept in my clothes and boots. Someone put a blanket over me in the night. I kick it off and go out to the toilet.

The inside of my mouth feels furry, bitter. I drink a glass of water in the kitchen, check the clock. It's way past when I'd usually leave for the school ride. I'm going to be massively late. Or maybe it doesn't matter? I can skip school today. One of my parents needs to phone in and let school know, though, or I'll get another detention.

My feet are comatose inside my shoes. I shuffle to my parents' bedroom and find my father filling a duffel bag with clothes.

I stop in the doorway and stare.

He pauses when he realises I'm there, before pushing

another folded T-shirt into the bag. 'It's not what you think.'

I'm sleep-stupid for a second, until his words and actions kick in and I realise he's packing to leave. He's got another son, another life, somewhere in another city. All the red rage inside me surfaces again. 'Well, what *should* I think?'

Even now, I want Dad to give me a solution to this problem. I want him to say, *This is all a misunderstanding*, or, *Don't worry, I'm going to sort this out. It's a mistake.*

But he doesn't.

'I have to go to Brisbane for a few days,' Dad says. 'I need you to take care of your mother and brother until I get back.'

My stomach bottoms out somewhere near my feet.

'Is it true?' I step into the room. 'Is Liam Pettifer my brother?'

There's a pause. Dad's hands stop moving.

'It's true,' he says finally, sighing. 'Liam is my son. He's your half-brother.'

My body starts to shake. My breath comes in short and fast, and hard to control.

Dad leaves the duffel and comes closer. 'Bo—'

'You …' I whisper. I push at him with my hands, as he tries to hold my shoulders in a gentle grip. 'You …'

'Bo—' Dad starts again.

But pushes turn to shoves, to slaps against his chest that get stronger.

Dad's grip becomes less gentle. '*Bodeen*. Bo, *stop*.'

'*You!*' I yell. I punch him in the chest, flail my arms to get free. '*You fucking*—'

I roar, because I can't even say what I *mean*: I can't even get the words out. The anger has expanded inside me like a giant

156

red boil. My thin skin is all that's keeping it from exploding.

Dad's still trying to hold me but I can't stand it. I can't stand him being near me. A year ago, I wouldn't have managed, but now I'm sixteen and we're almost the same height and build – I shove him off in one violent, thrashing surge, and he falls back against the dresser. He looks shocked.

'*BO!*'

I'd know the sound of my mother's voice even in an MCG crowd. She's standing in the doorway of the bedroom, holding onto the frame, static electricity making her black hair move like it's alive. She looks at me, horrified, looks at Dad.

I'm shaking so much my teeth are chattering. I don't know where all this explosive energy is coming from, but it's as though I'm full right up to the eyeballs with it. I have to let some of it out, have to *move*.

Mum retreats as I barrel out of the room. I hear Dad yell, '*BODEEN!*' but I keep running, out past the kitchen, through the flywire door, down the steps. I grab my bike, spin it around to mount, then I do what I wanted to do last night: I ride.

I'm not wearing my helmet or my gloves, but I pummel hard through the gate and out to the road. I don't think about which way to turn – I go left on automatic. The tyres feel like they're tearing up on the dirt road, and my head is full of white and red, and my whole body is cold and shaking.

A few kay from my house I realise where I'm going. My water bottle is still clipped to the bike frame, so I squirt some water – warm, murky-tasting – into my mouth as I ride. Then I'm on Fogarty's Hill Road, skidding down to the turn-off to Bowyer Track.

I'm forced to concentrate because of the condition of the

road and the speed I'm riding at. The path is so pitted and lumpy I feel seasick. I'm jouncing around on the bike, my guts sloshing, by the time I reach the Eden sign. I coast past, dodging gardens, riding as far as the Meeting House before screeching to a stop, dropping my bike, walking on. I follow the path that I remember, pushing my way through shrubbery and vines until I reach Rory's hut.

The garden around it rises up like a protective green wall, and Rory is outside, in a singlet and her cut-off overalls and some kind of leggings. She has a mug in one hand as she hunkers over one of the ripe-smelling beds, plucking at something. Seeing her there, something unhitches inside my chest – the rage I felt, the energy, it trickles away. All I'm left with is my rolling stomach and a pounding head.

When she hears my footsteps she rises, turns, sees me. Her face blossoms with delighted surprise. 'Bo! What are you—'

'Well, now I know what's up with my parents,' I say. 'Dad has a secret kid up in Brisbane.'

Then I spin around abruptly and vomit into the garden.

∗

'It's chamomile.' Rory eases the cup into my hand. 'I put some honey in it. It'll make you feel better.'

The end of Rory's camp bed is surprisingly comfortable. The mattress stuffing is thick and cushioning. She's got a pile of folded blankets here, too – army grey, red felt, rainbow crochet. She draped a green blanket over my shoulders when I couldn't stop shivering, but now I let it drop to my hips. I don't feel normal yet, but that first wave of nausea and cold dizziness has passed.

I sip the tea. 'Thank you.'

She smiles at me. 'You're getting some colour in your cheeks again.'

I nod and she rubs my back, and it's soothing.

'Do you want to talk?' she asks softly.

'I don't understand any of this.' The tea tastes like dried grass. 'How he could have another family? How he could even spend time with them, if they're interstate? It just… None of it makes sense.'

'You don't have all the information yet, though. You don't know what's really going on.'

'I don't want to hear it.' The idea of listening to my father try to explain all this away… My fists curl around my cup. 'He's a liar. He's been lying to me and Connor and Mum all this time.'

I try to summon the rage I felt before, but it won't come. All I have left is this dull, throbbing ache that makes me feel sapped and weak.

'You must think I'm pathetic,' I whisper.

'What? No way!' Rory slips her hand down my back, curls it around my waist and tugs me gently to lean against her. 'It's really hard when your parents do things that are outside your control. You feel like screaming at them, *Hey, this affects me too!* but they're caught up in all their own personal stuff…' She goes quiet for a minute, reaches for her cup on the log stump. 'When Ray and Star broke up, I was nine. I was too young to understand much. I only knew that my mum didn't want to live with us anymore.'

I stare at her. 'Ray is your *dad*?'

'Yeah. Didn't you realise?' Her eyebrows are lifted and her face is open, guileless. 'Sorry, I thought you knew.'

Um, NO, I want to say. I can't say that. 'But he's so—'

I cut myself off, cos I can't say those words either – 'old' and 'solitary'. Ray doesn't seem like the kind of guy who would have a family. I'm also amazed that he snagged a woman like Star – he must be at least twenty years older than her. Gross. Although he has a lot of presence, I'll give him that.

But now she's pointed it out to me, I can see it: the shape of Rory's face, her sharp cheekbones, her wiry frame. It reminds me of how I recognised my father's features in Liam Pettifer last night. I look away.

'He's so *Ray*. Is that what you mean?' Rory laughs. 'Yeah, he's one of a kind. But he was an okay father.'

She says it like he's not her father anymore. Maybe that's what it's like, when you live independently? Or maybe it's like that when your parents split? Maybe I'll be like that, when my parents separate? I don't want to think that far ahead.

I mumble at my tea. 'Sorry, I didn't mean to be rude.'

'You're not. Even if you were, I think you probably get a pass today.'

Suddenly all I want is to flop down on the camp bed with Rory. We could cuddle, and she could stroke my back, and I could close my eyes and pretend last night never happened.

But with my eyes closed, I wouldn't see her new fashion accessory. Now that I've noticed them, I can't help but stare.

'Ah – the leg warmers.' She snorts, looks down at herself. 'Sally knitted one and I knitted the other.'

They're clearly handmade. The wool is a mix of textures and weights. Bands of dark blues and greys and greens circle her legs, with the occasional uneven strip of red or pale yellow or cream. They go from her ankles all the way up to mid-thigh, which is where my brain seems to short out.

'Knitted leg warmers. Right.' My voice doesn't crack, but I need to clear my throat.

'Well, I cut off the legs of my overalls, didn't I?' Rory's eye-roll means she thinks it was a dumb move. She examines her leg warmers dispassionately. 'The knitting's not great, but I needed to get them done in a hurry, cos the weather's changing and my legs were cold.'

'Okay.'

'They'd be like authentic nineteenth-century stockings if I had tapes to hold them up. But that totally does not work, trust me, so I cannibalised the elastic from an old pair of shorts.'

I can see that. In fact, I'm basically staring at the elasticised tops like I'm hypnotised. The leg warmers are clinging to her thighs. They bunch all up and down her legs, and they look warm. But that strip of skin, between where her leg warmers end and where her cut-off overalls begin, is golden pale and exposed. I'm starting to think it's *too* exposed, like it might need covering up, with my hands, maybe…

'Oh,' Rory says.

I swallow hard, tear my eyes away. 'What?'

'Are they that bad?'

'What? No, no, they're fine.'

'You're staring at them.'

'Am I?' *That's because they're weirdly erotic.* I look her in the eyes. God knows what expression is on my face. 'Sorry. Your leg warmers are great. Really.'

'Okay, that's it,' she says, pushing herself up to standing. 'You have to come with me to Ilona and Sally's now.'

'Why?'

161

She answers my question with one of her own. 'When was the last time you ate? Your eyes are bugging out. You need something warm in your stomach, and Ilona always cooks a hot meal for lunch on baking day.'

She takes the cup out of my hands and urges me up. She's right, I *am* hungry – my stomach is growling around emptiness now, not gurgling with acidic anger. Rory pulls me to standing and we bump up against each other.

She leans to put the mugs aside and I catch her scent – lemon myrtle in her hair, plus the sun-smell on her skin. A hot surge rises inside me. My emotions are so close to the surface right now, and suddenly I want to touch her. I want to hold her. Draw her in, press my lips to the soft skin at the side of her neck, where the little ringlets lie…

'Ready to go?' She turns and looks up at me.

I've broken out in a light sweat. This is crazy. I can't touch Rory now, and I shouldn't. My head's too messed up.

I clamp my hands to my sides and nod.

Rory leads the way out the back door, and after a minute or two I get my voice back. 'So your mum and Ray weren't together when you moved here?'

'Oh, we were all travelling together, but their relationship had ended by then.' She slips her sandals on in the sun, shows me the curve in the path that leads to a set of log steps, winding up. 'They both wanted to be a part of my life, though, so we all moved around as a unit. I was born in New South Wales, in an ashram, I think – we shifted around a lot when I was little, so I don't remember all the places. One place was called Freedom Farm. Then there was a share house – I remember that one, cos it had flush toilets.'

'Wow. Luxury,' I joke.

'Yeah. A terrible waste of water.' She shakes her head. 'Anyway, I knew Ray and Star weren't exclusive, even when they were together. There was another woman, Carmen, who lived with us for a year at Freedom Farm – I didn't like her, though. She used to get really grumpy with me. But she found her own man and left, so it worked out okay.'

I'm squinting as we clear the log steps, trying to take in what she's saying. Her mum shared her father with another woman? For a *year*? I try to imagine my mother in that situation, can't picture it. Then I realise: I already know what that picture looks like. I've been living in it, for years and years, and I didn't even know. The idea makes me feel dizzy again. I try to stop thinking, to just listen to what Rory's saying.

'Anyway, Ray heard about Eden when we were up north, so we all decided to move here. Then Star met Stuart, when he came to Eden about four years ago. A year later, they had Daniel.'

'So your parents always had, like, an open relationship?'

'Sure.' She glances back. The sun makes her pale skin and golden hair dazzling. 'Marriage and monogamy are cultural constructs, right? It's something we've invented as a society – mainly it's about maintaining bloodlines and ownership.'

'You believe that?'

'Absolutely. If it was really about emotional connection, then why throw up so much resistance to gay marriage?' She waves a hand. 'In patriarchal society, women were traditionally married off or given away, like possessions, to solidify clan connections. In matrilineal societies, where women have

163

control over their own inheritance, you don't see the same emphasis on marriage and monogamy.'

'What about love?'

'Oh, love is real.' She smiles over her shoulder at me. 'Love is important. But conventional society has a pretty narrow definition of love.'

I think about my parents on the night I saw them sitting together on the verandah, laughing softly and pressed close. Wasn't that love? I used to think of them as halves of a whole – more than the sum of two. Was I wrong?

It's been the only understanding of love I've ever known. I thought it was real. But my father's deceit, and Rory's explanation of her family, has thrown everything I thought was true into shadow.

A high-roofed mudbrick cottage comes into view at the top of the log steps. Faded Tibetan prayer flags dangle like bunting under the eaves. Rory leads me past a mucky compost heap and a collection of forty-four-gallon drums, along a path to a wooden door decorated with ivy. We wipe our boots on a worn-looking grate in front of the door and go on in.

'Cooee!' Rory calls softly. 'Hello?'

A huge Coonara holds court over a collection of battered lounge chairs in an open-plan room with a kitchen on the right. A ladder leads to a platform loft. The house is warm and light-filled, large-windowed, with regal – if slightly moth-eaten – purple velvet drapes.

'Greetings!' Sally is sitting at the kitchen table with her glasses on and a mug in her hand, watching Ilona pound an enormous mass of dough at the kitchen island bench.

'You two up for visitors?' Rory asks, squeezing my arm in reassurance.

'No visitors.' Ilona grins, brushes at the flour on her cheek. 'But family is fine. Welcome.'

'Great, cos we're both starving,' Rory says.

'Ha – freeloaders. Should've known we'd see you here at lunchtime.' Sally pushes up from the table and starts collecting bowls and spoons from a tall cupboard stocked with Fowlers jars of preserves. It seems to take some effort for Sally to get around – she moves slowly.

'I can dish up,' Rory protests.

'But I do it better.' Sally waves a spoon at me. 'Hello again, Bo.'

'Hi.' I'm weirdly shy, even though I've met both these women before, and I know how easygoing they are.

'The stew is chickpea and silverbeet,' Ilona says. 'Hope that's okay.' She gives Rory a questioning look.

Rory keeps things simple. 'Bo's folks are on some heavy trip. He's come over here for a break.'

'Ah,' Ilona says, and that's all the questions and explanations I have to deal with, which is a massive relief. If I'd gone to anyone else's house, I'd have been given the third degree about why I'm not at school.

I'm not sure if my stomach is up to food yet, but after tasting the first mouthful, I find myself wolfing it down. The stew is rich and strange-tasting, with a faint hint of licorice – 'Star anise,' Rory explains. Ilona cuts thick slabs of bread to go with it. The bread is still hot – the loaf comes off a rack with about a dozen other loaves, all of them cooling outside on a towel spread over a table under the eaves.

'That's nearly a week's supply of sourdough for the community. And the butter is homemade too,' Rory says, grinning.

'Jesus, this is good,' I say, with crumbs and melted butter

dripping out of my mouth. Ilona and Sally and Rory all laugh, but it's no joke – I want to learn to cook from scratch like this.

Ilona keeps going with her bread-making. Sally comes around the bench to fetch something, and the two women exchange gentle smiles and touches. They chat with Rory as she scrapes up chickpeas from her bowl of stew. Nobody is making me converse. They get on with things, like everything is normal.

As long as I don't think about home, everything *is* normal. But if I let my guard down, my brain regurgitates images of my father packing his duffel bag, Connor's innocent face, Mum's horrified expression from this morning…I think the best thing to do today is not think at all.

Rory is admiring a felt rug on the back of one of the lounge chairs. 'Have you got any more of that dark green and red left? I'd love one with those colours.'

'I've got a bit,' Sally says. 'But maybe wait until I get the next mill delivery.'

I swallow my mouthful. 'You made that rug yourself?'

Rory answers for her. 'Sally's amazing. She felts them from the wool discarded by the mill.'

'It's not hard,' Sally says.

'Wow.' The rug is almost king-sized, with intricate patterns of drizzled lines. It's amazing to think it's handmade. 'That's a pretty useful skill to have.'

'It's *very* cool,' Rory says, licking her spoon. 'And Sal's teaching me how to do it.'

'Rory is becoming multi-talented,' Ilona says proudly. 'Rug-making, hand-knitting, pottery…' She holds up her own stew bowl. 'Do you recognise the work?'

It's the same earthenware, in the same style: mugs that are shaped to your hand, sturdy, fine-lipped bowls. I'd noticed the similarities between all the crockery pieces, but I hadn't put two and two together until now. The bowls we're using, like everything else, are Rory's.

I angle towards her. 'Do you supply everyone in the community with pottery?'

'Pretty much.' She shrugs, then raises her eyebrows. 'Although I can't keep up with the supply for Star and Stuart. Daniel breaks them faster than I can make them. Everything else I make is sold or traded.'

So Rory's more than self-sufficient – she's utilising her skills for the good of everyone. If she lived a regular teenager's life, she might be practising pottery as a hobby. Here, her work goes towards the community. She's sixteen, and she's contributing in a really concrete way.

'So … have you two got plans for the day?' Ilona asks.

'Ah, here we go.' Rory snorts. 'Bo, I think we're about to trade sustenance for labour.'

Ten minutes later, we're meandering through the garden, flicking away the gnats that hang around near the corn. Ilona has recruited us for bread delivery: Rory's carrying a string bag full of cloth-wrapped loaves. The clouds overhead make the sunny day hot and close.

'Ilona and Sally are pretty cool,' I say.

'They're the *best*.' Rory's string bag bumps around her knees as she walks. 'They really helped me a lot, after we arrived here. They're like my den mothers. Ray and I used to share another house, but then we needed more space, and when he moved out to his yurt—'

'His what?'

Rory laughs at my expression. 'A yurt – it's like a domed tent, made of canvas and hides and bamboo poles. It's actually a really efficient way to live.'

'Hey, no argument from me.' But I'm still getting my head around the idea that Ray is Rory's father.

'Anyway, after I moved, Ilona and Sally helped me get set up, and generally showed me how to be independent. Now, if I get lonely, I go crash there, or one of them comes over and sleeps at my place.'

I wipe my face with the bottom of my T-shirt, thinking of the way Sally interacted: she was chirpy, but moving around seemed like hard work for her today. 'Is Sally all right?'

'No.' Rory looks away down the path. 'Sally has aggressive late-stage lymphoma.'

'What?' My breath stops for a second. 'Shit. That's bad. Has she had treatment?'

'She doesn't want treatment.' Rory pushes through the leaves. 'She doesn't want to have chemicals injected into her, or have her hair radiated away, or be poked and prodded by doctors. She *especially* doesn't want to die in a hospital. She wants to keep on living as normal until she can't do it anymore, then Ilona will take care of her until the end. We'll all take care of her.'

My legs lock up. It's the matter-of-fact way Rory says it. Sally – this vital, happy woman, who I saw enjoying the river on my first visit here, who seems to make it her mission to be friendly to everyone around her – is dying? Like, really *dying*? How the fuck is that fair?

Rory turns and comes back to me, reaches up to squeeze

my shoulder. 'Oh, Bo, I'm sorry – I forget sometimes that you don't know what's going on with all of us. It's okay. We've known for a long time. Sally has accepted it. And she's made a decision about it, which we've all agreed to respect.'

I remember how Rory missed school last week. 'That's why she had to go to the doctor.'

She nods. 'It was to get some medication – analgesics, mainly. Pain relief.'

'Ilona's a nurse.' It's all coming together for me. 'She can take care of Sally until she …'

'… dies – yes. It's okay to say it, Bo. Sal and Ilona want people to be open about it. People die. It's normal. It's just life.'

My eyes are prickling, which is crazy. I've only just met this woman and her partner. But they've been kind to me. I clear my throat. 'It sucks, that's all.'

'I know.' Rory's face changes as she glances away. 'I get really sad about it sometimes.'

'They seem so happy.'

'Ilona and Sally have been together for seventeen years, and they'll be together to the end of Sally's life.' She looks back to me. 'That's what we were talking about before, yeah? What they have – that's not a social construct. That's love.'

*

It takes us more than an hour to deliver three loaves of bread, because at each house we have to stop and say hi, have a cup of tea, and shoot the breeze.

Allison's house is a round-walled hut with a thatched roof. Allison is a quiet, slender woman in her mid-thirties;

she's reserved, and seems a bit fragile. Apparently, she used to work in IT until about two years ago, when some kind of anxiety condition forced her out of the regular world to find simplicity and calm. Her garden is the most 'ordered' of all the ones I've seen here.

Star and Stuart, on the other hand, have a garden that is only one step removed from a jungle, and the most chaotic of all the houses – which is fair enough, considering they've got a little kid. It's Stuart's work day, but Star welcomes us in, plies us with strawberries in gratitude for the bread, elaborates some more about my aura and how purple it is today, offers to read my tarot cards, then changes her mind when Daniel totters into the room, having spilled water all down the front of his clothes.

We make it back out onto the path and Rory is shaking her head. 'Oh god, my *mother*.'

'Your mum's, uh, unusual,' I say diplomatically.

Rory's eyebrows go haywire, then her laughter settles. 'It's weird, y'know? Cos I haven't lived with her for years. She can be so full-on with the esoteric stuff…I used to believe in it all too, when I was younger. Some of it I still believe in, I think. I grew up with it. But my dad was always a rationalist, so I guess I ended up more like him.'

'She seems nice, though, your mum.' I grin as we pick our way through a forest of bamboo-cane tepees covered in runner beans.

'She's into good karma, she's always nice.' Rory breaks off a few young runner pods. We munch on the tender beans as we walk. 'And she's a pretty attentive mother, now. She wasn't quite as switched on for me back then as she is for Daniel…'

She glances at me. 'Sorry, you don't want to be talking old family drama today.'

'It's cool.' If it's not my family, I'm fine with it. 'Where are we going?'

'Back to my place? I have some pots to make. It's kind of boring, but if you don't mind hanging around…'

I'm tired, I realise. It feels like an age since I rode in past the *Garden of Eden* sign this morning.

I lift my face to the sun. 'There's no place I've gotta be.'

*

I flop into a sofa chair, watching Rory lug a metal bucket covered in a wet cloth closer to the pottery wheel. 'Is it much work to make all the crockery for the community and for trade?'

Rory's workshop is beside her hut, in the shady remnants of the mudbrick house. A foot-pedal-operated pottery wheel sits centre stage among makeshift shelves, a drum of water, and a lot of half-dried clay shards.

'Nah, it's okay.' Rory settles at a wooden chair beside the wheel. 'I do an hour or so a day, if I can. If I wasn't doing that, then I'd be out here mucking around with my sculptures anyway, y'know?'

In my world, teenagers don't contribute to the community like Rory does. I think of my friends, their energy and inventiveness, their opinions and ideas, the way they come at things from a totally different perspective to most adults. Why are we wasting that? It makes no sense – it's like growing a tree, but lopping off the branches once it starts coming into leaf.

172

'Hey,' I say, suddenly remembering, 'what about your tree?'

'The raku tree?' Rory gives me a sideways look. 'I don't know. I haven't gone back to see it.'

'You're missing double Art.' I watch her expression. 'Are you gonna come back to school?'

She dips her hands in a dish of water and sighs. 'I think I need a break from it.'

It's gutting, hearing her say that. It's like listening to a dream die. 'Ask you a question?'

'Anything.' She collects a double handful of clay from the bucket and dumps it onto the wheel.

'Why high school? You've got so much here. You're independent, you're working… You've already *got* a life. Why the hell did you ever decide to go to high school?'

Rory's cheeks pink up. 'It's going to sound weird.'

'The day I've had so far, weird is almost a relief.'

'Okay. Well…' She kneads the pedal at the base of the pottery wheel with her bare foot, and the flat turntable starts to spin. It makes a trundling, hissing noise, and her hands fill up with the soft, squishy clay. 'I was kind of thinking ahead. Eden is my home. It's where I belong. But after Ethan left, I realised that things go wrong. Things change. And I'm not equipped for a world outside Eden.'

'So you wanted to skill up?'

'I guess.' Her forehead creases as she concentrates on the clay and the words simultaneously. 'There's another reason. I've always supported the community in everything. I've always shared and given and sacrificed and let go. But I wanted something for myself. That's selfish, I know.'

'I don't think it's selfish,' I say softly.

'Here, it is.' She glances at me. 'Living in community is about compassion and surrender and trust. You can't think of yourself as an individual. You have to put the group ahead of yourself.'

'You're not a worker ant, Rory.'

She clears her throat, apparently compelled into full disclosure. 'One last reason – the most obvious one. Don't know if you've noticed, but except for Daniel, I'm the only person under thirty-five on the property.'

Of all the reasons, this one makes the most sense. 'So you wanted to meet some folks your own age.'

Rory lets the pottery wheel hiss for a moment before speaking. 'Have you ever felt all alone in the middle of a group of friends?'

It takes me a second to reply, cos something is stuck right in my throat. 'You were lonely.'

'I know it's crazy. I'm surrounded by people who love me, who look after me, every single day. But…' The look she directs at me then is raw.

'It's okay. I get it. You don't have to explain.'

'Turns out high school wasn't the cure for anything, though.' She dribbles water onto the clay with one hand. 'It's only shown me how much I don't fit in on the outside.'

I don't know where to start. Sympathy, sure, but *I'm* selfish, too. I want her to come back to school. 'I know it's been tough, Rory, but you'll fit in. You will. And come on, you've made a few friends. You're acing your subjects, and you got your kiln on in Art. You'll find your place in the world, I know it. The world's not all great, but you've gotta take the bad with the good.'

'I like the world sometimes, but I don't really feel as if I belong in it.'

I'm struck dumb by that.

Her eyes linger on the clay. 'There's one good thing, at least. I met you.'

I try to grin, to work with the positive. 'Well, yeah. That's right, you met me.'

'Will you go home tonight?' Rory drips another palmful of water onto the clay as she changes the subject.

I don't have to go home, I realise. I could stay here, in Eden. In Rory's hut. The idea jolts me, especially the fact that she's so comfortable with it.

But I know I can't. There's Mum to think about, for one. And for two, my head's still not right. I don't want to be with Rory like that, all confused and angry and unsure what I want. It might not be my ideal choice, but I should go home.

'Yeah.' My shoulders slump as I say it aloud. 'I'd better, hey. Mum will freak if I don't come home. I don't want to stress her out any more than she must be already.' At least I know a way to drag this out. 'I'll stay until after Meeting though, if that's okay?'

'It's okay with me.' Rory smiles, and I realise that she's already made a whole bowl – a small one, wide-rimmed and functional. She slices it off the turntable with a piece of sturdy wire, settles it on a nearby plank to dry.

'Wow, you're fast.'

'I've had a lot of practice.' She washes her hands, wipes them on a rag. 'I need to prepare some more clay – come help me?'

She moves away from the wheel, to one of the plank benches, and I sigh. 'Does that mean I have to get up?'

'Yep.' She waves me over, grinning. 'Come on, Bo. You're not scared of a little dirt, are you?'

My eyebrows lift, but I pull myself off the sofa chair and go to stand beside her.

Rory drags a cloth-wrapped lump – it looks like the bread in her hut – closer to herself, unfolds the cloth to reveal an untidy, rust-coloured mass. 'Okay, here. We're wedging the clay.'

'We're giving the clay a wedgie?'

She laughs. 'Not quite. We're working the air out of it, by ripping and kneading. Watch me.'

She uses the wire she had at the pottery wheel to slice off two chunks of mushy clay, then hands one chunk to me. It's cold in my palm. It's like holding a giant peeled orange, or one of Julie's tennis balls, the ones she loves chasing around in the backyard before returning them, clammy with drool. I make a face.

Rory laughs. 'Come on, it's not that bad! Stop thinking about the texture – it'll warm up as you go. First you tear it.' She demonstrates, ripping the chunk in her own hands into two like she's tearing a loaf of bread in half. She turns the pieces, slams them back together. 'Then you smash it. That part is pretty satisfying, especially if you've had a rough day.'

'Right. I can work with that.' I copy her actions with my own chunk, tearing it apart before slapping it back into a ragged shape.

'Then you knead it. It's a bit like making pastry, I guess.'

It *is* like making pastry – although you could never treat pastry with this much brute force. I get into the rough ripping of the clay, the force of impact when I slam it back, the way the clay warms in my hands, becomes more elastic.

176

'This is as good as hitting the heavy bag at training, y'know. I should wedge clay every time I feel pissed off.'

'Okay, gently now,' Rory encourages. 'We don't want it to dry out. Here.'

She sprinkles water onto my hands, and things get slippery. We're standing close at the bench, squeezing our fingers through the malleable clay, kneading in unison. When we bump shoulders, Rory smiles up at me, and I feel that sparking surge I got this morning in her hut – this time it's deeper, headier. I inhale, smelling the raw perspiration at the base of her neck, mixed with the lush muddy scent of the clay.

'That's great, Bo. That's really good,' she says, pushing down hard as she kneads.

'It is?' I watch the muscles in her arms jump, clear my throat.

'We should bundle this together. Here, let me slice this.'

Her wire makes quick work of the two separate lumps, and then she shows me how to layer them over each other, knead them into one mass. Our fingers move together on the clay, entwining. We laugh when our fingers tangle. Rory leans up against me, her hair tickling my jaw, her skin soft on mine.

My hands are filthy almost all the way to my elbows. 'This reminds me of making mud pies when I was a kid.'

'It's exactly like making mud pies.' Rory grins. She has a smear of clay across her cheek. 'That might be one of the reasons I like it so much.'

'Remind me not to scratch my face until I've washed my hands.'

'Damn, you shouldn't have said anything! My chin is itchy now…' She tries to rub her chin against her shoulder.

'Help you with that.' I rasp my thumb against her chin, leaving a terracotta mark.

'Oh, thanks a lot!' She laughs, slaps at me with her own muddy hands.

And then we're clay-fighting – snorting and daubing at each other. Rory adds more water to the mix, and the play gets messy fast. I press my damp fingers to her cheeks; she shrieks, laughing, and lifts her arms to rub her muddy fingers through my hair. I grab her hands and there's a bit of wrestling, our slippery fingers sliding together.

Rory wriggles in my grip, and suddenly I'm aware of her body against mine. My imagination starts to tumble fast. I want to grab her and press her back against the pottery bench. Shove bowls and clay aside as we bend over it to kiss. Slide my muddy fingers up her thighs, to where the leg warmers end. I want to tug the leg warmers down with one hand, as I streak clay-marks against her neck with the other—

'Um…I think I've got enough clay now.' Rory's voice is almost shy.

Air comes out of me with a shudder. All I can see is Rory's face turned up towards mine, the cool clay warming beneath our hands, the malleable texture of it under my fingers… I can't remember ever being this turned on in my whole life, and I'm glad I'm wearing jeans. Rory has gently lifted my hands away, and there on the bench is a squat, solid lump of the good stuff.

'I should call you in to do this more often.' Rory's face is one big smile. 'That's enough to keep me going for a week.'

'We wedgied the clay.' My words come out croaky.

'We did. You have natural talent.' She washes her hands in the dish of water.

'I dunno about that.' My voice comes out more level now. I keep my muddy hands lifted. I don't quite trust myself to move them yet.

'Sure you do.' She winks at me. 'It's easy as mud pies.'

I look at her face as she wipes her hands – her cheeks are peach-ripe. There's even a flush on her neck. I don't think all of Rory's enthusiasm is strictly about the clay, which makes me feel better. I wash my hands in the dish as she folds the clay back up in its cloth, tucks it into the metal bucket, turns back to me.

'Was that fun?' Her eyes are sparkling.

'Yes.' I can be completely honest about that. If I wasn't here for all the wrong reasons, if my head wasn't so flipped, I would've made a move by now. Even with my resolution not to kiss Rory today, the tug inside me is powerful. 'We should do it again sometime.'

She bites her lip over a grin. She knows what I'm talking about. 'Next time, we'll throw bowls on the wheel.'

'I think I should stick to my strengths. You make the bowls, I'll make the food to put in 'em.'

She laughs, pushes me on the shoulder.

16

I'm riding my bike home in the dark. The last twelve hours have been full enough to blot out some of the shit that was overwhelming me this morning. Ray's talk at Meeting tonight was about the original beauty of the world before humans started screwing everything up.

'Can you imagine what this place looked like before people arrived?'

He was sitting on an old beanbag by the fire-pit. We'd all eaten from the communal pots of roasted sweet potato and buttered corn and flatbreads. Lots of people were nursing steaming mugs of herbal tea. Daniel was lying across one of the sofas, fast asleep, with Star and Stuart sitting on a blanket on the floor beside him.

'This whole area used to be undisturbed bush,' Ray said. He cast a hand out to take in the darkening landscape beyond the edge of the Meeting House's floor. 'There was no cleared land, no paddocks. Water was plentiful. The feet of sheep and cattle hadn't bruised the topsoil into submission. Farmers didn't exist. Can you imagine it? Can you imagine this whole district, covered in red ironbark and manna gum, flourishing with life?'

He looked out into the twilight, as if remembering a time thousands of years ago. His face was made harsh by the light of the fire, sharp cheekbones and scraggy moustache thrown into shadowed relief. But his expression was wistful, and I *could* imagine it: trees even taller than the ones at the property's edge, mobs of wildlife, great flocks of birds in the wattle.

I sat on a cushion at ground level, leaning back on Rory's legs, relaxed in her presence in a way I'm usually not with other girls I've dated. Our fingers were intertwined, like they'd been while we were working on the clay. It felt as if we were kids holding hands in the playground, the way girls and boys do in kinder, then abandon with embarrassment as they get older.

'Our world used to be a very different place,' Ray said softly. 'Think of the original extent of the Amazon jungle. The extraordinary biodiversity that once existed. In much of the temperate zone – in Europe, North America, parts of Asia – forests were truly primeval, like something out of a fairytale. Ash, oak and linden trees soared a hundred and fifty, two hundred feet into the air. Mulch accumulated over millennia. The air was cool and dark, and smelled rich, like the amniotic fluid of the earth.' He looked back at all of us, gathered in rapt attention. 'It was a bountiful, beautiful place. An Eden in truth, not only in name.'

Caught up in the spell of the idea, I lifted my chin. 'You've created a beautiful place here, too. Eden isn't like any other property in the whole district.'

Ray turned to me, his eyes fixed and burning. 'We came here to create a safe space, a place to act on our convictions. We've made it a haven. A home.'

'Amen, brother,' Kell said softly.

'We've tried to practise an authentic way of life and being on the earth,' Ray went on. He was speaking to me, but also to the others. 'Our foundations are autonomy, sustainability, equality, respect. It hasn't always been easy – we've had to work at it. But we've navigated through differences of opinion and belief. We protect each other, provide support.'

People around the circle nodded in agreement. Star said, 'Yes, that's right,' and Jules murmured a gentle exhortation.

'Our aim was to nurture a cohesive group of radical thinkers,' Ray continued, 'and I think we've achieved that. We've created our own family. A place where we belong. Let's stay focused on that! Let's not concentrate on outside attitudes and ideas, but on what we've achieved here, and what's to come.'

When Meeting broke up, Ray walked over to where Rory and I were standing.

'You've come to spend more time with us, Bo,' Ray said. 'And Rory tells me that Eden has been a haven for you, as well, today.'

'Yeah, that's true.' I was holding Rory's hand – she was about to walk me out to the access road – and something about the moment felt sacred and quiet. 'You've all made me feel welcome. I appreciate it, hey. I didn't know where else to go.'

He reached out and shook my free hand in both of his. 'Bo, if this is a safe space for you to be, you're welcome anytime. But you already knew that.' He smiled. 'Whatever you're facing, you've got friends here.'

Rory beamed up at her dad – I could see in her expression how much she cared for him. I thanked Ray, for the meal and for the teaching, before finding my bike and walking out to the road with Rory. When she asked me if I was going to be okay, I could say, 'Yes,' with all honesty. My steps were firm and my heart felt light.

This has been one of the strangest days of my life. And Ray is not the guy I imagined he was. I don't know why I ever considered him intimidating. He's a good guy – smart, forthright, warm. The things he talks about, and the way he holds this community together... It's pretty inspiring.

And I can still feel Rory's hands on mine, the clay oozing between our fingers. It seems almost obscene, to feel so heartbreakingly alive when Sally is dying. That casts everything else into perspective – what does my family drama matter, compared to a death sentence?

My equanimity lasts all the way home, even gets me as far as the top of the front porch stairs. When I enter the house, though, Real Life pours back over me in a cold shock. Mum is sitting at the dining table under the fluoro light of the kitchen bulb, a mug in her hand. Her face is drawn, but she seems relieved to see me, I don't know why. When I left this morning, I must've looked ready to slash and burn.

'Where have you been, Bo?' she asks softly.

'I was with Rory.' The headache I had this morning returns. 'In Eden.'

'Yes.' I don't sound defiant. That would just make me seem childish. 'Dad's not here, is he.'

'His plane left at one.' Mum examines my face, in that way parents do when they're trying to psychoanalyse you. 'You're still angry with him.'

'You're not?' Now I sound defiant. 'Did you know about Liam?'

Mum places her mug carefully on the table. 'Your father told me about him last week.'

'But you didn't bother to tell *me*.'

'We didn't think you were ready.'

Mum's expression says that from the way I reacted, clearly, I'm still not ready. But it doesn't matter. It's done now. It's out in the open. It's not something I can un-know, no matter how much I might want to.

My head thumps with my pulse. 'Right. So that's it? Dad's gone, and we just sit here and put up with it?'

Mum rubs a hand across her face. She looks exhausted. 'Liam's mother, Lily, has a terminal condition. Aaron's gone to see her, before she…'

Suddenly I'm angry again. Is it the way Mum can't say the word? Or is it the fact that the word itself is so final, so devastating?

'Before she dies.' I have to say it. I have to speak it aloud. 'Is Dad with Liam?'

'Yes.'

Blood rushes in my ears, splitting my head in two. I swear and walk out. I leave my mother sitting at our family table, watching her cold cup of tea and wondering if my father will ever come home. That's when I know I can be heartless.

People die. It's normal. It's just life.

People die inside, too. It happens every day.

✳

I wake up. I don't have the headache anymore, but my skin feels tender, like I got beat up.

I lie in bed for a minute. I can't stop remembering stuff.

184

Not the fight with Dad, not the stuff with Liam – I'm thinking of other stuff, meaningless stuff.

Like that time last year, when Mum and Dad went away together for the night. Lozzie kept calling it a 'dirty weekend', which drove me spare, but it was right around when Mum got pregnant, so Loz probably wasn't too far from the truth. Me and Connor were looking forward to a heavy session of TV and gaming in our parents' absence from Friday night to Saturday afternoon. When I got home from school that Friday, Dad was loading the car, and Con told Mum that she should probably go pack, and Mum laughed and said, 'Stop rushing me. Packing will take five minutes. I'm only taking sexy nighties,' and Connor did that pretending-to-spew thing with his finger, because Mum said 'sexy', and he couldn't deal with the idea of Mum and Dad and sex in the same thought process—

I roll out of bed with a groan.

Will we recover from this? Will our family split up? What about the new baby? How does that fit into the picture? What the hell am I going to tell people? I don't know. *I don't know*. During the ride to school, I worry about the idea of telling people. It seems selfish, as if I'm concerned about my image or something. It's not about that.

Worrying turns out to be a pointless exercise anyway, cos when I walk into homegroup and Sprog says, 'Hey, sup dude?' I say, 'Nothing much,' on automatic. When Cam asks, 'What happened to you yesterday?' I say, 'Headache. Felt like shit, so I took the day off.' Lozzie examines my face with a little more attention, before shrugging, turning away.

Nobody seems to notice anything. A tearing feeling starts

up in my chest: how can no one, not even my friends, have realised there's something wrong with me? I'm not that good an actor, am I? But apparently I am.

Maybe I should be grateful. I don't want people to know about my family's business. Jesus – I'm getting a taste of what Sprog was talking about on Tuesday. But I don't want people to discuss my family situation, with me or anyone else.

That might make it real.

*

Heading for Humanities with Sprog and Cam, the conversation turns to Showalter.

'He's on leave again,' Cam confides. 'I did the collection yesterday – we managed to pull in a couple of hundred bucks for the family, which I thought was pretty good.'

This would normally be Sprog's cue to make a joke about how people are welcome to donate a couple of hundred bucks to *him*, but he keeps his lips zipped. Cam's attitude towards him has thawed – she makes eye contact with him now – and he's not going to risk it.

'So what's happening in class?' I ask. 'Have they got another teacher to replace Showalter?'

'Not yet,' Cam says, settling herself at a desk across the aisle. 'We had a sub yesterday for the double period. She was terrible.'

'She really was,' Sprog confirms. Man, if Sprog thinks a teacher is bad, that's saying something. 'This whole subject's turning into a total pile.'

'True,' Cam says, and I almost do a double take. Cam is *agreeing* with Sprog? They really have turned a corner.

We settle into our seats as Mrs Ramanathan sails into the room in a billow of scarves. My shoulders tense. I wait for her to make a beeline towards me, on a day when I haven't got any more excuses to give. But she moves straight across to stand at the head of the class, putting her notebook and pen on the desk. Maybe she's here to make an announcement about Mr Showalter? Nobody has reprimanded us, but I keep waiting for *someone* to.

But Mrs Ram doesn't do that either.

'Please stop talking and take your seats.' Her voice is clear, accented and firm. She waits for us to do as she's asked before continuing. 'Thank you. Now, most of you know me. I've taught almost all of you at different times. For those of you who are unfamiliar, my name is Mrs Ramanathan, and I will be your Humanities teacher in this class, from now until the end of the term.'

Okay, this is unexpected but not completely surprising – Mr Showalter can't teach, they can't hire someone new on such short notice, so it makes sense they'd give the job to a teacher already on staff. I didn't know Mrs Ram could teach Humanities, but just cos I've only ever associated her with Food Tech doesn't mean she's not qualified to teach other subjects.

People start sitting up straighter, tidying the books on their desks. Everyone knows Mrs Ram doesn't cop any shit.

'I take it back,' Cam says to me, under her breath. 'This class is looking up.'

'Miss D'Amato, do you have something to add?' Mrs Ram asks, raising her eyebrows at Cam.

'No, Mrs Ramanathan,' Cam answers promptly. 'Just glad

to have you on board.' She's grinning. Cam likes it when she can actually get work done in class.

Mrs Ram gives her a nod and a hint of a smile. 'Thank you. Now, I understand that you have been studying political and social movements of the twentieth century. Please get out your notebooks. We're doing a pop quiz.' When she hears sighing, she lifts her chin. 'You will be answering questions on what you should already know, so I don't imagine it will be too difficult. I'll collect the papers at the end of the lesson.' She positions her glasses, opens her notebook, and begins reading aloud. 'Question One. "The term 'Marxism' was coined after which…"' She stops, looks up, realises we're all still staring at her. 'Well? We have *begun*, people. Don't make me wait all day.'

Everyone suddenly cracks into action. People scramble to find pens, open books, and rack their brains for what little info they've absorbed in this class.

Mrs Ram waits for about ten seconds before starting again. 'Ahem. Question One…'

The quiz goes for the entire double period. In that time, I don't hear a single word from *anybody*, which has to be some kind of record. Mrs Ram could crook a finger at me at any time, though. When the bell goes, as papers are being passed to the front, I grab my backpack and make a quick getaway.

I jog to the lockers to grab my gear for the ride home, and get another surprise: Rory's at school, right here in the hall. She's abandoned the overalls today, in favour of a pair of jeans and a brightly coloured scarf that she's modified into a top. Seeing her, I get an immediate rush of warmth, and an undeniable sense of relief. Someone I can talk to, someone who knows what's going on …

'Hi!' Her face lights up as I trot over, and she pulls me into a hug. 'I hoped I'd run into you.'

My whole body vibrates with the contact. 'You're back at school? That's ace, why didn't you tell me?'

But she's already shaking her head. 'I'm not really. I'm collecting work from the teachers, so I won't fall behind if I do decide to come back. And I saw my tree! Oh, Bo, it's so beautiful.'

Her expression loses all animation as she sees something over my shoulder. I turn to see Sprog barrelling up the hall.

'Wait!' He lifts his hands – he isn't going to let an opportunity like this pass him by. 'Rory, please don't bolt, okay?'

'I'm not bolting.' Rory crosses her arms.

'Look, I'm sorry,' Sprog says, and blushes, as Cam arrives.

'You had a speech worked out,' Cam says to him, one hand on her hip.

'I did.' His expression is contrite as he turns back to Rory. 'I had a whole speech. But it sounded lame, and I'm just … I'm real sorry. That's it.'

Rory uncrosses her arms, but her posture is still stiff.

Cam rolls her eyes at Sprog. 'That's all you've got?'

'I said I'm sorry, didn't I?' He looks at Rory again. 'I was a dick. Sometimes it happens. I act like a dick, for no good reason. It's a character flaw.' He flinches when Cam thumps him on the shoulder. 'Rory, please forgive me or this mad chick never will!'

Rory glances between him and Cam, snorts. 'Okay, I forgive you.'

'Thank god.' With a dramatic sigh of relief, Sprog collapses onto the hall lino like his strings have been cut, as Lozzie rocks up.

'What's Sprog doing on the floor? Can we kick him while he's down there?' She makes a few pretend jabs, while Sprog writhes and abuses her good-naturedly. Before we attract too much more attention, I hoist him up.

'So, where to?' Sprog asks, hitching up his jeans. 'It's Friday arvo, what's the story?'

'Well, I'm still on house arrest. You don't wanna go to the skate park while you've still got the chance?' I'm hoping no one will try to rope me into anything; I need to get home.

'I'd like to go, hey, but I get too devo.' Sprog makes a face. 'Then I end up commiserating with Jem and the boys, and before I know it I'm crying into my beer.'

'I thought you did that every night?' Loz jokes.

'Fuck off,' he says. 'If they were closing down the riding trails, you'd be having a full-blown spasm.'

'The skate park is closing?' Rory asks.

'They reckon it's too dangerous cos it's so rundown. Council wants to redevelop the site, maybe for a supermarket,' Cam says. She jerks a thumb at Sprog. 'He's been moaning about it for ages.'

He shrugs. 'There's nowhere for teenagers to go in town. The skate park is pretty much it. If the council's turfing us off to make way for a supermarket, where're we gonna go?'

'So you want to make a place for teenagers to hang out in Lamistead,' Rory says. 'Maybe get the skate park restored?'

'Yeah.' Sprog blinks as he realises what he's said. 'I mean, *I* don't wanna restore it. I can't do that. But the council should—'

'Why can't you?'

'What?'

'Why can't you talk to the council about repairing the skate park?'

'Y'know, that's not a bad idea,' Cam says.

Sprog squints at them both. 'I'm a teenager. They don't listen to teenagers.'

'Start a petition,' Rory says. 'Then it wouldn't be only you talking, you'd have everyone backing you.'

Sprog is gaping. 'A...what?'

'A petition.' Rory notices his expression. 'It's easy. You write up a page, with a description at the top explaining what you want, then you ask everyone who's interested to sign it, as a show of support.'

He frowns. 'And, what, people would sign it?'

'Most of the kids at school would be interested in keeping the skate park open, right?'

'Well, Lamistead council provides facilities for seniors in town,' Cam points out. 'Shouldn't they have to make a space for teenagers too?'

'You could talk to your mum about it,' I suggest, and Cam nods.

'I dunno.' Sprog rakes his hand through his hair. 'Dealing with the council sounds kinda complicated.'

'Start small,' Rory urges. 'Just make a petition saying that you object to the council removing the only teenage-friendly space in town, and you want to suggest that they renovate instead of redeveloping. You get everyone to sign it, then you present it to the council, and say, hey, it's not only me, every kid in Lamistead wants this. It's proof there's a need.' She shrugs. 'I'll help you draw it up, if you like.'

Sprog looks flabbergasted. 'You'd do that?'

'Sure.' She snorts. 'My mum used to take me to rallies and stuff when I was a kid. I've had plenty of experience with petitions, believe me.'

Sprog looks from Rory's face to mine, as if he's asking me what I reckon.

I don't know why he thinks he needs my permission. 'I think it's a bloody excellent idea. Even if they knock you back, at least you can say you put up a fight.'

Sprog turns back to Rory. 'Then ... that would be awesome. When can we do it?'

Rory glances around at all of us, grins. 'Anybody got a piece of paper?'

Saturday morning, Mullet snags me at the end of the game.

'Consistency – that's the thing.' He slaps me on the back. 'Just keep doin' what you're doin'. And make sure you're here for everything, all right? Every training session, every game. This could be your shot.'

'Um, okay.' I nod, break for the change rooms where Sprog is walking around with a piece of paper and a pen, collecting signatures. His approach is pretty basic: he goes up to people and says, 'Sign this,' while shoving the paper in their face. But by home-time, he's got another thirty signatures.

'This is sweet.' He's grinning as he clutches the petition. He hasn't even changed out of his jersey and boots yet. 'I'm already on my third page. Wanna help me trawl around town?'

'Can't.' I keep my face down as I pull on my runners. 'I'm grounded, remember?'

'Grounded.' He snorts. 'When's your dad gonna come to his senses, hey?'

'Got me.' I shrug, as if the mention of my father hasn't sliced right through me.

Mum's resting when I get home – she had to take Con to footy this morning, in Dad's absence. I can't keep ignoring Mum. We should be comforting each other, supporting each other. Problem is, whenever I see her, I feel like bursting into tears. It's like Mum is connected to my heart, and right now my heart is crying.

Connor thinks Dad's travelling interstate for work, and he's somehow decided that this week is a great time to be a total pain in the arse. Right now, he's in the kitchen singing, 'I'm-so-fucking-hungry,' to the tune of 'Everything is Awesome' while I wipe the bench down.

I dump the dishcloth, whack him on the back of the head. 'Mind your language.'

'You say "fucking".' He glares at me.

'I'm sixteen, I'm allowed. And I still don't do it at home.' I stir the big pot on the stove, hip-check him as he tries to muscle in front of me to butter his toast. 'No one wants to hear a nine-year-old swearing, Con. It's gross.'

'You're not Dad,' he says, shoving back.

'That's right. Dad would've whacked you harder. Here, take this cuppa in to Mum.'

'Can't you take it?' he whines. 'You made it.'

At the door to my parents' bedroom, I inhale deeply, release, before knocking and walking in.

'I've made a pot of bolognese sauce.' I place the cup carefully down on the bedside table, avoiding eye contact. 'You and Con can have it with pasta, or on toast, whatever.'

Mum's lying in bed with a book. She looks tired, although she looks tired all the time lately. 'Thank you, Bo. You don't need to fuss, though.'

'Yeah, I do.' I've been trying to think of how to phrase this, remembering Sprog's 'speech' from yesterday. 'Listen, I'm sorry about last night. I was pissed off, and you were there, and I didn't mean to—'

'You don't have to explain. Although I appreciate the apology.' She pats the bed for me to sit near her. 'You're trying to figure all this out, same as me. And you don't even know the full story.'

'I know the story.' I perch on the edge of the bed, my spine straight. 'You don't have to give me all the gory details. Dad's got himself another family up in Brisbane, and he—'

'What?' Mum stares. 'No – Bo, that's not it at *all*. Is that what you've been thinking?'

Hot bubbles rise up inside my chest, make my eyes water. 'Well, what was I supposed to think?'

Mum takes my hand, squeezes it hard. 'Bo, listen to me. You father has a child from an old relationship. It's not ideal, and I wish he'd had the guts to tell me about it a long time ago, but we're dealing with it. Aaron and Lily Pettifer split up while she was still pregnant with Liam, because…' She plucks at the blankets with her free hand. 'Well, it's complicated and—'

'You know what?' I let her hand go and spring up off the bed. 'Don't tell me. I don't think I want to know.'

I'm not being obnoxious. I really *don't* want to know. Mum's always going on about how sometimes when you speak the truth to somebody, they don't want to hear it. You can say something a million times, but if the other person isn't ready for it, it won't sink in. It's only now I've figured out what she means. This, I'm not ready for.

'Okay, it's a lot to take in,' Mum concedes. 'Maybe

your father needs to talk about it with you himself.'

'So Dad's not going to leave us and move to Brisbane?' I ask gruffly. My bottom lip is quivering, which is embarrassing, but I can't help it.

'Oh, love, no. Come here.' Mum holds out her arms. I have to kneel on the floor to hug her. 'Your dad and I… We need a little time. We have to have some uncomfortable conversations, but we're not done yet. We've been talking on the phone, and his intention is to come back. You have to trust that we're working on it, okay?'

I stand up unsteadily. I have an older brother, and Dad's taken off, and apparently he *wants* to come back, but Mum and Dad need to hash things out, which won't be easy—

'Are you going to Eden again?' Mum asks.

I focus back on her. 'Yes. I want to see Rory over the weekend.'

I'm expecting Mum to say, *Your father told you not to go*, or something like that. Instead she sighs and sinks back into the pillows. 'Well, you're sixteen, Bo. You have to start making your own choices.'

That was exactly what I thought when Dad first laid down the prohibition on visiting Eden. Except deciding to make my own choices was easier, somehow, when other people wanted to make them for me. I should be happy – I've won. But now I feel like a shit, standing over my mother.

This doesn't taste like a victory.

✳

'What about this one?' Rory taps at my phone.

Without the benefit of speakers or headphones, the song

intro sounds like it's beaming in from Greenland. 'NERO. More dance-y.'

Shoeless, shirtless, jeans rolled up, I'm standing at the edge of the river with my arms plunged in to the elbows. We've dug up clay from Rory's river deposit site, sieved it into a metal bucket for 'weathering', whatever that is. I pick at the grit stuck under my fingernails while Rory sits on the bank, checking out my song list. With no reception, music's about all my phone's good for in Eden.

'You dance to this?'

'On occasion.' When she side-eyes me, I laugh. 'All right, no. It's good for cycling, though. Anything with a good drop is great for cycling.'

'What about...' She scrolls with her finger, a little awkwardly cos she's not used to it. '...Drapht?'

'Hip hop,' I say. 'I love that song.'

She keeps scrolling, squints at another title. 'Nickelback?'

'Ah, maybe give that a miss.'

'Kurt Vile?'

'That one's old but awesome.'

The sun is descending into the trees to our left. In a few minutes, Rory will have to go help in the Meeting House kitchen. Everyone in Eden seems to have about ten different chores on the go at one time. Kell was fixing an old gate to a new post at the property entrance as I rode in; Virginia was in the kitchen of the Meeting House; Stuart seemed to be scavenging something from the broken-down bus. Things are busy in the community, life is happening. It's a far cry from my place, which feels as if it's in a state of suspended animation, waiting for my father to return.

'Powderfinger?' Rory says.

'Old again.' I hear the guitar and drums at the start of the track, focus on my fingernails. 'That's one of Dad's.'

'You miss him.'

I glance up – Rory's looking at me. 'I don't want to, hey. I feel like he doesn't deserve it.'

'You can't help missing someone.'

I give up trying to get clean, wade up out of the freezing water and flop down next to her. 'I get angry – it comes and goes. I can't always sustain it.'

'Maybe you shouldn't keep hanging onto it. The angry, I mean.'

I shrug, reach for my shoes.

She settles my phone onto my T-shirt, which I abandoned on the grass when things got muddy, and sits facing me, cross-legged. 'What do you know about your dad's situation up in Brisbane?'

'Not a lot. His old girlfriend is dying. Liam's their kid. For some reason, my father's never spent much time with them. It's another family, though. One he's never been that involved with.' I voice one of my deeper fears. 'Maybe he wants to start *being* involved.'

'You don't feel like Liam is someone you could fit into your family?'

'I don't know. I guess.' I pull my socks over my wet feet. 'He was nice enough when he came over. It's just weird, y'know? Like, oh, here's this total stranger, he's your brother. Mum knows more, but she says it's complicated.'

'So you're really waiting for your dad?'

'Basically, I'm in a holding pattern.' I snort, pull on my

runners, knot the laces. 'That's what it's like, being a teenager in the regular world. You spend all your time waiting: until you're old enough to drive, drink, vote, get a job. You've got to tread water for eighteen years before you can even start to have a life.'

'It's not like that here.' Rory leans back on her arms, extends her legs until her toes are nudging my thigh.

'No kidding.' I'm trying not to get distracted by those toes. I roll my jeans down over my wet shins.

'Here's a question. D'you think it's affecting you more cos it's your dad, rather than your mum?'

'What, like a father-son thing?' I collect my shirt, pull it back on. 'I don't know. Maybe. Me and Dad have always been tight until now.' I stand, pocketing my phone, extending a hand for Rory.

She pulls on my arm as she clambers up off the grass. 'I wonder if you'd feel differently about it if Liam was your mother's son?'

I think about that. I guess I'd be … disappointed? Sad, probably. But I don't think I'd feel as betrayed. I frown towards the river. 'Maybe I'm pissed I'm not my father's firstborn son. Maybe it *is* a guy thing. That's sexist, right?'

Rory grabs the heavy, clay-filled bucket. 'I don't know, Bo.'

We wander back along the river path towards her hut, taking turns carrying the bucket.

'You're quiet.' Rory's been keeping an eye on me as I roll the conversation over in my mind.

'I'm trying to nut it out.' I lug the bucket the final distance, dump it under the eaves of the workshop. 'I always figured that I thought about my parents in different ways cos they're different people. I never thought gender had anything to do with it.'

'Maybe it doesn't.' She guides us both through the garden, onto the path to the Meeting House.

'But it's…' I scratch my head. 'I dunno. You've made me look at it in a new way.'

'A lot of our ideas about gender are learned. We don't think of it as sexism. It seems normal.'

'You question *everything*, don't you? Doesn't that get really confusing?'

She laughs. 'I guess for someone who's grown up in the outside world, it'd be confusing. But I was never taught that way.'

We climb up the back steps to the Meeting House. Rory gives me a quick tour of the kitchen. The set-up is basic, but there's a storage area for tubs of flour, pottery jars full of dried lentils and grain, hanging bundles of herbs. A bucket of clean water stands in one corner, for washing hands and rinsing dishes.

Rory shows me what she's supposed to be doing – making pastry for cheese-and-spinach parcels for tonight – and I find a bowl and start on that, while she gets the fire going in the pit at the room's centre. Once the flames kick up, things feel more homey.

I measure flour, add herbs, salt, shortening. But I can't let our earlier conversation go. 'So sexism, all that stuff. You don't have that problem here?'

Rory feeds extra slivers of kindling into the range. 'We try not to replicate outside-world binary attitudes here. Black and white, male and female, queer and straight, abled and disabled, young and old – everybody is supposed to be equal.' She shuts the door of the range with a padded cloth. 'But sexism is tricky. Even here, it keeps sneaking in somehow...' She looks over my shoulder. 'You've got the texture just right there.'

'I want to learn how to make new stuff, so it's good, doing this.' I turn out the pastry, kneading gently. Here comes that blush again. 'I'm actually thinking of changing subjects. Studying cooking. Mrs Ramanathan's been hounding me about it.'

'That'd be fantastic, Bo. Are you going to do it?' She starts chopping parsley and spinach for the filling.

My fingers have sunk into the pastry – I smooth it out. 'Ah, I dunno, hey. I'd have to swap out of PE, and I think everybody would freak. The cooking thing...I've been kinda on the down-low about it. It's not something guys like me do.'

'Guys like you?'

'Sporty blokes. Footy guys.' I grimace. 'Blokey guys.'

'But why would you put yourself in a box like that?' Rory looks genuinely confused. 'You've got more than one talent, Bo. Don't waste it. See, that's what makes sexism so ridiculous. It limits men as much as it limits women.' She tips the chopped greens into another bowl, turns soft, handmade cheese through the mix, adds seasoning. 'And it's so easy to fall into those patterns. Me and Ilona are always ragging about how the women in Eden do more of the cooking and housekeeping stuff. Ray keeps saying that there are no stereotypes when it comes to hard work, *but* each job goes to the person most gifted in that area.'

'So women are more gifted at cooking?' I half-believe this. It's what I've always been told.

'I know, right?' She nudges me with her elbow. 'You could argue the toss with him on that one.'

I tumble the pastry into a neat ball, hunt for a rolling pin. But it's the other thing she said that grabs me. 'Does Ray set everyone jobs?'

'Mostly it's voluntary, but sometimes he allocates, yes. Stuff has to get done.' She selects a metal baking tray, smooths oil across it with her fingers. 'People think that living here is one big bludge, as if we all lie around peeling grapes and playing guitar, or something idyllic like that. But we have to work hard, follow the rules. It's pretty disciplined.'

'There are *rules*?' I roll out my pastry, slice it into rough squares. 'Nobody said anything about rules. I want my money back.'

'Haw-haw.' Rory makes a lopsided smile.

'What sort of rules are we talking about?'

She shoves me over so she can scoop out the cheese mix onto the pastry. 'Come on, you know some of them already – what Ray said at Meeting. Autonomy, sustainability, equality, respect. There are other guidelines, but you might not get them.'

'Like what?' I fold the pastry to make little parcels.

'Okay, well…' She wipes her sticky fingers on a cloth, nods at the parcels taking shape. 'Vegetarian food only, obviously. And organic food – nothing processed.'

'You ate salt and vinegar chips at the river party.'

'Shh. I'm a teenager. I'm supposed to be rebellious.' Rory grins, transferring the finished parcels onto the tray. 'Also, no plastics. Avoid synthetics and mass-produced items.'

I fold and tuck. 'So that's why there's no IKEA in your hut.'

'Shut up. We all practise yoga or deep breathing every morning.'

'Before coffee?'

She gives me a fake glare, continues. 'We use river water to wash every day. We never keep money on our person – Ray deals with all that. We practise mindfulness.'

'What's that?'

'Being fully present and aware of what you're doing. Being in the moment. Like with driving – we walk around the car three times before getting into it, then wait two minutes before turning the key to start the car. That lets the driver focus on the car and the act of driving, not on some hectic schedule. We also only travel in groups.'

'What about you going to school? And what about Stuart?' I wipe my hands and lean against the bench while I watch her put the tray into the oven. 'He goes to work in town three times a week.'

'Well, Ray wasn't excited about me going to school on my own, that's true,' she admits. 'And Stuart has an exemption. But Kell often goes with him. Stuart drops him off part way into town and Kell walks back.'

I had no idea about that. 'Okay.'

'We also don't sleep too much. I usually go to bed at midnight or one, and everybody's up at about five.'

I gape at her. 'How are you not dying? Seriously, I don't think teenagers are medically advised to sleep less than eight hours a night. It affects your growth or something.'

She shrugs one shoulder. 'It's fine. I get tired, but there's a lot to do early in the morning. And evenings are late cos, well, there's chores, then Meetings, then homework…'

'Jesus, Rory.'

'There's one more thing, but it's not really a rule, just something we all do.' She selects a piece of herb from a bunch hanging above the bench, wafts it under her nose. 'Whenever we leave Eden, we take a leaf or a pinch of dirt or something from the property with us. To remind us where we've come from, and where we're going back to.'

'You do that?'

'Yes. I take a sprig of my favourite herb from the garden.'

'Okay.'

She grins. 'You have to ask me what's my favourite herb now.'

'Rory, what's your—'

'Rosemary.' She hands me the leaf she selected. 'I love the smell of it and the sturdiness of the plant. And according to old legends, rosemary grows best where a woman is strong in her own house.'

I smile, but I'm thinking about this. 'I guess some of those rules make sense, like the focusing-on-driving one. But some of the others… Do people in town look at you funny when you're walking three times around your car?'

'Probably. But they look at us funny anyway.' She turns to wipe the bench down. 'The rules don't have to make sense to outsiders. They make sense to us, and that's the only thing that matters.'

I'm about to ask another question, but there's a kerfuffle near the back door: Star and Ilona enter the Meeting House, carrying big, wrapped bundles.

'Ooh, it's swap meet!' Rory's face lights up. 'I'll put the kettle on.'

'Hello!' Star waves at us as she dumps her bundle near the brown couch. 'Rory, I've got those purple leggings you like, and the green pants.'

Rory grins. 'Keep the leggings for next time, but I've got dibs on the pants.'

She rushes over to the two women, and there's a lot of excitement as the bundles are unwrapped and random clothes fall out. A few seconds later, Kell wanders in with an armful of his own.

'Work trousers and jumpers, mainly, but there's a vest, a couple of belts, some socks I haven't ever worn...' He drops his load near the fire-pit, nods at me. 'Hey, Bo. If we're making a pot of tea, I'll have a mug.'

'For sure.' I hunt around for tea things, as Rory comes over with green cotton cloth – the pants, I guess – bunched up in her hand.

'We don't get to buy things,' she explains, 'except at the op shops in Lamistead every now and then. So we pool all the clothes and stuff we're not using to give each other some variety and make sure everything's being recycled. Are you okay to sort out the tea while I run back to the hut? I've got to grab a few things to contribute.'

'Go for it.'

'Oh, and check the parcels in the oven!' Rory grins and dashes away.

Swap meet turns into quite an occasion. Everyone who comes to Meeting carries a bundle, which could contain anything from clothes and shoes to books and blankets. Virginia brings along some embroidery threads and needles, and while Rory and I prepare the dipping sauces and vegies, folks pore over the pile of clothes and even do some on-the-spot alterations to things they've discovered.

I see Rory's pink cardigan pulled from the pile and claimed by Sally, who tugs it on straight away. I nudge Rory as she stacks parcels on an earthenware platter. 'That's your cardigan.'

She glances up. 'It's Sally's cardigan now.'

'I thought you liked it?'

'I do. But every swap meet, we give away one thing that we're really in love with. That teaches us not to become attached to material things.' She shrugs. 'I'm happy that Sally got it. And she might bring it back next month, who knows.'

After the swapping frenzy is over, Allison and Stuart pull the couches and rugs closer to the fire, and Rory and I bring out the food. Ray arrives, bringing a bucket full of ginger beer bottles. The atmosphere is festive; people compliment me and Rory on the food, which gives me a warm feeling. I've never cooked for a large group before, and it looks like I did okay.

Songs start up, with Stuart, Kell and Ilona taking turns on the guitar. Rory is laughing with Virginia as they darn some holes in the green pants – they're holding a leg each – and Ray is talking to Jules and Sally, who smile as they watch Ray's expansive hand gestures.

'Good stuff,' Kell says, lolling back on the grey couch beside Daniel, who's still munching on the crust of a cheese-and-spinach parcel. Kell pats his belly appreciatively. 'Great food, nice company, tired from a solid day's work… What more could you want, hey, Ray?'

Ray looks over, grinning. 'For me, nothing else. For the world, I'd like a little more, but right now, I'm happy.'

Kell smiles. 'We got our own slice of heaven here.'

Ray angles himself towards the fire. 'That's always been my argument with people who say we shouldn't worry about the problems with this world, that we'll all experience a perfect world in heaven. Why should you wait until you're dead? We've made a heaven right here – we know it's possible, because we're the example. I want to see *that* happen all over. I want to see every man, woman and child enjoy the kind of life we live.'

Kell nods. 'I like the sound of that.'

'People outside say, *But living zero impact is hard work!* Like driving through gridlock, working nine-to-five, isn't hard work.' Ray slaps a hand on his dusty, jeans-clad knee. 'Things worth having are worth working for. I believe that.'

Stuart walks over and gathers Daniel up, sits with him on the rug near the fire. People shift and settle into seats to listen.

Ray stares into the flames as he goes on. 'It's a question of values, though, isn't it? Values out there are so skewed, folks don't realise what's important.' He throws a hand towards the 'out there'. 'They think they want dishwashers, and giant TVs, and all the crazy consumer trappings. They assume that's what they want, cos it's so normalised – I'm gonna be a sixty-hour-per-week wage slave for the next thirty-five years so I can pay off my car, my house! I want that, right? Isn't that what everyone wants?'

Ilona nods, putting her plate aside. 'Society has become corrupted.'

Ray shrugs. 'People have been heavily conditioned. We all have, except for Rory and Daniel here.'

He lifts his chin at them. Rory smiles and keeps plying her needle on the pants.

'We've been conditioned to obedience, compliance.' Ray catches the eye of every person in turn. 'Our wild self has been suppressed so deeply, we don't even realise it was ever there. Our instinct was broken, replaced with civilisation. And now we're enslaved to it. Civilisations like ours, they don't want to look at the bad things that are happening. They want to console themselves with the positive – all the benefits we've acquired from chopping down our rainforests, or mining the world into Swiss cheese to feed our fossil fuel addiction. *Look at what we've gained!* they say. Advances in communication and science. Better cars. Better houses. Better standards of living. And we accept these things as god-given – they're ours. We don't think about the irreparable damage we've done to bring it all about. Think about the situation in Bangladesh, for instance...'

Ray's voice travels on from here, from our tight little community circle, out and beyond to touch places and things I've never seen. Rory sits across the other side of the fire, her head tilted, watching her father as she tucks up against Sally, who's now wearing the pink cardigan. Rory's cheeks are rosy from the heat of the flames, her hands reddened from the clay-work and the cooking. Her face is smudged with flour, and there's a streak of dried mud up the side of one of her legs. I can't remember seeing her look more beautiful.

I've always thought Rory lived an insular life full of restrictions, but I realise now that's not it. Her world is bigger than mine. I've lived for sixteen years without giving too much thought to the world beyond Lamistead – I might've thought as far up the Australian east coast as Brisbane, but that's it. Rory's thinking about everything, every place, every ecology on earth, all at once.

Her whole life philosophy is about action and consequence, how these little actions impact on a much larger scale. How the plastic bag you use for your supermarket shopping ends up being picked over by seagulls in the Atlantic Ocean. How the petrol you use fuels more than your car – it fuels an oil war in the Middle East.

I've never thought on a global scale. My life and vision have always been bounded by family, by my local community, by the mini-dramas at school. It almost seems too much for my head to fit in the rest. But in Rory's head, it fits. It all fits.

I like this girl. I've known it for a while, but watching her now, I feel it sounding, deep inside. *I like this girl.*

209

As I feel it, Rory's attention drifts sideways, away from Ray's monologue. Her eyes meet mine, and I don't look away. Across the red and gold flames, she shares a soft, private smile with me, and I feel it again: my heartbeat drumming, warm under my ribs. There's no sound – of two matching components clicking into place – but that was only ever something I'd imagined.

And suddenly I'm remembering the way Mum and Dad sometimes hugged each other, for no reason at all. Ray was right. Your mind doesn't want to linger on the shitty things, the unhappy memories. When things are bad, it latches onto the good things – the good times you experienced, in what now feels like a past life.

Right now I'm hoping that maybe, if I wish or pray or dream hard enough, those good things will come back.

✳

Monday morning I come out into the kitchen and find Mum talking on the landline. She's standing at the glass doors to the verandah. Her voice is low, but I catch the gist.

'...don't know. Well, I can't tell you that. All I can tell you is that I don't *know* how I feel...'

I want to duck back into my room, but it's too late, and I have to get ready for school. I put the kettle on, not wanting to hear but straining my ears.

'...so, yes. Have you thought about how this is affecting Bo and Con?' Mum crosses one arm in front of herself, holding the receiver with the other hand. 'Of course I have. Well, what did you— Don't talk over the top of me, Aaron, you know I can't stand that bullshit...' Her gaze flicks over to me, flicks back.

'Fine. Yes. Yes, he's right here. D'you want me to put him on?'

I shake my head like a lunatic. *No* – no way. The last thing I want to do is talk to my father right now. I wouldn't even know what to say.

Mum sees me, bites her lip. 'Okay, he's … he can't talk right now … Yes, I'll ask him. Okay, call me tonight. Right. Talk to you then.'

And that's it – there are no fond *goodbye*s or *I love you*s. Mum thumbs off the call and drops the handset onto the kitchen table. 'That was Dad.'

'Yeah, I got that.' The kettle's coming to the boil. I grab a mug.

'Look, I have to make a few more calls …' Mum rubs a hand across her forehead. 'Are you right to get Con organised for school? Then I can drive him.'

'No problem,' I say. 'I'll get him up and fed.'

Mum reaches for the phone again. 'He asked how you're going. Your father, I mean. He asked how you're going with footy.'

I nod. Of course he did. Cos footy's the only way my father and I can relate.

∗

'Mr Mitchell. Wait.'

I've done pretty well – about as well as could be expected, really – but now it's end of first period and as I'm about to slide past to the door, Mrs Ram raises her finger in my direction.

Oh shit.

She's wearing a peacock-blue blouse with small gold

flowers along the hem, and the colours make her eyes seem really fierce when she gives me her full attention. It's a Maximum Blast stare from a teacher, and cos it's Mrs Ram, it carries even more weight. I want to sink into the floor.

'Speak,' she says.

There's nothing I can say, and whatever I say, it won't be enough.

'I haven't decided yet.' I don't hang my head, I stand straight. I don't want to keep dodging Mrs Ram. I just want to get it out in the open, get it over with.

'Forget the subjects.' Mrs Ram flaps a hand. 'What's going on?'

'What?' My bottom lip goes slack.

'*Bo*. Please don't treat me as if I'm stupid.'

'Mrs Ram, I don't know what you—'

'Friday, in my class. Today, in my class.' She ticks off the days on her fingers. 'Other teachers tell me you've been withdrawn and distracted. You look as if you are either coming down with an illness, or going through some kind of personal trauma. Now, which is it?'

None of your business – that should be my immediate reaction. I should take refuge in *I don't know* or *it's nothing* or *I can handle it*, but I'm overwhelmed by such an enormous sense of relief that someone has actually noticed.

I swallow, uncross my arms. 'My dad has taken off for Brisbane. I don't know if he's coming home. I met my older half-brother for the first time last Wednesday night. Everything is … Things are a mess right now.'

It's crazy, making a *teacher* my emotional safe house. But I have to trust somebody outside of Eden with this.

Mrs Ram sighs, looking as relieved as I feel. 'Thank you for telling me, Bo. I had a sense there was something going on.'

I give a curt nod.

'I'm sorry your family is going through this.'

'Yeah, me too.' My throat is clogged tight.

'This is a hard thing, a very hard thing. And it's understandable that you're unable to make complex decisions right now.' She pats my shoulder gently. 'Who is supporting you? Have you explained what's happening to your friends?'

'No.' I shake my head. 'Except for Rory.'

'You've been visiting her at the Eden community?' Mrs Ram's brows knit together.

'Yeah. I just … need a break from home sometimes, hey.'

Mrs Ram taps her thumb against her pursed lips before speaking. 'All right. There are three things I need to say. First – we are still on an external deadline. I want you to do your best to consider a subject decision. Meanwhile, keep up with your schoolwork. If you do that, I will try to ensure that none of the other faculty interferes with punitive consequences. Do you understand?'

I nod. Knowing that I won't be hounded with detentions or extra homework is a weight off my back.

'The second thing – you should explain this situation to your friends.' She sees my expression. 'I understand that this might be uncomfortable for you, but believe me, if the teaching staff and myself have noticed that something is "up" with you, your friends have noticed too. Your friends are there to support you, Bo. That is what friends do.'

'But I'm already talking to Rory about—'

'And this is the final thing I need to say.' Mrs Ram clasps her hands together in front of herself. 'It's good that you are talking to Rory Wild – it's good you are talking to *somebody*. But the community in Eden is…perhaps not as benign as you've been led to believe.'

'They're good people,' I counter. 'They work hard, and they share everything—'

'I am not saying that the intentions and purpose of the Eden community are wrong,' she goes on. 'In fact, I admire their environmental focus. I've visited the site – Eden was a much larger group when it first started, and it had strong connections to the community in Lamistead. But now numbers have diminished, the group has become very insular, and they are led by one powerful man, a demagogue. This concerns me. As a discerning student of history, it should concern you too.'

I still don't get it. What is everyone's problem with Eden? 'Ray's an okay guy, Mrs Ramanathan. I don't think you understand how—'

'I understand very well, thank you.' Her expression softens. 'Bo, I don't like to see any vulnerable student of mine led astray by—'

'I'm not being led astray!'

She sighs. 'And I'm not here to dissuade you. You have to form your own opinions on the matter. But you should have all the facts, so you can make an informed choice. The Garden of Eden community is under scrutiny for issues related to the education and well-being of children within the community, and I've heard there's also a problem with the leasehold on the Bowyer property.'

'Eden is under investigation?' My gut feels suddenly cold.

'Rory has no registration, no record of birth or education, no immunisation schedule… It's as if she doesn't exist. The principal had to report it, and there had been concerns about other children in the community. Now social services and the council are making preliminary enquiries. That is what I have been told, and that is where things stand for the moment.' Mrs Ram locks eyes with me. 'I know what you're feeling, Bo. You believe you have found a refuge in Eden, a place free from the flaws and divisions of the outside world. But that is the thing – there is no "outside" or "inside". It is all one world. And Eden is a part of that world, no matter how much the people there would like to believe otherwise.'

The rest of the day is a blur. Does Rory know that Eden is under investigation? Does anyone in the community know? I need to warn them.

In every class, in every free moment, I'm thinking about Rory, and Eden, and *Rory*. What would she do if the community folded? How would she cope? And what about Allison, who can't cope with the outside world, and Sally, whose plans for a peaceful death all rely on the autonomy of the community, the respectful understanding of the people there? I try to imagine Sally at the mercy of doctors, dying without dignity in some sterile hospital bed…

I can't picture it. I honestly can't picture *any* of the community members living in the outside world. Eden has become more than a home for them: it's part of who they are. They've built it with their bare hands. Even more important than the greenery and the homes and the land, their identities are bound up in their communal lifestyle, the values and camaraderie they share.

And as far as I'm aware, none of them have any money

or resources they could use to create individual lives for themselves outside. They've pooled everything they have to build a life *together*. Thinking of Rory and the others being thrust out into the regular world, living in disconnected suburban houses, shopping at supermarkets… The whole idea seems fundamentally wrong.

When Sprog punches me on the shoulder at the end of sixth period, I'm miles away. 'Whadidja do that for?'

Sprog rolls his eyes. 'I dunno where your brain is right now, mate, but can I get your attention for, like, two seconds? Then you can go back to being a distracted miseryguts.'

'For what?'

'I want you to check over this petition-submission letter. I'm taking it in to the council straight after school.'

I rub a hand over my eyes. 'Sure. Sorry, man. Gimme a look.'

Suddenly I notice how cleaned-up Sprog is. His jeans don't have holes in the knees, and he's wearing a neat T-shirt. His windbreaker is just a windbreaker, no hood. He even looks like he's brushed his hair.

He thrusts the paper into my hands. 'There. What do you think?'

'Gimme a sec.' I scan through it, feeling Sprog's eyes on me.

'So what's your problem, bro?'

'No problem.'

'Girl trouble?'

'No. No girl trouble.' I glance at him. 'You're not emailing this?'

'Cam said it's better to present it in person.' He shuffles his feet beside me. 'No problem. No girl trouble. So what, you're not gonna tell me?'

'No, I'm not gonna tell you.' I hand the paper back. 'The letter's fine. You got enough signatures?'

'Totes.' Sprog grins, temporarily diverted. 'I got four hundred and thirty-two names.'

'Shit. I didn't know there were four hundred and thirty-two teenagers *in* Lamistead.'

'Some adults signed, too – parents and teachers and stuff.' He slaps his backpack. 'All in here. Hey, I gotta go catch the bus into town. I'll see you at training, yeah? Then you can tell me what's going on.'

'Sure.'

I give him a wave as he heads off. I won't tell him. There's too much happening, and my brain feels too jammed up to explain it all. Real Life Overload.

About two seconds after I get rid of Sprog, Cam ambushes me near the senior wing. 'Why was your brother in the Roscoes' car at the bus loop?'

I shrug on the other strap of my backpack. 'He's mates with Ebony's little brother, Garrett.'

'It's Monday. Doesn't your mum usually pick him up from the primary school?'

'Yeah. Um, what?' The key to my bike lock is wedged deep at the bottom of my pocket. I finally focus on what Cam's saying.

'I thought it was weird, because I know your parents don't let him sleep over at friends' places mid-week, so...'

She's looking at me expectantly, waiting for me to provide a valid explanation. Only I haven't got one, because I don't know what the hell's going on. I have to get home.

'Cam, I've gotta go.' I try to push past her as gently as I can.

She narrows her eyes. 'Bo, is there something happening at your place?'

The last thing I want is to have this conversation now. 'I'll talk to you later.'

She snags my T-shirt sleeve. 'No, you won't. You've been tight-lipped for days.'

'Cam, I will. Lemme go.' I jerk loose. 'I *will*, okay? But not now.'

I run to the bike racks, fumble with my bike lock, get free, ride. Overcast skies make all the clay-dirt colours fly up off the road. The whole countryside has been touched up by X-Pro, and my breathing seems overloud, disturbing the picture-perfectness of it. Then I'm home, staggering on the stairs cos my legs are emptied from riding so hard.

Inside, Mum's folding laundry at the kitchen table. She looks up as I burst into the house. 'Hey, love.'

'Hey.'

I stand there for a second, torn. Mum squares and smooths one of the bathroom towels, fishes another one out of the basket. Julie is flopped on the floor of the kitchen, asleep, in her usual fashion. The only thing that's out of whack is me.

'Aren't you supposed to be getting ready for footy training?' Mum asks.

'Yeah.' I stand for another second. 'Okay ... I'm gonna do that.'

'Here's your jersey.'

Mum tosses, I catch. It all seems so normal, so calm. Too calm.

'Where's Connor?'

'Hm?'

'Where's Connor?'

Mum selects a blue T-shirt, eyes on the basket. 'He's gone to Garrett's place for the night.' She folds the T-shirt. 'Actually, he might stay there for a few days. Just until things settle down.'

'What?'

'Until we work a few things out.' Mum chooses another towel, tucks and smooths methodically. The towel is an easy problem to straighten out. 'It's too much for him, Bo. He's still too young to understand.'

I feel my face screw up. 'What about *me*? There's still a shitload of stuff *I* don't understand.'

'Connor needs to have some normal for a while,' Mum says. She puts the folded towel on a stack of others.

I narrow my eyes. 'Do the Roscoes know that Dad's gone?'

'I just said that Aaron's away for work, and I'm not feeling so great…'

'Mum…'

'It'll be okay,' Mum says. 'I know you're worried, but it'll all work out.'

I'm rooted to the spot, but inside, I'm spinning. *How?* I want to scream. How the fuck will this work out? Dad's gone, Connor's been farmed out to another family, I'm going mental, and Mum seems to have slid into some quagmire of self-absorption. She didn't even tell me to mind my language.

This separation is wrong. I complain about Connor, but I don't want my little brother staying at some other family's

220

house. I don't understand that. I don't understand anything. Most of all, I don't understand this situation that's pulling our family apart.

✻

For the first time in history, I blow off footy training.

Consistency. Every training session, every game . . . Mullet's voice echoes in my brain, but I push it aside. Sprog will be at training, and I'm not ready to answer his pointed questions.

My bike turns on instinct: left, then left again. Jules is at the Eden sign when I pass through; he's sitting on a log stump beside the new gate, whittling something.

'She's on the harvest side!' he calls, giving me a wave.

He means the fields on the other side of the river: Rory's taken me on enough back-garden detours now that I know the way. I park behind the Meeting House and follow a trail around the large, thatch-roofed chook pen, then past a patch of land that's been left fallow. Mellow, the jersey cow that Kell tends, is cropping the tall grass; she raises her head as I wander onwards.

Skirting around Allison's hut, I glance over just as her front door opens, and Ray steps out.

Ray and Allison stand in the doorway, facing each other as they speak. Allison is wearing a long bottle-green robe – it doesn't look as if she has anything on underneath. Her straight blonde hair is caught up in a dishevelled bun. Ray cups her cheek with his hand as he says something to her, and she nods, looks away. Looks at me.

I turn my head quickly. I didn't mean to be an observer, and I don't want to make any assumptions. But I'm pretty sure I know what I saw, and I'm pretty sure they both saw me. I keep clomping forwards, hoping to get a bit of distance.

It's actually none of my business. And it's not like there's a lot of options for people in the community – only Allison, Ray and Kell are single, and I can't imagine any one of them getting involved with outsiders. But it still gives me an uncomfortable feeling. Ray looked old enough to be Allison's father, when they were standing together like that…

On the slope down towards the river, I hear boots on the path behind me.

'Bo, wait up.' Ray's long strides reach me in no time. 'Hey.'

Ray's work shirt is hanging loose over a faded, threadbare T-shirt and a pair of jeans. I'm struck again by how fit he is – his gait is firm, certain. As he gets close, he smooths back his moustache, then his hair, tying it into a ponytail with a piece of leather thong.

'If you're looking for Aurora, she's harvesting,' he says. 'But I guess you know that.'

'Yes, sir, I do,' I say.

'Just Ray, Bo. Not sir.' He lifts his chin, urging me to keep walking. 'I've been counselling Allison. She's been going through a tough time, lately. A very tough time.'

'Okay.'

I don't know why he's lying. I'm surprised, cos I didn't think people here were into keeping secrets. Or maybe he's not? Maybe he really was counselling her, and I read it wrong? I only caught a glimpse. The rules around here are different, and I don't know or understand them all. Besides, it's not my place to judge, and I have something more important to talk to Ray about.

'I heard a rumour today – it got me worried. Someone told me that the council and welfare are investigating the community here. Is that true?'

'Mmm.' Ray scratches at the stubble on his cheek as we walk, which reminds me of how he cupped Allison's cheek. But he seems to have recovered his chill. 'Yeah, we know about that. We've known for a while. Bo, there are always going to be people who don't agree with what we're trying to achieve here – that's pretty much a given. We've been on watchlists, we've been persecuted before. I think Eden's been on the authorities' radar ever since it got started.'

'So you're not worried?'

'No.' He claps me on the shoulder. 'There'll always be haters, Bo. In fact, in my experience, if you've got people hating on you, you know you're doing something right.'

'True.'

'You're not letting a few misguided rumour-mongers get to you, are you, Bo?'

'No, sir,' I say, forgetting. 'I mean, no way.'

'Glad to hear it.' We've nearly reached the turn in the river, and Ray slows his steps so he can face me. 'You're a good man, Bo. You know, I don't believe in much woo-woo stuff, but I do believe in fate, and I believe in people. And I think you were drawn to this community for a reason. There was something predestined about it, don't you think?'

'I guess so.'

'For certain. Through Aurora, you've come to Eden at a time in your life when you needed it. And when we needed you. There's a purpose to you being here, I can feel it. It gives me a lot of energy to see you at Meeting, to see the new spirit you bring to the community. And if there's ever anything you need, you let me know. You can talk to me anytime.' He glances across the river. 'Now, I should stop rambling, let you find Aurora. I'm sure she's looking forward to seeing you, and she'd probably appreciate an extra hand or two with the harvest. We'll catch up tonight at Meeting, yeah?'

'You bet.'

He claps my shoulder once more, nodding as he holds my gaze, then he turns and takes the divided path upriver. I'm not sure what just happened. I've been warmed by Ray's blessing, but warned by it, too. And I'm still not sure what's going on with Allison.

But my worries float free as I look across to the other bank of the river. The fading sunlight glows on the corn, with Rory a pale blue figure in among the green and gold leaves. She has her hair tucked under a broad-brimmed hat. She's wearing cut-offs with a loose white shirt over the top, and work gloves, and a kangaroo-pouch bag is suspended from her shoulders for holding the cobs. She waves at me, and I wave back as I cross the bridge, make my way closer.

'You have excellent timing,' she says, as she takes off her gloves. 'I've been at this for four hours, and I'm over it.'

'Will Stuart and Ilona mind if you knock off?' I lift my chin at the others. A small pile of unhusked corn sits like a mounded sculpture over to one side. It doesn't look like enough to feed a community of eleven people, but what do I know?

'We're finished for the day,' Rory says. 'The light's going. We'll come back tomorrow for the rest.'

She grabs for a brown bottle on the ground and takes a

long swig, liquid dribbling into her mouth, down her chin. Unhitching her pouch and putting it on the corn pile, she steps back to sluice her face then passes me the bottle.

I take a pull – the water is cold, probably from the river – then Rory leans forwards, puts her damp hands on my shoulders.

'It's good to see you,' she says, smiling. She kisses me on the mouth. It's not really a romantic kiss, more a chance to brush cool, wet lips. Fireworks fly under my skin all the same. When she pulls back, we're both grinning.

And I have a definite feeling of predestination.

'Sorry, but I don't understand. You told me how things are with you and Ray and Star. You're their kid, but you all seem really…separate. And you just seem so chilled about it.'

We're sitting on the couch in the garden, enjoying the last of the sun, and in Rory's case, enjoying not being on her feet picking corn. Her white shirt is balled up on the couch beside her; she wiped her face with it, and now she's in a tank top.

She teases corn silk out of her hair as we talk. 'I grew up differently.'

'I could never be that detached.'

'It's not detachment, it's…' She tugs at her hair. 'I don't know if you'll get it.'

'Try me.'

'I'm not theirs.' She sees my face and clarifies quickly. 'Not in the same way you are with your family, I mean. Ray and Star both believe that your children are part of the earth. Your children come from you, but they don't *belong* to you, like some kind of possession. Ray and Star relinquished me to the earth, to Gaia. I belong to Gaia.'

'What does that even mean?'

She leans forwards, shaking corn silk from her fingers. 'It means I have a photo of me, in a calico singlet dress, with flowers in my hair, sitting in a circle with Ray and Star … They did a whole ceremony – well, Star likes to ritualise everything. But it means that the way I was raised was different. It was part of my parents' philosophy that I be raised as naturally as possible. That's why I was given this surname – Wild. The earth is my guide, my protector, my mother and father, my everything, and ultimately the earth is the place I'll return to. Ray and Star interfered as little as possible.'

'So they didn't take care of you? How does that even work?'

Rory uses a box of matches on the stump nearby to light a candle in a tin holder. 'Well, I was left to my own devices a lot. Ray and Star were there to feed me, and make sure I didn't hurt myself, but they just…' She shrugs. 'I don't know, they've always been kind of hands-off. They didn't want to push any of the traditional parenting rules, because that would mean I'd be picking up all *their* conditioning, from the way they were raised in conventional society. So they kind of … left me to make my own decisions.'

'But how can you make decisions for yourself when you're just a little kid?'

Rory shrugs again. I think I'm meant to take that as *Well, I'm still here, right? I survived*. But the whole idea makes me feel sad for her. Maybe it's not like I'm imagining, but did her parents look out for her? Has she ever had a parent who actually *parented* her? I'm pissed with my father, and frustrated by my mother, but at least they've always been there for me.

And now I'm thinking about the welfare investigation,

what that might uncover. What would all this hands-off parenting and homeschooling look like to the inspectors?

'Star's been more involved with Daniel, though, hasn't she?'

'Yes,' Rory admits. 'She's been really different with Daniel. Her ideas have changed over the years.'

'What about Ray?'

She frowns. 'He's there to provide advice, if I ask for it. But his ideas have changed too. He doesn't believe in human procreation anymore. He advocates for VHE.'

'VHE?'

'Voluntary Human Extinction. He believes that the best solution for the planet is for us to simply stop having children.' She glances at me. 'It's not cos he doesn't like people! It's an ecology issue. The earth's overcrowded – at the rate we're reproducing, our population is outstripping our natural resources.'

I gape. 'So he thinks we should all stop having kids?'

'If everyone chose to limit their families to one child, we might have a chance. But it's probably too late for that. Humanity hasn't exactly been a great thing for the planet, y'know? If there were no more children, then the ones we have now would actually be valued, and with the time and resources we have left, every person could live a good-quality life.'

'Ray believes that humanity should let itself die out.' My face must look a little freaked as I take this in. My mind immediately flashes to the memory of Mum's belly-nudge a few weeks ago. 'Okay, that's … pretty radical.'

'"Radical" is considered a complimentary term around here, y'know.' She picks at the candle wax as it starts to pool.

'He doesn't think it might be hard to convince people that human extinction is a good idea? That it might be a little unrealistic?'

'I would say "idealistic".'

'Okay.' This is obviously part of a larger conversation, and I don't want to veer off track yet. 'But putting all that stuff aside ... Star had Daniel.'

'I know.' She examines her own wax-capped fingertips, crumbles the wax away. 'Star is her own person. Not everyone holds the same opinions as Ray.'

Rory's expression is deliberately neutral. It's not the first time I've seen her wear this look. I remember it from the day I came here for her birthday, when I was introduced to her dad, who I didn't know was her dad at the time.

Rory's pissed about something.

It's so unlike her – she gets passionate about stuff, but rarely angry – that I want to unpick it a little. 'You said you were okay with it, but was Ray okay with Star having Daniel?'

'He advised against it,' she says evenly. 'On a philosophical level.'

'But Star didn't take his advice.'

'It'd be a banner day if Star took advice on something.' Sarcasm – another rare slip. She's upset.

I think I might have overstepped, and I don't want to fuck this up. I put my hand on hers, twine our fingers together. 'Rory, you don't have to keep talking about this.'

'What?' She starts when our fingers connect, but she doesn't pull away. 'I'm fine.'

Then I think of something really obvious. 'Are you jealous of your half-brother?'

Her lips press together. She blinks at the candle. 'You can't be jealous of a three-year-old.'

'But he's had all the parenting and care you missed out on.'

'People cared for me.'

'But not the people whose care meant the most.'

'There are all different ways of showing love.' She says it like she's trying to convince herself. There's a long pause, before she shakes her head, brushes her cheeks roughly with both hands. 'We should go to Meeting. It's getting late.'

I help her carry the candle and water bottle back to her hut. Rory wraps the bread in calico and dippers water from the barrel into her big cast-iron kettle on the range, while I load some more wood into the fire, bank it down.

She grabs a chunky hand-knitted jumper, which I think is an old one of Kell's, and pulls it on. 'You ready?'

I snag her wrist as she's heading for the door. In the dim shadows of the hut, her face seems haunted. 'Do you wanna skip Meeting?'

'I can't skip Meeting.' She looks scandalised. 'And I'm hungry. Aren't you hungry?'

Something feels different, though, when I'm sitting around the fire-pit circle tonight. The stars above the Meeting House are dazzling, but my appetite for dhal and oatcakes isn't what I thought it would be.

At first, I think I'm stewing over that scene between Ray and Allison. But Allison seems completely relaxed – she's not looking pensive, or throwing meaningful glances at Ray. Maybe I'm rattled because of the situation with Connor, or still naggingly worried about the threat of the welfare investigation. But that's not it, either.

Rory sits beside me, picking at her food, smiling at Jules as he displays his newest carved piece, waving to Star and Daniel. I watch Ray presiding over a conversation with Virginia and Kell. The first time I met Ray, I had no clue that he and Rory were connected. He barely acknowledges their relationship at all. Perhaps, because of his role in the community, he doesn't want to be seen to be showing favouritism or something. Maybe Rory's right. There are all different ways of showing love.

But what if your way is so different it's unrecognisable? It makes me angry on Rory's behalf. Does she really feel unloved, unwanted? Who in their right mind wouldn't want to tell the world that this smart, talented, gorgeous girl was their daughter?

I'm also thinking about what Rory said about Ray supporting VHE. I would have said a belief in human extinction is at odds with the kind of community Ray's encouraging here. But I don't know what to think. I don't have all the facts.

I put my plate aside, and wait for a lull in the conversation before asking my question. 'Ray, is it true you believe that humans should let themselves die out?'

Ray's smile doesn't fade as he turns towards me, but I see him glance sideways at Rory. 'You've been talking to Aurora.' He nods, looks back to me. 'Yes, that's true. I believe *Homo sapiens* is basically a failed experiment.'

My voice comes out a little too hard. 'So how does that work, when you're leading a community of people?'

'Ah, Bo, it's a tough one. I mean, I love human beings.' Ray's expression is full of compassion as he looks around the fire-pit. 'I love all of you. People are wonderfully creative,

231

inventive, adaptable. We're beautiful.' He returns his gaze to me. 'But we've been indoctrinated with this idea that we're the pinnacle of existence – that human beings hold a special position as the crown of creation. We have to fight that conditioning. Wildlife has as much right to existence on this planet as people do. And frankly, the planet would be better off with fewer people on it.'

'But VHE? Seriously?' I stare him down. 'My parents are having another baby in April.'

'Well, that's unfortunate.' Ray spreads his hands. 'Bo, I understand the loyalty you have – that all human beings have – to their own species. But I really think that's just privilege talking. In lots of ways, humans have been terrible for this planet. We grow and spread like a cancer, and we seem to destroy every natural thing we touch. And what have we really contributed to the earth? Let's weigh it in the balance – what have we ever given back?'

I think about the question. 'Well… music, and art, and culture.'

Ray shakes his head. 'We've reproduced the beauty of the natural world in art, then trashed the very thing that's inspired us.'

'What about science, and knowledge?'

'What about war?' Ray counters, leaning forwards. 'All we seem to do with our scientific knowledge is militarise it. And we haven't even been able to successfully share that wealth of knowledge around. There's a vast group of people on earth whose lives are defined by poverty and despair.'

'But we've improved a lot of people's basic lives, with stuff like running water, and hygiene, and vaccines—'

'Don't get me started on immunisation,' Ray says.

'Okay. But what about medicine? Brain surgery? Heart transplants?'

'Well, I actually have a problem with that. It's about extending human life beyond its natural course. Days gone by, if you had a dicky heart, you died. That was nature's way of weeding out the weak from the strong. I mean, if you've got a dicky heart, should you be procreating? Producing more children with dicky hearts, who go on to produce dicky-hearted children of their own, and so on, down the line?'

I can feel Rory's eyes on me, and the heat from the fire in my cheeks. 'So you think we should just let those people die?'

'Well, I think you need to consider all those medicines and hospital beds and doctors, all that time and money, those resources, used to keep one person alive. Don't you think we could've used those resources more effectively? We could've invested in solar energy, or reforestation, with the millions of dollars it takes to keep a handful of people alive.'

I'm very aware that Sally is sitting in the circle right now, watching this whole exchange. 'I'm sure those people in hospital think the resources are being well used.'

'That's the thing, though. Do they?' Ray shakes his head. 'People give their dogs fifty-thousand-dollar hip replacement operations. Our general standard of living in this country is so high, we don't even realise how much we're wasting. Throwaway appliances. InSinkErators. Happy Meals. Is this the beauty of humanity?'

'But you still think we should let old and really sick people die?'

'Bo, I think we should all consider what's best for the

233

planet.' Ray's eyes bore into mine. 'Our society can't go on like this forever. And I'm saying there's a time for everything. Even death. Barely a generation ago, people got sick, or their babies were born sickly, and they just died. And there was an acceptance of that. There was sadness, and grief, but people moved on. These days, folks fight to hold onto life with everything they've got, with the whole arsenal of modern medical weaponry. They're fighting death. Making a war on death. Making it the enemy. Can you see the futility of that? I mean, none of us gets out of this alive, right? We're fighting the inevitable, like trying to keep the waves from crashing against the shore.'

Ray stands up to walk the perimeter of the fire-pit. He knows he's got everyone's attention now.

'The death saddhus in India, they clothe themselves in rags, dress in ashes from funeral pyres, drink from skulls they've scavenged. They live with death every day. They understand it.' He holds his hands above the flames – maybe it's to warm them, but it looks strangely like he's holding fire in his fingertips. 'Our society has no real understanding of death, which means we've got no proper understanding of life. That's why we place so little value on it. None of us live in the moment, we're all distracting ourselves with devices and screens, ignoring the way we're ruining the planet. I mean, the planet is our lifeblood, and we're shitting all over it. We're trying to stave off death with medicine every day, fighting it as individuals, but collectively we're destroying the very thing that keeps us all alive. D'you see the irony?'

Across the other side of the circle, there's movement.

'Can I say something?' Sally stands up on shaky legs,

keeping a firm grip on Ilona's hand. Standing looks painful for her. 'I've been thinking a lot about this issue over the last few months. And I think Ray's right – as a society, we've made death the enemy. Whether that's out of fear of the unknown, or the sadness of grief, or a primal urge to cling to life … I'm not sure of the reasons, and it doesn't matter. But I've decided it's something I don't want.'

She looks down at Ilona, who's squeezing Sally's hand, giving her the chance to stand upright to say these things, even though tears are tracked down Ilona's cheeks. Sally leans and kisses Ilona on the lips. I can't help but feel my throat tighten.

Sally straightens again and talks on. 'You're all my beloved friends. And I want death to be a friend to me, as well. Not an enemy. I don't want to go towards it with fear and anxiety. Passing back into the life force of the planet, becoming one with the earth again … that should be a time of celebration. And I'd like you all to celebrate with me. So I've made some … arrangements. And I'm setting a date – a time of my own choosing. Will you all be there to support me?'

'Of course we will, darling,' Virginia says, her voice thick with emotion.

She stands, then Jules stands, then the whole circle erupts as everyone gets up to go to Sally, to offer her love and support, to give her their strength. Ilona gets a lot of love too. Sally stands in the middle of a starfish of enveloping hugs, as the entire Eden community expresses their desire to be there for her.

Daniel weaves in and out between the legs of all the adults. I wonder if he even understands what's going on. Caught up in the hug-fest, I find myself pushed in Sally's direction.

She sees the expression on my face and gives me a sympathetic pat as she reaches for me. 'It's okay, y'know. I want to say goodbye on my own terms.'

'I don't want to say goodbye,' I mumble into her shoulder. 'I don't want to celebrate your passing. I don't want you to pass at all.'

'Oh, Bo.' She pulls back to smile softly at me.

I've only known about Sally's condition for a short while. Everyone else here has had more time to deal with it, find peace with it. Maybe that's why I find this whole thing so unsettling.

But there's another reason I'm unsettled: me and Ray never got to finish our conversation. We never got to the meat of it. I'm nowhere near convinced that humans are a blight on the planet, that extinction is the best way, but Sally's announcement seems to have somehow affirmed Ray's philosophy to everyone in the community.

Rory takes my hand. 'Let's go, Bo,' she says quietly. At least there's one other person here who understands how I'm feeling.

We don't interrupt everyone to say goodbye, I just grab my bike and Rory walks me out to the gate.

'Are you okay?'

'Um, yeah.' I push the Cannondale around the gatepost, lean it against the *Garden of Eden* sign so I can pull on my gloves. 'I wasn't expecting Sally to announce she's planning to top herself, but yeah, I'm fine.'

'It's her choice, Bo, and we have to respect that choice,' Rory says. 'If you were in her situation, wouldn't you want to be able to decide?' She angles her head. 'Are you sure this is only about Sally? It doesn't have anything to do with what Ray said?'

Away from the fire, my arms are goosebumped with cold. I look up at the sky. 'I don't feel like I really understand what's going on. Ray's position on VHE is…'

'He rattled your cage.'

'What? No.'

Rory smiles. 'Yes, he did. Ray does that to everyone. Challenges your ideas. Turns them on their head. It's a bit disconcerting if you're not used to it.'

'Disconcerting' is the word for it. But I can't help thinking this hasn't got anything to do with Ray challenging my conditioning. I think it's cos I saw him and Allison. Maybe even cos of my relationship with Rory.

'I don't understand how he can believe that stuff.'

She rubs her biceps, her hands brisk against the grey wool of the jumper. 'You have to remember, Ray pushes every idea to the extreme end of the spectrum – that's the way he is. But he's right about the way humans have wreaked havoc on the planet. Can't you imagine how the world would look if we hadn't been here to drill for oil, or cover everything in plastic, or burn everything up? There'd still be untouched rainforests in Borneo, and an ozone layer over Australia, and old-growth forests in Europe. There'd be clean air and water and—'

'Yeah, but we wouldn't be here to see it.'

She shrugs. 'Humanity will end up extinct anyway, the way we're going. We've already destroyed whole communities of animals and plants – and if we keep using up our resources, like we do now, we'll make the world uninhabitable.'

'I just… I'm sorry, hey.' I exhale, and my breath clouds

between us. My eyelids are dry and sore. 'I believe in rainforests, and the ozone layer, and all those things, all right? I do think about them. But I don't know if you have to sacrifice things like medicine and art and people's lives to achieve them.'

'Desperate times call for desperate measures.'

I baulk. 'What does that mean?'

She looks at the moon. 'Only that sometimes you have to make sacrifices for the things that are important.'

'Jesus, Rory. Don't you think you've sacrificed enough?'

She stares at me. 'I think you'd better leave.'

I might have screwed this up big-time. 'Rory, look, it's late and we're both tired…'

'You're right. I'm tired of talking about this, anyway.' She smiles tightly. Her lips, the side of her nose, are limned with moonlight.

'All right, then.' I pull the Cannondale upright. 'G'night.'

'G'night.' She steps back so I can sling a leg over my bike, bumps against the gate. 'Ow. I keep forgetting this is here.'

It *is* kind of bizarre – there's a gate across the path, but no fence either side. It's obviously not to keep Mellow in check. 'What's with the gate anyway?'

She rubs her elbow. 'Oh, Ray heard that there might be inspectors coming, so he put the gate up as a precaution. So we don't have people randomly driving in. We take shifts to keep an eye on the gate and the driveway.'

'Like a security detail?'

'More like an early warning system.'

'So Eden is being investigated?'

'Yes, it's true.' She frowns, kicks at the dirt with the toe of her sandal. 'Stuart's been helping deal with it. I don't know why they can't leave us in peace, it's not like we're hurting anyone.'

'Rory...' The neckband of the oversized jumper slips off her bare shoulder. I lift it back up. 'I'm sorry if what I said offended you. I don't want to leave and worry that you're stressing about it.'

Her nose-stud looks black in the shadows here. 'It's kind of you to think about me, but I'm okay.'

'I always think about you,' I say. It's an easy thing to admit.

Rory blinks at me. 'You... You should probably go.'

She stands back to wave, and I cycle away. On the ride home, I don't think about human extinction, or fathers who don't love their children, or friends with lymphoma, or the act of dying, or death itself. I think about a little girl in a calico dress, and a girl with a corona of golden hair, and a girl pulling off her work gloves after picking corn, and kissing Rory on the lips, and life, and life, and life.

21

'They've thanked me for bringing the issue to their attention.' Sprog squints at the words on his phone, reading from the official email he received from the council after recess. 'But they don't have any plans to restore the skate park or create a new space for teenagers at this time.' He lets his phone-hand drop to his side. 'Well, that sucks.'

It's Tuesday. Last night's discussion with Ray is still stuck between my teeth, but I don't have the headspace to think about it right now. Me, Sprog, Cam and Lozzie are grouped around our usual lunchtime bench. I've piled hot chips from the canteen onto a piece of notepaper to cool them down. Cam is sitting on the tabletop, her feet on the bench seat. Lozzie is doing her seagull impersonation, eyeing off my chips.

Cam finishes her calzone, wipes her fingers on her socks. 'Well, that's a bit pathetic. Don't teenagers deserve a space, like everybody else? What are we supposed to do?'

'Sit on our hands, I guess.' Sprog sighs up at the shade cloth above the senior area. 'Shit. It was a good plan. Restoring the skate park was a good idea.'

'You haven't got any choice,' Cam says. 'You'll have to fundraise for skate park repairs.'

'What?' Sprog looks from the shade cloth to Cam's face. 'You mean like that GoFundMe shit online?'

Cam shakes her head. 'Look, I talked to Mum, and she said that the council's always scratching for project financing. They're much more inclined to approve a project if you donate, or contribute locally-raised funds, at least enough to match the anticipated expenditure.'

'Say that again in English?' Sprog says.

'Give them some money, and the council will probably say yes,' Lozzie translates, swiping a handful of my chips.

Sprog looks blank. 'But I haven't got any money.'

'Stage an event and *raise* the money,' I say to Sprog, before frowning at Loz. 'You're nicking my chips now.'

'Idiot tax,' she says, grinning.

'Jesus.'

'Well, I guess we could do that.' Sprog chews his bottom lip for a second. 'We could put a gig on – a dance party.'

'Nice,' Cam says, as she hops down off the table. 'Live band or DJ?'

'DJ,' I say, munching on a chip and guarding the remainder.

'I reckon DJ too.' Sprog pockets his phone, rubs his neck. 'It wouldn't be that much different from setting up a gig at the river, yeah?'

'It'd be a bit different,' Cam says. 'You'd probably have to make it in town, like at the pool or something.'

'Pool's closed,' I point out.

'Oh shit, I forgot about that.'

'No booze.' Lozzie points with one of my stolen chips. 'In

town means families. You can't have booze at an all-ages gig.'

'Have it where the skate park is now,' Cam suggests. 'That's right on the main drag.'

'Passing traffic on Gough Street,' Lozzie agrees, nodding. 'And you'd have the dais. You could set up a stage and rope off room to dance, people could pay to join in. Maybe get some stalls happening, and ask them to donate some of the proceeds.'

Sprog squints. 'D'you think the local craft-y folks would get in on that?'

'Like for the Growers Market,' I say. 'Yeah, I reckon they would. Give people a bit of notice – how long have you got?'

'Twelve days until they close down the park for good,' Sprog reports glumly.

'Oh oh oh, I've just had an amazing idea,' Cam says, turning to Lozzie and clutching her arm. *White Night*.'

'Ohmigod, *yes*.' Lozzie clutches Cam in return. 'I saw all the pics on Instagram. Ebony said it was amazing.'

'That was in Melbourne, right?' Sprog asks. 'Where they decorated the buildings in the CBD with light shows and stuff?'

'We could do a local version!' Cam says, squeezing Sprog's shoulder.

'Um, how complex are we talking here?' Sprog doesn't look too unhappy about the shoulder-squeezing, although he's obviously not quite sure about an event on that scale.

'Not that big,' I suggest. 'A stage for the DJ, some dancing, stalls. Maybe some of the shops in town might stay open?'

'All the coffee shops and takeaways, like The Codfather, would,' Lozzie says. 'A skate park revamp would bring teenagers back into town, so that'd be more business for them, right? So you could ask them to donate some of their takings on the night. And if you wanted the artistic stuff, there's a few kids from AV Media who'd probably be happy to set up some light shows on the buildings near the park.'

'Lindsay screened big vids and stuff for the school fete last year, remember?' Cam says. 'And Jem would DJ, wouldn't he?'

'Yeah, he would,' Sprog says, grinning. 'Jem's a sick lad.'

'My mum could probably run pony rides in the park for a few hours,' Lozzie says. She sees Sprog's expression. 'Mum'd donate her takings, and you've gotta have something for the younger kids.'

'Can we at least *try* to keep things within the realms of sanity?'

'Skating demos?' I suggest. 'You could get the guys to put on a display.'

'Holy shit.' Sprog rubs his face with both hands. 'Okay, this is starting to sound larger than life.'

'I still think you should do it,' Cam says. The look she's directing at Sprog now is positively glowing. 'We'll all help out – everyone will.' She spreads her hand across the air in an arc, like she's revealing the banner for the event. '*White Night hits Lamistead – a dance party to raise funds for a new and improved skate park.*'

'*Local traders open till midnight. With food, and pony rides, and light displays.*' Lozzie smiles. 'It sounds brilliant. I'd go. Let's face it, it's not like there's anything else on, is there?'

I raise a hand. 'One thing.'

Sprog groans. 'What else?'

'We should have proper recycling.' I stare him down,

243

which is no easy thing to do with salt and tomato sauce on your fingers. 'I mean it. We'll need to take responsibility for garbage anyway. We can set up big recycling bins, for plastics and bottles and paper plates and stuff. I'll organise it, if you like.'

He raises his eyebrows.

'What?'

'Sounds like something your girlfriend would be more interested in doing.'

'Nah, I've been thinking about it more. Everyone should.' I ball up my hot-chips notepaper and throw it at the senior area recycling bin. It goes straight in.

'This all sounds awesome,' Cam says to Sprog, 'but you've got to get permission from the council to make it happen, and you haven't got much time. Mum might be persuaded to help move things along, but your best bet would be to write up another letter, outlining the fundraiser idea, and submit that, like, today. Otherwise, it'll be a fortnight gone, and we'll be having our dance party on a supermarket construction site.'

'That won't work.' Sprog frowns, then his expression brightens as he turns to me. 'Help me write the letter? I could take it in this arvo.'

'Right now?' I walked into that one. 'Um, okay. Sure.'

'And I'm going to start asking around.' Cam hoists her bag, lifts her chin at Loz. 'Come on, you can help me sound out the AV people.'

She drags Lozzie away. I think this might have been some kind of strategy to give me and Sprog some space, and Sprog's innocent expression, as he sits beside me and rummages for a pen and notepad, confirms it.

'Right. Letter writing.' He dumps the paper and pen on the table in front of us. 'I hate letter writing. Don't you hate letter writing? Let's talk about something else. What's going down at your place, bro?'

I roll my eyes and start lifting myself off the bench seat, but he grabs a fistful of my shirt and sits me back on my arse.

'Seriously, Bo, what's going on? Every time I call you lately, you're unavailable.'

'I've been hanging out in Eden with Rory. No reception.'

'No reception in Eden, right. And your dad's cool with that? Cos I know how he is, with the grounding, and the term-time socialising…'

'He's fine with it.' My jaw is set. I stand up again. 'Look, if you want to—'

'Man, it's all good. I'm just thinking, y'know, that *you're our mate*, and *if there's a problem, we want to help.*'

I can't say anything then, cos he's replaying my exact words from when he was having his own family issues. I sit myself back down, wet my lips. How can I talk about this? Where do I even begin?

'It's not…' False start. My courage dries up. 'Look, it's okay. We're dealing with it.'

'Really? And little powwows with Mrs Ram are helping us deal with it? Blowing off our friends and footy training is helping us deal with it?'

'Sure.' I swallow hard. It's too late. I've pretended everything's okay for too long, and now I can't take it back. What will Sprog and Cam and Loz think about me, that I've concealed this from them?

'Right. Mullet wasn't impressed, by the way. Although me

245

and the boys appreciated the chance to show off for the scout in your absence...' Sprog's eyes are worried. Then he softens. 'Mate, get real. Whatever it is, you're not dealing. Will you please just tell me, so I can tell the others, and then we can all get with the program and sort it out?'

My chest constricts. 'Dad's...' My mouth gets dry, and I stop. Sprog shoves his can of Coke in my direction. I take a drink, try again. 'Dad... He left.'

Sprog stops dead. 'He what?'

'He left for Brisbane. And he's got another kid. A son. Older than me...'

Then it all comes out, like I've yanked my finger out of a hole in the dam. Words tumble and flow around me, and while I talk, Sprog gets very sweary. By the end, he's quiet.

'Well, fuck.' He pulls two jelly snakes out of his bag and passes one to me. 'Go on, you need that.'

'Thanks, man.' A jelly snake might actually help. I feel drained, and the sugar might give me some energy. 'Anyway, we're all just waiting. Dad said he'd be gone a few days, but it's been nearly a week.'

'How's your mum coping?'

'Yeah, she's kind of going about things like it's business as usual, but when she's not doing stuff, she collapses. She's spending a lot of time in bed.' I chew, look at the notepad in front of us. Blank, like my head right now. 'I've been trying to help out, with meals mainly, but it's hard.'

Sprog shakes his head. 'You shoulda told us sooner, bro.'

'I know. But...' I let myself droop. 'I didn't know what to say. Even after I gave you that whole speech about how talking makes you feel better, I didn't know how to tell you.'

246

He gives me a wry grin. 'Yeah, it's different when you're in it, hey. But it's kinda a relief to talk about it, right?'

'True.' I catch his eye. 'Thanks.'

He slaps my shoulder. 'So...I got no solutions right now. Gimme a minute to think. D'you wanna keep talking about this, or do you wanna write the letter?'

'Letter.' I'm happy for the distraction. There's only so much soul-baring you can do in the course of a normal day. I rub a hand over my face, pick up Sprog's pen. 'Okay, what are we gonna say? *Dear Mrs Whittaker. Further to your letter regarding the petition I submitted on Monday...*'

*

Another piece of paper in front of me – not a letter.

The deadline for subject changes is looming. Mrs Ramanathan has given me a second chance, and a second second chance, and now I've actually got to make a decision. I already tried flipping a coin, but that didn't work, so I've made a list of pros and cons, because...because I can't think properly with everything that's going on, and I need something concrete to help me figure this out.

On the plus side, if I change to Food Tech: I like it. I'm good at it – I've kind of accepted that now. Mrs Ram will be rapt, Rory will give me props, and it might even lead me into some kind of satisfying work when I finish school.

On the downside: sport has always been my fallback. If I switch out of PE, that will be gone. I don't know if I'm good enough to pursue cooking as a career. I've only really thrown myself into it in class. Mrs Ram has been the sole voice of encouragement. Plus, everyone's picture of me will change, and I'm not sure how to deal with that. There'll be some weird conversations at home. I've only just let on to my mum that I'm into cooking, so I have no idea how my parents will react – Dad has only ever associated my future with sport. He thinks it's a done deal.

I chew the end of my pen. I don't know why I'm even worrying about what Dad thinks, he's not *here*, he's in *Brisbane*. I shouldn't give a stuff about his opinion – he doesn't seem to give a stuff about mine.

'Bo!' Mum's voice rings down the hallway. 'There's someone here to see you!'

Dad. My heart lurches, and I have to take a few deep breaths as I walk out of my room. It won't be him. I'm pissed with him anyway. Even if it is him—

'Hey, Bo!' Cam's standing in the doorway with her mum, Mrs D'Amato. They're both carrying casserole dishes.

Something under my ribs withers. Cam must see it in my face, cos she bustles through the door with forced cheer.

'Could you help me with these?' She loads her casserole dish into my hands, turns to take her mother's. 'Me and Bo will tuck these in the fridge, then I have to ask him about school stuff. Mum, you and Mrs Mitchell should have a cuppa – we'll be a little while.'

Lena D'Amato is a short, neatly put-together lady who looks as if she's come straight from the council offices, dressed in nice shoes and a skirt suit. Cam got her height and long limbs from her father, but her colouring and poise from her mum. With a practised motion, Lena pushes Julie out of the way with her knee, then steps over the threshold to clasp my mother's hand. 'Liz, it's lovely to see you. Camilla and I made

248

a *lot* of beef stroganoff yesterday afternoon, so I thought you might like to take some of it off our hands.'

Mum is pink in the face. I know she wouldn't like the idea of people seeing her in trackpants, with her hair unbrushed. 'Lena, that's … that sounds wonderful.'

'Come on, Bo,' Cam says, tugging my sleeve.

'Would you like a cuppa?' Mum says to Lena.

'It doesn't sound as though we've got any choice,' Lena says drily, directing her eyes at Cam. 'I think we've been set up.'

Cam and I dump the food in the fridge, then Cam pushes me into my room, closes the door behind us and whirls around.

'I can't believe you didn't tell me!' She whacks me hard on the arm.

'Ow.' I rub the sore spot. 'Look, I'm sorry, but I didn't know how to say it.'

'You say it like, *Oh god, Camilla, my dad's walked out and the whole family's going to hell. I* told you about it when *my* dad cracked it, and he and Mum got divorced!'

'You were ten! It's … different.'

'How? Guys are so stupid sometimes!' She throws up her hands, but just as I'm starting to feel angry, she envelops me in a hug. 'Oh, Bo, I'm sorry. I've been so worried about you. It drives me crazy when I don't know what's going on. Dominic called me and told me about your dad – are you all okay?'

'We're surviving.' I pull back and let myself exhale. 'I mean, we're crappy. But, y'know, we're fine. Thanks for coming over, and bringing the food. I don't think Mum's had a chance to talk to anyone about it, so it's good your mum's here.'

'Do you know what's going to happen?'

'Mum keeps saying Dad's coming back.' I shake my head. 'But I'm not sure, hey. I'm actually not sure about anything.'

'That's totally shit.'

'Nothing I can do about it.' I scuff the rug, think for a second. 'Cam, there's something else. It's about Garden of Eden.'

'Rory's community? Are you still in touch with her?'

'Yeah, I've been going over there to see her.' I blush, get past it. 'Anyway, I heard a rumour from Mrs Ramanathan that the community is being investigated by welfare, and there's a problem with the leasehold. I thought you might be able to find out for me?'

Cam shrugs. 'Why not? I might not be able to get much out of Mum, but I can be a bit sneaky about it.'

'That would be awesome, thank you.'

She squints at me. 'Your dad's taken off, but you're worried about Rory's hippie commune?'

'I'm worried for Rory,' I counter. 'Whatever affects the community, affects her. The atmosphere there is…kind of tense right now.'

I don't have words for the uneasiness I felt about Ray's talk last night, and Sally's announcement, and everyone's response. Explaining the situation out of context would make it sound darker and more ominous than it really is. I remember how Sprog reacted when I first tried to explain Rory's situation – I don't want Cam to make this into a big weirdo deal.

'Then sure,' Cam says. 'If it'll make you feel better, I'll try to get some info.'

'Cam, you're the best.'

'I'm glad you think so,' she says, grinning. 'It's all part of my plan to butter you up so you'll help with White Night.'

'No problem – I want to keep busy. Load me up.'

'Great.' Cam pulls a piece of paper out of her jeans pocket and unfolds it. The list of stuff on it is long enough to make me wince. Cam notices. 'Come on, Bo, don't wimp out on me now. Okay, here's what I was hoping you could do…'

22

'I'm being swamped. Seriously, I've got eighteen juniors who want to help out already, and it's only recess.' Lozzie looks harried.

'They know they can't come to the river shindig, though, right?' Sprog's hands are on his hips. 'I can't guarantee that people won't bring booze to the river, and I don't wanna get parents of junior kids offside.'

'No, it's cool,' Lozzie says. 'Only seniors are coming to the river, right, Bo?'

I nod. Sprog and Cam have worked out a plan to get everyone together at the river tomorrow night to gauge support for the fundraiser. 'We'll have most of the year on board by day's end, and Teo and Joel are talking to the Year Twelves.'

'Good,' Cam says. 'How's the speech going?'

'I told you, I'm not giving a speech,' Sprog says. His hands have dropped; he shoves them in his pockets. 'I'm just gonna, y'know, talk. Ask for a show of hands, maybe send around a sign-up sheet for people who'd like to help out if council gives us the green light.'

I flag Sprog's attention. 'Any word from them?'

'Not yet.' His brow furrows.

Cam puts an arm over his shoulders. 'You won't get a response in twenty-four hours. Come on, be realistic.'

'Yeah, I know.' Whether he's taking strength from the advice or the physical contact, Sprog's expression clears as he turns to me. 'Okay, what've we got next period?'

'Biol,' I say. 'Double.'

'Great. I can ask Phil Marcel about speakers.'

'And I've got AV kids to sweet-talk,' Lozzie says with a grin. She grabs her bag and takes off.

Sprog closes his eyes for a second, opens them. 'Am I doing this right? I've never done anything like this before. Am I fucking it up?'

Cam rounds on him. 'Dom, look at me. You're doing fine. The important thing is, you're giving it a shot. Like Bo said, at least you can say you put up a fight. That'll mean something, right?'

'Yeah.' He looks into her eyes. 'Yeah, it'll mean something.'

✳

By the afternoon, almost every senior has signed on to come to the river. The only downside is, I can't ask Rory to the party. On Mum's request, I cycle into town and check on Connor while he's at Under-10s footy training. Then I cycle back to do homework, check the Event page for the river party and send messages online, and eat dinner with Mum, because I don't like the idea of her sitting alone at home, picking over a plate of reheated lasagne.

But it means I don't get to see Rory. I've wished about a

hundred thousand times that she had better access to a phone. I'm still wishing it on Thursday, after footy training, but I know I'll have to ride over and see her if I want her to come tonight.

'She might not be keen, though, after her last river party experience.' I towel off, slide on my jocks and shorts, reach for the T-shirt in my locker.

Sprog shakes his head, and wet drops fly everywhere. Training was brutal tonight, although I've had some pats on the back from the boys – I think what Sprog said, about giving the rest of the team a chance to show off for the scout, has earned me some brownie points with the other players, if not from Mullet.

Sprog spent longer recovering in the shower than he probably should have. He's still got to run back to his place to pick up the sign-up sheets, which he forgot, and the trays of sausages in his fridge. Just quietly, I think he's hoping to get his hands on more of Curtis's booze as well, but I doubt he'll get as shit-faced tonight as he did at the last party. He's got too much to do.

'Mate, Rory'll come or she won't,' he says. 'Not much you can do about it. At least you can tell her that she's got people keen to see her, and they'll be keeping a close eye on Shandy and Todd.'

'True.'

'And the swing's still broken, so there's no danger there.'

'You are so full of lols.'

'I'm so full of *nerves*,' Sprog admits, his cheeks colouring as he scrapes at his wet hair. 'I hate public speaking. I always fail that shit in assessment.'

'Then don't think of it as public speaking. Imagine you're…mouthing off to Mr Small in English or something.'

'I guess that could work,' he muses, as he grabs for his jeans in his locker.

'*Dominic! Dom!*'

At the sound of his name, the familiar voice, he turns. In the act of pulling my shirt over my head, I spin around in time to see *Cam*, of all people, burst through the door of the change room.

The collective reaction to the presence of a girl inside the footy club change room is instantaneous: like a scurry of cockroaches when the light goes on, blokes dive for their clothes, hotfoot it back into the shower stalls. Almost everyone is semi-naked, including Sprog, who's standing, frozen to the spot, in a towel, when Cam barrels up to him.

'Dom, you did it!'

'What the hell are you—'

Cam slams into him for a hug. She's in her netball skirt, with her black hair loose, and a helluva lot of brown leg on display.

'Cam.' I yank my shirt fully on, tap her on the arm. 'Don't know if you're aware, but this is the *boys* change—'

'You *did it*!' Cam pulls back, cheeks flushed as she holds Sprog by the shoulders. 'Mum just rang me – the council has agreed to let us stage White Night!'

'What?' Sprog looks dazed. I'm not sure if it's the effect of the news or of Cam's hug. 'We got it?'

'He got it?' Even I'm shocked.

Cam goes on breathlessly. 'The council has said we can put on the fundraiser, and Mum has persuaded them to match what we make dollar for dollar! I ran over here as soon as I heard. Oh my god, this is *so amazing*!'

She flings her arms around Sprog, and for the first time, he seems to recover enough to actually hug her back. He looks at me over the top of her shoulder, as she jumps up and down in his arms. I wish I could bottle the expression on his face.

'I still can't believe it!' Cam is bouncing, she's so happy. 'Dominic, you bloody legend!'

Sprog clears his throat as he pulls back carefully. 'Whoa. Okay, I'm ... Wow.'

'That's fantastic news, Cam,' I say. 'Now it's time for the ladies to wait outside while Sprog gets his clothes on, yeah?'

'What?' Only now does Cam seem to realise that she's been hugging a large, wet guy dressed exclusively in a towel. 'Oh. Oh, goodness, I'm ...' She steps back, flaps her hands. 'Okay, I'll ... I'm just so happy! Ohmigod.' She crosses herself twice in succession, her face turning beetroot red.

'We'll see you outside in a sec,' I say, cos Sprog seems to be incapable of forming words.

'Right. Sure.' In spite of her embarrassment, Cam's smile is bigger than the moon. 'Okay. See you outside.'

When she skips out the change room door, blokes all over the room return to normal programming. Sprog is still standing there, staring after her as if he's been struck by lightning.

'You right there, mate?' I say, grinning.

'What?' He scrubs a hand over his face, through his hair. 'Clothes?'

'Clothes. Oh, yeah.' He spins around and grabs for his jeans, which have fallen on the floor.

'That's amazing news about the council.'

'Hm?' He pulls on his gear. 'Oh, yeah. Shit. Wow, huh?'

I shake my head. 'Mate, you'd better start kissing that girl soon, or you're gonna do something like accidentally walk in front of a bus.'

He flushes, tugs his T-shirt out of his locker. 'I'm not that bad yet.'

'You're getting there.'

Cam is waiting near the car park when we finally make it out, talking to Lozzie on the phone. She disconnects as we come closer, and the three of us head towards Trout Street, with me wheeling the Cannondale.

'It'll be all over town by the end of tonight,' Cam says. 'Will you guys be at the river before seven?'

'I'm going to Eden first, to see if Rory wants to come.'

Sprog nods in the direction of Trout Street. 'I've gotta go home for a sec, then I'll probably hitch. Bo, can you come with me and give me a hand with the stuff for tonight? I swear I won't hold you up.'

'Sure.'

As we walk, we talk about all the things we need to organise for White Night in the next week – tonight is going to be the clincher. Sprog will be asking people to help with stage set-up, and Loz will collect gold-coin donations towards the cost of the insurance. But the beauty of the event, Cam explains, is that everyone's enthusiastic. We've all been talking about it at school so much that most of the players are already on board. People really *want* the skate park restored, and now they can do something to make it happen.

'This is gonna be big,' Sprog says, as we reach Trout. He's

looking towards his house like a guy who's not really seeing much except the things in his head.

Cam nudges Sprog's arm. 'Stop worrying. You've got a whole school full of people ready to help. You've *got this*, Dom.'

'Right.' He takes a deep breath, exhales.

'Do you need a ride?' Cam asks him. 'I was going to get Mum to drive me and Loz.'

'Nah, I don't mind hitching. There'll be loads of people heading that way.'

'We might see you on the road. We'll stop for you, yeah?' Cam says. She and Sprog exchange looks that I feel embarrassed to even be observing.

'Sure, that'd be ace,' Sprog manages to get out.

We leave Cam – reluctantly, on Sprog's part – and walk towards his house. Talking about White Night has got my blood moving. And I reckon Sprog's excited, too, despite his anxieties. His eyes rove the street as he talks market stalls, the AV displays Lindsay and her mates want to set up.

'We need to ask local shopkeepers if they'll agree to stay open until midnight,' he says. 'And we need to sort out sound equipment.'

'Yeah, but after tonight, you'll have a team to help.'

'I'm still shocked the council said yes, to tell you the truth. I never figured they'd listen to a teenager.'

'Why wouldn't they?' I lean the Cannondale against the hurricane fence near the Hamiltons' gate and we walk through the front yard.

Sprog shrugs as we go up the porch steps. 'I dunno. I mean, who the hell am I? Just a local footy boofhead. I'm a nobody.'

Before I can open my mouth to object, the flywire door of the house practically flies off its hinges as it slams outward.

'*Didja just say you're a nobody?*' Curtis Hamilton looms large in the doorway. 'Too right you're a nobody, you little *SHIT*.'

Curtis swings, and Sprog stumbles back, clipping me as he goes. His brother's punch sends him tumbling down the steps. I fall to the side, smack onto the floorboards of the porch, winded and gasping.

Sprog lifts his head, his nose streaming blood. 'Curtis—'

'*You little cockhead!*' Curtis looks demented, his face red with fury as he strides down the steps and grabs Sprog off the dry grass. He holds his younger brother's T-shirt in a throttle-grip. '*You* told them I belted Heather? You'd rat out *your own fuckin' brother?*'

'*Lemme go!* Curtis!' Sprog wards off his brother with both hands, half-glazed eyes spinning wild.

'I'm gonna fuckin' *END* you!' Spit flies out of Curtis's mouth as he pulls his fist back to hit Sprog again. Cowering, Sprog turns his head, and the blow glances off his skull.

Curtis raises his fist again and the paralysis that's descended on me suddenly disappears.

I vault off the porch and jump onto Curtis's back. '*No!* He's your *brother*—'

Curtis roars like an animal, throws me off, rounds again on Sprog, who's scrabbling desperately towards the gate on hands and knees. Curtis crosses the distance in two long steps, kicks Sprog viciously in the side. Sprog flies back against the fence. His skull connects with the fence pole with a sickening clunk.

'*STOP!*' My head is spinning as I pull myself up off the grass. '*Curtis*, stop! *You'll fucking kill him!*'

This finally seems to penetrate Curtis's blood-red state of mind. He looks up, looks around. Two people in the street have witnessed the scene in the Hamiltons' front yard. I think I recognise Justin Fromer's sister, Breanna, break for her house at a run.

Sprog is lying against the fence in a bloody sprawl. Breathing hard, Curtis steps in and grips his brother's shirt again. '*Get the fuck out of my sight.* You come back to the house and I'll rip your fuckin' head off, to hell with the cops.'

Then he releases Sprog, spits on the ground, and stalks back inside.

23

I'm already running for Sprog. I roll him over, frantically searching for signs of life.

"M fine.' His eyes are fully glazed now. ''S okay, 's all right...'

I think he's in shock. Blood is trailing all over his face from the nosebleed he got with that first punch. He tries to get up, lurches, falls back onto all fours.

'Stay still, man.' I try to check the red torrent gushing from the back of Sprog's head. His shirt is already covered in it. 'Ah, shit—'

''S okay,' he rasps. Leaning on me, he manages to pull himself upright. 'I gotta... We gotta...'

Too much is happening too fast: Sprog's weight falling against me, Curtis still raging in the house, the street spinning in my vision, the late afternoon sky all over the place, too blue, too high. We've got to get out of here. Curtis could come back for a second attack at any time.

I manhandle Sprog out the gate. My bike's been knocked on its side from the collision of Sprog's body against the fence.

I need to get my shirt off, put it against his head wound, but he's too heavy.

'Jesus. Bo, put him down for a sec.' Breanna Fromer is suddenly here – denim mini, Havaianas slapping the pavement – and I'm incredibly glad to see her. She's got a tea towel in one hand. 'Use this.'

I grab the tea towel as I ease Sprog to the ground, lean him back against the fence. I press the folded towel onto the wound above his nape, my blood-sticky fingers trembling.

'Baz is bringing the ute down.' She's talking about her eldest brother, Barry.

'Christ.' I smear my sweaty, throbbing forehead against my shoulder, press the tea towel more firmly as Sprog groans. 'We can't stay here. Shit. We've gotta move.'

'Yeah, let's get him outta Curtis's way,' Breanna says, before jumping up to wave into the street. A white ute pulls up at the kerb and she yanks the passenger door open. 'Baz, he can't really walk.'

I'm concentrating on Sprog. His eyes are open, and some awareness seems to be returning. He lifts a shaking hand, tries to touch the back of his head.

'Get him up.' Barry Fromer appears on Sprog's other side. He's nineteen, with the same dark hair as Breanna and Justin. 'Here you go, mate. Let's get you up. That's it.'

Sprog sways dangerously when he's pulled to his feet. We all work together to wrangle him into the passenger seat of the ute. I hold him in place with one hand, propping the door with my shoulder.

'My bike—'

'Got it.' Barry hoists the Cannondale, settles it into the

tray. 'Brea, get home. If you see Curtis in the street, stay out of his way. I'll text, okay?'

'Breanna, thank you,' I say.

She shakes her head. 'Shit, don't worry about it. Let me know if Sprog's okay.'

With a last worried frown, she takes off back to her place, and I bundle into the cab of the ute. Sprog sits in the middle of the bench seat; he looks as if he's turned to marble, he's that white. The tea towel has dropped to his shoulders. I press it back into place, as Barry jumps into the driver's side.

'He right?' Barry puts the ute in gear, glancing at Sprog. 'Make it to the hospital, y'reckon?'

Sprog seems to come back to life at that, although his voice is barely a mumble. 'Not the hospital. Not the—'

'Sprog, you've had a knock on the head, mate.'

'Hospital'd be best,' Barry agrees, as the ute heads down Trout.

'No.' Sprog is becoming more animated. He bats at my hand holding the tea towel. 'Mum was there. The cops already know about Curtis.'

'He whaled on your mum? That's how she ended up in hospital?'

Sprog says nothing, just closes his eyes tight, head down.

'And now he's whaled on you. But you don't want to report it, even though you need medical attention. Well, that's fantastic.'

'Do you *want* my brother to get arrested?' Sprog looks up. His eyes are bloodshot, but his face is set. 'If I show up at the hospital like this, they'll make another report.'

'*Fuck* Curtis!' My anger spills over the sides. 'He fucking *deserves* to get arrested!'

'No,' Sprog says. He looks decided.

Me and Barry exchange glances over Sprog's shoulder. Barry shrugs – *what can you do?* Family's family.

I sigh. 'Well, shit. Where then? No hospital, and you can't go home. Better come back to mine.'

The trip doesn't take long. At the bottom of the driveway, Barry pulls the ute over to idle, gets my bike out of the tray while I help Sprog out of the cab.

'Thanks, man. We owe you.' I'd clap Barry on the shoulder, but I'm still propping Sprog up.

'Forget about it.' Barry stands my bike against the stump holding our letterbox, nods at Sprog. 'Just patch him up so we can get that White Night shit happening, yeah? It's all Juz and Brea have been talking about.'

He grins and takes off, so now it's just me and Sprog standing at the bottom of the driveway as the sun starts to fade. Sprog presses the tea towel to his head. I steady him with my arm. 'Hey, come on. Nearly there.'

His face is pasty, the smeared blood trails like a gory mask. A rapidly blackening bruise is developing on his forehead. I worry that he's going to spew. If he throws up, he might not go the distance.

But he makes it. I help him climb the stairs, as Julie goes off her nut, then I'm turning the doorknob, pushing Julie out of the way, and we're inside.

Sprog leans into me, his voice low. 'Don't say nothing to your mum, I don't wanna—'

'*Mum!*' I call.

Sprog hisses. 'Fucking hell, Bo.'

'I'm not *not* gonna tell her, am I?' I look at him. 'Come on, man, seriously.'

'She doesn't need—'

'She's fine. Mum!'

'So much yelling,' Mum says, coming into the kitchen. Her expression changes when she sees Sprog. She moves pretty fast for someone carrying around about ten extra kilos of baby in front. 'Dominic, what happened?'

'It was his brother,' I say, ignoring Sprog's glare.

Mum grabs the tea towel, presses it more firmly to Sprog's head, lifts his chin to examine his face. 'Let's sit him at the table. Fetch me some towels, and the big torch from under the sink.'

While I grab all of these things, Mum settles Sprog into a chair.

'Bo, I'll need you to hold the torch, but get Dominic a drink of water first.' When the water arrives, she pushes the glass into Sprog's hand. 'Sip slowly.' Sprog's sips turn into gulps, and she stills him. '*Slowly.*'

'I'm fine, Mrs M,' Sprog says, but his voice is rough, grateful.

'You will be,' Mum says. 'Let me have a look at this.'

As Sprog leans over his forearms on the table, Mum shows me where to direct the torchlight. She examines the cut: it's nasty, but clearly not fatal. I fetch a bowl of warm water and a clean cloth, the medical kit. Mum's been patching up me and Connor since we were both big enough to get into strife, and Dad before that. She'll defer to the hospital for breaks and infections, but she's otherwise pretty good with emergency first aid.

'I don't think it's too deep,' she says, frowning. 'You've bled a lot, but head wounds do that. I think it'll be all right with some butterfly closures. But are you sure you don't want to see a doctor?'

Sprog wets his lips. 'If I go to the hospital, I'll get Curtis in big sh—' He cuts himself off, amends quickly. '—trouble. So I guess we gotta fix it here.'

Mum's eyebrows lift. 'I can't say the thought of Curtis getting into trouble bothers me, but it's your call.'

While the patching-up is underway, I go out on the verandah and call Cam. The first thing I have to do is calm her down. 'He's not dying, Cam. He took a bad knock, but he's okay.'

She makes an effort to settle her voice. 'Have you asked him about tonight? Does he want to cancel?'

'I think it might be too late for that.' I check inside through the glass doors: Mum has finished the cleaning and disinfecting, started on the taping. 'But we might need a ride from my place. Can you set that up?'

'Oh my god, yes, of course. Are you sure he'll be okay?'

I grimace. 'Once we get him cleaned up, I think he'll be all right. We'll just have to look after him.'

When I go back inside, Mum's finished sorting out the cut.

'Give him a couple of paracetamol, Bo,' Mum says. 'And he'll need a sweatshirt to get changed into. I'll make you a cuppa while you have a shower, Dom. You should go get washed up. Actually, Bo, could you take him to the bathroom? I don't want him walking around on his own right this minute.'

Sprog doesn't shrug me off when I help him stand up. We walk slowly to the bathroom.

'You never told me about your mum and Curtis,' I say softly.

'I forgot about them.' Sprog's voice is raspy.

'What?'

'I forgot about Mum and Curtis.' He stands in front of the bathroom mirror, looking at his bloodstained reflection. 'It was like, when I was thinking about the skate park stuff, all the organising and the council, I kinda forgot my family even existed. That's why Curtis surprised me, back at the house. I been so preoccupied, I didn't even think about him being there.'

I spin the shower taps, pat him on the shoulder. 'It's okay, mate.'

'It's like I thought the rest of the world had disappeared while I was busy.' He meets my eyes in the mirror. 'But they're still there. My mum, and my brother. They haven't gone away.'

The bathroom is filling with steam. Sprog looks defeated. It unnerves me, seeing him like this.

I push him gently towards the shower. 'Water's running. Have a shower and you'll feel better.'

'Yeah, okay.' He doesn't sound convinced.

Later, I sit on the kitchen bench while Sprog drinks his cuppa and we both wait for Cam. Sprog's wearing one of my hoodies; it pulls a bit across his shoulders, but at least it's clean. His jeans are the ones he had on before and his hair is still damp from the shower. He seems relieved to have all the dust and blood off his face. No way to get rid of the bruises, though.

I don't want to make a big deal about it. 'You've come up all right after a drench.'

'Yeah, cheers,' Sprog says. I don't think he wants to make a big deal about it either.

A car horn sounds outside – Cam's here. I ease off the kitchen bench and walk into the bedroom, where Mum is propped under the covers, her tablet balanced on her tummy.

'Our ride's here. Don't wait up – I'm not sure what time this will finish, I'll text and let you know. And thanks for helping out with Sprog.'

She puts her tablet on the nightstand. 'Has he got somewhere safe to go? If he hasn't, you should bring him back here after the party.'

I nod, kiss her on the cheek before leaving. 'I'll see what he says. If you wake up tomorrow and find Sprog on the couch, don't be surprised, okay?'

My concern that Cam would turn this into a melodrama is unfounded. She swaps seats with Lozzie, though, so she can get in the back with me and Sprog. 'We've got extra sausages – Mum stopped and got a meat tray from the supermarket on the way here. And I've reprinted the sign-up sheets, so don't worry about that either.' She presses her lips together, looking at Sprog as she buckles her seatbelt. 'Are you all right?'

'I'm good,' Sprog says.

Cam does a scan of his face, taking in the bruise, and the dressing at his nape. She swallows, looks away. 'Okay.'

From the driver's seat Lena D'Amato eyes Loz and then the rest of us in her rear-view mirror. 'Belts, please. Dominic, congratulations on the council approval. You're doing a worthwhile thing.'

'Thanks, Mrs D'Amato,' Sprog says quietly, looking out the window.

The trip to the Harvey property threatens to be mournfully silent, but Lozzie takes over, going through the plans for tonight, drawing us all into talk about White Night options, cracking the odd joke. Sprog starts to loosen up a bit. He still pauses in too many moments, his face brooding, but we all work to fill the gaps. When we get to the river, people have started gathering. The bonfire is already alight, and a few brave souls are actually swimming.

'I'm going to drop you here,' Lena says. 'Camilla, text me a half-hour before you want me to pick you up.'

We thank her and pile out. Sprog walks over to Justin and Breanna Fromer, who've obviously done a sneaky drive – Justin's only on his Ls – in Barry's ute to get here. Sprog must want to say thanks to Brea.

Loz turns to me. 'Jesus, he looks wrecked.'

I sigh. 'Yeah, he's a bit wrecked. And he can't go home. I can put him up for—'

'He can stay at ours.' Cam's watching Sprog talk to the Fromers. Her chin is lifted, her colour high. 'I already asked Mum about it.'

'So what are we supposed to say to him?' Lozzie asks.

I rub a hand through my hair. 'I dunno. Say nothing. Act like, y'know, everything's normal. But just be a little kinder.'

Regardless of how Sprog or the rest of us are travelling, the party itself seems to be going well. Joel has taken command of the barbecue again, and folks are having a good time. There don't seem to be any junior kids here, which is a relief, cos I've had enough dramas for one night. The only person missing is Rory. I never got the chance to ride over to Eden and invite her. I have a feeling she'd understand.

But Sprog's got to make a speech to the gathered masses sometime in the next thirty minutes, and he's not exactly bursting with good cheer. Pushing past a knot of kids near the blaring dock, I search for him in the crowd, finally spot him on the far side of the gathering.

In a quiet corner, where all the cars are parked, he's nursing a beer and looking at his reflection in one of the car windows. It's Barry's ute, the same one that carried Sprog over to my place after the fight. It's hard to make out Sprog's expression from this distance, but the way he leans towards the glass and examines the bruise on his forehead speaks volumes.

I should go over and say something. The attack was a crap thing to happen, and now it's over – he should give himself permission to let it go. I don't want him to still be carrying around that melancholy feeling he had back at my place.

There's a splash from the river, and I glance away from Sprog. When I look back, ready to march over to him, I get a shock.

Cam is walking up behind Sprog. She takes his beer out of his hand and puts it on the bonnet of the ute, her lips moving as she talks. I have no idea what she's saying to him, and quite frankly, I wouldn't want to know – that shit is private – but Sprog's looking away. Cam reaches up mid-monologue, brings his face around. She slides her hand further to touch the bandage at his neck, and her fingers linger there.

Which is when Sprog seems to crack.

He reaches out and puts his hands on Cam's hips. They both go still. Their stillness reminds me of the way possums freeze in place when you startle them. For a moment, they stand there, staring at each other.

Then Sprog pushes Cam firmly, walking her backwards; he is guiding them both. A few short steps and they're safe in the shadowed area between Barry's ute and another four-wheel drive. Cam's arms slowly curl around Sprog's neck. His head dips in darkness, their faces come together—

'I guess Sprog's getting a pep talk, then.' Lozzie has crept up on my other side.

I flush, look away. 'Crazy timing.'

'*Perfect* timing. He's going to give the speech of his life. And also, come on, *thank god*. I was starting to think they'd never get their act together.'

I laugh. 'Blossom, I swear, you are the most sarcastic, hard-arsed—'

'Talented, beautiful—'

'I honestly don't know why I'm still friends with you.'

'Cos you adore me?' Loz clasps her hands together under her chin, bats her eyelashes.

'Ask you a question?'

'Shoot.'

'Does it bother you that I'm going out with Rory?'

She drops her hands. 'Well, considering neither of you actually leave the Eden property, I don't know if it can be technically termed "going out", so—'

'Seriously.'

Loz pouts. 'It doesn't bother me that you're going out with Rory.'

I feel lighter. 'Good.'

'It bothers me that Rory's going out with *you*.' She glances away, then shrugs. 'She's cute.'

My mouth opens. 'What? Really?'

271

Lozzie nods, looking bashful.

'Since when?' When she shrugs again, I have to control my smile. 'Wow. Okay.'

'Stop smiling!'

'I can't help it!' I raise my hands when she starts whacking me. 'Okay, okay. Cam knows?'

'For ages.' She bites her lip. 'I wasn't sure how you'd take it. I was worried you'd think, y'know, that dating you had put me off guys or something.'

'Did it?'

'No, of course not, dork. It did help me work a few things out, though.' She leans forwards and pecks me on the cheek. Then her eyes stray sideways, and she tugs on my sleeve. 'Oh – it's happening.'

Sprog has emerged from behind Barry's ute, with Cam beside him. He strides towards the group of people around the dock, pushes through and flips the music off. Lozzie clutches my sleeve, grinning.

Without preamble, Sprog jumps up onto the tray of Teo's Hilux and lifts his hands. '*Yo! People!*'

Everyone looks up. Sprog stands there in his borrowed hoodie and scuffed jeans. His hangdog expression and his self-consciousness about the bruises on his face seem to have disappeared. Cam is beaming at him.

'Folks, this afternoon we got council approval to stage White Night.' The whole gathering breaks into cheers, clapping and whistles. Sprog waits for it to quiet – he looks relaxed, and his voice is clear and strong. 'The event will be raising funds to rebuild the skate park, which goes under in nine days' time.'

Mass groaning. Sprog nods, palms raised.

'I know, I know – I feel ya. But we're gonna make sure Lamistead has a place for us. It's gonna take a lot of work to make White Night happen, and we need your help. So…who's with me?'

Hands and fists are thrust high into the night, and the cheer that goes up then is deafening.

24

'Okay. I've decided. I'm gonna change to Food Tech.'

Mrs Ram eyes me like I'm from outer space, and possibly explosive. 'Are you sure?'

I slump. 'Shit. Sorry, I mean – no. I'm not sure. Not a hundred per cent.'

'So how did you arrive at your decision?'

'I dunno, hey.' I rub a fist against my stomach, glance at the floor. 'It's just a gut feeling. That's all I've got.'

Mrs Ram smiles. 'You are following your gut into cooking. There's a certain poetic irony in that.'

'Well, I'm glad you think it's funny.' My mouth twists like I bit on something sour. Hey, this is only my *life*. That's always good for a laugh.

'Calm down, Bo.' Mrs Ram's amusement shakes free. 'I am not laughing at you – I'm happy. This is a good choice, I know it. You are feeling unsure because you are at a junction, and there is no way to see what lies at the end of this road you've chosen. But in my own experience, trusting your instinct is never a bad thing.' Her expression switches gear as she looks over my shoulder at the students flowing into the classroom. 'Ah, we are out of time. I will collect the paperwork and get it back to you for your signature, all right, Bo?'

'Yes, miss.'

'Excellent. And I'd like to hear how you are going with that other situation we discussed, but it will have to wait. Class is about to start.' She claps her hands as she stands and steps away from the desk. 'Good morning, everyone, please take your places quickly, we have a lot to cover today.'

People are still on a high from last night – Sprog receives a lot of back-pats and thumbs-up gestures from people as he walks in with Cam. They take seats near the front. Cam's not into PDA, so there's no hand-holding or smooching. The only visible indication that something has changed is that Sprog is sitting beside Cam, when he'd normally sit closer to the back. There's also the expression on his face, of course. His bruise has flowered into a sensational purple mess, and it doesn't seem to bother him in the slightest.

I slide in on the other side of Cam. 'Did we get final numbers?'

'Donations totalled two hundred and seventy-nine dollars and sixty-five cents.' Cam settles her notebook on her desk. 'That'll cover the insurance, and give us a bit to help pay for extra expenses.'

'Who put in the sixty-five cents?'

'That was me,' Sprog admits. 'It was all I had on me.'

Mrs Ramanathan calls for attention. 'Miss Thomas, Miss Woodliffe, please sit down…' She walks around to the front of the desk and props herself on the edge of it. 'Thank you. Today we are continuing the unit on political systems, focusing on social movements. Grassroots community movements and political action are a critical part of the development of any society. You should remember Charles Tilly, who said that social movements play a critical role in the way citizens engage in public politics. And I understand many of you have already begun participating in grassroots community action...'

She arches an eyebrow at Sprog, whose confused face becomes comprehending. He grins around the classroom, accepts a fist bump from Nikki.

'Yes.' Mrs Ram nods. 'This is how it starts. Change comes when ordinary people decide to take action – to right a wrong, to resist an injustice, to defend a truth. But first you must recognise wrong and injustice and truth when you see it. The ability to make ethical choices comes from within you.' She looks right at me, continues on. 'The opportunity to enact change comes from social and political movements. And the society that emerges from this is the combination of many ordinary people speaking with multiple – but unified – voices.'

She scans the room, commanding every eye.

'*You* are those voices. *You* are the future of this society. That is why this is important. And that is why we study it in this class.'

✳

Friday night, I hung out with Mum at home. I was desperate to see Rory, but Mum was low, and lonely, so I stuck around. We watched two episodes of some show that I would never usually watch voluntarily. Then Mum started crying when the woman on the show got separated from the guy she was hot for, so I switched off the TV and sat down beside her on the couch.

'Oh god, I can't watch this stuff anymore. I'm too hormonal!' Mum wailed, pulling another tissue from the box I'd brought over. I let her cry on my shoulder for a minute, before passing her a glass of water.

'I'm sorry.' She sniffed. 'I don't like to do this to you…'

'But you miss Dad.' I patted her on the back gently.

'Of course I miss him.' Mum blew her nose. 'That doesn't mean I'm not angry with him.' She saw my face. 'What, did you think love was easy? It's not like it is on TV. Love can be bloody hard work, and we're working our guts out at the moment.'

'Have you been in touch with Dad?' My voice was quiet.

'Yes.' Mum straightened, sipped her water and handed it back to me. 'Lily Pettifer… She died, Bo. So your father is staying for the funeral. I'm waiting to hear sometime in the next few days about when he's coming home.'

I was sorry to hear about Lily, although her death didn't have a lot of meaning for me. Dad was staying for the funeral, then coming home – even that meagre news was something. But I didn't want to get too lit up about it. Trusting Dad again would be a bit premature.

I nodded at my knee before looking at Mum. 'Okay. But can you do something for me? Can you ring the Roscoes and get Connor home? It's not right that he's with another family. It feels like… like we're falling to pieces.'

Mum stared at me. 'It really bothers you? Having Connor staying elsewhere?'

'Yeah, it bothers me.'

'All right.' Mum brushed my hair off my face. 'I'll get Connor home. We should all be together. A unit.'

Saturday morning was footy – Sprog didn't rock up at all, which I think was on Mrs D'Amato's insistence, cos of his knock on the head. Cam said her mum was fussing over Sprog a bit, but that he didn't seem to mind. Considering he's been staying in the D'Amatos' spare room, with the opportunity to see Cam in her PJs at breakfast every morning, I can see why a bit of fussing wouldn't worry him.

He was a loss at footy – we nearly got our arses handed to us by Tarrakan in the re-match, and only Joel managed to save the day. Mullet got stuck into me for lacking focus, but my head was too wired. News about Dad, Connor coming back, changing my subjects, thoughts of Rory ... I was actually giving myself props for concentrating on the game at all.

After the game, I pulled Mullet aside and had a quiet word.

'You don't want to go up for the rep squad?' He seemed flabbergasted.

'I'll play as long as you'll let me. But I'm not looking to get scouted.' I remembered what Rory said to me about it, and tried to let him down gently. 'I still love footy, hey, but I've got more than one talent. I wanna see where it'll take me.'

'Well, good luck to you, Bo. And if you ever change your mind ...' He shook my hand. 'We'll still see you on the ground next weekend, though, right?'

I grinned. 'For sure.'

I spent the afternoon making a really nice dinner, in anticipation of Connor coming home – Mum said we should all eat together. 'A unit!' she reminded me, and I couldn't very well say, *Thanks but I wanna go see my girlfriend*, after I'd given her the big 'family values' speech. So I focused on the flour, herbs, shortening...rolling out the pastry...the aroma of the lamb-chickpea-ricotta mix...chopping and slicing for the salad. Simple food, simply made, but it was enough to calm my brain, the routines of cooking somehow always more than just momentarily soothing.

The cooking settled me, but seeing my brother get out of the car was even better.

'*Bo!*' Connor swooped up the stairs and jumped for me to catch him.

Luckily, I did. 'Oh my god, you've turned giant, mate. What has Garrett's mum been feeding you, hey?'

'Ice cream,' Connor said, grinning.

'Right,' Mum said, as she clambered up the last stair. 'Come and have some real food, then. Bo's put on a spread.' She checked my face. 'What is it?'

'Nothing.'

'No, there's something.' Her eyes narrowed. 'When was the last time you saw Rory?'

'Last Monday.' I cleared my throat. 'Mum, I know it's gonna be late by the time we finish dinner, but I was hoping—'

'Yes.'

'What?'

'I said, *yes*. You should go see her.' She squeezed me on the shoulder. 'I'm sure it must be difficult when you can't call.'

'It's a *nightmare*,' I said fervently.

'Then go. I mean, eat dinner with us first, but then you should get out of here.' She grinned. 'I'll get Connor to help me with the washing up.'

'Not the washing up!' Connor groaned.

I remember the dinner. The food worked out pretty good, and Connor was in great form, and Mum seemed more relaxed and happy than she'd been for ages, but after that my whole awareness started to narrow to *leaving soon, leaving soon*, and I could only think about one thing.

Now it's eight-thirty, and I'm on Bowyer Track, my bike light flaring on the scrub, arms pulling at the handlebars of the Cannondale like I'm coaxing the reins of a horse. Legs straining, lungs working, my whole body tingling. I'm going to see Rory. God knows, it could all go to hell – I could show up to find her still pissed at me from the argument, or angry at me for not coming earlier in the week – but something is fiery in my blood, something that was warm and soft is now urgent.

I take the crest of the hill and ride past the gate – curiously unstaffed, given that Ray's supposed to have people posted for security detail. The light from the Meeting House draws me, and I drop my bike near a patch of comfrey and walk on, pushing branches and leaves aside. It's not until I get within earshot of the house that I feel unsure, because I can hear Ray's voice, mid-speech.

'…not the time to back down,' he says. 'We have to fight to make a difference, we have to do something radical.'

Someone interjects, but so quietly I can't hear.

Ray's reply is scathing. 'You really believe that? They don't care about *us*, they don't care about the welfare of our children. They don't even care about their own welfare, or they wouldn't be doing these things to the planet we're living on.' His words calm. 'All we've asked, all we've *ever* asked, is to be left alone. To live life our way, by *our* rules, not the rules some government or corporation has imposed on us. To exist the way Nature prefers – the way we, as individuals and as a community, prefer. The way that's best for the planet. But they can't seem to stop interfering.'

Another quiet response.

'Right here, right now,' Ray says. 'I'm asking you to consider a choice. If we stand together in this, there's no way they can ignore us, there's no way they can change our minds, or misinterpret our message.'

I know I'm walking in on a dialogue that I can't understand out of context, but again I experience that strange sense of unease. The atmosphere in Eden is dreamlike in this leafy darkness. It's like having vertigo. I look away from the light ahead, blink at the path at my feet, to get my bearings.

Closer to the Meeting House, I realise that everyone in the community is gathered for the meal and Meeting like normal. The fire illuminates figures, faces. Ray is standing – he holds up his mug and pours a dollop of ginger beer out of the brown bottle, in a kind of demonstration.

'Not tonight, but another night to come.' He glances around the circle. 'Who's with me?'

They're Sprog's words, repeated back here, but under very different circumstances. It gives me a shiver. Everyone around the circle raises their own mugs. It looks like they're toasting Ray, or each other, but nobody looks festive. Ilona looks grim. Kell and Allison seem confused. Star's expression is uncertain, and Stuart seems to have turned to granite. Virginia and Jules are nodding, looking at each other. Only Sally appears calm.

281

When Ray drinks, they all drink as one. Rory's hand falters: she's staring at her lap. Her mug is thrust out, her hand trembling.

'Aurora,' Ray says softly. 'Come on, sweetheart.'

As Rory lifts the mug to her lips, I finally make it to the stairs, break into the light.

Stuart clears his throat. 'Hey, Bo – welcome back.'

'Bo!' Rory looks up, then she dumps her mug on the floor and races over. She slams into me, and I'm enveloped in warm girl.

'Man, it's good to see you.' I lift her chin. 'You okay?'

'All good,' she whispers. 'Come on, let's go.'

'Aurora …' Ray calls.

Rory tugs my hand, doesn't turn around to her dad when she replies. 'Meeting's over. G'night, everyone!'

She seems to be in a major hurry to get me out of the Meeting House and down the path to her place. Her grip on my fingers is tight, insistent, drawing me on. I'm only now registering what she's wearing: the grey woollen jumper, her cut-off overalls, her leg warmers. Her face is flushed from sitting close to the fire and her skin is dewy. Her hug is still imprinted on my body.

'Rory, I'm seriously sorry. For the argument, for being away so—'

'No, it's all right, really. I'm sorry, too. And I'm glad you're okay.' She whacks low-hanging creepers aside as we barrel along. 'I wasn't worried – I mean, I was worried about you, but not that you'd—'

'You don't need to be worried I won't come over. I'd never—'

'I know, it's fine. It was just a heavy Meeting, and I'm—'
She blows out air, like she's been running. 'Anyway, it's done.
And I'm so glad you're here. I've been wondering what's
going on with you and your family, and Cam and Sprog and
Lozzie, and—'

Her words fall over the top of each other, and I grab her
other hand. 'Hey, slow down.'

She stops, catches her breath. 'I've missed you.'

'I've missed you too.' I smile in the shadows of the path.
She's here, right in front of me. I can smell her scent, mixed
with the perfume of night jasmine nearby.

'Come on,' she whispers, and when she leads I follow,
helpless.

Her hut is close; there's a tiny candle in a jar propped on
the windowsill outside, making the approach seem friendly.
I spot another jar twinkling in the garden, near the couch,
and I squeeze Rory's fingers. She marches for the door.

'Hey, you don't wanna sit outside and relax in the—'

'It's warmer inside,' she says, and I have to admit, it's
definitely cosier in the hut, with the range banked and soft
candlelight spreading from the window to the bower of
furnishings in the room. Rory pushes the door shut. 'Now we
won't have any interruptions.'

I grin. 'Right, cos when everyone leaves Meeting, they'll
be—'

'I don't wanna talk about Meeting,' Rory says, and she
shoves me against the dresser and kisses me.

This is not a peck, this is not a brush of cool lips – this is
jet fuel. The whole world pinpoints down to *kissing* and *Rory*
and *kissing* and *wet* and my eyes snap shut. Rory's mouth and

hands fix me in place, and a sudden *whoomp* of detonation goes off throughout my entire body. Everything turns hot and rich and immediate.

My arms go up instinctively, squeeze hard – too hard. Rory makes a noise into my mouth. I pull back, breathless. 'God. Sorry. I didn't—'

'You didn't,' Rory gasps, and pulls me down again.

Her lips are so *soft*. There's not a single nerve in my body that isn't stretched taut. We kiss for a long time, pressing and kneading, and I hear myself groan.

Rory's eyes are glassy. 'Is this okay?'

'Yes.' I draw on her bottom lip again and again. 'Yes. Yes.'

She laughs softly. 'That's pretty definitive.'

'I have definitively wanted to kiss you for a definitively long time.'

'Bo …' She wraps her arms around me, hugs me tight.

'You're shaking.' I rub my cheek against hers. 'Did something happen tonight? At Meeting?'

'No talking about Meeting.'

'I can hug you as long as you need me to.'

That makes her squeeze tighter.

When she eases back, her hair is a golden corona, and her cheeks are pink in the candlelight. Her nose-stud is a tiny black-green spark. She looks at me, leans back and tugs her jumper off, over her head. Then she reaches up and touches a finger to my lips. Slides her finger across to the line of my jaw, and in an instant, it's like I'm inside the candle flame.

I lean and brush my lips against hers. *Soft, soft, soft*. I trail my hand up her back, down her side to her thigh, reach the elastic of her leg warmers and slide my fingers under the wool.

It's so much like my fantasies that even as I'm doing it, I have to remind myself that this is *real*, this is really happening.

Rory quivers.

I kiss her again. 'It's all right. We're not in a hurry.'

'We're not?'

My blood accelerates, and I have to focus. 'We're not.'

I kiss behind her ear. She gasps, and I could do this forever – hear her make these sounds, watch her expressions change as her head falls back. I could do it all night.

She clutches the front of my shirt. 'I think I need to sit down.'

We go to her bed, lie on the nest of blankets. She presses her forehead against mine. 'I've fooled around before. But I've never—'

'Me neither.'

'I don't know why I feel shy.'

'It doesn't matter.'

We kiss some more, and it's warm, luxurious. I find her leg warmers with my fingers again. It's like I'm so close to her now that we're feeling in unison; I can tell all the places on her body that she wants me to touch, and where she wants me to touch next.

'I like the touching,' she whispers.

'It feels good, touching you.'

She smiles with her eyes closed. 'Then keep going.'

It rains in the night. I wake up and hear a faint patter blending with the sound of the trees murmuring outside. I don't know what time it is; the light inside the room is dim and pink. Rory stirs beside me.

'Is that rain?' Her voice is soft, her head cocked to one side.

I listen. 'Yeah.'

We lie there, cuddling, then Rory drops back off to sleep. For a moment, it seems bizarre, that I'm lying here in a girl's room listening to the gentle rain outside, not scoping for the sound of parental footsteps but just lying here, completely relaxed.

I could stay here like this. I could be happy. We've created a little oasis here, in this moment. Soon we'll have to move, go outside our protective bubble into the larger world, but right now, we're self-sustaining.

Suddenly I understand the appeal of a place like Eden. I'm still thinking that when I fade back into sleep.

When I wake up again, the room is lighter, and Rory is standing by the range, wrapped in a crocheted blanket.

'Hey.' She smiles, sleep-tousled, and passes me a mug. 'Here – regular tea and milk.'

She looks adorable with her hair all mussed like that. I blow on my tea, put it on the log stump-nightstand to pull on my shirt. 'You sleep okay?'

'God, yes. I actually slept in.' She settles her own mug next to mine. 'One sec.'

She goes out the back door of the house, maybe to pee. I pick up my tea and sip, look out the window. The world is glittering after the rain. Sun is sprinkled over the green, and a cobweb in the vine archway outside is lit up like a diamond waterfall.

I see movement further away. Ray Carl is heading for the river with a little pail in his hand. He's shirtless and barefoot, with an old towel wrapped around his waist, and probably bare-arse naked underneath. He's got the tanned stringy muscle that comes with hard work, and his flat stomach reminds me of the guys from senior footy, only they all lift weights to get a sixpack, and Ray is way ahead of them.

In the real world, a guy his age with a body like that would probably still make women stare, like they do with my dad sometimes. I wonder if Ray goes into Lamistead on occasion and walks around, and if the women of Lamistead stare. I wonder if Ray stares right back.

His greying hair streams over his shoulder like cypress moss as he strides fast for the river. He makes me think of a story Mum used to read to me when I was little, about Rain Woman and Fire Man. Fire Man was leathery and lean, always running, throwing embers into his sharp mouth. In the illustrations, his flame hair licked behind him as he ran.

Rory shuffles back into the room, and I forget about the view out the window. 'Is it cold out?'

'Damp, not too cold.' She clambers back onto the bed, lays the blanket over our knees. I pass her tea over and she takes long swallows before passing it back. 'This is warmer.'

I put both our mugs on the stump, so we can burrow under the blankets again. I have Rory in my arms – *in my arms*. I got to wake up with her. I press my lips into the vee where her neck and shoulder curve together, and she makes these cute noises, and my heart feels all coloured in.

Rory sighs and shudders and smiles. 'I love it when you do that.'

'Good. Cos I love doing it.'

'Do you have to go home?'

'Soon.' I clear my throat. 'Actually, Mum was probably expecting me back last night.'

She sighs differently this time. 'I wish you could stay. I wish you could lie here with me all day.'

I kiss her lips quickly. 'You can't even lie here yourself all day, let alone with me. Are you harvesting?'

'The corn's done. We didn't really get enough in the harvest, but Ray said it'll do, so we're grinding it today.' She brushes a finger down my cheek. 'I still wish you could stay.'

I put my arms around her. 'All day today. And all day the next day. And every day after that. And we'd make our own garden, and I'd cook you mouth-watering dishes with the vegies, and build you a little cabin in the woods.'

She laughs. 'I've already got one of those. You don't want to go for a bit of variety?'

'A cabin in a field, then. Near a silver creek, with wildflowers growing.'

'Bo.' She presses her hand to my chest, her expression becoming still. 'You don't really want to become a member of the Eden community, do you?'

Wordless, I shake my head. I've thought about it heaps. It's beautiful here, and I don't think I've ever met a group of people who are so incredibly supportive and community-minded. I wouldn't mind the hard work, and I agree with what they're trying to do – to make themselves an example of how it's possible to live on the earth without destroying it.

I've got to be honest, though: if Rory wasn't here, I wouldn't be as eager to participate. And Ray's influence is getting harder to ignore. I like Eden, but I'm not really sure what direction the community is going in.

Rory's expression is sad, but it's mixed with relief. 'That's okay. I wasn't sure, but I didn't think so.' She puts a finger on my lips when I open my mouth to apologise. 'You don't have to say sorry. You don't have to say anything like that – it's not about us. It's about what *you* want.'

'You,' I say impulsively. 'I want you.'

She kisses me, long and deep. I spread my hands across her back, span her waist, stroke my fingers around to her front. Things start to get faster, more intense. I don't know if I'm touching her right, if I'm doing this right, but Rory says, 'Oh god,' at some particularly amazing moments, which seems to establish that I basically have an electric line straight from my ear canal to my groin, but Jesus – how are girls' noises not sexy?

Rory puts her hands on either side of my head. 'It's late. Oh god, you should go.'

I kiss her neck. 'Keep saying "oh god" and I won't give a shit.'

She blushes. 'We should stop.'

'We should,' I agree. Then we kiss again for a long time.

Then I realise it *is* late, she's right, and I have to push myself away. 'Stop. Oh shit...' I scramble for my bike gloves, sit up to tie my boots. Rory kneels behind me and runs her fingers across the hair at the nape of my neck. I finish with my bootlaces, pull her into my lap. 'I have an idea. Come back to school. We could see each other every day. I could kiss you every day.'

Rory bites her lip.

'Cam and Loz and Sprog are keen to see you. The teachers love you.' I lip my way down from her ear to her collarbone, lift my head to meet her eyes. 'But it's not about the teachers. Or Cam and Loz and Sprog, or even me. You have to want it. Would you like to come back? Give it another try?'

Rory looks at me with solemn eyes for a long moment. 'Yes.'

I want to cheer. Instead, I kiss Rory. Which quickly scales up to the point where it's hard to leave – again.

I wriggle my way off the bed. 'Goddammit, I've gotta go.' I touch her cheek with my gloved hand. 'I'll see you tomorrow morning. On Bowyer Track.'

'You will. Now go. Don't get in trouble cos of me.'

I press my lips to her forehead and leave.

Dozens of millipedes have come out to drown themselves in the puddles from last night's rain. I make my way back through the wet undergrowth. The earth is steaming in the sun – there's a tang of iron, a smell like grass clippings, and that feeling of freshness that excites you.

I go past the Meeting House, retrieve the Cannondale from the comfrey patch, jump it around a bit to get the wet off as I head for the gate.

'Hey, Stuart.'

Stuart's sitting in an old, collapsible camping chair that's been repurposed for the guard station near the Eden sign. Of all the community members in Eden, Stuart is the one I find the most easygoing and straightforward. Maybe because he has a job in the regular world, so he knows what it's like to live 'outside'.

'Bo, you heading home?'

'Yep. You're watching the gate today, huh?'

'Yeah.' He shrugs. He was reading a book when I arrived; now he leans and selects a gumleaf off the ground to act as a page marker.

'That looked like an intense Meeting last night.' I veer around the gate to get onto the road.

'It was.' He positions the leaf marker carefully as he stands. 'Bo, are you catching up with Rory again soon?'

I grin. 'She's meeting me tomorrow morning. We're riding in to school together.'

'She's going back? Well, that's great.' He leans on the *Garden of Eden* sign. 'It's good you're looking out for her.'

I shrug and smile. Why wouldn't I?

Stuart scuffs the dirt with his boot. 'Bo, things are getting ... kind of heavy here right now. With the investigation, and Sally and everything. So maybe it's better you and Rory are meeting outside of Eden. Ray's been talking about restricting visitor access, so...' He squints. 'Do you understand what I mean?'

By 'visitor', Stuart must mean the welfare inspectors, and he wants to keep Rory away from them – I get it. 'It's all cool.'

'Okay, great. So I guess I'll see you when I see you. Take it easy, Bo. Ride safe.' He extends his hand for me to shake, which seems kinda formal, but whatever.

'Cheers. See you round.'

The ride home is muddy and slippery, but there's a reservoir of energy inside me – the crystalline buzz you get from being really happy – and it makes the cycling easy. I'm aware that the sun is rising higher with every minute, though, and my chances of sneaking back into my room are decreasing exponentially.

I have no plan for what I might say to Mum. *I spent the night at Rory's* – that seems like the most efficient and simple answer to give. But it'll also create more complex questions. And it'll be hard to keep the smile off my face when I tell her.

I park my bike under the stairs, check my phone for the first time since last night. Fuck, it's after eight. Connor has a footy game at ten, so he and Mum are sure to be stirring. I'm gonna get busted.

I squeeze through the door. The house is strangely quiet. Julie is snoring and farting on her bed in the corner of the hall alcove.

'Christ, Julie, you stink,' I whisper.

She doesn't even look up.

I sneak down the hall. Tiptoe into the kitchen, watching for the boards that really creak – the ones nearest the island always groan like a concertina. I'm wearing the worst possible shoes for this. I take one more creeping step.

The floor cracks on the *other* side of the island. I look up.

My father is standing directly opposite me. He's wearing daggy dad sleepwear – T-shirt, trunks – and he's in a sneaking pose identical to mine. We're probably even wearing identical expressions of shock.

'Wow,' he says in a low voice. 'Looks like I'm not the only one who had a big night.'

Surprise homecoming – right.

'Bo, could you make us all tea?' Mum asks. She's tucked up on the couch, with Dad a measured distance away, while Connor replays his proudest moments of this morning's footy match.

Dad took him to the game. Mum got a chance to lie in. And me... I dunno what I'm doing, just kind of lurking in the background, I guess. It feels incredibly weird that my father is home.

'...so I gave him the bump,' Connor says, hip-checking an imaginary opponent, 'and he fell over! Then I went straight for goal.' His hands describe the victory – I flash back to all the times I've replayed my footy games for Dad in this exact same way.

'You did good, little man,' Dad says.

Will he say *You did good* when he finds out about my subject change? The idea of telling him makes me nauseous.

'It's great you made it home in time to see me play.' Connor gives Dad the hugest grin, as Dad takes his hands.

'I was really happy I could see it,' Dad says. 'Now, me and Mum and Bo are gonna have a cuppa, so what are you gonna do?'

Connor shrugs. 'Well, I'm still reading *The Ruins of Gorlan* – Mrs Barton says I should try to finish it this week.'

'Well, you go and read for a bit, while we chat, and then I'll take you out for a kick, okay?'

Connor tootles off. I bring over the mugs, hand them out, go stand by the window.

'D'you want to sit down, Bo?' Mum asks.

'I'm fine.' I'm not going to sit on the other couch with my parents staring at me like this is some kind of intervention.

'I'm glad I'm home,' Dad says simply. He looks up at me. 'Of course, I'd be gladder if you were glad I was home too. What's happening, Bo?'

'Nothing much.' The garden out the living-room window has a sun-washed paleness.

'Mum said you had Sprog over here after a blue with his brother.'

'Yeah.' I angle towards him, cupping my mug. My back is stiff and my face is set. 'Curtis had a pretty good go. Barry Fromer helped me get Sprog here, and Mum cleaned him up.'

'That's a bad scene. It's a big improvement, then, if Sprog's staying at the D'Amatos'.' When I make a noncommittal noise, he goes on. 'So footy's going okay?'

I sigh. 'Yeah.' No point explaining now that I've pulled out of the rep squad tryouts. That could be a long conversation, and I'm not up for it.

'And you're all organising some fundraiser thing?'

'To fix up the skate park for teenagers in town, yeah.'

'Sounds like a good idea.' Dad seems a bit formal, a bit awkward. I'm not the only one having trouble coping with the weirdness of all this, then.

'I'm doing okay with my schoolwork. I didn't put in my best effort at footy yesterday, but we still won, and we were a man down. I've been trying to help Mum as much as I could, with Con and dinners and stuff.' I take a swallow from my mug. 'I did what you asked. I looked after things while you were away.'

'What about things with this girl?'

I stare at him. 'With Rory.'

'With Rory, yes.' He looks at me seriously. 'You were there last night.'

'Yes.'

'You're looking after her? Treating her right? With respect?'

My back straightens further. 'Yes.'

Dad frowns. 'You're using protection?'

'It's not like that!' I glance away. 'Okay, yes, it's like that. But it's not like *that*. We haven't… Things haven't reached that point.'

'But they're getting there.'

'Yes. And I'm not stupid, of course we'll use protection.' I blush just saying it.

'That's good to know,' Mum says. The expression on her face reminds me that this is actually a part of the conversation that concerns her, too.

'I'm being careful,' I say to her. I don't know why I say it, cos it's really nobody's business except mine and Rory's. But the words make Mum visibly relax.

'Okay.' Dad nods. 'So all that's left to cover is the fact that you've been spending time in Eden.'

'That's not going to happen anymore. I've convinced Rory to come back to school.'

'You must be happy about that,' Mum says, slipping her feet up onto the couch.

'Yeah. I'm going to meet her tomorrow and we'll ride in together.'

'And if you want to hang out after school hours?' Dad asks.

'Then we'll figure that out when we come to it,' I say, jaw clenched.

'She's always welcome to come over here,' Mum says.

Rory and my dad in the same orbit – two diametrically opposed forces. Yeah, that sounds great. I keep my expression neutral. 'Okay, thanks.'

'It's important you've encouraged her to go back to school,' Dad says.

I nod. There's no way I'm going to mention the tension in the Eden community right now.

There's a long pause.

'It's really good to see you, Bo,' Dad says. His voice almost sounds wobbly.

I take another slug of tea, forcing it down cos there's something in my throat that's making it hard to swallow. 'It's good you're home.' I swill the remainder in my mug; it's getting cold. 'Okay, I've got homework to finish, I better get into it. Mum, give me a yell if you want a hand with lunch.'

I go to my room. That seems like the safest option right now – for me and for Dad.

*

297

I'm supposed to meet Rory at the T-junction of Bowyer Track and Fogarty's Hill Road at eight-fifteen the next morning. She's not there when I arrive. Fifteen minutes passes, and nada.

Well, shit.

I consider riding up to Eden to find her, but that'll make me late and score me another detention. Why isn't she here? Maybe she got held up. I jig on the spot. Maybe she can't come. Things might be locked down in Eden. Rory might be having trouble cutting loose…

I can't wait any longer. It kills me to ride away, but I have to do it. When I get to school, Cam is stuffing around with insurance paperwork for White Night, but she still has time to baulk when I rock up on my lonesome.

'Where's Rory? You texted last night to say she was going to—'

'Dunno.' I shrug, but my shoulders are too tight for it to look casual. 'She didn't show up this morning.'

'Damn. D'you think she's changed her mind?'

'Jesus, Cam. I don't know.' I see her face. 'Look, I'm sorry. I'll ride up there this arvo and find out what's going on.'

After Cam retreats, Sprog snags my sleeve. 'I got your text. So your dad's back?'

'Yeah.' I glance away.

'That must be fun.'

'It's a hoot.' I roll my eyes. 'What about you, man? You going okay at the D'Amatos'?'

'Yeah, good.' He *looks* good – better fed, and his bruises are fading. His eyes stray to Cam. 'I mean, Mrs D'Amato talks a lot, but small price to pay, yeah?'

'What's happening with Curtis?'

He shrugs. 'Breanna Fromer passed word on. Mum's home, Curtis is home, no charges were laid. Everything's kinda gone back to the same old. I dunno if they've even noticed I'm not there. They're just caught up in their own sad world, y'know?'

'Not much you can do about it, mate.'

'Tell me.' He sighs, then snorts. 'Anyway, you and Rory are ... what? Is it official?'

I give him a bump. 'None of your beeswax.'

He grins. 'I notice you haven't grown a hipster beard. So does that mean—'

'It means I'll snot you if you keep talking about it.'

'Well, she has armpit hair, so I'm assuming—'

'*Sprog*—'

'Dom,' Cam calls, 'have you got the list of all the traders on Gough Street we've already called?'

'Saved by my woman!' Sprog laughs, backing away with his hands up and a massive smile on his face.

I can take my mind off Rory's absence from school and Dad's presence at home when we all get our heads together to talk about the fundraiser. There's still shitloads of work to do, and the countdown is on for this Friday. According to Sprog, Jem is good to go, the equipment is organised, and we have a sound engineer. Cam reckons the shopkeepers in town are game on – not all of them will stay open, but we've got enough – and all the paperwork for the council and police and St John Ambulance are being processed. I talk to Lozzie about how to handle the garbage-and-recycling aspects, and whether we should get a ute with a big water tank, so people can rehydrate while dancing.

Everybody's on a high. But I don't start to feel good about it all until I get to the junction after school and see Rory standing there beside the Titanic in her cut-off overalls, a tie-dyed scarf covering her head.

I pull up, and she steps forwards, and I push the kickstand down on the Cannondale, and then we grab each other, and hug, and kiss and kiss and kiss.

'This could prove distracting,' Rory says, as we pull away.

'No kidding.' I find her lips again. It's still a surprise to me every time, the softness, the eagerness and sense of wonder Rory brings to kissing. But there's something a little desperate in it for both of us, and I have to draw back.

'What is it?' Rory asks.

'It's … Nah, you go. What's happened?'

'I asked you first,' she insists.

'My dad came home.' Her expression is shocked, and I nod. 'Yesterday morning – well, it was probably Saturday night, hey, only I was with you all night so I didn't realise…'

'Oh, Bo. How are you coping?'

'It's a bit…complicated.' I scuff the dust. 'Enough about me, what's going on with you? And what's with the scarf?'

Rory swallows and meets my eyes as she reaches up and tugs at the scarf. The rainbow-coloured material slides, slips away, and… My breath catches. Her champagne curls are gone, replaced by a soft golden fuzz. It's basically a buzz cut.

I don't know how to react. But I know that my reaction is important. 'Wow. You … cut your hair.'

'Yup.'

I never know what to do in these situations, when the girls come to school moaning about fashion or hairstyle disasters.

Not that this is a disaster. In fact, without all the curls, Rory's face looks regal, high-cheekboned and elegant. She has a leather string around her neck with a gumleaf for a pendant, which kind of completes the look. It's radical, but everything about Rory is radical.

It's not up to me, anyway – it's her hair, she can do what she likes with it. She still looks good to me. But her expression and manner are both subdued, like the haircut isn't something she's crazy about.

I don't want her to feel bad, so I do the only thing I can think of to comfort her.

'You look gorgeous,' I say, and I step in again, slide my arm around her waist.

'Thanks.' Rory runs her fingers over her head. 'Bo, Star and Stuart have left Eden.'

'Left? As in—'

'As in gone.' She composes herself with effort. 'They took the van and went to Adelaide last night. Daniel's gone with them, of course. There was an argument.'

I'm shocked, way more shocked than I was about the haircut. Star and Stuart seemed like some of the most heartfelt, committed members the community had. But more than that, it looks bad, especially during an official investigation into whether the community is serving the best interests of its kids.

Rory presses her lips together. 'We had a long talk about it last night at Meeting, and we've all basically decided … Look, things are happening right now at Eden. And I need to be there. I can't come back to school. Ray thinks—'

'Rory—'

She holds up a hand. 'Let me finish. Eden is my *home*. It's where I belong. We've talked with the inspectors … If things settle down, then I do *want* to come back to school. But I can't now. Do you understand?'

It's like I've copped an elbow in the guts during a match. The worst thing about it is, I do understand. Tensions in the community are obviously running at an all-time high, and – as Ray and Star's daughter, plus the last remaining kid in Eden – Rory would be caught right in the middle.

All I can do is nod. 'I get it. I do. Ah, shit … So that's it? You're decided?'

'Yes.' She looks heartbroken. 'And you can't come to Eden until this is all over, so—'

'We have to figure out a place to meet up.'

'Yes.'

I frown at the ground, at Rory. 'Star and Stuart really just pissed off like that?'

'Yes, but they said goodbye. They …' She looks as if she's holding back tears. 'I'm sorry, I can't talk about it.'

I fold her into my arms. 'Is that why you cut your hair?'

She tucks her face against my shoulder. 'Yes.'

Suddenly I remember Stuart's formal handshake yesterday. That was no accident. He knew they were leaving. And Star must have known – so Rory's own mother didn't give her any advance warning. Which is pretty fucked up, if you consider it from Rory's perspective.

I hug her for as long as I can, until neither of us have a choice but to separate. I don't want to leave her. I don't understand what's going on with the community, but Star and Stuart's departure seems like a bad sign.

Later I'm on the phone to Loz, talking about the recycling, and I can't help but tell her about Rory's situation. She's completely confused. 'That's freaky. No, seriously, Bo – leaving your kid behind like that? Come on, that's weird, right?'

'Dad left us behind when he went to Queensland,' I say.

'But he came back. Is Rory okay? The hair-cutting thing…'

'She's stressed, Loz, her mum left the community. Give her a break.'

'Hey, I'm not down on her or anything,' Loz says. 'If you think she's okay, then it's all good.'

27

Dad's already home when I get back from school on Tuesday, but he's making phone calls, so I go to my room and fill out the paperwork for my subject change while I wait for Mum to get home with Connor. My mother and brother have both been a good buffer over the last few days. Being around Dad is awkward. Nothing he says seems believable to me anymore, and when we're in the same room, there's a buzz of tension, like we're both standing under a live powerline.

What shits me the most is that nothing has been said, nothing has been discussed. It's like his absence never happened, and we're all going to pretend that Liam doesn't exist, that everything's dandy. Mum seems quietly happy to have Dad home, which gets up my nose too. Doesn't she care that he abandoned her, abandoned *us*, and then waltzed back in again without comment?

Dad's been trying to slot back into normal life – sorting out new jobs, taking Con to sport, helping Mum around the house, tinkering in the shed. It's only in the quiet moments that you notice things aren't quite right. Meals, for example, have been a nightmare of forced civility and good cheer.

I make tonight's dinner, with Connor 'helping', which basically means he's bent on one knee in the kitchen, watching the sausages under the grill, while I sort out the salad and chop potatoes.

'Bo, these snags are really spitting. Wow, look at 'em go.' His head tilts up to me. 'You should cook dinner every night.'

'I *do* cook dinner every night, sport.'

'You've been helping Mum with meals, Bo?' Dad's lacing his runners, before taking Con out for a kick. 'That's great.'

'Someone had to,' I mutter.

'Pardon?'

'Nothing.' I lift the lid off the pot to roll in the spuds.

When we're sitting around the dining table, it's all *Please pass the potatoes* and *Excuse me, could I have the tomato sauce?* and then the fun really starts.

'Connor, take your elbows off the table,' Mum says, reaching for the salad bowl.

'What's wrong with elbows?'

'Well,' Mum says, eyeing me and Dad, 'it seems we're all being especially polite right now, so I'd say elbows are a no-no. Also chewing loudly, and speaking with your mouth full.'

'Liz—' Dad starts.

'Did you notice that smell in the back garden?' Mum interrupts.

'Is it the whiff of sarcasm?' I ask, looking at my plate as I saw at a sausage.

'Oh, Bo, what a funny fellow you are,' Mum says. 'No, it's not that.'

'Is it in the back corner, near the bottlebrush?' Dad asks.

305

'That's where the overflow pipe for the septic tank runs under the garden.'

'The grass around there has been looking very green.'

Dad sighs. 'Then the pipe has probably burst. I'll fix it tomorrow.'

'Actually, it's really making me nauseous,' Mum says. 'You and Bo can fix it together. This evening.' She smiles sweetly at both of us.

Which is how I find myself sliding on rawhide gloves, and lugging spades and a mattock over to where Dad is pacing out the space in the back corner of the garden. Mum was right – it really stinks over here. The grass is lush, too, which is a dead giveaway.

I drop the tools in a heap. Being this close to Dad is making me tense. 'We can't do this with the bobcat?'

'It's too shallow and delicate.' Dad slides on his gloves. 'There'd be no pipe left. Nah, we'll have to do it the hard way.'

'Joy.'

It actually takes very little digging to unearth the pipe – the ground is really soft – but we have to dig carefully around the pipe itself, and then clear about twenty centimetres underneath so we can do the repair. And yes, it's disgusting. This is our septic pipe we're dealing with. There aren't any solids, but the water leaking out of the pipe and into the soggy ground around it is tea-coloured and smells rank.

'I'm gonna hold the pipe. You dig out that last bit there, on the left,' Dad says.

We're knee-high in reeking black mud. I grab the spade.

'Not the spade, Bo! Jesus. Clear it with your hands.'

'I'm not gonna use my hands!' I throw down the spade. '*You* clear the fucking mud, I'll hold the pipe.'

Dad glowers. 'Bo.'

'You can't order me around anymore! I'm not the fucking village idiot, y'know!'

'Bo…' Dad sighs. 'Okay, son. You hold the pipe.'

I debate whether or not to just leave him with the whole revolting mess. But something in his face makes me stay.

I get down on my knees, grab the slippery PVC. The stink is so much worse up close. 'Ah, this is gross.'

Dad's expression softens as his lips quirk up at the corners. 'Yes, it is. I guess your mother wanted us to sort out our shit.'

He hunkers down beside me, starts digging with his gloved hands. After a minute or two of listening to the sound of sloshing mud, and enduring the putrid air of the leaking pipe, I'm ready for a distraction.

Dad provides one when he starts talking.

'I don't know where I was born.' He doesn't meet my eyes, keeps scooping. 'I was dropped off at a hospital in Gatton, in South East Queensland. It's a country town, a bit like Lamistead. I imagine I was some poor girl's unhappy secret. At least I didn't end up in a garbage bin. Whoever my mum was, at least she left me at a hospital.'

I don't interrupt. I watch my father dig with his hands, listen to his words. He's never shared these details of his life with me before.

'Anyway, I was raised in a couple of places in Brisbane – not great places. They weren't the kinds of homes you'd really want to be in, if you had a choice, but they provided enough. Hot meals, dorm beds. A tough culture, but no serious abuse.

From what I've heard, I got pretty lucky. Rigid places, though – lots of rules, strict schedules.'

Rules. Strict schedules. I look at Dad as he speaks, but he still doesn't meet my gaze.

'I guess I got sick of it after a while. Became a bit of a tearaway. I ended up going out to a couple of different foster families – same deal, not fantastic places to grow up. Some people were kind. But I'd gotten nearly to the end of high school, and I wasn't cute anymore – I was just another awkward rebellious teenager. Then I was placed with this family in Mount Coot-tha.' Dad stops scooping, rests his hands on his knees. 'Pass me the hacksaw, Bo. I think that's enough space for the repair.'

I nod, pass him the saw. Dad starts cutting off a section of pipe from the spare piece he's brought down.

'Anyway, they were a good family, the Pettifers. It was unusual, y'know? To be fostered by a family so late. They took me in when I wasn't expecting it. I'd figured when I was eighteen I could cut loose from the system, go my own way. But they took me in, made me feel welcome.' He drops the hacksaw and the piece of pipe next to the hole we've dug, wipes his brow with the back of his arm. 'I didn't repay their kindness too well. I was knocking around with a group of guys by then, all older than me – some of them I'd met in the system. We were getting up to strife, trawling up and down Brisbane, going to see bands, sneaking into pubs, getting pissed and hanging out in Fortitude Valley. My best mate was this guy, Patrick. He was a good bloke – a year or so older, but we hit it off. We were thick as thieves. Patrick had this job in a factory, screwing pallets together, so we had some cash to spend – me and Patrick had a good old time.'

'Sounds like me and Sprog,' I say quietly.

'A bit like that, yeah.' Dad catches my eye – a quick, intense glance – then looks back to what he's doing, cutting the pipe section lengthwise to make a cuff. 'So, here's me, living with this family. They were trying to do right by me, and I was slipping off all the time to hang out with these guys. But I kept coming back to the Pettifers, to see Lily. She was their eldest daughter.'

I keep my grip on the pipe as Dad reaches for the PVC primer and glue in their red and blue bottles. 'I think I know where this is going.'

Dad sighs, looks down into the hole in front of us, puts his filthy gloves aside and starts wiping down the septic pipe with a rag. There's a clean, obvious split about a palm's-length long, close to the top.

'Yeah, maybe you do. Now, I know it's not supposed to happen. You don't get involved with foster siblings – in some states, it's the law. But sometimes you meet someone, and you can't seem to help it. Something tugs inside you, and you follow.' Dad wipes and talks and wipes. 'Something tugged inside me, tugged hard, when I met Lily. And she felt it too. It's easy if one of you takes a shine and the other's only so-so – those things always resolve quickly. But when you're both looking at each other, and you can't seem to look away …'

I think about me and Rory. I know what that tug feels like.

Dad nods at the expression on my face, goes on. 'Patrick and Lily and me, we used to get around together. Her family weren't too happy, but we were teenagers, and Lily was

309

a wild thing. We used to go out on the cheap most nights. Sometimes we'd be hanging in the street, or at the park, sitting on the kids' swings in the dark. Then one night Patrick got incredibly pissed – he flaked out, and it was just me and Lily…'

'You got together?'

Dad's eyebrows lift as he starts painting the split in the pipe with primer and glue. 'If "got together" means the same thing today as it meant in the nineties, then yeah.' He shakes his head. 'But it went deeper than that. It wasn't just a casual hook-up. It meant too much. And it should never have happened, but yeah, we kept seeing each other. There was a lot of sneaking around, of course, but we were so sure…We really felt like Romeo and Juliet, y'know? I mean, we weren't any older than you are now.'

'Her family found out, though, yeah?'

'Well, it got more complicated than that.' As I hold the pipe, he holds my eyes. 'Things get more complicated when your girlfriend falls pregnant.'

I knew it was coming. I knew, but I still can't control my reaction. 'That's heavy.'

'Yeah, it was. Well, we decided to run away together. Get married, maybe, raise the baby. We knew we'd need cash, so I signed on at Patrick's factory. Worked the pallet lines. It wasn't great money, but it was enough for what we had in mind.'

Dad fits the cuff around the split part of the pipe, over the two-toned colours of the primer and glue. I keep the pipe steady as he positions the cuff. We're both sitting in the smelly mud, septic water seeping through our jeans, but we're silent, working the job, contemplating the part of the story that has to come next.

'Me and Lily had these dreams, we used to talk about it…' Dad says softly. 'Anyway, one day I came home from work to find that the Pettifers had locked me out of their house.'

Dad clears his throat, wipes the glued cuff with the rag. He sits back on his hands, and I release the pipe and brush my palms on my shirt, waiting for the rest.

'I knocked on the door,' Dad goes on, 'because I thought it was a mistake, y'know? I didn't think they'd changed the locks on purpose. But then Lily's dad opens the door, and he's standing there, looking at me. And that was when I realised Lily had told him.'

I'm thinking about what it would feel like, if Rory was pregnant, and I had to explain that to my parents, her family… Now I understand why Mum breathed easier when I told her that me and Rory were being careful.

'There was a massive blow-up, of course,' Dad goes on. 'The Pettifers were threatening to press charges for incest, statutory rape—'

'What?'

Dad nods. 'It was their right – in Queensland it's the law, and Lily was only fifteen. Her parents were furious, as you can imagine. The argument got ugly. Lily was hysterical, I was…blazing, I was that angry.' Dad shakes his head at the memory. 'But it didn't seem like we had a lot of choices. I'd just turned eighteen, I could be tried as an adult in court, and Graham Pettifer knew that. He knew my life would be over if I went through the system. So he offered me an out. He'd give me a lump of cash, drive me to the train station, and I'd take off. Get lost. But there was no way I could take Lily with me – that was the price I was going to have to pay.'

'What did you do?'

Dad shrugs. 'I left. Lily didn't want me to, but I had no choice. Her family promised to support her and the baby. So I left this girl I loved, while she was pregnant with my child, and I hopped on a train.' He looks away from the pipe, out of the garden, into the soft light of early evening that's draping itself over the back paddock. 'The hardest thing was letting go of the future – the plans we'd made, the ideas we had about how things would spool out. It wasn't hard to let go of the present or the past, cos they were crap. But it was hard to let go of the dreams we had ...'

Dad's gaze lands back on me, back to the job at hand, and he shakes himself like he's shaking off a heavy coat. He stands up, and I do the same, and he hands me a spade. What's done is done – now it's time to shovel back the soil we've lifted out.

He makes the first cut with the spade's blade into the heap of mud on the ground beside the hole. His voice is gruff. 'Lily's parents were deadset against us having any contact. I was a no-hoper – a foster kid, a factory labourer at best, who didn't even know where he'd come from, or where he was going ...'

I shift my own first spadeful. 'So where *did* you go?'

'First I went to Sydney, then out into the country. Different states, different jobs. I tried to contact Lily, but I had to send all my letters to the Pettifer home – I didn't know if she got them. I travelled for about two years, working casual jobs, fruit picking, carnie work, never settling anywhere. I felt like I'd failed Lily, failed the baby. Failed myself.'

My voice is quiet. 'How did you keep going?'

Dad keeps shovelling. 'It was tough. Travelling like that, staying low to the ground, you get disconnected from everything. You don't make friends, you don't put down roots. I felt like I was on the moon. It was a very lonely time. I reached a point where I was so lost – life didn't seem to have a lot of meaning, y'know? I couldn't stand it anymore. Then I met this guy who told me about a job going in Victoria, with this bloke who had his own business ...'

The understanding comes to me, clearly outlined, like I'm looking through a telescope that's only now come into focus. 'Harry Krane.'

'Harry didn't judge. I fronted up for the job, he took one look at me, sat me down with a coffee and asked me what I'd done, and I told him. It all came pouring out. He said that if I wanted to start fresh, he'd give me a chance. He was a good bloke, very patient and matter-of-fact. So I worked my butt off here, and I finally got back in touch with Lily. She told me ... She told me that I had a son.'

The grief on Dad's face when he says this is something solid, something tangible and real. It's such a new expression on him it makes me stop digging.

'I sent money back to Lily when I could. When I asked to see my son, she sent me a photograph. I knew I couldn't go back to Brisbane without risking arrest – the law there has no statute of limitations on things like that. Lily and the boy, they'd had to put everything behind them and start fresh, like me. It haunted me, that I was only a plane trip away but I couldn't go back. But I'd made my bed, I had to lie in it.'

I take a breath, resume shovelling. The hole is half-full now.

'About four years after I came to the district, I met your mother,' Dad says. 'We hit it off. I'd been alone for so long... I'd been avoiding getting involved with anyone, cos I didn't want to wreck things again, y'know? I'd been keeping my head down – lower than a turtle. But here was your mother – this vivacious, gorgeous woman who dragged me out of my shell...'

I look towards our house – Mum's up there, probably watching us through the glass doors of the verandah.

'I didn't talk to her about Lily and the boy. I knew it was a mistake. But I didn't want Liz to think badly of me. I didn't think I could handle being rejected again. And after a few years, with babies and life and everything that happens, I convinced myself that the old part of my life was over, and it was easier not to talk about it.'

'But then the truth came out,' I prompt.

'A few weeks ago, Lily got in touch with me to pass on the news that she was terminally ill. That she was going downhill fast. And she wanted to see me, wanted me to meet Liam. Her parents passed away about five years ago, and I guess she wanted to make a connection between me and Liam before she ran out of time.'

'And you had to tell Mum.'

'I had to tell your mother, yes. I gave her the whole sorry story. How I'd ended up here, and who Liam and Lily were, and why I'd never been able to go back.' Dad snorts. 'She was angry. I knew she would be. But it was a relief to tell her. And she was actually worried for *me* – that I had a child I'd never met. She's still... We're still working things out. There's the issue of my silence, for all these years. She feels betrayed,

314

and I can understand why. But at least we're talking about it.'

We've reached the present, the now. Our hole is nearly filled in. Before, I'd wanted this job to get done fast, but now I wish it was taking longer, so Dad has enough time to tell me the whole story.

'I knew if I went to Brisbane, I'd be leaving you all here with lots of big feelings. But time was getting short, because of Lily's health.' Dad clears his throat again, taps some of the dirt in the hole with his boot. 'I wanted to see Lil. I wanted to connect with my son. Liam convinced me to go to Brisbane, in the end.' Dad smiles softly. 'He's a persuasive bloke. And part of me decided that I'd been running and hiding long enough. It was time to deal with it, to let the secret out. I felt like it'd been burning a hole in my heart for years.'

The hole in front of us is no longer a hole, just a slightly sunken depression in the ground. Dad and I are standing here with our spades, both of us filthy, both of us exposed.

I look down at the dirt. 'You should've told me. You should've told *us*.'

'Yes.'

My voice is thick. 'I thought I was your eldest son.'

'You are. In every way that's relevant, you are. But you're right, Bo. I should've talked about this with you before.'

My face lifts. 'So ... what happens now?'

Dad sighs, pushes on his spade to straighten up. 'I never met Liam before a fortnight ago. I've been a stranger in his life. That knowledge has racked me for over twenty years.' He looks at me. 'But I don't want to be a stranger in your life. I want you to know the truth about me, so you can see me as a whole person. As a man, not just as your father. I've made mistakes. I've got history, like everyone – it's what makes us who we are. But I don't want to run away again.'

I bite my lip. 'D'you want Liam to live with us?'

'Liam's grown now, he has his own life. But I'd like him to feel welcome in this family, yes.'

'He seemed like a decent guy.'

Dad nods. 'Lily was a good mother. She didn't take out her anger and frustration on our son. I'll always be grateful for that.'

And now I have to ask. It's like the question has been boiling inside me, trapped for so long it's a roar. It churns up my throat, turns my voice into a muddy croak.

'Do you still … love me the same as before?'

Dad throws his spade down, steps right in. 'Bodeen … You and your mum and Connor brought happiness back into my life.' There are tears in his eyes. 'Do I still love you? I loved you from the moment I knew you existed, and I've never stopped, mate. You make me proud every single day.'

28

'All right, everybody, settle down please,' Mrs Ramanathan says.

She checks the connections on her laptop as we all bustle around finding seats. Wednesday morning, and Sprog isn't in class – I mime 'looking for Sprog' at Cam as she walks in, finds a seat beside me.

'He's in the AV area,' she says quietly. 'He's talking to the juniors who volunteered to set up on Friday afternoon.'

'What's the problem?'

'They're juniors.' Cam rolls her eyes. 'And I have to keep reminding myself that we're dealing with the bozone layer.'

'The what?'

'The air surrounding stupid people that stops intelligent ideas from penetrating.'

'Right.' I grin. 'Did you think that one up yourself?'

'Actually, I got it from a Mensa website,' she says with an embarrassed smile.

'Thank you, that will do,' Mrs Ram says, as she extends a hand for quiet. 'For the last few weeks, we have been examining social and political movements. Now we are going to talk about some social movements that went wrong.'

People settle and look up. I've gotta say, attitudes in this class have totally altered. It used to be a classroom where the only thing you were guaranteed was an entire period of boredom, but things have changed. Mrs Ramanathan commands the room. After her last speech, we're all paying attention.

'For various reasons, in human history, people have gathered in groups to enact social change. But some of these attempts have failed.' Mrs Ram looks over as Sprog enters the classroom.

He looks apologetic. 'Sorry, Miss, I got held up.'

'Take a seat, Dominic.' She narrows her eyes at him. 'I'm glad you could make this class, in particular. You will understand why shortly.'

Sprog slides into the seat Cam has saved for him, and Mrs Ram returns to her explanation.

'As I was saying – social movements that went wrong. Often these situations arose because the ethical basis for community development was unbalanced or absent. We talk a lot about the Cultural Revolution, and Fascism under Hitler, but sometimes the communities involved were on a much smaller scale.'

She moves away from the front desk so we can see the images she's clicking through up on the whiteboard. The first is of a man with dark sunglasses. Then we see pictures of young people and families standing together with placards, all of them wearing outdated clothes.

'I'd like to talk briefly about Jonestown,' Mrs Ram says. 'The community was founded by Jim Jones in nineteen fifty-five – it had socialist precepts of racial equality and humanism when it first began. But then the tone changed. The People's Temple, as they were called, emigrated en masse to Guyana, in South America, to escape perceived persecution in the United States at around the same time that Reverend Jones began a slow decline into what sounds, from all reports, to be a state of serious mental illness. The community became more cut-off and dictatorial in nature, culminating in nineteen seventy-eight in the mass suicide of nearly a thousand people, including Jones himself.'

'They topped themselves?' Sprog looks flabbergasted. 'A thousand people?'

'Yes.' Mrs Ram's expression is both sad and grim. 'They drank a solution of cyanide in a type of cordial called Kool-Aid. Many drank willingly, but some accounts suggest that the ingestion of cyanide was not voluntary for all. More than three hundred of the community members who died were children.'

'How does that even happen?' Nikki asks.

'It happens when people in a community become too fixated on their leader – that creates a type of totalitarian mentality. All or nothing.' Mrs Ram gestures to the pictures on the board. 'The people came together in a spirit of social equality, utopian harmony, but the dream soured as Jones became more and more paranoid. Records indicate that the group had practice runs for what Jones called "revolutionary suicide".'

'That is seriously screwed up,' Bailey Debert mutters.

'Indeed. And it might interest you to know that those practice runs had a code name: White Night.'

A murmur runs through the class. Sprog and Cam look horrified.

'Yes.' Mrs Ram nods. 'So you can imagine my distress when I heard about your fundraiser being given the same name. But don't worry – I believe the term has since "gone viral". White Night celebrations are held worldwide now, perhaps as an attempt to reclaim the name as a force for social good. But as a student of history, it's hard for me to view the name with anything but revulsion – and now you understand why.'

Sprog bites his lip. 'They really killed all those little kids? The ones in the photos?'

Mrs Ram nods. 'That's the thing about social movements, Dominic. It is not like a technological or scientific experiment, when failure only involves loss of time or money or resources. If *people* are part of the equation, when things go wrong the results are often tragic for the individuals involved.'

✳

I explain all this to Mum in the afternoon, when she gets home from work. Dad's taken Connor to footy training, so it's only me and Mum hanging out – me on the verandah, giving the Cannondale a service, and Mum at the foot of the verandah steps, weeding the garden.

'So what are you going to do?' Mum asks. 'Is it too late to change the name?'

'Yeah.' I spin the bike's back wheel, checking the brake pads. 'Anyway, Mrs Ram said that now the name is being used as a force for social good. So even though it's kinda icky, Cam has convinced Sprog it'll be okay.'

'That must be a relief.'

'Yeah.'

I wipe the gear cogs, and glance down at Mum – she's pulling up onion grass from around the rosemary bush. The smell of the herb makes me think of Rory. I'm worried about her dealing with all the stuff going on in Eden lately. Plus… I just miss her. It's not only the kissing – we should be hanging out more, doing the stuff that regular teenagers do.

'Are you thinking about Rory?'

I look at Mum, then back to the rag in my hand. 'You've really got that mind-reading thing turned up to eleven this week, haven't you?'

She shrugs, grinning.

I frown, trying to figure out how to say this. Simplest is probably best. 'How do you know when you're in love?'

Mum pauses with a handful of onion grass. 'You really like this girl.'

'Yes.'

'Oh, Bo.' She smiles. 'You've got a long way to go before you have to worry about being in love.'

'How do you *know*, though? It's all… formless feelings, and not being sure what's going on. D'you know what I mean? How do you recognise it?'

'How do you recognise love? Well, goodness.' Mum sits back on her haunches, pushes away hair that's fallen loose from the untidy bun at the nape of her neck. 'Look around you. You want to know what love looks like, watch the way your father and I live every day.'

'But… you guys are fighting.' I shouldn't say it, but I do.

Mum laughs. 'You think that means we don't love each other anymore? I told you, Bo. Love can be hard work. Your

321

father and I...we'll get there. We're straightening out the important stuff.'

'So what's the important stuff?'

Mum contemplates her gardening gloves, then reaches for the secateurs. 'It's four things. First of all, you have to talk to each other – that's incredibly important. Talk about everything, the trivial stuff and the profound stuff.' She cocks her head. 'Even the painful, embarrassing stuff. That, especially.'

'Okay.'

'Secondly, have trust.' She starts pruning the bush with gentle snips, placing the cut rosemary pieces on the step beside her. 'Trust your partner, and trust yourself – the decision you made to choose the other person, the feelings you have for them.'

I squint. 'The trust thing sounds like it has a lot of moving parts.'

Mum nods. 'It does. Sometimes trust is shaky, and sometimes you have to build it up again. See *talking*, as I mentioned. But you have to remind yourself why you chose the other person. What attracted you together in the first place? Because remembering *why* you fell in love can be important, especially if you're in it for the long haul.'

'What's the third thing?'

'Thirdly, have good, regular sex.' She glances at me. 'Don't blush, Bo, if you want to know the truth of it, that's the truth – intimacy is important.'

I'm trying to control my face, while still getting my brain around the fact that I'm as bad at handling the 'parents-have-sex' concept as Connor. 'Okay, so what's the final thing?'

Mum smiles softly as the bush she's tending takes shape. 'Well, the fourth thing is plain kindness. You have to be kind to each other, as much as you can.'

'That's it? Kindness?'

'Kindness is the key to everything. You have to be kind in every circumstance – even when you're both angry, or stressed. Kindness is…' She looks around at the green life in the backyard. 'It's like water on the garden. You can plant a seed, make it germinate, fertilise it. But it won't become lush and bear fruit without a sprinkle of compassion.'

An understanding finally reaches my heart. Our family will be okay. The crisis is over – we're gonna make it. And Mum is right. We survived by being kind to one another.

It's like a heavy black bird inside my chest flies free. I look around the backyard, following Mum's line of sight, and realise something else. All the time and work we've put in here, the effort Mum's put into the garden, it's all been worth it. Hakeas and westringia and roses intermingle. Things are growing well, especially after the recent rain. Our place, it's a good place. It's not like Eden, but it's still beautiful.

*

I don't know what happens to Thursday. Between classes, and making phone calls about last-minute details for the recycling, and meetings with Cam and Lozzie and Sprog about how the festivities are going to run, and realising that I've double-booked Thursday afternoon – I'm supposed to have footy training – and remembering to bring in my subject-change papers… The day is just really busy, and underneath it all is the humming thread of wanting to see Rory. I have to push

323

away that distraction all day, then one last time as I remind Sprog about training right as the bell goes.

'Mullet will be pissed.' I gnaw my thumbnail.

'Don't worry about it.' Sprog flaps a clipboard full of running sheets in one hand while he chews a jelly snake in the other. 'I'm not going, either – I can't, hey, there's too much happening.' He considers. 'Look, d'you want me to call the club?'

I breathe out, force my hand to drop. 'Yeah. That'd be good. We should tell Mullet this afternoon might be a bust, footy-wise.'

'No problem.' He sticks his jelly snake between his teeth, fishes a pen out from behind his ear and scribbles a note on his clipboard. Looks at me sideways as he takes his jelly snake back. 'The bell's gone, man. Don't you have somewhere more important to be?'

I don't need another invitation. My bike is free, and I'm away.

But when I get to the Bowyer Track junction, there's no Rory. I stand there for a few minutes, but then my foot starts tapping. I'm not waiting uselessly again. My mind is already made up before I get back on my bike.

The ride in to Eden is marked by interruptions. At different points along the track, fallen tree branches block the way; I have to get off and move them aside to pass through. It's not until after I've shifted the third branch that I remember there hasn't been a storm. These branches have been put here deliberately, to restrict access, or at least slow it down.

I ride on grimly.

Here, the rise, and here, the gate. I'm relieved to see a

friendly face – Kell is sitting in the camp chair, writing something in a notebook.

'Hey, man.' I dismount, push the bike up to the gap at the side where I can slip through.

Kell stops scribbling and stands. 'Hey, Bo. Dude, you can't go through there.'

I scan the gap. 'Have you planted something?' I back up the bike to change direction. 'That's cool, I'll go through on your side.'

'Nah, man. I'm real sorry, but you can't come in.' Kell stands firm, hands by his sides. 'We're not letting outsiders onto the property right now.'

I gape. 'Seriously?' I try to compose myself. 'I'm here to see Rory, okay? We were supposed to meet at the bottom of the track, but she never showed up.'

Kell shrugs. 'No strangers, man. That's what Ray and the rest of us have decided.'

'I'm not a stranger!' I dump my bike and open out my hands. 'Kell, you *know* me. I've been here loads of times – I've been to Meetings!'

'Not for a while,' Kell says, his eyes unblinking.

'This is bullshit.' Losing patience, I start to walk through the gap, but Kell blocks my path. He steps in front of me, using his body to bar access the same way he'd muscle in front of Mellow to get her to change direction.

I look up at him. He's mid-thirties, and significantly taller than me. 'Man, get out of my—'

'*Kell.*'

Cheeks fiery pink, nostrils flaring, Rory marches up to the gate. The green fisherman's pants she's wearing snap against her ankles at the hems. Her shorn head makes her look like an Amazon, and her fists are clenched. Even though I'm pissed at Kell, I can't help but smile when I see her.

She whacks her hand on the gate near Kell's arm. 'Let him in, Kell. Stop being idiotic.'

Kell frowns. 'Ray said no outsiders.'

'I don't give a shit what Ray said. It's *Bo*. Let him in.' She glares at Kell's expression of indecision. '*Right now*.'

He sighs and moves aside.

I pick up my bike and wheel it through the gap. I can't help smirking at Kell as I go by. 'Saved by my woman.'

Rory grabs the bike off me. 'Come on.'

She wheels in front, I follow behind. We weave through the paths, and I can't help but notice that the property seems a little wilder than usual. Nobody's been cutting back the vines, or the spots where jungle has started encroaching on the pathways. I guess they've been busy with other things. But the whole place seems deserted.

'Where is everybody?'

'They're … getting things ready.' Rory has to squeeze the bike through the undergrowth. A blackberry runner hooks on her arm; she shoves it away. 'I'm sorry about the gate. Things are crazy here.'

'It's okay.' I push bamboo leaves out of my face. 'Are we going to your place?'

'No. Kell will tell Ray you're here, and he'll come looking for you. Bo, I'm so sorry I didn't meet you. I couldn't get away.'

'I get it.' I don't really, but I know that something serious is going on.

'We've all been directed to stay within the boundaries of the property.'

'By Ray?'

She nods. 'And there's something else, too, but… Wait until we get to the river.'

Giant trees, the downhill slope, cornflowers in the grass on the way… We make it to the river, cross the bridge and walk fast, up past the bathing area to the bank where Rory gets her clay. That's where she finally settles my bike against a tree and turns to face me.

'Oh, *Bo*.' She hugs me tight.

I return the hug, clutching her against me. 'Rory, what the hell's going on?'

'Shh. I'll tell you. But I just need this for a second.'

She stands on tiptoe, rubs her cheek against mine, angles her face so our lips fit together. She's not the only one who needs this. Her body is warm, and I feel as if I've been on simmer all day, thinking about her. My hands smooth down her back. Her mouth makes soft, moist promises against mine until my knees start to weaken and we both sink down together.

Her hair is mouse-fur short – I can feel the contours of her head with my fingers as we kiss. She sits straddling my lap, facing me. Her hands roam over my arms, squeeze my shoulders, stroke my neck, my chest. I'm getting uncomfortably fired up, and I have to pull back for air.

'Time out. Whoa. God, you feel fucking amazing. I've missed you so much. But you've gotta tell me what's happening.'

She closes her eyes, opens them. Now we're face to face

I can see how tired she is, the large circles of fatigue darkening her eye sockets, the hollowness in her cheeks. She looks as if she hasn't slept for days.

'It's… Things are crazy, like I said. When Star and Stuart left, Ray was hopping mad. But the other big thing is that Sally has chosen her leaving day. It's tomorrow, Bo.'

'*Tomorrow?*' My immediate thought is *Not on White Night!* which seems selfish and grotesque, but maybe it's because the thought of Sally dying at all is grotesque. 'That's… that's too soon.'

'I know.' Rory picks at the collar of my T-shirt, her fingers unsteady. 'Everyone's upset. This is all happening so fast… And I can't come to the fundraiser, Bo, not on Sally's leaving day.' Her chin is wobbling. She presses her lips together.

I cup her jaw in my hand. 'Rory, you shouldn't be alone tomorrow.'

'I won't be alone. We'll all be together.'

'I mean, *I* want to be with you. You'll be grieving, and I want to be there for you. Somebody needs to be looking out for you – have you been sleeping? Eating properly?'

She shakes her head. 'I've been up nights, talking with Sally and Ilona. And the Meetings have been going so late, until two or three in the morning…'

'Oh, babe, that's so nuts.' I curl my arms around her – she seems to soak up the support. 'Rory, this isn't normal. I'm serious. And you don't have to deal with it all on your own. You should get out for a while.'

She frowns. 'Get out?'

'Yeah. Take a break from Eden, while you're coping with

Sally's leaving.' Now I've suggested it, I'm possessed by the idea. 'You could come to my place. Just pack a bag and come over.'

'I don't know…' Rory's brow furrows.

'Listen. Do you know when everything is supposed to be … you know … *happening* tomorrow?'

She pulls back. 'Sally wants it to happen as the sun goes down. So that's about seven o'clock.'

'And you'll need to be here for Ilona for a while after that, yeah?'

'Yes, of course.'

'Okay. Then I'll come get you. It'll be late, about ten.'

She's shaking her head again. 'No, Bo. You're not allowed on the property.'

'*That's right.*' Another voice breaks through the quiet talk between me and Rory.

Ray Carl is standing near the tree where Rory has propped the Cannondale. His face is stony, and he's wearing something different – trousers under a pale collarless shirt. It gives him an air of gravitas, although that could also be because of his glowering expression, and the way his arms are crossed.

'Bo, I believe Kell told you that we aren't admitting visitors to Eden right now.'

'Yeah, I was told.' Rory has already jumped up; I push off the ground to stand.

'But you didn't respect that,' Ray says.

I brush dirt off my hands. 'I made a promise to meet Rory today. I had to respect that promise first.'

'Fine, you've met,' Ray says, with a thin grin. 'Now it's time to go.'

329

I hesitate, look at Rory, but her lips are pressed together and she's nodding. I don't want to cause trouble, and I don't want to start a fight with Rory's dad, right here in the middle of Eden.

Rory walks with me all the way to the gate, Ray shadowing us. I can't leave her like this, though.

I glance at Ray. 'So, you guys are on high alert or something, is that it?'

Ray makes the thin smile again as we walk. 'Things are moving, Bo. I wasn't happy about the child welfare investigation, but then I realised – it's time to shake things up. Stir the pot. It's like evolution. Like the earth revving its engine, you know what I'm saying? We've all been called to meet the challenge. Have you felt challenged these last few weeks, Bo?'

'Yes, sir,' I say, my face set.

Ray snorts, shakes his head. 'You never did lose that desire to bow to authority, did you, Bo? See, that's why you never truly accepted the call. You never really let go of the false self – the conditioning you were raised with that blocks your spiritual awakening.'

I look at him now with open eyes. Ray has lost the plot. I don't know if he even understands half the stuff that's coming out of his mouth – *I* sure as hell don't. But I know that whatever is happening here, it's hurting Rory.

'Have you looked at your daughter lately?' I say quietly. 'Have you seen how tired she is? She's—'

'None of that is your concern.' The lines on Ray's forehead and around his mouth are pinched. 'Bo, we're not hurting anyone here. This is our choice, our free will, our pledge to

330

the earth, our message. We're part of something important, and none of us can go back. Your selfishness makes it impossible for you to understand.'

He gestures for Kell to let me pass out of the gate. Rory pushes her way forwards.

'Aurora—' Ray starts.

'You said we have *free will*,' Rory spits back, before turning to me, helping me with my gloves. She leans in close, her voice a whisper. 'Tomorrow night, at midnight. I'll come to you.'

'Rory—'

She kisses me quickly, hugs me in order to deliver another whispered message. 'I'll be at the skate park. Count on it.'

We pull apart, and I give her one last anxious look before getting on my bike and cycling away.

As soon as I get home, I do the only thing I can think to do: I call Cam.

'Oh crap, Bo,' she says. 'I meant to tell you earlier. You asked me to find out what I could about the Eden thing, but then I got caught up in all the White Night stuff and—'

'What is it?' I'm chewing my thumbnail.

'I'm sorry, Bo, I completely—'

'Cam, let go of your Catholic guilt for one second and tell me what the hell's going on with—'

'They're closing it down,' she blurts. 'The welfare investigation was just the start. Council checked the leasehold, and found that the community is way behind on its rent. The Eden community is going to be evicted.'

29

'Have you got everything?' Dad asks.

'I think so.' I pat myself down, haul on my backpack.

He checks his watch. 'It's nine-thirty. I'm gonna take your mother and Connor home. I know you'll be out late, but try to keep me updated. Let me know when you're heading back home.'

'I'll make sure to text. I'll be on my phone all night, Dad.'

'Great.'

We're standing out front of The Codfather, and there are people *everywhere*. Up and down the street, banners are flying and folks are moving around, getting food, coffee, talking, laughing. Mum waves at me from a bench seat a few metres away – she's chatting to Antonia Lanzzi. Connor leans against her, weary from all the excitement.

Light displays swirl lava-lamp patterns on the walls of buildings all along Gough Street and behind the stage at the skate park – it's an amazing contrast with the dark of the night. Music from the speakers bounces around in the air, the bass thumping into the pavement.

White Night is going *off*.

'Dad, I've gotta go. They're starting the announcements in an hour, and I've gotta help Loz with—'

'Okay, go, go.' Dad grins at me. 'Enjoy yourself.'

I smile at him. 'I will. And I'll text.'

'Okay. Good luck!' But as I turn in the direction of the skate park, he reaches for my shoulder. 'Bo – this is a great night. It's a good thing you've all done. A good thing for the whole town.'

I smile. 'Thanks, Dad.' Then I remember that talking is important, and there's something I still need to know. 'Dad, are you sure you're fine with me changing subjects, and pulling out of the tryouts for the rep team? I know I kinda sprung it on you.'

'You're kidding, right?' He snorts. 'I've been eating your dinners for the last week, mate. You can really cook.'

I feel my face warm up. 'I didn't know if you thought I'd made the right choice. My whole life up until now has been about sport. I thought maybe you'd be disappointed.'

'Bo.' Dad clasps my shoulder. 'It's your life, and your choice. You can never disappoint me if you do what you know in your heart is right.'

I take a deep breath, release it. 'Okay. And Dad? If you ever want to go back up to Queensland, to see Liam, maybe do some digging to find out where you're from…'

'Bo, I'd … I'd like that.' Dad blinks hard. Then he gives my shoulder a final squeeze, before we both get too overwrought. 'Now, you're sure Rory's meeting you tonight?'

'Yeah, she said she would.' I'm clinging to that thought. 'I told her it's okay to stay at our place, so she doesn't have to go home.'

Dad nods. 'She's welcome to stay. You tell her it's all right by us.'

Rory's coming – she said she would. And once she's out in the world, away from Ray, I'm going to give her a refuge, like she once gave me.

*

The rest of the night consists of dancing, and coordinating, and dancing, and more coordinating. Donations are flowing in fast. The music is fantastic, even after Jem Reynolds takes a break and hands over to one of the younger guys. I'm not as lost in it as I'd like to be – I'm always keeping my eye out for Rory. I talked with Dad about going to collect her from Eden, but we decided that would probably only create conflict. I don't want to cause Rory any more stress than what she's dealing with already. Better to wait for her to come to me.

So my focus isn't really on enjoying myself. Plus, there's always something I'm noticing: like that the recycling bins need to be emptied, then Cam needs a hand locating Lindsay about pulling the plugs for the light shows, then Sprog wants me to grab the guy from the council and tell him that he's needed to say a few words about the skate park project on stage. Announcements are made, lost friends are located, microphones are stage-managed. Being part of the event organisation team is harder than I thought it would be.

But there's a moment when Loz drags me into the moshpit and Cam hugs me, and Sprog chest-bumps me, laughing. For a few minutes we're all together, dancing like lunatics, slamming it hard, screaming at the tops of our lungs right along with everyone else as the street crew sprays water over the crowd. Our sweat steams on the night air. That's when I feel like I know exactly what the spirit of White Night is about, when – for one brief, pure moment – I let everything go.

I look up and see Jem Reynolds has taken back the DJ spot. Two other guys from the skating crew grab the mic and start beatboxing as the riffs from 'Whatta Man' by Salt-N-Pepa bounce out of the speakers. Cam pushes past us and climbs up onto the stage. She's flushed in the cheeks, smiling broadly as she grabs the other microphone.

'There's someone we need to thank for all this!' she yells. She looks ridiculously happy. Her arm goes out like she's trying to embrace the whole crowd, and the cheers coming from around me are enormous. 'You all know who really made this thing happen, right? Well, if you don't, you should.'

Whistles and whoops from the crowd go off like a series of firecrackers. Cam's smile gets even bigger, then she turns towards the moshpit.

'Dominic Hamilton, get up here,' she says, but whoa, her voice has gone so breathy and low it sounds like a different kind of command.

Catcalls now, mixed with the applause and cheers. The crowd starts chanting, '*Sprog! Sprog! Sprog!*' and after a bit of shoving from people behind him, Sprog vaults up onto the stage. He's sweaty, and his hair is ratty, and his T-shirt's limp, like he's been dancing for hours – which he has – but the glow on his cheeks is real. He stands there like Bashful Dwarf until Cam tugs his sleeve to step closer.

'Do-o-mini-ic…' Cam singsongs into the mic.

Sprog clears his throat as the mic comes his way. 'Um, yeah?'

There's a few laughs at that, but it's all good, the people in the crowd are on his side. He's grinning with it, the energy of the night, and the feeling of being among friends.

Cam slips an arm around his waist, faces the crowd. 'Dom, we all wanted to say thank you. Because of you, we've raised nearly *five thousand dollars* for the skate park restoration, and the council is on board to make it happen.'

Mad cheers. Sprog's eyebrows hike, and we all see him mouth, 'Seriously? Five grand?' at Cam.

She nods and grins. 'It wouldn't have happened without you. You've worked your butt off for this cause, and we need to show our appreciation.'

'Yeah, show him!' some wag calls out. More laughter.

That seems to be all the encouragement Cam needs. She yanks on Sprog's shirt front with her free hand, brings his face around, and there – in front of a screeching, wolf-whistling audience – she kisses him hard. It takes him about one second to catch up, then his arms lift as he scoops up her hair and kisses her back. The crowd goes absolutely nuts. When the kiss finally ends, when they both pull back, Cam's cheeks are even more flushed, and Sprog looks punch-drunk.

I turn to Lozzie, who's laughing and making thumbs-up signs at them with both hands. 'Okay, what time are we closing down this snog-fest?'

'Um, now?' Loz checks her phone. 'It's after twelve, so that's officially it. But we've still got the pack-up.'

'It's after twelve?' I look around. I can't see any shaved heads nearby.

'Yeah, why?'

'Rory's meeting me. She said she'd be here by twelve.'

Lozzie shrugs. 'Maybe she's up the back? Have a squiz around. I'll call time.' She pushes forwards towards the stage, signalling Cam to make final thankyous and wish everyone goodnight.

I pull back, scanning the crowd more intently. There's still a lot of people moving around, which makes it hard. A few figures are staggering here and there – it's an all-ages gig, so no booze on site, but I know some folks snuck in their own.

I'm still looking for Rory when Sprog bumps up against me, laughs and gives me a high five. Cam is a few steps behind him, talking to Loz.

'What'd you think?' Sprog asks.

He's got such a wolfie grin on his face that I've got to grin back. 'This... this could be the most amazing night I've ever seen in Lamistead.'

'It was *incredible!*' Cam yells, and she throws her arms around Sprog's neck. Now that she's kissed him so publicly, it's like she's got a licence to just go for it anytime from here on in. Which, okay, I'll give them both a pass on that one.

But something's missing, *someone's* missing, and I'm getting a creepier and creepier feeling about it.

Lozzie leans in and fixes her eyes on me. 'Where is she?'

'I don't know.' I shrug, but I must look helpless, cos Lozzie frowns.

'That's not good.'

'No.'

Cam detaches from Sprog for a second. 'Did Rory make

it?' There must be something in the way I look back at her, because her expression changes.

'She didn't show.' And there's no denying it now – this feeling inside demands movement. Only I'm stuck in place. My joints are glued with indecision.

Loz grabs me by the shoulder. Her eyes have a worried set. 'I think...you need to go find her.'

'Yeah.' I remember the look in Ray's eyes, the last time I saw Rory in Eden. Loz's anxiety collides with the anxiety inside me, and that's when the flame finally ignites, burns away all doubt. 'I think I need to go find her. I think I need to go right now.'

Cam's concern has got Sprog's attention. 'Mate, how was she getting in?'

'She was cycling,' I say, but I'm already pushing past them. I make one spin to orient myself, then jog for the parking area on Gough Street.

But the others are keeping pace with me.

'Could she have had a bike malfunction?' Cam asks, struggling to pull on her backpack.

'No way.' Sprog helps her with the straps. 'Fennelli does good repair work, that bike was solid.'

'She could've walked it in, if it came to that,' Lozzie points out.

'Could it have been something to do with the community eviction?' Cam says. 'An official meeting or something?'

'On a night like tonight?' Lozzie counters. 'With all the town council members and officials here at the fundraiser?'

'I'm gonna go to Eden.' I can't think with all this chatter around me. The anxious fizz in my blood is loud enough. We've reached the pavement fronting the parking area, and

338

there's nobody here but us. I wave my hands. 'Riding's too slow. I need a car. Shit, where's all the fucking car jockeys when you need them?'

'One sec,' Sprog says. He squeezes Cam's shoulder and dashes away.

'I don't think this is urgent,' Cam says, wringing her hands. 'It can't be something serious. She would've found a way to let you—'

'She doesn't have a *phone*, Camilla.' My voice has taken on this low, brutal earnestness as I sweep my eyes around the car park. Lozzie holds my arm, as if she's trying to stop me from taking off. If someone doesn't give me access to a car in about five seconds, there's a chance that could happen.

Sprog comes back at a run. 'Found someone.' He rests his hands on his knees, panting. 'You won't like it, but I found someone.'

I pull at my hair. 'I honestly don't give a fuck who drives at the moment, as long as they can …'

Three people break out of the bushes, a way behind him, and I groan.

'Oh, Jesus Christ,' Cam says, and she actually forgets to cross herself.

'Take a deep breath,' Lozzie says to me quietly.

'Where's the emergency?' Shandy says, hiking her designer-knock-off handbag onto her shoulder and twirling her keys in her hand as she comes closer. After hours of dancing, she's looking a bit dishevelled in the fashion department, but her make-up is still perfect. Kaylah trails behind her, appearing surprisingly sober.

The tall guy on Shandy's other side sighs loudly. 'Shan, the whole point of getting the car tonight was that I'd get to drive the bloody thing—'

Shandy swings around to stare down her brother in a way that would make lesser mortals turn to stone. 'Davey, that car is mine in a year. And if you think I'm going to let you behind the wheel, after all the beers you've had, and *wreck my car*, then you're a fucking idiot.' She turns back to all of us and puts a hand on her hip, her voice flat. 'I drive, or nobody goes anywhere.'

It's not much of a decision. I'm already moving. 'Shandy, I'm up front. I'll have to give you directions at the turn-off to Bowyer Track. Are you in the four-wheel drive?'

'You think my dad's giving me more than one car? You are seriously deluded.' Shandy walks me down towards a bright blue Nissan Patrol, her heels clacking on the pavement. She thumbs her keys and the car's indicators flash. 'I'll take you, but no more passengers.'

We've separated to go either side of the bonnet. Sprog and the others have suddenly realised they're not coming.

'Shandy—' Kaylah starts.

'Stick with them,' Shandy says to her, lifting her chin at Sprog and Cam and Loz. She gets in the driver's side.

Sprog puts a hand on the bonnet. 'What if you need back-up?'

'I'll wing it,' I say, swinging open the front passenger door.

'Getting in or getting out?' Shandy says in a bored voice. She's already buckling her seatbelt.

'In.' I baulk at the sight of Davey Patterson clambering into the back. 'Hey, what about him?'

'My brother has to come. It's the law or something.'

Shandy waves a hand, like, who knows what *that's* all about, as she slips the key into the ignition and the engine kicks over. 'Tell everyone to back off. I'm still not great at reversing.'

I make a pushing-away motion at Lozzie and Sprog as the Patrol squeals backwards out of the bay. Shandy straightens the car, flicks on the headlights. Cam gives me a tight, anxious wave, Shandy throws the car into gear and then we're coasting down Gough Street.

'So Hippie Girl didn't show up to meet you, is that it? Maybe she's broken up with you.' Shandy taps her nails on the steering wheel and her charm bracelet jingles. She's driving surprisingly well after her initial hoony reverse.

I clench my hands on my thighs. 'Thanks for that theory, Shandy, and for the way you just threw it out there, but actually I think Rory would dump me in person.'

Shandy sighs as we turn off onto Trout. 'Yeah, she probably would. I got dumped by text once, but that doesn't seem quite her style.'

'Not to mention the fact she doesn't have a phone.' But I'm surprised to learn about Shandy's romantic pratfall, and even more surprised she told me about it.

'So how do we get to Eden?'

'Go Martigan's Road, then take Fogarty's Hill Road.'

'Shan, put the heating on, would ya?' Davey calls from the back. 'This car's bloody freezing.'

'Oh, shut up,' Shandy calls back, but she punches the buttons for the heating anyway.

I can't look out the window as the dark houses and trees flash by. Everything inside me feels blurry and raw – it doesn't help to have blurry visuals as well.

'Thanks for this,' I say stiffly.

Shandy does that thing with her pinkie finger and her hair. 'I would've said no, but Baz and Teo were too pissed to drive, and Sprog said you were desperate.'

We cruise without talking. Beyond the celebration at the skate park, the whole town is still and silent. It's weird, driving around while everyone else is at White Night. Everything feels abandoned. No pedestrians, no movement except our car. I think of Ray's vision of a world without people. This is what it would be like: silent, breathless buildings, everything empty in this strange, heartbreaking way.

That only makes me think of Rory. 'Can we go faster?'

'Not unless we want to get a ticket. And I don't want to get a ticket.'

'She could've had an accident on her bike. She could've been hit by a car—'

'And she could be sitting at home, reading a book. You don't fucking know. I know you want to make this into some kind of drama, Bo, but this isn't the Batmobile, okay?'

'Fine.'

'I mean, who doesn't have a phone? Jesus.'

'They're off the grid.'

'It's stupid.'

'There's no reception anyway—'

'It's *stupid*.' She slaps her hand on the wheel. 'You're *both* stupid. See, time has moved forwards, and now we're in the *modern world*. If I wanted to live in a commune, and weave my own clothes, and grow my own food, and have a dozen babies by the time I was twenty, I'd kill myself and ask God to send me back to the eighteenth century. I bet they don't even have

342

running water. I mean, what the fuck is wrong with people? It's, like, it's not enough that we've progressed as a society, we've gotta feel *guilty* about it, too.' She grips the steering wheel, scowling.

I didn't realise Shandy even had an opinion about it, except to think that Rory was a bug to be squashed underfoot. I raise my eyebrows. 'Wow.'

'Oh, shut up.'

'You feel better, now you've got that out?'

She glares at me.

'Tell me more, if you like. I'm a captive audience.'

'Whatever. Let's just go find your GF, then you can get the hell out of my car.'

For some reason, Shandy's grating honesty feels like an improvement on everyone else's anxiety. I'm being driven to the rescue by someone who not only hates me and my girlfriend, but hates everything my girlfriend stands for.

Weirdest. Night. Ever.

We get onto Fogarty's Hill Road, and the Patrol grumbles fast over the dirt. Shandy's gunning it now she's outside the town limits – there must be a plume of dust behind us about a mile long. The stars above are beautiful, like a wide, glittering net, but I'm not really enjoying the view. Davey seems to have dozed off in the back seat, but he wakes with a grunt when Shandy follows my directions onto Bowyer Track and the car hits the first of many potholes and loose branches.

She shifts down a gear. 'This road is the pits.'

'You should try it on a bike. Keep going until you get to the crest of the next hill.'

'If my suspension drops out cos of this, you're totally paying the repair bill.' But now we're getting close, and Shandy peers through the windscreen. 'Hey. That looks like a fire up ahead.'

She's right: there's a red glow hanging over the site of the Eden property. Frowning, I lean forwards as far as my seatbelt will allow. 'They have a fire-pit in the Meeting House. But it's not that close to the access road.'

'Is that a bonfire?' Davey asks blearily from the back seat.

Shandy grimaces. 'Maybe they're all dancing around the bonfire with flowers and body paint or something.' She glances at me. 'But that looks too big. Bo, if this is a real fire, we should get out of here. Go call the CFA.'

'Let me find out what's going on first.' I point. 'There's the entrance. Stop here.'

She pulls the Patrol up in front of the *Garden of Eden* sign, and I shove open the car door, cursing the gate and Ray's paranoia, cos if it weren't there then we could have driven in. But I've got other worries. The red glow from the property is unmistakeable, and now we're stopped and there's no dust swirling, I can see the smoke in the air.

'I think I should go,' Shandy says. 'I think I should call.'

I cling onto the car door. 'Please just wait. Give me five minutes, okay?'

'I'm not dying in a fire cos of your dumb girlfriend, Bo.'

'*Five minutes*. If I'm not back by then, take off.' Which is when *I* take off, running to the gate.

Shandy yells out the driver's side window. 'I hate you for this!'

'You hate me anyway!' I call back, but then I ignore her

cos I've passed the gate and I'm running towards the Meeting House, running towards Rory.

Leaves and branches whip me in the face as I bolt along the path. I inhale, and the air is smoky. I barrel around a moonlit corner, vault a pumpkin vine, and look up to see—

The Meeting House is on fire.

I skid to a stop. The floor is stone, but the walls and what's left of the roof are flaming. And I can hardly comprehend what's in the middle of it all: the fire-pit is glowing, and a few lumped shapes are grouped around it. Are *people* sitting there? That can't be, it can't be right...

But I inch closer, shying from the radiant heat, and there *are* people. I can see two shapes, shapes I don't want to recognise, that I can't believe.

The unmistakeable white swirls of a period dress – Virginia. Beside her, Jules's waistcoat. They're leaning against each other.

The whooshing roar of the flames is loud, and the inside of my head is loud, too. What are they doing? Why aren't they moving? Where's Ray, and Allison and Kell and Ilona and Sally? Where's Rory?

I step as close as I can, shouting at Virginia and Jules. Close enough to see the brown glass bottles strewn around the edge of the pit – ginger beer. Close enough to see the mugs that have fallen and smashed. Close enough to see closed eyes, and slack faces.

How can they be asleep in the middle of all this?

But they're not asleep.

And suddenly everything Mrs Ramanathan said fits together and smashes me in the face.

Mass suicide…they drank a solution of cyanide in a type of cordial called Kool-Aid…

My mind can't take that in, can't handle it. This can't be real. This can't be happening.

The people came together in a spirit of social equality, utopian harmony, but the dream soured… So, Bo, have you come to drink the Kool-Aid with us?

This is happening. Jesus, god.

Nausea in my stomach. I back off, and the fire is gaining momentum so fast that my face feels sunburnt. Black spots in my vision. I can't worry about that now. I can't worry if the Meeting House and the two people inside it burn. The others must be here somewhere. I have to find them. I have to find Rory.

Oh god – *Rory.*

I take a wide path around the fire. I have no way of knowing if she's at her hut, but that's the first place I think to go.

I run.

My feet are moving so fast I can't feel the thump they make on the ground. The reverb of my feet is absorbed into my whole body – my pounding heart, my gasping breaths – all churning together until I'm vibrating from the inside out.

Most drank willingly, but some accounts suggest that the ingestion of cyanide was not entirely voluntary…

My skin's been pulled off and I'm running bare and vulnerable, wet with blood and sweat, fear rising up off me like steam and blown away with the rush of my pace, to reach the hut, to find my girl.

The group had practice runs for what Jones called 'revolutionary suicide'… White Night… White Night…

All I can feel now is the burn in my calves and the heat in

my lungs, this asthmatic wheeze coming out of me as I run through green plants made black and red by night and fire. I sprint around a corner so fast I skid, and I—

Hit a leathery wall, bounce off it, fall back sprawling in the bracken.

'*You*,' Ray says.

His clothes are blackened and his face is haggard, lips violet in the fireglow. Compared to other times I've seen him, full of energy and charisma, now he seems withered.

I stagger up off the ground. 'What's happening? Virginia and Jules ... the Meeting House ... *What have you done?*'

He looks at me through rheumy eyes. 'We wanted to shake things up. We were stirring the pot. If Aurora hadn't—'

He grimaces suddenly, lurches sideways and throws up on the grass nearby. I step back in disgust, in horror. Maybe Ray drank the ginger beer too. Right now, with the heat in the air roasting my lungs, I don't really care. There's only one thing I care about, and this isn't it.

'Where is she?' I step in again. '*Where's Rory?*'

'Our message ...' Ray mumbles. 'Humans are a cancer on the earth ... we tried to tell them, to be an example ...'

I grab him by the shirt front. 'An *example*? You wanted to be a fucking *example*?' My voice is cracking. 'People are *dead*,

Ray! People you loved! You tried to kill your whole fucking family, and for *what*?'

He pulls at my hands, and as I let him go, his expression contorts. 'They wanted to evict us! They forced our hand! And you're an outsider! You'll never understand, you'll never...'

I'm sobbing for breath. 'Jesus Christ... There's no "outside" and "inside", Ray. It's all one world. *Where's Rory?*'

He shakes his head at the ground. When he tries to snag my T-shirt sleeve, I yank away. Talking to Ray is a waste of time. I need to find Rory and get us out of here before the whole place ignites.

I turn and run.

The leaves slapping at me are dusted with ash. Then the hut and its garden come into view – the hut is intact, no fire here.

'Rory!'

I push through the front door. Everything is the same as the last time I visited. The bed with rumpled blankets, the kettle and the dresser, the crystals at the window. Only the flicker of the fire outside lights the darkness. The range is dead, and the inside of the hut feels cold.

'*RORY!*' I scream it out, even though I know she's not here.

I dive back outside, around to the pottery workshop. Nothing. Just the round bodies of abandoned sculptures peeking out from behind finished bowls on the shelves, like moons behind clouds. I grab at my hair. Goddammit, where *is* she?

Think, Bo.

The crackle of fire sounds louder. She could be at the

river – it's where I'd go if there was a fire. She even said it herself: *we can always retreat to the river*.

I jerk in that direction, thrust past grabbing vines. The burble of water is almost drowned out by the snapping pops of the fire, the pounding of my feet on the wooden bridge. My heart pounds louder.

When I spin around the boulders near the washing place, I hear a desperate shriek.

'*Stop, it's Bo!*' Allison's face is white as moonlight, her hand clutching Kell's arm.

I see the thick branch Kell's wielding, and rear back, almost falling on my arse.

'Jesus.' Kell blanches, lowers the branch. 'Fuck, man, I thought you were Ray.'

'*What the fuck is going on?*' I grab his arm, panting.

'The whole world's turning to *shit*,' Kell moans. He throws the branch down, grabs at his hair. 'I didn't want this. None of us wanted this…'

Allison splashes out of the river edge towards me. 'We came back from Sally and Ilona's, and Ray started going on about it… What we'd all agreed to do.'

'To drink the ginger beer together,' I say. *Drinking the Kool-Aid*. I get a sharp stab of nausea.

Allison just nods. 'Virginia and Jules were already…' Her eyes cloud, and she swallows hard. 'They were drinking when Rory showed up. And we had our cups—'

'I lifted it.' Kell's voice is shaky. 'I just couldn't…'

He gags, and Allison continues. 'Then Rory started arguing with Ray, and he went ballistic. He kicked the logs out of the fire-pit, began throwing bottles around.'

'He said we'd wrecked everything.' Kell has tears in his eyes. 'We'd lost the faith. He said we were selfish.'

'We just wanted to live.' Allison turns to him, folds him into a hug. 'It's not your fault, Kell.'

It's nice they're supporting one another, but the fire's almost on top of us, and my most important question is still unanswered. 'Guys, hug later. *Where's Rory?*'

'I-I don't know.' Allison wipes her damp face, smeared now with ash and mud. 'Ray grabbed her, and she pulled away, then she just ran.'

I make a desperate, frustrated groan. She could be anywhere.

Then I remember something. The Meeting House. I don't want to think about it – about Virginia's swirling dress, Jules's waistcoat – but I have to, there's something important. Ray's staggering around the property, Allison and Kell are here, Virginia and Jules drank the poison…

Ilona and Sally.

They're like my den mothers.

They're more than that – Rory loves those women like they're her real parents. And they weren't at the Meeting House.

I think of Sally's awkward, painful movements the other night, her fateful announcement. If I was going to die, I'd want to die in my own house, with the things I loved around me and my family by my side.

I can't be sure. If I'm wrong, that could be my last chance gone. But I think I know the best place to look.

I grab Allison's arm. 'There's a car just outside the front gate. Can you and Kell get there?'

Her face becomes determined, and she squeezes Kell's slumped shoulders. 'I didn't want to die at the Meeting House, and I'm sure as hell not going to die in a fire. What about Rory and Ilona?'

'I'll find them.' I turn.

Kell snags my arm in a death-grip. His eyes are watering, and he's gasping from the smoke. 'You can't go back in there, man. The whole place is going up!'

'I'll be okay. Get yourselves out!' I shake him off, start back the way I came, call over my shoulder. 'Dunk yourselves in the river! Go wide around the fire!'

The path leading away from the river feels hotter than before. I strip off my hoodie as I run, lash it around my waist, take the log steps two at a time. Running uphill steals the breath right out of me. Or maybe it's smoke – that means the fire's closer. All I can think of now is Rory. There's the cottage, at the top. Please, god, let this be where I find her.

I dash around the forty-four-gallon drums, nearly slipping on detritus from one of the compost heaps. I thrust through the wooden door, past the ivy wreath and into the main room.

'Rory! *RORY!*'

The inside of the cottage is dim; everything is quiet. Panic catches up with me. My chest and legs are burning, and my knees shake as the adrenaline burst tails away. I lean over, coughing, wanting to cry. She's not here, and I don't know where she is, and what if she was behind the couches in the Meeting House? Fuck, I didn't check. What if Ray found her? What if she's—

'Bo?'

Light flickers: a candle, up above. Someone is coming

down the ladder from the loft, in a white shirt and a pair of green fisherman's pants—

'Oh fuck, thank *god*.' I squeeze Rory tight as she tumbles into my arms.

'*Bo*.' She hugs me hard enough to bust a rib, but I don't care. The soft golden fuzz on her head brushes against my chin, then she pulls away, desperate. 'Ilona's upstairs with Sally, and—'

'You didn't drink it.' I clasp her arms. 'The ginger beer.'

'Of course not.' Her face is drawn and her eyes are red-rimmed, but she looks whole, she looks together. She squeezes my biceps. 'Sally didn't drink it either. But...she had something else prepared. And now Ilona's up there with her.'

'Oh.' It flows over me, this knowledge that Sally is gone. I can't deal with it yet, can't retain it.

'And I need your help. We have to get Ilona out of here.'

'The Meeting House is on fire.'

'I know. I was there.' She looks even more exhausted, saying that.

'I found Allison and Kell. They're heading for the gate. The gardens are going up.'

Rory presses her lips, touches a hand to her forehead. 'Then we really need to go.'

'Now,' I say. 'We need to go *now*. I have a car out front.'

'Can you help me get Ilona there?'

'Absolutely.' We'll have to get back through the fire. It doesn't matter. Rory is here, and alive, and she needs me. 'What can I do?'

'Come up with me and help bring Ilona down. She'll

be…resistant. But once we've gotten her away, I think she'll be okay. Is the fire really bad?'

I nod. 'It's close.'

'Come on.'

Rory tugs hard on my hand and I follow. I clamber up the ladder behind her, not thinking much about anything except *she's alive*. I can see her pale hands on the rungs. I can see the back of her neck. I want to shout, I want to celebrate, but we don't have time for that.

My feeling of gratefulness and relief evaporates when we reach the loft. It's a simple room. There's a rocking chair, a table, a clothes basket. A lit candle stands in a saucer on the nightstand, and on the low futon bed, a woman lies as if she's asleep. Ilona sits beside her, holding her hand.

It's Sally on that bed. It's Sally with the sleeping eyes, with the grey static skin, with the expression of absence. I can't just see it – my heart demands to know it, too. Sally is dead. Her body rests, but her soul has flown away. She won't wake up again. She won't smile, or offer me stew, or give me a hug, or *be* again in this life.

I haven't ever seen a person in death before tonight, but now I've seen three. I'm dizzy for a second, and Rory seems to sense it. She steadies me briefly before walking closer to the bed.

'Ilona.' Rory puts a hand on Ilona's shoulder. 'Lonie, it's time.'

'No,' Ilona whispers. She's hunched, holding Sally's hand, her face stripped of colour.

'Lonie, Bo is here. He said the fire is coming. We have to go now.'

'Ilona, I'm sorry.' My voice breaks. 'I'm so, so sorry.'

'Lonie, we have to leave.' Rory hunkers in front of her den mother. 'Right *now*.'

'You leave,' Ilona whispers. 'I'm going to stay.'

'No, you're not.' Rory's tone is dripping with anxiety. 'You have to come, Ilona. You have to come with me.'

'Where are they?' Ilona straightens, looks around. 'Sally took the pills, then while I was holding her, you—'

'I buried the rest of the pills in the compost,' Rory says.

'Why did you *do* that?' Ilona wails. 'I told Sal... I told her I'd be right behind her, and now you've—'

'Ilona.' I step in, squat down beside Rory. 'Ilona, please. I'm sure Sally didn't want you to go with her.'

'Yes, she *did*!' Ilona throws her head back, her face twisted with grief. 'She... No, she didn't... Oh, Sal!'

Ilona sobs, with a gasping sound that reminds me of Mr Showalter, and collapses forwards. Rory holds her close, patting and rocking.

Then I smell it – the smoke in the air. I stand up to give myself some space. Is it on our clothes? No, it's not our clothes. If I can smell it here, inside the house, we're in trouble.

I squat down again. '*Ilona*. We need to get out of the house. We need to go to the road.'

'I *can't*,' Ilona gasps. 'Sally—'

'Mama, please come,' Rory says, clutching Ilona's knees. Her expression is suddenly distraught, displaying the full horror of what she's been through tonight. 'Please. I *know* Sal wouldn't want you to stay. You told me that some things you just know, and I know this. She would want you to come with me. *Please*, Mama. Don't make me say goodbye to you too.'

Tears run down Rory's cheeks. Ilona sits, looking at Sally, and the pause is so loud and long I want to scream.

Then Ilona stretches out a hand. Her voice is hoarse from crying.

'Help me up,' she whispers.

✳

Outside we discover the flames are eating their way towards Rory's hut. We won't be able to get out the way I came in. The light from the fire is incandescent on Rory and Ilona's faces, and Rory looks away as the front of her garden starts to go up. I watch as the Narnian couch catches alight, and it's not just smoke that's making my eyes smart.

'Your sculptures,' I say to Rory.

But she shakes her head. 'There'll be more sculptures.'

'We need something to cover us. The smoke, and the radiant heat—'

She grabs my arm. 'Wait with Ilona.' Then she dashes back inside before emerging with two blankets. I recognise the swirling greens and reds straight away.

'Pure wool.' She has to raise her voice now over the sound of the fire. 'It's flame-retardant.'

She strides across to one of the forty-four-gallon drums – the roof overflow pipe feeds right into it – and dunks the two blankets in the water, soaking them completely. I help her drape the wet blankets over herself and Ilona and me. Ilona's face is dull, her actions slow, like she's moving underwater.

Rory takes Ilona's arm on one side, and I take the other. 'Let's go, let's go!'

We have to run far to the left, towards Star and Stuart's old place, skirt wide around the fire zone. But there's no way to avoid the main track from the Meeting House if we want to get to the gate, and that part is creeping with flames. I run under one blanket with Ilona. Rory goes ahead, covered with the other blanket, beating at flaming tufts on the path, embers flying around us. The bright red sparks are everywhere, falling like fireworks.

The gate itself is hot when we pass through. Then I'm staring at the downhill stretch of Bowyer Track, at the absence of Nissan Patrols in it.

'*Goddammit*, Shandy!' I spin on the spot.

Rory is sheltering Ilona. '*Shandy* has the car?'

'Yes. Shit. She said she'd wait, but ...'

Suddenly, there's the sound of an engine gunning, and the Patrol bounces up the rise. I see Shandy, white-faced in the driver's seat, then hear her as she winds the window down. 'Jesus, what are you waiting for? *Get in the car!*'

Davey Patterson isn't in the back seat anymore. I don't ask questions, just bundle Rory and Ilona and myself inside. Almost before the doors are closed, Shandy's spinning the wheel to do a sharp three-point turn. As she backs up, I hear the clang of metal as she hits the gate.

'Whoops.' Shandy checks her rear-view, gives us urgent, glaring glances. 'Buckle up, this is gonna be crazy. Christ, you all stink of smoke. Bo, your *hair*!'

I reach up quickly, feel heat, brush my fingers madly through my hair. 'What happened to five minutes?'

'I had to take the others out.' Shandy clings onto the wheel as we jounce downhill. 'Kell was coughing too much from the smoke – Kell's his name, right? And I drove to Fogarty's Hill to call the CFA.'

'Then you came back.' I'm impressed.

Shandy nods at me in the rear-view, clocks Ilona, who's slumped against Rory in the back. Her eyes meet Rory's. 'Hey.'

'Hey,' Rory says.

They share a look I can't decipher. Then there's a jolt. Shandy straightens the wheel and drags her eyes back to mine. 'Where are we going?'

Jesus, I don't know. I grab my hair again, shake my head. 'My place – they can all come to mine. Where's your brother?'

'Davey's with the others, they're waiting for the CFA.'

So we drive, Shandy speeding the Patrol along Bowyer Track, dodging branches. We collect Allison and Kell at the bottom of the track, and there's a sad reunion in the back. Rory seems so calm. It's got me worried.

Fogarty's Hill Road, back the way we came in. Shandy has to pull over to avoid the fire trucks that come screeching along the dirt. When I look back, I see a red haze glowing in the crowns of the trees, far behind.

Shandy doesn't make snarky comments, or ask questions, which is good, because Rory and Ilona and the others aren't up for that. When we get to my place, Shandy pulls the car up and we stumble out.

I lean in through the passenger-side window. 'Are you gonna be okay?'

'Why wouldn't I be?' Some of the usual haughtiness

is returning to Shandy's face. 'Stand back, I have to go get Davey.'

'Thank you. We would've been stuffed if you hadn't helped us.'

'Forget it.'

'Well, thanks anyway.' I'm about to turn when I remember something. 'And Shandy?' She looks at me, putting the car in gear. 'Whoever dumped you by text was a loser.'

She tries not to smile, revs the car, and takes off.

The quiet, after Shandy tears away, seems stranger than the madness we just left. Ilona leans on Rory, Allison and Kell look lost. I take Rory by the arm. 'Come on. This is my place.'

We all support Ilona, who's almost a dead weight now, up the stairs. Everyone looks horribly tired. It's not only weariness and gravity pressing on them: Rory and Allison and Kell seem shell-shocked. I can't imagine how Ilona must be feeling. I get them all through the door, down the dimly lit hall, walking slow, with Julie slavering and wagging her tail like mad.

'Bo? Is that…' Dad rushes forwards, helps us with Ilona. 'What happened?'

I hardly have enough energy left to gesture. 'Dad, this is Ilona and Allison and Kell. And this is Rory. The community is burning down. It was… There's a fire…'

'Jesus. Come and sit, all of you.' He ushers us to the dining table. 'Rory, hi. Are you okay, love? A fire, god almighty. Is it close?'

I shake my head. 'It was heading towards the river, so further east. And the CFA will be there now. I think they'll get it sorted. Dad…' I'm not sure how to say this part.

'Sally's dead. Virginia and Jules are …' The tears on Rory's cheeks could be from the stinging smoke or grief. Her voice hitches, steadies. 'They took poison. The eviction notice spooked them, and then Ray worked on them.'

'He nearly worked on us,' Allison confirms. She's still holding Kell's hand. 'The CFA will find bodies, near the Meeting House, and at Sally and Ilona's place …'

Dad goes completely still. He looks from Rory, to the others, to me. 'Is that true, Bo?'

The solemnity of his voice makes my eyes well up. I have to work hard for control. 'Yes. Yeah, it's true.'

'How many?' Another voice – Mum has walked into the room, her hair sleep-tossed, a shawl wrapped around her shoulders. She's in her pyjama pants and a T-shirt, her belly straining against the fabric. In the spare light of the kitchen bulb, she looks defined and solid and *alive*.

'*Mum*.' I hug her then, because I need to be hugged more than anything. And because she's Mum, she hugs my girl when she's finished hugging me.

'You must be Rory,' she says, smiling sadly.

Rory nods, sobs once, claps a hand over her mouth.

'It's all right,' Mum says, rubbing Rory's back. 'Let's get you sorted out. Bo, put the kettle on. Aaron, we need a jug of water, mugs, towels and blankets.'

It's Mum's response to everything – *put the kettle on*. That alone makes me feel more normal. I grab the kettle, eavesdropping as Mum sits down at the kitchen table with Rory and the others, teasing out the details of what happened.

Ilona finally talks, her voice rough and distant. Allison and Kell step in at the moments where she can't go on. They talk

360

about Jules and Virginia's despair at the idea of the community breaking apart. They explain how Sally was the one who made the choice to end her life, and how Ray exhorted the whole Eden community to band together in one final act of radical revolt. Rory talks about how hard it was to stand up to him, how desperate she felt.

When they finish, there's silence. I don't know if Mum and Dad can take in the enormity of it all, but neither can I. Three people confirmed dead. The destruction of the community, the razing of the property... I can't get my head around the horror of it, even though I was there to see the finale.

'Bo?' Rory clasps my hand, so I raise my head. 'What about Ray? What happened to him?'

I don't want to tell her. But it would be wrong not to. 'I saw him. He looked... I think he was sick, Rory. I think he took the poison.'

Rory nods calmly. Then her whole face crumples. I pull her into my shoulder as she starts shaking.

'I shouldn't care.' Her voice is muffled, gluey with tears. 'He chose that. I shouldn't care.'

'He's your father.' I stroke her hair, as Allison pats her on the other side.

'That's right. He's my father.' Rory shudders in my arms. 'Oh god—'

I hold her tight as she quakes; I hold her tight as she cries. My chest feels too full right now. It's hurting me to hear my girl sob like this, like her heart's gonna break. Her father and her den mother and her whole community, all in one night...

I don't hear the knock on the door, or Julie barking. Only when Dad comes back into the room do I look up.

'Hey.' Cam is biting her lip, her arms laden with a huge casserole dish. 'We heard about the fire. Shandy got on her phone and told the entire world, as usual. And Barry Fromer got the CFA call – he had to go in half pissed.' She plonks the dish on the kitchen bench.

'*Half* pissed? He was fully wrecked.' Sprog pushes forwards, his arms full of blankets. 'Anyway, we thought you might need a hand, hey.' He and Lozzie carry their loads towards the couch in the living room.

Mrs D'Amato is lugging carry-bags full of food. 'Liz, Aaron, hi. We bought extra supplies. They said everyone came back here. Where do you want all this?'

'Um, the kitchen is fine. Oh goodness...' My mother stands up, as people start pouring through the door.

Julie is going off her nut. Lozzie puts the kettle on again, ferries blankets to Allison and Kell, whose expressions are simultaneously shocked, grateful, and maybe a little freaked out. Lena D'Amato sits down beside Ilona, taking her hand gently. I feel like I'm in a whirlwind.

Dad taps me on the shoulder. 'You should come see this.'

He walks down the hall to the front door, beckons me forwards. Rory comes too, clinging to my arm.

Cars are pulling up in our driveway, people walking closer: the Lanzzis, the Reynoldses...holy shit, is that Mrs Ramanathan? Everyone is carrying bundles of supplies, bags of food and clothes.

We stand in the doorway and watch the bobbing line of headlights approaching our house in the dark, as the sound of talk spills out of the kitchen behind us.

'Looks like Lamistead's coming out in force,' Dad says.

Rory's breath hitches. 'Oh my god. Bo.'

'You thought your community was gone?' I pull her against me, grinning despite the thickness in my throat. 'Think again, babe.'

EPILOGUE

Weeks later

'Homework diaries, people! And I want your final essay on NGOs on my desk, or in my staffroom pigeonhole, by this Friday, are we absolutely clear? Please don't forget to attach your *name* to the essay...'

'Yes, Mrs Ramanathan,' everybody choruses, then the bell is ringing and we're outta here.

Sprog snags me before I can sprint for the bike racks. 'Wait up, man. I need your signature on this.'

'We're not submitting it until Wednesday!'

'Mrs Franklin said we need the organising committee's names at the top of the list.'

'Jesus, Sprog, you'll see me at training at five, get it then.' I check the time. 'Shit, I've gotta go.'

'Bo, come on.'

'Goddammit – okay, fine.' I drop my backpack, jog back. Sprog has the letter with the petition for the new recycling program for Lamistead Secondary. I tap the names already listed. 'What's the hurry? You haven't got Shandy yet. Or Lozzie.'

'Shandy's meeting me at the bus. Lozzie's… shit, I never know where Loz is now. She and Kaylah are always pissed off somewhere. Pashing behind the girls' toilets, probably.'

I sigh, dig in my bag for a pen. When that proves fruitless, I appeal to Sprog. He doesn't have one either. I'm about to start fuming when a black biro lands on the letter in front of me.

'Sign away,' Cam says, grinning as she walks closer. 'Move it, Bo. You're going to be late for training.'

I glare at her, and at Sprog for good measure, as I sign the bloody letter. Then I bolt.

Twelve kay of dirt roads later, I'm ditching my bike at the front steps, leaping up them two at a time, banging the door open, throwing my footy stuff together. I've just finished slathering a slice of bread with butter and jam when Mum walks into the kitchen, holding her tummy down low.

'Food food food,' she says, putting the kettle on. 'My god, I think my entire maternity leave pay is going to go on groceries. And what is it about cereal? I've never known two boys who eat so much cereal.'

'We're expanding,' I shrug. 'Turning into giants. You should be proud to have produced such alarmingly enormous specimens. The tallest men in all the land.'

'I am proud,' Mum says, smiling. She tucks my hair back behind my ear. 'Are Rory and Ilona still coming over for dinner?'

'Yep.' I fold my bread in half. 'Rory texted at the end of lunch to confirm. She sent some pics of the block. Ilona wants to talk to Dad about drainage. She and Allison are sussing out the best places to site the houses or something.'

'And firebreaks,' Mum says.

'Yeah, and firebreaks.' I nod, my voice sombre. We don't talk about that night much anymore. It was all anyone in Lamistead talked about for weeks, and I got pretty sick of it. 'Anyway, they met with the land council today and got permission, so it's all systems go.'

'The first Lamistead community-living site …' Mum smiles, shaking her head in wonder. 'It's going to be amazing. A lot of work, but amazing. Now seriously, Bo, are you really going to have time to cook dinner between the end of training and our guests arriving?'

'Did you get the supplies I need?'

'Yes, Monsieur Cordon Bleu.' She grins.

'Then watch me.' I grin back. 'Now I gotta move or I'll be late. And Mullet's only just forgiven me.' I pick up my bread, my training bag. 'Whatcha doing now, anyway? Where's Dad?'

Mum nods her chin at the verandah doors. 'Digging me a new vegetable bed. I think it's time we put your homegrown food plan into action.'

'Really? Sweet.' I step over to the verandah doors, check through the glass. 'Oh look, Dad and Con have got the bobcat out, what a surprise. Well, I guess that's the last we'll see of them for the next five or six hours—'

I turn when I hear a sound. A gasp.

'Mm.' Mum's got a hand against the kitchen bench, her head angled down. 'Ooh, I felt that.'

'Another kick?' She looks up at me, and I take a step back. Take a step forwards.

Mum rubs under her belly. 'Call Dad in from the garden, would you?'

'This is a joke.' I stare at her. 'You're screwing with me. This is a joke.'

'Bo, I never joke about—' Mum gasps again, steadies herself, rubbing more firmly. 'Hm. Wow.'

'Nonononono…'

'Yesyesyes…' She smiles sweetly at me.

'*Now?*'

'Well, it had to happen sometime.'

I rush closer. 'Oh god, what should I do? Oh, shit—'

'Bo, language. Call your father and your brother.'

'What about dinner?'

She blows out through another pain, rolls her eyes. 'And don't ask stupid questions.'

I grip her by the arm. 'What do you need? Oh, this is weird, shit, shit.'

Mum laughs through a huff of exhaled breath. 'Relax, Bo. It's a baby, not a national emergency. Call Rory and tell her we need a raincheck. I'll call the hospital—' She squeezes my arm suddenly, and her face tenses, her eyes close. After a second, she opens her eyes, looks straight at me. 'Okay, maybe it is a national emergency. Go get your father.'

'I don't want to leave you here!'

'I'll be fine.'

'Are you *serious?*'

She looks up at me, shaky but smiling. 'This is it, Bo. Are you ready for your world to change?'

Acknowledgements

Many thanks to the team that always makes the magic happen – everyone at Allen & Unwin is ace, but my deepest thanks to Eva Mills, Sophie Splatt and Jodie Webster for their encouragement, long talks about fictional people and communities, and infinite patience. If there are any screw-ups here, the fault is all mine. Thanks also to my agent, Catherine Drayton, who guided me from this story's inception.

I'd like to thank Blossom D'Onofrio, who gifted her name to this book, for her trust and goodwill. My gratitude also to Jared Thomas, Angela Savage and Clare Atkins, who steered me right on representation issues, and especially to Auntie Kath Coff and Auntie Julie McHale, who were kind enough to read parts of this manuscript.

Without support, I would achieve nothing. The friends and writers who supported me during this book's creation are many, but I'd like to say thanks to a few people in particular. The women of The Vault prop me up, and put up with my whingeing, and generally make writing a more pleasant, less solitary activity every day – you are all my heroes. Retreat buds and YA community friends – Amie, Jay, Cat, Lili, Will, Eliza, Nic, Kat, Ebony, Peta, Skye, Dave, Dani, Adele, Melissa, Bec…yeah, this could turn into a shopping list, but let me just say, 'You all rock!' and leave it at that.

Finally, the biggest thanks, as always, goes to my family – Geoff, Ben, Alex, Will and Ned. Love you all so so much.

What if Sherlock Holmes was the boy next door?

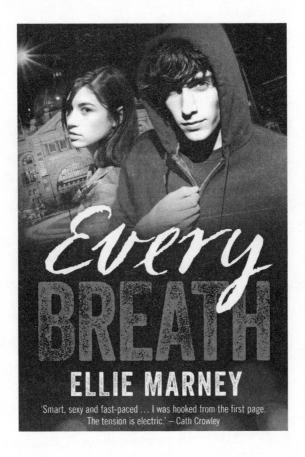

'Smart, sexy and fast-paced … I was hooked from the first page.
The tension is electric.' — Cath Crowley

'A smart, contemporary take on a timely classic that
is sure to please Sherlock aficionados of all ages.'
– *Kirkus Reviews*

Sparks fly when Watts follows Mycroft to London in this second sophisticated thriller about the teen crime-fighting pair.

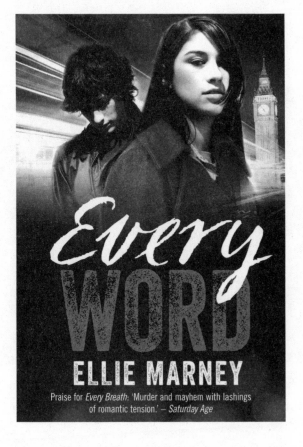

'A tense mystery full of edge-of-the-seat situations and hair's-breadth escapes all lit with a romantic gloss.'
– Katharine England, *Magpies*

Watts and Mycroft are back in another crime-fighting romance
...and this time they may not make it out alive.

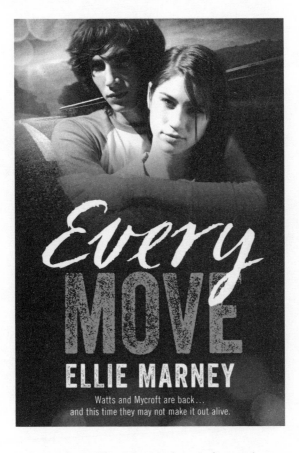

'Author Ellie Marney keeps the reader
spellbound until the very end.'
– *Good Reading*

About the Author

Ellie Marney is a teacher and author of the Every series, *No Limits* and a contributor to *Begin End Begin: A #LoveOzYA Anthology*. In 2015, her first book *Every Breath* was named as one of the top ten most-borrowed YA books in libraries nationwide. Ellie is an advocate for the #LoveOzYA movement, runs #LoveOzYAbookclub online, is an Ambassador for the Stella Prize Schools Program and speaks regularly at schools and events. Born in Brisbane, Ellie has lived in Indonesia, India and Singapore. Now she lives in a very messy wooden house on ten acres in north-central Victoria with her partner and four sons, who still love her even though she often forgets things and lets the housework go. *White Night* is her fifth novel for young adults.

Find Ellie online at www.elliemarney.com